"J. Daniel Stone's debut novel proves that he is a valuable addition to the genre. He has a magical talent for harmoniously weaving words with a beauty and grace I've never encountered until I picked up *The Absence of Light*. His passion is poetic and sings right off the pages. This book is truly a treasure you can't afford to miss!"

—Stacy Bolli, author of *Ollie*

"J. Daniel Stone's prose is so poetic it sings to me. Reads like Edgar Allan Poe."

—Nate D. Burleigh, author of *Sustenance*

"J. Daniel Stone is thought-provoking, provocative, and always highly controversial. His stories are a backstage pass to the intricate workings of a nefarious thinker."

—Donna Lyons, owner/founder of Dopamalovi Books
and author of *The Angel Maker*

"J. D. Stone has arrived on the scene with his debut novel, and seriously, it rocks on so many levels . . . J.D.'s style forces you into this fictitious world without remorse, without a chance to escape as you're propelled to turn each successive page . . .

J.D.'s Novel has it all, my friends. Suspense. Chills. Thrills. Hell, the evil Jester in-the-box, after reading this, went on a rampage in his dingy abode, clearly upset he missed this one for his own collection . . . Nonetheless, he popped out of his box with a big grin, two bony thumbs up, and a special ringing of the Jester's bell. Get this book when it's released, you're going to love it!"

—Charles Day, owner of Evil Jester Press and author of the YA novels *The Legend of the Pumpkin Thief* and *Book 1: The Hunt for the Ghoulish Bartender* (winter 2013)

"*The Absence of Light* manages to walk the fine line between suffocatingly eerie and tear jerking beautiful. J. Daniel Stone gives his characters life in a bleak world resonating with song . . . which you will never want to leave."

—Jonathan Moon, author of *Heinous* and
Stories To Poke Your Eyes Out To

"The world needs Goth boys and girls—who better to guide a reader into a good ghost story like that of a black-clad bearer of angst and pain? J. Daniel Stone's *The Absence of Light* offers a horde of such morbid youth as well as satisfying haunts."

—Steve Berman, owner/founder of Lethe Press

The Absence of
Light

J. Daniel Stone

The Absence of Light
Copyright © 2011 J. Daniel Stone

First Edition February 2013
Published by Villipede Publications
ISBN: 978-0615740911
       061574091X

Cover art and design by Madoosk Design, madoosk.net

Interior title page photo by Patty Picket Photography

Villipede.com

For My Enemy–

You Know What You Are

Sources of Inspiration:

Maynard James Keenan, Otep Shamaya, Black Sabbath, Christopher Balzano, Trent Reznor, Requiem for a Dream, music, Emily Dickinson and MUSIC.

I don't want anybody to ever say '*That was nice, that was a good read.*' I don't give a fuck for a good read; I don't want to read a good read; I don't want to write a good read! What is a good read? A RIPPING YARN?

—Kathe Koja

Language is a virus.

—William S. Burroughs

Author's Note

This book was conceived in 2008, written very slowly between 2009 and 2010, and edited fully in 2012 and early 2013. Places and people and scenes may seem skewed, but I saw it fit to leave it all alone as to not take away from the original aesthetic I was trying to capture. Long live being yourself.

My full gratitude goes out to my beta readers and to all who have said good things about my work and/or have supported me in any shape or form, which includes, but not limited to: Jonathan Moon, Kathe Koja, Charles Day, Stacy Bolli, Nate D. Burleigh, Andrew Wolter, Steve Berman, Vince Liaguno, Donna Lyons, Frances Dead, Jessi Munoz, James Jetstream, Greg Amaral, Stephen W. Roberts, Nick Medina, the staff over at Abomination Magazine and Pink Narcissus Press, J.R. Rodriguez, Justin T. Coons, Mema, all the folk on Twitter, and many more. Thank you mother, for as much as you've complicated my life, you've also been a great cheerleader of mine. A huge thank you to Villipede Publications for believing in this book strong enough to make it their inaugurating novel. But the biggest thank you of all goes out to Matt Edginton, for without his sharp eye, his clarity, ferocious respect and inherent talent for ART, this book would not be as beautiful as it is. And to the Mystical Maggots that writhe in my brain and keep me a slave to the muse. Keep being your slimy selves.

Peace in Rage,
J. Daniel Stone

Prologue

The absence of light is darkness, and deep within a heart is cradled. 1989 and New York City had every reason to be *alive;* frayed city weighted with the world's shame, its dishonor: pick pockets, murder-suicide, unemployment and a black market in the red.

Gloom lush as oil pulsed through the four a.m. nightscape, through the bowels of subways, slippery as the spray paint that spread graffiti full of hate. Dreary colored ink, tags like *ALL YOU NEED IS LOVE?* and *STOP THIS!* Words by artists with no families to love them, with minds numb to society. Signs of the times, signs of the state of mind.

The artists ran amuck like sketches slashed across bad comic strips, bane forms dressed in thrift shop rags, sad youth dreaming their listless dreams, already sick of life, sick of the world. The happiness of letting loose on the frilly 80's dance floor had come to an end; the psychedelic fervor of the 60's was an ash of memory.

Unease. Alive.

There was a boy who knew all of this, dark little boy with the dark name: Arkham, like the asylum. A black shock of hair crossed crazily across sapphire eyes; a dirty leather jacket ripped at the shoulders revealed skinny arms and sinister tattoos gaudy as costume jewelry.

The city was a hectic maze in his mind: turn one corner and a new light could show you a whole different world, turn another and you'd wish you weren't born. Each neighborhood was distinctly different: a jigsaw of eight million stories to tell, eight million diseases to spread, eight million beating hearts connected by a single artery.

Arkham knew that his city was very much *alive.*

He believed that there was more out there than meets the eye, so

3

many things between the dimensions to make people *believe*. Madness was rampant in New York City, madness that could only be caught with the click of a shutter, the flash of a bulb. He wanted to show this to the world, to introduce the city to *Them*.

Arkham wanted to capture it all.

On this side of town you could run on one end of the street and be safe, but cross the other and you sure just bought yourself a one way ticket to hell. Everything from buildings to people was crunched together; the windows were black and the stoops were slathered in vomit and beer. *ANARCHY!* was painted across tenement windows; *DiE DiE DiE MY DARLING!* thwarted psychedelic letters into your eyes.

The Continental straggled across 3rd Avenue black as sin and clear as daylight. Kids filled the bar wearing battered jeans and leather jackets, clutching liquor bottles and downing every bitter drop. The drinks were cheap but they much preferred their own temptations. Black and orange finger nails tapped across the bar top demanding to be heard, to be seen. Dark makeup pooled in eyes like bruises; straight razors were worn as charm bracelets on ropy limbs; mops of hair hung like dark delicate curtains across sharp little faces. If fingers ever came to brush it to the side, all they'd feel was the song of a secret hurt, of primal erotica.

When his Docs hit the pavement Arkham felt the city reach up with an oily hand and grasp his ankles, imploring that he never leave. But why would he? The night air was mystical, flavored by smoke from the open bar doors and the Jägermeister on everyone's tongue; flavors of the times, of the youth that coursed into the bar scene a half decade below the age limit.

That's when he saw the band leaving: Bone Crushers. Arkham knew their sound, had seen them on stage before: thrashing skeletal bodies and heavy metal electro-industrial explosion of a stage show that made kids drink until they puked, made them dance until their feet bled. It was well known that they cut their wrists on stage and threw the blood onto the crowd, and that the kids drank every fabricated drop that was offered to them. The power of music was strong, especially when its listeners were sad kids with nothing to look forward to in life, the razor scars already three layers deep in their own skin.

Sick of life. Sick of the times.

THE ABSENCE OF LIGHT

The band filtered through their crowd of pious fans silent and grim, arms draped around one another's neck nervously, all waiting for an autograph. His camera began shooting before he could even think, flashing like some crazed paparazzo. Through the lens Arkham thought he saw one of *Them*, fluttering dark moth, but once his eyes focused it was gone.

Kids in town paid Arkham in hopes that an orb would appear in their black lace bedrooms, in the silent three a.m. puzzle of the subway stations. They even gave the orbs fancy names: *ectoplasm, vortex, roundabouts;* the existence of life after death between the planes. To the kids the orbs were mystifying; it meant that something was paying attention to them for the better unlike a parent or a teacher telling you how sad you've become.

Arkham didn't know much about orbs, how they developed in film, but they were always there: phosphorescent roundabouts like crystallized rain. This convinced him that the earth could tip over at any moment, unraveling a long black carpet for *Them* to walk across and invade our reality. Perhaps that wasn't such a bad idea.

And then Bone Crushers' long faced fans scurried to the bar in a smear of rouged lips and mossy black hair. Arkham followed and sat in the middle of the bar watching the pale faces get drunk beneath a sheen of swirling smoke. Eyes surrounded him like all the orbs in his pictures. Kids scuttled into their velvet-clothed caves, scrawling poetic dusky dreams on their skin and transferring them to lyrics. Another underground band played; the melodies spiraled over crunching guitar riffs, songs about magic and the end of the world, the perversion of De Sade, the demons of Dostoevsky.

Waiting.

Arkham ordered a round of Guinness, a shot of Jameson, laid a toothpick atop the filmy head, and then picked it out with one long white finger. When he sipped, the carbonation bubbled over his tongue, delicious black stout washing the taste of pollution off his palate. He imagined a field of endless wheat and barley being fed into giant machines to make this heavenly drink. Then suddenly a hand gripped his shoulder; an array of silver rings covered the short fingers.

"Juicy fruit," Arkham said.

"Like the commercial!"

Arkham saw platinum blonde hair shaved down to the scalp but not before it was dyed three different shades. Crystal blue eyes lathered in black liner, and a dusty leather jacket pinned with bottle caps. Myriad metals ran through the wide face: sterling silver, surgical steel, gold. Arkham especially liked the thin black filigree chain that connected Juice Box's labia to his left ear lobe. One wrong move and he could be left lipless.

"Drink?"

"Of course."

Arkham slid the glass of Guinness and a shot of Jameson over to his best buddy. Juice Box resembled that need when you're craving a sweet snack, and how indescribable the feeling is after the first bite. His presence simply made people trippy. No one really knew why. Maybe it was the sugary name, but it beat the hell out Hans Diederich any day.

"I missed the fucking show . . . was in the dark room again."

Juice Box sipped his drink. "Well, no worries. It was the usual. Screamers and goonies left dripping wet with fake blood."

"Mhmm."

"I've done my homework like you asked," he leaned in close.

It was said through word of mouth that Arkham's work was tainted, that a roll of film was easily ruined by dirt or a sliver of light, the oils from a fingertip. Gossip was as common as hair dye in this part of town, but Arkham knew he was onto something greater, and so did Juice Box. He was the best friend anyone could ask for and no sooner to prove it he took out a thick notebook from his silver-spiked messenger bag and opened it to a page scribbled with red ink.

"The first ever paranormal photographer was W. Campbell . . ."

Juice Box's mind was a sponge for knowledge; he remembered things that no other twenty-two-year-old could dream of. It was one of the many reasons he never even finished high school, nor dreamed of going to college: he had an answer for everything and his teachers found it degrading. Then Juice Box spoke again.

"He took a photo of an empty chair while testing his camera and when he developed the film there was a little boy in the photo alongside the chair, leaning on it to be exact, a little boy with crazy eyes."

"Creepy." Arkham began to chew on peanuts and took out his own notebook, a scrappy bible filled with cut out passages from novels about ghosts.

"Don't be sarcastic."

"I'm not."

"He could never do it again as long as he lived and that, my friend, sparked the tradition today known as paranormal photography."

"So fast . . ."

"All it takes is one man's obsession to flower into something huge. Think of electricity, or the telephone."

"Are you saying I'm obsessed?"

"Well . . ."

"I'm a ghost hunter. I show the world that there's another kind of life walking around here at all seconds of the day, a life that everybody pretends doesn't exist because they're scared . . ."

"You've got big dreams, Arky! You can put your work in every gallery around the city!"

Arkham thought about the galleries he visited, the connections he made, but became sick of it all quickly: the in-crowds and wannabe denizens who slept in posh lofts and bathed with rose pedal soap, the drunks who talked in pompous art-speak, blowing their pride right up their own asses.

"It's deeper than that, Juicy. Do you ever question the dark?" Arkham's eyes were huge and crazy-blue, accentuated by the kohl liner.

"Not really . . ."

"It's amazing what we think about when we turn out the lights. Ever try it?"

"That's why I don't—"

"Well you should try it. Stand in your room with the lights on, and then turn them off. You'll notice the difference right away. Darkness . . . the absence of light . . . a whole new world. It's beautiful."

"Right . . ."

"And . . . sometimes I think I hear them, you know . . . *Them*." Arkham clicked his dark fingernails against his teeth. "Just because this reality is the one you see in front of your face doesn't mean it's the *only* one . . ."

Juice Box paused for a moment. "And what if you fuck with the wrong ones, the kind that're out to hurt you?"

"Fire."

"Well then. To discovery and dark promises!"

Juice Box laughed and then yelled *car bomb* after dropping the whiskey shot into the beer and chugged. Arkham did the same and they both walked out of the bar and into the brisk December night. Punks ran like mad in filthy converse sneakers; sharp teeth were concealed beneath powdery skin, but they kept walking, talking about music and girls and life until they were home and back to being weirdos.

Saturday when he got the call, Arkham busy in his bedroom working on a new batch of film, wet pictures strung on clotheslines crisscrossing door to window, the single bulb branding the room a devilish red. A fan blew lightly around to dry them quickly, making his posters of bony rock stars wave like flags. The stink of photographic chemicals pierced the air; a smudge of the gelatin layer was drying on the walls.

A sweet sounding girl. Her name was Helena Addams, and of course he had to ask if she had any relation the famed family. She said no, but asked if Arkham knew about *The Elliotts*, and when he said yes she asked that he come see her. She was a great fan of his work and simultaneously curious about her own encounters with *Them*.

"Real Ghostbusters shit," she said.

Helena talked about her windows opening without being touched, her bed sinking in from an unexplained weight as she slept, and footsteps that seemed to crawl around her bedroom walls from fathomless directions. Bright dots sometimes flashed in her peripheral vision. But she wasn't frightened as much as she was turned on, left dreaming of a ghostly body pressed against hers, ectoplasmic hands spreading her legs, a cold mouth opening against the moist cleft of her pussy as if drinking from a sacred river; a wispy tongue claiming her own.

Arkham listened to her stories and fell in love, imagining that she looked like a black haired Judy Garland. Helena lived in Queens and so it wasn't a bad train ride to go visit. Arkham stared down the archaic warehouse that took over the entire block, scorched by smog and grease vapors and the noise pollution of the 7 train. The entire town was a slum.

Insects darted across the streets; construction projects lay half-finished, and garbage bags reeked as they lay open and wet, pungent stench like that of the East River. He soon realized that the same river bordered this town: Long Island City. Arkham couldn't help the urge but to take pictures; maybe he'd catch an orb unexpectedly, the pissed off spirit of a slum lord, or a horde of cockroaches and rats with bejeweled eyes and sharp buck teeth.

Knocking on the huge warehouse door, locks springing open with heavy clicks, and Helena was just as he imagined her, only taller: big black eyes, black silk dress slit up the sides, pale legs delicious as Sigourney Weaver's when possessed by Zuul. Her corset scrunched her torso as if elongating it and her hair was soft as velvet. It made him feel dangerously perverted, his crotch instantly swelling.

"You can come in, Arkham," said her sultry commanding voice.

"The Elliotts," Arkham said proudly, "are Bradbury's family of ghosts and monsters who live in and love the dark."

"Exactly," Helena smiled. "Now won't you come in?"

Arkham moved forward. "Wow, I didn't' expect it to be so . . . *dark* in here."

"I prefer it that way."

"How old are you anyway?"

"Nineteen."

Her voice opened up his senses like smelling salt.

"And you live alone?"

"Yes, a bit of an inheritance if you will."

Arkham truly felt closed in. Buildings here were notorious for being small and dusky and old, the kinds of places that hoarded evil. Helena's place was no exception. Ugly colored brick walls were covered in decorative lace and half-stenciled drawings. Thumb-tacked posters crowded the ceiling; the shelves along the walls held books about the dark arts. Arkham smelled musk incense, patchouli and the dry licorice smell of Jägermeister. On the ceiling was Helena's flamboyant handwriting in dark purple ink.

GHOST: A seat of life or intelligence; a disembodied soul, spirit or demon; a faint shadowy trace or a false image imprinted upon a photographic negative.

"Over here is where Shadow Man usually comes by me," Helena said.

SHADOW PEOPLE: Dark humanoid forms seen in peripheral vision. They watch out for other spirits or ruthless demons; they are not harmful and are described to have red eyes and wear fedora hats.

She showed him into the open bedroom, one small window covered by heavy curtains, black armoire draped with funeral lilies and a lone absinthe colored skull. When Arkham peered out the window all he saw was faded cobblestone and garbage bags filling the rusted fire escapes. Then he turned to the bed and powered on his camera. Helena sat by the edge as if knowing he was ready to just press the button and shoot.

"This side is where he sits."

He?

She pointed at the huge bed, the light in the room growing fuzzy and purple. Arkham saw the faint indentation of what could have been the weight of a human. A warning? The light at the end? But his eyes were focused on the window which had a paragraph scratched into it.

Dreams are often precursors to other hauntings past or present. Ghosts may use them to communicate.

TIME SLIPS: The universe operates on different directions and angles. These doors can be triggered open by an array of many things.

Did Lovecraft foresee these time slips? They were insinuated in his *Dreams in the Witch House* story: impossible angles and fifth dimensions that could transport a person from one end of the universe to the next as if walking into their own home.

"And it looks like he's here now," Helena whispered, licking her black rimmed lips.

Come out, Arkham thought. *I need to impress her; I need to be taken seriously.* And then he saw it: the dash of something bright and round, an illuminated insect without wings.

I SAW IT! Arkham heard her voice. But she didn't say it aloud.

"Is Shadow Man your Captain Howdy?"

"I guess . . . though my Shadow Man is not a violent thing. But the others might be."

"Others? There's more? I don't hear anything . . ."

"You can hear them, too?"

"Sometimes."

"*They* never come around when I want to play; only Shadow Man returns."

Arkham felt his pants tighten again. "Lay yourself down. And turn off the lights."

Helena lay down, her body moving slick as a fish out of water. Arkham pulled out his camera, battered black thing, sticker-scarred, and put it into snap shot mode, taking as many pictures as possible. He filled the room with intermittent luminescence and his own lust. As each flash erupted like blazing sunlight, he saw the lingering scarecrow body between the dark, its face, and the strange eyes.

But he couldn't stop imagining Helena lifting her dress, ripping the fishnet stockings to shreds so he could see the deep wet curves between her legs, her flower, her everything. When he was done Helena sat cross legged, revealing just enough thigh to make any guy jump the gun and ask a girl out.

She said yes.

And then they grabbed one another, tongues invading tight lips, the taste of beer and lipstick on his palate, hands scrambling to remove ornate clothing. Soon Arkham's hands were between her legs, trembling white fingers, honey haired delta opening like a bag of secrets, his mouth throbbing. They made love in the dark, while Shadow Man and whatever else roamed around as their only audience.

They drank Jägermeister until their tongues were stained dark brown, drank one another's soul until their hearts exploded. Left only was the bitterness of the city air and the sweaty taste of angst. The feel of your lover's breath upon your face is that of heaven and hell; their skin is the secret map to the heart.

They lived the life.

Time blinked.

Helena was nine months pregnant now, fraternal twins that she said she had visions of. Her stomach was swollen as edema, swollen as Arkham's dick every time he watched her comb her hair, or rub oil on her long pale legs. If for any moment of those nine months he thought he found peace in the dark, everything had turned upside down. The voices came back, too close to Arkham's ear to see, too deep inside the hills of his brain to ignore.

"It's the dark masses in our peripheral vision that try to make contact," Helena said. "Not voices."

Arkham saw many of those, black clouds and shapeless materializations. He recalled great fat red things spying on him at night, glistening snake eyes watching a sunset, portals into a worse place.

Dangerous times.

"That's what Shadow Man does," Helena would tell him. "He just stares with his red jealous eyes."

Then she'd press her liver colored lips to his forehead, making the thought of danger vanish. But not for long. Arkham knew that it was *Them* trying to take Helena away. Arkham imagined *Them* hiding behind her eyes, moving through her black splay of hair like the hand of an adulterer, and that she liked it. Thinking of Shadow Man sniffing the fine juncture of her pussy pummeled him with jealousy, fed fuel to the fire.

There's a lonely dark place in paranormal research and investigation, inhabited by things that stretch beyond what is known about paranormal activity. These entities hide between ghosts and are slow to make themselves known. They attach themselves to people, places, and their intentions are never positive.

Tonight he let four sheets of an Alphabet City hallucinogenic dissolve under his tongue, a blotter called Rat Salad. Arkham knew that this was the only way to contact *Them:* shave away conscious control and let the unconscious seep through as if turning your brain in to a portal for your soul to rise out. But Arkham saw no apparitions, no orbs, just himself in the mirror looking quite wicked and enraged: ripped fishnet sleeves, arms furrowed with scratches.

He was waiting for her to come home. The burn in his chest told him what to do, the drugs fueling his new mission, and the ghosts trying to put out his fire. Arkham turned out the lights, questioning the dark no more.

Brightness glissading, teasing his face with warmth, and Arkham couldn't believe it was morning already. Pushing the curtains aside he let daylight flood the room to soften the headache. He stared at his arms and his torso before the mirror. He was bruised; bite marks were scattered across his pale chest, a bead of gleaming meat shown where his nipple ring once was. Arkham did not know what had happened, could not even recall the sun rising—*nothing.* But what he did know was that all this blood was not just his, that it was tinged with a familiar, rich and metallic scent, fresh. It was *hers;* he could taste the bitter-sweetness as if champagne left too long in a tin can, the saccharine flavor, the velvet flood of Helena's milky-red monthly blood.

It was then he saw the coarse black hair fanned out by his feet, roped across the floor. Globules of clotted blood streaked the walls, faintly *warm* as his finger grazed the jellied mass. Deep in his brain her voice echoed, shrill screech to stop, but he didn't listen. He couldn't stop; something had wormed into his blood and controlled him. And then he saw her. Face down, head twisted at a painful angle, two cavernous eyes searching for something, mouth a frown of meat, smashed lips sinking into her skull. Huge portions of hair had been ripped from her head, tugged so hard Arkham saw a glistening sliver of skull. There was a clear fluid drying on the floor, sticky underneath his boots.

Placenta.

And then he remembered the babies. Running, praying for them to be safe, and her body made an awful suctioning sound when he turned her over. Flat stomach, pale thighs slimed with gore. But that's when he heard the gentle suck of air through tiny nostrils, the squeak of infantile vocal chords; his vision cleared, seeing a boy and a girl, clean as a whistle, identical faces, sweetly cute. Arkham ripped down the black mesh that covered his bed and wrapped the babies up to keep them warm. There was no sign of any broken bones, any blood; just healthy, hungry infants. He scooped them up, kissing their soft foreheads and walked down the stairs and out into the parking lot.

A few stragglers loomed as he lay the babies down and slumped back to his loft. Back inside he lit a match and cradled his dead girlfriend. The flame grew instantaneously, licking the curtains, then his pant leg: a bright burning mouth to swallow him whole.

There was a finite, shapeless presence watching him. *The alive of the city*. It was the thing that had brought him and Helena together and what ultimately tore them apart.

22 years later

part One

There are moments when one has to choose between
living one's own life, fully, entirely, completely, or
drag out some false, shallow, degrading existence
that the world in its hypocrisy demands.

—Oscar Wilde

1

The L train bolted through the dark wet underground; intermittent flashes glowed against the night's solemn faces. There were seldom awake, most were bums. The hum of metal and electricity felt magical, like a full night of drinking and not having to wake up in the morning; a morning darkened by the whorls of tunnels and fetor of the squatters collecting mountains of beer cans, their drunken mumbling like a scary song to whatever bystander would dare listen.

Three friends were returning from Saint John's cemetery in Queens, a borough that spreads its greasy legs like a sinful lover between Brooklyn and Long Island. Saint John's is the perfect place to capture *Them*. It is a place of great reverence; you don't need to look to know that dead people are there. After all, it's the city of the dead. But you must go in with a clear head and respect for the manifestation to happen. The dead are so picky.

Clive led the pack with a black and silver Nikon FM10 gripped by thin white fingers poking through thief's gloves; mousy brown hair covered his Dresden blue eyes, corduroy pants his stick-like legs. He preferred film cameras over digital, even though he was living in the heart of the technological era. Digital cameras proved to be faulty when backtracking through the catalogues. Anything from water vapor to dust mites could trick the eye as solid evidence of ghosts. 35 mm film and an SLR lens were ideal for mode of capture. Evidence is best found on film negatives.

Lynk controlled the full spectrum HD camcorder, his sharp nails clicking the sticker-scarred surface, his yellow eyes weary of the supernatural. The full spectrum camera allows one to see light that is not visible to the human eye—UV, IR—at a greater sensitivity by spectrally transmitting the rays onto film. It's the only way to see *Them* as they are seeing you. But you can't always trust what you see; sometimes you need to watch through different eyes, namely your

17

ears, and that's why Rez was with them. He could hear things others could not.

"You think Glenn Danzig ever went ghost hunting?" Clive asked.

"Oh, Clive, come on. He doesn't need to find ghosts; he's practically ol' LUCIFER himself . . ."

"I think we got some great shots tonight."

"Yes, we did. The night was full of THEM."

"Thanks to Rez . . . King Spooky!" Clive said, dipping the flask into his lips, rotgut Jägermeister smelling of cinnamon-candied heaven.

"Gimme some of that!" Lynk said.

Sharp features broke free of straggling orange and black hair; an apex chin stuck out like a sore thumb.

"Take what you want. Anything good on the full spectrum?"

They all had the look of typical ghost hunters and artists: overtly pale and thin, clutching their equipment, their pens, and their creativity tight in the palm of their hands like selfish children. These are the traits molded by hours spent working alone, listening to EVP sessions and reading the measurements of Geiger counters bent over a coffee table or a computer; these are the traits of obliging one's self into a happy solitude for the sake of art.

Nobody or nothing could come in the way of their work.

Tonight's mission was simple: capture a panoramic view of the cemetery, the beautifully rotting stones, the tombs encased in mummy-tight vines and laugh at strange engraved names. A waiting game. But what lay a sweeter thrill than to prove the existence of everything that you're told is only bound to the story books and bad movies?

But as it always seems to happen, like the touch of a slimy apparition, night faded to creamy daylight and it was time to go. But the reading needle on the antique Geiger counter still bounced crazily; the EVP recorder was dead center in the middle of a conversation between the deceased. *Tea at sunrise? Coffee at dawn?* It all translated into a heavy set of white noise, a hectic snap, crackle and pop in the air; whispering particles of dust.

"Nothing that I see yet," Lynk said. "Rez, did you hear anything tonight?"

Rez rolled over wretchedly on the dirty plastic seat, the Jägermeister swirling in his stomach, the licorice flavor still sticky on his palate. Thick black hair fanned across his vision, obscuring the earth as he knew it; his eyes were sapphires that could pierce light through any darkness. *JAMESON WHISKEY* and *HEALTHCARE?* screamed the advertisements; *LiZ WuZ HeRe* and *BaCk OFF FuCkErS* read the terrible permanent marker graffiti. But Rez wasn't really focused on any of that. His mind was lost inside *The Place of Dead Roads* by William S. Burroughs, a ragged paper back copy he lifted via five finger discount from a downtown thrift shop. He still smelled the ancient shelf dust.

The wind is rising, ripping blurs and flashes of russet orange-red from the trees, whistling through tombstones.

"Didn't hear a thing," Rez quipped.

He thought about the cemetery again, about the warm October wind and the leaves piling high. It was Rez's special place to think, to gather thoughts without a live audience other than the dust of bones beneath the soil. There were two mausoleums there as big as Staten Island: one made of marble, the other of wood, and both were tinged with the smell of altars and pale funeral lilies. One could wander inside them for days, traveling through the labyrinthine hallways lit only by candlelight offerings, not remembering the need for sun and air. It's said that one could hear heavenly music spiraling above, or sometimes the distant recoil of a pissed off ghost if one could tune his ear to it. Rez constantly heard full fledged conversations, leaving him to wonder if it was nice to be calm bones, nice to slowly decay and hang out with the worms.

"Well that's too bad," and Lynk sucked Clive's flask with a loud slurp, always an inch away from Clive it seemed.

"Did you thank them, Lynk?" Clive asked.

"Thank who?"

"The spirits. We owe them thanks when they show up. It's a sign of respect, bidding them luck on their forever journeys."

"Journey into my own fucking head," Rez said.

The train halted; beer cans fell with metal a ping to the floor, rolling toward Rez's skate shoes like the song of steel drums. The robot conductor announced *THIS IS FIRST AVENUE* and they all went running. Rez's black and red flannel stuck to him like glue it was so tight, and it stunk like all hell. The florescent lights beamed upon his exposed pale chest as he ripped some of the buttons away, cutting into the dark curly hairs that scattered down to his groin. He caught Lynk staring. What did he want? A little skin? A little suck? *Fuck that*, Rez thought.

The three stumbled up filthy stairs and across a fresh puddle of piss, flaring clove cigarettes to life, Djarum Vanilla, the kind only sold in smoke shops. The air of 14th Street smashed into their lungs: charred pretzels, the brine of dirty water dogs, sweet roasting peanuts and whiskey laced nights. Dawn was opening its crepuscular eyes, stretching neon across the sky and reflecting off the oily streets as they descended upon Alphabet City. They zipped past storefronts and bodegas marked *cLoSeD FoR BuSiNeSs*. A chain of big red stop signs with a mutated rodents read *RAT INFESTATION!!!* It was a literal sign of the times. Stale economy, stale people, stale hopes and dreams. These were the streets of loss and deceit.

The FDR drive was loud as a rooftop party in the distance; the smell of wasted youth was potent. They stumbled across Oval Park until they reached the front of Clive's building. Rez could see pale light slipping past the benches now, mottled through the discolored tree leaves and sparkling across the crazy fountain where coins clattered as if a wishing well. He never liked the sun, never liked to tan like all the cool kids did. Rez found daylight to be too exciting; it meant that night was close again, and it's always better to write at night too. At least it used to be that way.

"Oh for fuck's sake, my keys are gone," Clive said.

"I got a spare," said Lynk.

"Funny how *you* have a spare to my own flat."

"An *apartment*, you British fuck-face. Get it right."

"Fuck off, wanker," Clive stuck out his tongue.

ArT SaVeS! was spray painted across the glass doors, and as Lynk opened them Rez saw a tunnel of darkness. Up the stairs, roach motel hallway, and you could see the little beasts darting up the walls: silver leggy things fast as bullets. So quiet in the apartment, discomforting. Anything could be waiting between the silence to snatch you. The old Salvation Army curtains were drawn, shadowing the band posters and magazine cut outs, their eyes bright and staring them down. *YOU'RE LATE!* They screamed. *GO TO BED!*

Never, Rez laughed to himself.

The stench of hangovers and stale beer whispered from the back of the apartment, soured by cigarette smoke. The living room was polluted with Sutter Home wine bottles, crushed PBR cans and spicy cigarette ash. They always drank until morning, not worrying about work or parents or school. It was the good life. Across the back wall were shelves packed with perverse William S. Burroughs novels,

Kathe Koja, the poetry of Bradbury and the existential terrors of Mark Z. Danielewski. DVD racks displayed Masters of Horror, Italian Splatter, films directed by Rob Zombie, Tim Burton, black and white horror classics: a vast collection of the macabre.

"Awright, time to light up and develop this batch," Clive said.

Rez lit a joint with his favorite jet-flame lighter that glowed green. The Lower East Side blend pummeled his lungs sweetly, relaxing his soul. He exhaled it across the teal musical scale tattoo on his one forearm, the black raven quill on the other covering his suicide ghosts. Patchwork flesh that burned whenever he heard the voices; razor into forearms because the blood amused him, because Rez was called weird his entire life. The pain of the blade always outweighed the one in his heart, a nice little vacation from life. And the ghosts in his head liked to show up when he was at his most vulnerable: it's the easiest way to penetrate the mind.

Lynk disappeared behind the spicy cloud and the fact of the matter was that it was better off that way. Rez wasn't too fond of Lynk because he wanted to see Clive happy. He found that Clive's strangely close friendship to Lynk kept him from truly flowering as a photographer. Clive could move on to do greater things than New York, was good enough to go on real ghost hunts with the greatly respected paranormal societies that had made it to television and had written books: The Massachusetts Paranormal Crossroads, The Atlantic Paranormal Society, and the Paranormal Research and Investigation of Southern Maryland. New York didn't have any of that kind of respect, funny because it's one of the major necropolises of the world.

Hopeless, his mind said. *Ridiculous*.

The dark room harbored all of Clive's developing tools, his passions concentrated into one small space. Rez saw myriad metal trays against the flat grey wall in the back littered with band posters and magazine cut outs. The shelves held chemicals such as the mixer and developer, silver-halide in little glass bottles, poisonous if one spent too much time hovering over a tray inhaling. A white machine called "The Enlarger" resembled a freakishly huge microscope; it was for creating photographic prints from film negatives. Rez had seen Clive turn film negatives into huge portraits so many times; he'd been taking photos of Rez for years now.

There was one lone window for ventilation, painted with a huge black hex and the words *FuCk THE wOrLd FoR ALL IT'S WoRtH!* scratched out. Piles of tattered photography manuals lay in the corner; post it notes scribbled with Clive's signature chicken scratch were indecipherable, and one lousy shelf held more scrap paper. There was the one cheap laptop Clive had bought for his digital work because it made the editing process easier when he wanted to taint hues and angles, or make light twirl like water colors through the subjects he photographed. But it didn't give Clive the same high as traditional silver. There was some kind of unexplainable power that came with shooting your own work. Transforming the film from small brown negatives and watching it grow was like raising a child, a small square child. It was rawer, the traditional way; Lynk felt the same. They both lived for photography.

Clive's latest shots were pinned to the wall: decaying structures of the five boroughs, Alphabet City locals—beatniks and gentrified dwellers—the dying music culture of downtown and gutted tenements. The East Village turning into another Soho inspired Clive to capture the town as much as he could before the next record store was closed and replaced by a Japanese Noodle shop, before the next dilapidated brickwork was refurbished and the rent skyrocketed, kicking out the punks and tradition for the cookie-cutter complacency of the Midwest.

Rez turned on the safe light and a red drunken glow sat atop everything. Something flickered; strange phosphorescence darted in his peripheral vision, but as soon as he focused he saw Lynk standing around stupidly. Clive unraveled the Nikon's film and loaded the EVP recorder tape into the player, and the full spectrum tape into the VCR. Rez heard no noises, nothing but their own footsteps crunching gravel and dried leaves, and their maniacal conversations about music, booze and sex.

Maynard James Keenan sings like the devil on steroids, Rez heard his own voice say.

Craft beer is a blessing in America. That was Clive.

Music can set the soul free . . .

Of all the pussy in the good green world, New York has the best. That was Clive again.

Last week the trio had broken into a burned down tenement on Orchard Street and did an entire photo shoot there. They strung cameras from the broken walls, the crumbling cabinets, the broken windows. Tripods were in every corner; Geiger counters and EVP recorders were in hand. Every livable space had to be occupied with equipment; they didn't want to take any chances of not capturing the dead on film. Rez remembered how the apartment echoed with its sad past of tortured immigrant life, of twelve people squished into one bedroom, of sleeping and eating roaches, of watching your family suffer with the mumps measles and tuberculosis, and nothing could be done about it because mom was a housewife and dad couldn't speak enough English to get himself an office job.

Dirt in their hair, in the air like soot, their eyes clouded, their teeth yellowed from malnutrition. Death was more than rampant; it was culture in this part of town. The children were always the loudest; their short life shielded them from judgment in death with a forever adolescence. It was the adults that kept themselves back as if with a ten foot pole; it was the adults who knew when to strike, knew to stay quiet. You could taunt them, call them out, but they only showed themselves when they were ready.

Clive was preparing those photos for the Cabal Gallery. A portfolio that would juxtapose the madness and serenity of the city. Rez was the model for a lot of his work. And there he was in all his emo grandeur, strung up like some freezer meat on taut clotheslines zigzagging across the room. Soft whitewashed face, sapphire eyes blotted in kohl, black hair drizzled in red and posing as if he didn't know the bones beneath his own skin, but a grin like that of the evilest bird in the world plagued his face.

That's when Rez noticed the little shining dots surrounding his body in the photos: orbs. It seemed the things were alive, not just water vapor or dust mites, but like vortexes trying to suck you into their weird spineless worlds. It's why Clive loved taking photos of Rez, why he always asked him to listen carefully for the susurration between the darkness of the city.

"*Sanity's Abyss.* That's what I'm going to call that one," Clive said sternly.

"A choice name if you ask me."

"Dago will be stoked to see how well I did, and how good you came out. And how good *They* came out."

Then Rez heard a small crashing sound, the spill of a thick juice and equipment toppling.

"FUCK!" Clive said. "My work Lynk, you bloody imbecile!"

"I didn't do it!" Lynk's face was haggard in the dim red light.

Clive's English accent was strongest when he was pissed off and drunk; it made Rez jump to his senses like a taser just shocked him in the ass. Lynk had spilled silver halide all over the table where Clive had film negatives lined up to be developed.

"We're all fucking loaded. Get out, both of you."

The way Clive was standing at the door, the hallway lit by the rising sun, and the safe light penetrating his body, made him look almost scary, inhuman. His dirty brown hair was skewed across his bold features; Rez could smell his odors, the oils of his skin and armpits: it was the badge of skipping the shower this week. Clive's Dresden blue eyes screamed for alone time and he was soon leading Rez and Lynk out of the dark room. Whatever Clive says, goes. It was his apartment after all. Neither Lynk nor Rez paid any rent, not that Clive minded anyway.

"You asshole, Lynk. Always screwing things up; always attached to his hip like a fucking puppy dog."

"Fuck you, Rez. Just fuck you."

"Whatever, man."

Clive came out of the room and lazily apologized, grabbing a handful of beers and plopping himself on the couch. But Rez only saw Lynk: turning away awkwardly, his honey colored eyes burning into Rez, thin hands clawing at his hips as he followed Clive to the couch.

"I'd like to go out later," Clive said, reading from his notebook and a new MTA map. "I've a few new places I want to hit up. Especially Queens."

"Whatever you want, Clive," Rez said.

"Yeah. Now come drink . . . and rest. We'll go out tonight."

Rez forced himself to sit on the couch, watching Lynk grin like a son of a bitch, happy little bastard, and he laid his head down to read again. There was nothing left for him to do. He hated listening to the conversation of hunting ghosts, hated to remember that he couldn't look into any of his notebooks. He wasn't a writer anymore and that hurt. Maybe sleep wasn't such a bad idea after all.

2

It was the kind of Pennsylvania moment when summer slithers into fall, but when fall yearns to be called autumn. Nightfall, and the winds whispered with the change of seasons, pruning leaves to pale colors, piling at the edges of nameless roads and forest peripheries.

Jimmy drove like a fucking lunatic, his yellow puffy hair battling the night wind as he cut the pickup through shaded side roads to get to The Skeleton Grin. Electric Orchid had howled dozens of their shows there, earning pennies, but still, playing music was what it was all about. At The Grin kids with no places in society could join together and let out the strife of life. It was their release from the brainwash of American advertising that said you had to be skinny to be pretty, had to smile to be accepted and be straight to not be a sodomist. They didn't have to be like everyone else, nor did they want to be. Jimmy cranked the stereo louder. Nine Inch Nails; "Dead Souls" coiled through the ratty speakers, too much bass and not enough treble.

Delilah Dellinger was relaxing herself in the back of the pickup. Skinny pale limbs wrapped in fishnet were stretched across amps and chords; pink and black dreadlocks slashed the air like pythons battling the cool star-wind; the vintage black Docs she wore were her only pair. Her eyes were sapphire jewels marking the trees that sped by like burnt sticks, the Amish style housing sprinkled across the land old as colonial times itself, creaking like arthritis in the calm wind. Each one of them dreadfully the same.

It wasn't as cold as Delilah expected, but everyone's blood in Violet Hill is a tad thicker—*perhaps that's why people are so thickheaded here*—but it's what you come to expect living in a patch town. Built upon a mine smack-dead center in the Pennsylvania Coal Region, Violet Hill was not as pretty as its name. The stores and houses bulged like bones picked clean; its people were mindless except for the judgement they passed. Their only source of pride was within its anthracite production, known locally as "the black diamond." It supplied power to the people's electric gods and entertainment systems; it supplied heat during the grueling Pennsylvania winters, keeping them safe in their dens and ultimately ignorant to the world around them. And then there were the Amish, an entirely different demon-clan that Delilah preferred not to think about.

"The perfect hair . . . perfect wife . . . perfect kids and perfect life," Delilah said. "*I . . . will finally . . . be somebody.*"

"Shut up and drink the wine!"

Her best friend Alex Zweig was in the back of the pickup too, his dark hair snapping against his sharp face and his chin moving quick while he worked a new stick of gum to freshen his breath. Alex's androgynous face was shrouded by pale green eyes that were said to be the spitting image of his mother—though he'd never met her—and his long sharp chin was that of his father's, but he'd never met him either. He had two jagged front teeth by the luck of never wearing braces, and whenever Jimmy hit a bump he'd draw blood on his own lip; sometimes Jimmy did that on purpose.

The bottle of Jägermeister was in his lap via a double-thigh death grip; his fingernails were the color of pearls, and he was slowly teasing them along the soft pale cheek of a very young boy to get his mouth open before pouring some of the spicy brown liquor in. Alex's fingers played the boy's features like they did the piano: with sinful sexuality.

He was a ravenous natural, had slaved happily over his piano since Delilah could remember; but these days he took command of Juno synthesizers as if he was Bach or Beethoven risen from the dead and evil as sin itself. They'd been playing together since they were sixteen: Delilah, a capella natural, and Alex, the piano maestro. Whenever Alex played the piano it lulled Delilah into a crazed dreamy state as if an intravenous dripping black glitter into her vulnerable vein.

"Sutter Home is the Zinfandel of dreams," Alex said to Delilah. "Now take a sip!"

Delilah completely forgot she was holding the bottle, too focused on Alex's tattoos inked across his chicken bone arm, glowing under the moonlight: the tattered band logo on his wrist, a scarlet-swirled orchid on his bicep, the one he kept dead and dry in a jar. That orchid helped form one-half of the band name. Delilah sipped the pale wine and gagged a little bit. It wasn't the best in the world, but it was cheap and did its job of fucking her up. She studied the boy next to Alex.

He looked just as lost as the rest of Electric Orchid: fake black contact lenses, hair spiraling out of control in the dark wind, kohl rimmed eyes that spoke of solitude and the displacency that plagued many youth in Violet Hill. Human pollution. When the boy called for more Jäger, Alex cringed. He'd called Alex a *he*, the evilest of pronouns. Though born a biological boy, Alex became a pious gender queer when he hit puberty, discovering that it was more interesting to lose the pronouns that categorized people like sheep. He didn't believe in that bullshit ornate red line that divided girls and boys, gays and straights.

Being referred to as your first name made people think twice about you. It took away the judgment they'd love to cast upon a boy with a girlish face, or a girl who wears boy's shirts. Sexuality was like the seasons, changing every now and again, so why choose a side? And Alex was a name that screamed androgyny anyway, so he took advantage.

"This wine goes down like demon piss," and Delilah drank straight from the spout again.

"I wonder if Trent Reznor drank this wine."

"Nah, he loaded up on better shit than this white trash drink."

"But he was once the pioneer of *all-i-want-to-do-is-eat-glass-and-die*. He led lots of kids out of their dark closets."

"Key word is *once*," Delilah shot back. "People eventually get over it . . . change . . . evolve."

"I bet Ozzy could finish off twelve bottles of this shit in his Sabbath days."

Delilah thought about all the Nine Inch Nails posters in her room, thought about how many limbs she would sever just to see them play live. Not that she had a problem with cutting herself anyway; she'd been doing it for years, the skin so scarred not even her crow colored tattoos couldn't hide the ruined tissue.

"Fuck yeah!"

Alex had the mouth of a sailor, the heart of a dear friend, and a German's beer tolerance. He rarely was ever drunk, but one pull off a bong and he was high for two days talking about psychedelics, remaining hypnotized by splatter movies and white noise that singed your ears after watching a good horror flick on the VCR. Delilah loved him. They were best friends, and the only person she considered family. Sure, she had the rest of the band, but she couldn't trade secrets with them like Alex, couldn't talk about her nightmares; they said she was a moment away from the loony bin.

"You gunna keep doing that?" Delilah said.

"Does it bother you?" Alex's grin was halfway between naughty and nice.

"I like it," said the boy. "Can I blow you?"

"Yeah, when we finish our set."

"Mmm. All sweaty."

"WHAT!" Delilah hissed. "What's your name anyway?"

"Tommy."

"Tommy," Alex said, putting his arm around the boy, spider fingers clutching his bony shoulder, "is my date for the night."

Alex's voice was soft and monotone, threatening yet soothing, just like his persona. The other band members, Billy the drummer, Sheigh the bassist, and Jimmy the guitarist, were crunched in the front smoking a joint of typical Pennsylvania ragweed, sipping Colt 45 from brown paper bags and talking nonsense that translated into a dictionary of slurs. Sheigh's arm hung lazily out the window, covered in tight purple and black lycra, her hand fishing through the night air. Delilah grabbed the joint and smoked away. It tasted fucking good, must have been a Philadelphia strand because nothing in Violet Hill ever flowed this sweet. Then she looked up and saw the moon out like a golf ball, the stars becoming clearer as the streets widened and the trees faded. They were closing in on Steeraway Street now, the main boulevard.

"I wouldn't mind making out with you, Delilah," Tommy offered. "The more the merrier."

"Touch me and I'll rip your dick off," Delilah snapped.

"Whoa, whoa—no need for any of that. Tommy's just playful," Alex said after his tongue became free from Tommy's dark lips and lit a clove cigarette.

"You still smoking that rat cancer?" Delilah obviously changed the subject.

"Djarum Vanilla. Sweet until the last pull. Best after sex."

"Ew."

Tommy made a snorting sound; Delilah saw a trace of powder by his tiny nose.

"Oh, for fuck's sake—and he's a *coke head?*"

"Tommy is whatever Tommy is."

"HEY NUMB SKULLS!" Sheigh yelled. "How about some of our music?"

"Good way to wake up the dead!" Alex said. "But I wanna hear Sabbath instead."

"We'll be doing plenty of that at the show, fucker. Here we go!"

The music cued and Alex's familiar, intense key boards blurted sepulchrally; Jimmy's Warlock grunted, and Sheigh's dragging bass beats smashed into Billy's drumming head on: a freakish time signature for a song called "28 Days," inspired straight from the movie. Delilah recalled the dilapidated studio in which they recorded their first single. It was on a piece of shit multitrack recorder in the basement of Sideshow Music Shop where the sulfur smell of Lacuna Lake and fermented beer poisoned their lungs, where the tales of horror and mystery of drownings and mutated fish roared like campfire tales. When the studio scored enough money to switch to CDs, they'd made a dozen. Delilah drew the covers herself; twisted psychedelic pattern in hues of grey and black, littered with chunks of anthracite and bats flying over a huge cratered moon. Then Delilah began to sing the lyrics.

Stinging English rain lit by a dead sun . . .
Put the devil on wholesale
Now you've nowhere to run . . .

This was a tactic to get the band ready to play. Delilah felt the muscles in her chest rise, her shivering skeleton becoming one with pale skin. That was when she saw the road rip open and belch up something black and twisted, something attracted to the song. It was no secret that Electric Orchid's music disturbed the afterlife, but Delilah closed her eyes and ignored it. She laid back and listened to her own voice slide this reality away from the mountains and into one of pollution and cavernous buildings higher than anything she'd ever dreamed of, where one could jump off the rooftops and fly: New York City, the place she was born. Electric Orchid had finally been given the chance to leave town . . . but it all depended on this show.

Suicide lies, we still seek
Knife in the eyes . . .
Never been so meek
We shall RISE and CREEP!

"Wanna go egg bombing? You always used to like that," Alex said.

"No. We're growing up; we can't waste food like that anymore."

"Twenty-two is hardly old; twenty-one is perfectly sweet."

"Too dark out there Alex. I don't like it as much as I used to. It's—"

"The absence of light: so dark that you're forced to question your own visual perception. I know."

Before Delilah could answer Jimmy began to yell. She heard the gallop of horses, saw the familiar black and white pilgrim lace outfits: Amish women riding in a carriage full of vegetables and homemade jams. Jimmy slowed the pickup down to a grueling hum and opened his window wider. For some reason he had a hate for the Amish, most likely because their Anabaptist religion plagued too many minds in Violet Hill, ruined too many families with Puritan code of dress, their insidious dedication to the *one and only god*, which naturally cut the freedoms of a woman in half.

Good of you to be so kind, Lord!

Jimmy was mixed race: Louisiana black on his mother's side, and golden haired Amish on his father's side. It was the sin of all sins to breed with English people, with anyone outside of the Amish circle, and so Jimmy's father had been excommunicated. But it was for the better. Thanks to his mixed heritage, Jimmy had the soul of jazz in his blood and the complacent patience of the Amish to hold a steady thought and write music. Though he hated his Amish side, he was a new kind of breed in this part of Pennsylvania and it made him a small celebrity.

But Jimmy's hate for the Amish truly came from the fact that they were people who deemed anyone that didn't believe their Christian world view an English sinner; these were the same people who picketed for peace and simplicity in a world where none of that existed. They were so backwards. You could throw rocks at them and soak them with soured milk and they'd never throw a punch or cause a fit. But Jimmy knew that there was a fine line dividing insanity and composure, and any second it was going to snap; if Jimmy could help it along he would. He used that same excuse for his drinking problem, too, never being able to top off the tap at any bar he went to.

Plus, Jimmy was best friends with Sheigh, who was everything he wanted in a girl: psychotic wrapped in a bow laced with beer, all the things proper Pennsylvania girls were not. Sheigh loved all the attention Jimmy gave her, and they were known to fuck around a little, but nothing more. Falling in love could mean ruining the band, could mean an inevitable break up. Emotions plagued many bands that they loved—underground and successful—which ultimately ripped them apart, so they marred any chance of emotional attachment. But it wasn't uncommon for them to cuddle the nights away, backbone to stomach, dirty feet wrapped together in a sweaty knot, sunlight drenching them in the wee morning hours, hands clenched together, still sticky with the night's last brewski, the last drop in the bottle.

"Hey you little leg-spreading slut . . . wanna make me a happier man?" Jimmy said.

The Amish girl just stared straight ahead while Jimmy and Sheigh nearly died of mocking laughter, shoving handfuls of Spree into in their mouths and washing them down with warm beer. Sheigh's crazy brown eyes grew huge, a little jealous.

"Cut it out Jimmy!" Delilah slapped the side of the pickup.

"Fine, ladies—your loss. I got a big dick," and out came his wriggling pink tongue.

"ENGLISH SINNER!" one girl howled.

He sped away and blasted dirt into their faces. Delilah watched them choke on the cloud; the horses shook their heads. She pitied them for a moment, but lost the thought as The Oasis strip club blasted her eyes with sensual purple light at the beginning of Steeraway Street's run down section. *Not enough of them*, Delilah thought.

She saw women's metal nipples shine sweet as California oranges and the doorway packed with smoke. The No Catch dry cleaners had the most powerful lights on the boulevard and it caught Delilah's undivided attention, reminding her of the *hit your head against the table* shifts she had suffered there for chump change. If you took Steeraway Street down to the end, you'd hit the giant Ghelligg anthracite factory: the biggest supplier of jobs in Violet Hill, and the biggest supplier of pulmonary failure. Delilah's "father" worked there.

They parked illegally in front of The Skeleton Grin, but who the fuck cared. The Grin's mascot was just as creepy as the namesake, giant skull glowing green as absinthe with black hollow eyes and a cigarette being fed into its mouth right after the bony mechanical arm poured the whiskey. The sign in the window was scrawled messily in blue-black ink and read *ELECTRIC ORCHID TONIGHT!* Everyone in town knew them and came out to support, if not just for a good show and cheap beer.

Delilah stepped out of the truck, dizzily high but ready to play.

Sheigh and Jimmy were arm in arm; Billy was writing on the pickup with a foul smelling paint pen. If he had never picked up the drum sticks in his life, Billy most certainly would've been a bohemian painter, selling his work like a gypsy at the Steeraway Street flea market.

Alex huddled into a dark corner with Tommy, his long trench coat open, their hands rubbing one another's swollen crotches, their ripe asses. Delilah saw Alex's birdcage torso, saw that Tommy's tongue had already left a slimy trail of spit down to Alex's groin. Jimmy opened the door, from which the dry smell of beer and a great cloud of opaque swirling smoke greeted the band.

They walked in together.

3

"It's about time you grew up and got over it, old man. They ain't ever coming back, and you're drunk again," Hans whispered to himself.

Been whispering to himself more than ever these days. He'd been staring at the old warehouse for over an hour, the smell of paint and truck exhaust like poison in the heavy air. Ugly brick fortress of aerosol portraits: bloodied zombies in glittering air gun finish, drab skulls with top hats in sketchy brush; a countdown until the end of the world, 2012, bold-white.

How many times had he crossed this heavily worn pavement? How much of his own essence, his alcohol spit and sweat and vomit scarred this place? How much of Arkham's life still coursed through here? Each year it obviously became less and less. There was nothing left as far as the human eye could see, only stains long since faded, specks of ash from a fire that had been put under control more than twenty years ago.

Two decades had slipped past him like trying to grasp a fish out of water. Left only was a thinning mop of feathery blonde hair atop his head; crow's feet spread like peachy strings each time he frowned. Stress lines ringed his face. Though time had moved on as much as the fashion trends, Hans still wore his cracked leather jacket with pins and bottle caps sewn into the lining, his impossibly black jeans and Docs as if they were still in style, as if it was 1989 and the punks still roamed free, as if the metal heads still smoked hash all night long singing to Black Sabbath and Iron Maiden.

His old habits had yet to die hard.

Do you question the dark? Arkham always asked him. *Sometimes I hear Them!* Had he? Was Arkham so wrapped up in his work that he'd truly found the key to unlock the chains between the dimensions? If so, that same key had opened the door to his casket and buried him.

Just because this reality is the one you see in front of your face doesn't

33

mean it's the only one.

Oh fuck, this ghost hunting thing. Hans remembered how much Arkham obsessed over it, how much he slaved in that dark room to find any scrap of evidence, writing ghostly findings in journals and reading novels about *Them* all night. The smell of photo-chemicals was pungent; Helena's patchouli incense made you think of heaven, and the Jägermeister flowed free as the smell of cigarette smoke and the dark music that filtered out the stereo system.

What if he went in there now? What had remained through the incineration? Dead flame . . . ghosts . . . ectoplasm? Invisible vampires would surely burst through the walls and envelope his body, knotting him up in a sinister silky spider web, violating his skin, his mind, and ultimately feasting on his brain. After all, he was sure that's what they'd done to Arkham. Then again, he was drunk . . . still. *And what if you fuck with the wrong ones?*

"I kill them by fire!" A voice ricocheted in his brain.

Hans remembered that fucking fire. A bright vengeful blaze that shot Ferris wheels of burning light into the sky; nobody understood why it started, and why this place. Since then it hadn't been lived in. 5Pointz was the new name, graffiti capital of Queens, a haggard place where drive-by shootings were just part of the day, where Riker's Island inmates used to be dropped off and let back into society to rob and deal drugs again.

But now, it was a new world.

Hans watched the shadowy kids slash their aerosol murals of werewolves and goblins and comic book characters of all walks of life across the crumbling brick walls. He saw them scale the fire escapes like twiggy acrobats and shoot spray paint upon the highest factory style window as if over the moon. Most of all he saw how easy it was for them to just walk in and out the doors, a simple task he couldn't do. So he just watched.

Every day since Arkahm's death Hans had been haunted by fever dreams of a new, different life. A life that hadn't left him alone like some vagabond, a life that hadn't buried him alive with regret, with all of the notebooks and photos. *The Shining, Amityville Horror, Poltergeist,* and *Carnival of Souls.* It's all Arkham read. Did Arkham want to *be* a ghost? Was it not enough to be the hunter?

There were Arkham's journals too. His signature scrawl slashed the pages. Some entries were dotted in red like a great smear of blood; the Burroughs-esque poetry could sing right off the pages if only teased the right way. Arkham formed collages as well, pasting words like *GHOST* and *HAUNTING* and *DEATH* and *REDRUM* and *MADNESS* side by side as if spinning together his own book. When Hans read them all he thought about how William S. Burroughs used that same technique in his writing. It's called the cut-up method, created by taking a fully linear text, cutting it in pieces and then pasting the passages back together in a new order, which in turn makes a new text, lyric, poem, anything. *When you cut into the past, the future leaks out*, Arkham had told him. Hans swigged from his flask, took a pull off of his Pall Mall and he was good to go. One battered notebook lay in his bag and he took it out, flipping open to a random beat up page.

Like burning autumn leaves our overwrought fancies had been reading into every wind howl, and standing hard against the bank, the laughter close. The plain text was pasted together like a bad puzzle, but Hans shoved the scrappy pieces of papers into his bag and prayed that they'd disappear. He felt as dismal as the last drop of liquor at the bottom of the dreaded bottle: the realization that everything means nothing and that you have to wake up and face it all again.

Then something shot past him, bullet-speed, dark gibbous thing, and for a second he thought it was the glimmering shadow of Arkham. But then he saw it was only a rolled up carpet, and that an old Mexican man was pulling it into the dilapidated parking lot. He breathed heavily, trying not to scare himself.

Hans thought about his life in the East Village, how he'd done nothing but drink his regrets away for two decades, watching the original badness fade away. Typical of Manhattan these days, the village was plagued by gentrification. Any area that is discovered by artists and bohemians will often attract affluent residents, subsequently increasing the housing prices which then drives out the people who first instilled culture and sanity into the neighborhood.

Like in Hell's Kitchen: the Sharks and Jets were no more, the dusty windows of Italian social clubs and gambling rings were gone; the bakeries no longer wafted the fresh smell of bread in the morning. It was replaced by the crayon smell of make up and the bitter stench of expensive hairspray. It pained Hans to walk down 9th avenue these days, finding that Hell's Kitchen was not so hellacious anymore. The windows were marked *CLOSED!!!* and *RENOVATION!!!* making way for new posh eateries and fancy yuppie bars.

The same crap was happening in the East Village. The punks have nearly disintegrated; dive bars are far and few in between, and the sweet sound of music is being asked to quiet down. The corner gangs have been replaced by tight lipped business folk, the feeling of dread replaced by an ephemeral happiness. Conformity is the game. Identity is now a mere number, guided by the next social media craze. Trends and scenes come and go so quick these days it was a marvel how anyone kept up, but that was part of the plan: keep clear of any emotional attachment and follow the leader. Compromise and ease is the way of life, no work necessary.

The gentrification plague with no phoenix in sight.

But Hans could never imagine living anywhere else except here, not in the darkness of another city, nowhere that a sunless ocean could take him; nothing. New York was his home, no matter how much it had changed. The soul of mob life and extortion still lingered here; cigarette butts and broken glass glimmered in the alleyways, and the rats hadn't yet left to find a new nesting ground. Music was still the city's lifeblood. He held onto that much withered hope, at least.

If only Hans could only accept his age and the realization that things change, for better or worse. But of course this was a world where technology brainwashes people to follow the next trend and buy buy buy whatever the hottest commodity is. People make hobbies of sitting behind I-phones, servants to Netflix and hypnotizing laptop screens, all trying to outdo one another's machine craze. Isolation could be bought and sold now. To Hans it made no sense. Facebooking about how one wiped their ass was now the most interesting way to start the day. It was so *fun* to read about. It seemed no one wanted to take the time to read a book or create decent tunes anymore; nobody wrote things like *Junky* or *Dandelion Wine* these days. Those were the kinds of books that turned kids into readers, thinkers, but nobody wants to read today. They want to simply gaze into tiny LED screens because they're too afraid to be challenged.

Even books are electronic and that made Hans' temples burst! No longer do phone calls exist; text messages are the way to go. Who would ever think that the world would come to digital voices instead of the real thing? Back to morse code? Robots talk to you on the phone, electricity snaps like jaws if you touch the wrong metal; even mail is sent through the computer. And people talk in their own digital language! Abbreviated words reconfigured with upper and lower cases, a U in place of YOU; R in place of ARE. Cyber-talk: a secret tongue that millions of people speak, except for Hans. He didn't have a cell phone, didn't want one.

Nobody did things for the feeling anymore, for art. No one understood art these days. Being yourself had evolved into a misunderstood trend rather than a rebellious movement. It gave him a sick sense of reality. A man in his forties *should* have been married, he knew, should have been a father and not just some crummy barkeep in a rock dive. But was that the way his life was supposed to end up? He guessed not.

Hans had forgotten all about women, about love. Perfect hair, perfect wife, perfect kids, perfect life. What was that? He needn't a woman's curves, needn't to know how they would taste or smell. He didn't want to see the fluffy sliver of sex between their legs, or their smiles that could melt candles without ever lighting them. He didn't want anything but for his life to make sense.

Hans could only think of Arkham, how he smelled, tasted. Sweaty and crunched over his tables of photos, skin sweet as freshly washed laundry. Surely this leather wearing creature wasn't attracted to his best friend; surely he didn't miss the *special* way Arkham touched him, always warm and wet with the faint trace of photo developing chemicals on his lips, his cheeks. Surely he didn't miss the way his hair stuck to his face when they got drunk together, the way he kissed Hans on the cheek when he discovered a new orb, the way Hans imagined the twisted white rope laying between two skinny legs . . .

No. Hans wasn't supposed to miss him that way.

Then the 7 train exploded above his head, pulling his mind out of his own deranged dream. The junkyard at the end of the block all of a sudden screamed with the youth of his old life of getting into trouble and not giving a fuck about anything. *Old life*, he thought. *Exactly*. The thought spoke to him with some kind of strange clarity. Change has come, but it was time to get the bar and wait for what, he didn't know.

Rez spent twilight alone at the fountain in Oval Park throwing coins into its watery depths and making a thousand wishes he knew would never come true. He picked through a cold falafel and was amazed that no matter the temperature, the verdant flavor of fried chic peas and fresh tomatoes was magical, and the taste of his clove cigarettes enhanced it. There were two left in the pack; his lungs felt good and charred now, his throat sore, his palate tainted with the everlasting dry stench of sweet smoke. With that, Rez decided to make some more wishes.

A family. Ephemeral happiness. A lover.

One . . . two . . . three . . . the coins were tossed, rusted dimes, and the lucky nickel he'd kept with him since the day he decided to hit the streets, all dropped like the Heart of the Ocean into the fountain's murky water. There was a pen in his grip, but no words rolled off the inky tip. There hadn't been words in a long time, so he pumped the volume up on his iPod and let his head fill with the sweet revelations that lie within music.

Music always soothed the soul.

Rez touched his skin, admiring the feel of his own bones, the feel of his fingers traversing the tattoos three layers deep, the faint razor scars. He let the last rays of twilight wash warmth against his face, into the cracks of his half-smile. Then it was gone. What remained above was cloud like chitin that spread over a wide-white city moon. Emollient winds swept past the park benches marked up with ancient graffiti scratched into the surface, with hardened gumdrops that would never be able to be scraped off no matter how hard the parks department worked.

He'd been thinking about the streets. Overcrowded back then and no change today. The mouths still chatter about riots and pick pockets and drug busts by the light of garbage can fires. The beatniks and the homeless, families that learn to recognize one another by dirty faces, by pockmarks and certain stenches. It was a familiar past life.

Rez had plundered through the murky depths of the careless New York City Administration for Children's Services for most of his life, a tug of war over what family would receive the government's money for his caretaking, with Rez never seeing a mere dime of it. Rez had no idea what his social security number was, no idea if he had money in some secret bank account waiting to take him out of New York City, but what Rez did know was that you didn't need any of that to live in the streets.

Sixteen-years-old and he fell into homelessness headlong, sick of foster life, sick of the way those pseudo-families stared him down with cold judging eyes: the strange non-blooded son, the flimsy artist who didn't fit in with their morals, their Catholic constrictions. It was very easy for Rez to move around the city without an identity; he was used to being invisible. And so he settled. He learned to *survive*, learned to eat food lying at the bottom of trash bins when he had no money, fighting for the last piece of half chewed chicken against the whorls of maggots and roaches that engulfed his hands, his arms, skidding down his spine until he was one large living blanket.

Nobody taught Rez what stability or trust was when he was a growing boy, when a child needed it the most; nobody doused him with affection when a child of four or five was supposed to be drowning in it. This helped him realize that you could sum up life as pure bullshit, that religion was tainted and the seasons died as fast as they were born. You could count the seconds and watch the skin on your face wrinkle; you didn't feel the same hope each morning your eyes opened.

He had grown up.

Holidays became gaudy past times (not that he cared for any), another excuse to exchange pointless gifts and collect candy from strangers; celebrations invented to distract people from actually understanding that they meant nothing in the end. Everything means nothing in the end; everyone is doomed to take the same dirt nap.

It was then he found out that ghosts were real, and that believing in them was not such a bad idea. Real ghosts; not the puppeteer in the sky who judges cursed souls to pass into his golden spire kingdom, that is, as long as you believe his illusion of life. Rez could hear them too; faint voices not like a whisper and not like someone far down a tunnel, but muffled sounds; voices from inside his head, his mind.

Sometimes they penetrated the membrane between reality and dream, trying to latch onto his brain and take him for a ride. They'd been following him since he could remember. The nightmare had been following him forever: a pale woman yelling all that is known as agony during childbirth. Back then he drank those demons away, not giving a fuck about life or wandering ghosts. Then again, he was writing too. Without it there was nothing else to do but think about how much he sucked at life. Writing was his lover, his best friend, his wool blanket when it got cold. The talent of jotting down dreams and turning them into stories was no longer there. His creative conscious was paralyzed, in need of something that he just couldn't figure out.

Rez knew his own mind, his own soul. He'd been living in it its hectic landscape his entire life. Most of all, he knew nothing was going to fix the writer's block at the moment. That beautiful microburst of art was gone; the magical bridge in the shape of the written word stemming from brain to fingertips had crumbled. Forcing his psyche to change only excused Rez to numb his mind with alcohol, falling into a greater creative paralysis.

These days writing meant scratching his dreams across notebooks with ink so black it ate through the paper, a catalogue to use later on—how ever long that would be remained a mystery. There were nights of riding the trains and drinking stolen bottles of Jäger, marking up his notebooks like leper spots with themes, jagged plots and crazy characters; the sights of the boroughs and the people on the train were inspiration all in their own fucked up right. There was always a free show, from fist fights to Opera singers, to steel drum masters, and even a man who told jokes that sounded as if Dirty Harry and George Carlin had been lovers and had an illegitimate child. *A FUCKING DONUT!* But no one laughed; no one filled his pitiful change cup. Those days were dead. Inspiration was dead.

There used to be readings, small get togethers brought to the world by ragged would-be's, their thrift shop clothes, their oily hair that glistened like raven's wings; kids who hung out on stoops all hours of the night staring into the sky, just waiting for that one right person to connect to the sad poetry they ripped from their own heads and scrawled down into linear sentences. They spoke in fancy, writerly speak, but it wasn't good enough. No big name conventions wanted them, and who said their own city even wanted them? But they put on their puppet shows anyway, their readings, offering their thoughts of the world and their view of reality to small underground crowds.

Some people loved it. Others hated it. Opinions ran amuck, but opinions are sharp as blades, cutting you without even knowing it. Opinions are too unique to say who's right. Plus, these kids weren't anyone Rez could seriously remember anyway, just the locals who wanted attention. They were John's and Kristi's, hipsters, punk princesses and devil-doll stool pigeons. Nobody wrote anything of mere relevance, mere insight. The stories and poetry came out of their mouths like jumbled, forced attempts at being a vagabond artist. Their flaunts only made them seem tacky; their pompous attitudes got them nowhere in life. But to Rez, art was life.

Art is not some kind of dodge or hustle, it's a sacred duty.

KGB Bar hosted local readings, anywhere in Williamsburg too, and so the writing crowd had thrived like a nest of hungry arthropods, but died all at the same time too. They lost out to the musicians, to the ambient crowds, the indies and the gypsy artists living strictly by the code of *Viva La Vie Boheme*. The writers just couldn't compete; most of them were sad little pups that lived on the streets like Rez, who slept with candles in their grip so it would chase away the rats and the roaches, so it could warm them.

A lot of them fought like little Down syndrome teenagers. They couldn't throw a fist faster than they could spit, but they did have weapons: pens, books, and their own introverted ways of tormenting speech. Rez once saw two little vertebrates arguing over something as benign as a cheap paperback copy versus hardcover, a Gibson versus an Ibanez, and one of the guys stabbed the other with a ball point pen in the shoulder; ink exploded in a crazy sheen of metallic black mixed with blood. Some of the true nerds knew how to sharpen knives into old school quills, and they used them not only to write their work, but to protect themselves from the people they were afraid of. Who they were, Rez would never know.

But that fucked up crowd and the waned hope for the craft didn't stop Rez from what he did best. Rez wrote *Rivers End*, and *Ambigrams & Palindromes*, from hanging out with that crowd. Two stories he managed to sell to a professional magazine. He thought about his favorite part of *Ambigrams & Palindromes*.

And so the music swelled beneath his grip, his heart a filthy cauldron of notes and figures pouring like lava as his fingers met the bone-white keys. He knew they'd never leave; his limbs took control and his mind opened into a black hole.

Then *Rivers End*.

It was now or never, the bottle glimmering in the soft afternoon light, and so his hands wrapped around the wet edge, and he opened his mouth to feed.

Gods, it hurt to think about that, but Rez couldn't help himself. The memory of how dedicated he used to be to the craft made his blood simmer, his heart race. Remembering the books with cigarette burns, the pens he'd kneaded down to mere nibs made Rez want to escape the world even more. The life of an artist obliged him into loneliness, but a comforting one at that. Without it, he wasn't able to distract himself from that burning question.

Family? Bloodlines? A Past? A lover?

It was all ever Rez thought about. Most of his characters never found full-scale happiness when he typed THE END. It was a characteristic derived from being given away at birth. Having been ripped from the first pair of hands that were supposed to keep you safe from the world's evil; without the first pair of lips that were supposed to whisper how much they loved him left a huge gap in his heart. Constantly searching for blood ties could be so exhausting, mentally more than physically.

That came with an identity crisis as well. Sometimes Rez was a wannabe musician, playing rookie chords on a dollar store guitar; other times Rez was a sinister photographer, a lyricist, a would-be painter and even, though he failed miserably, a junkie. It depended on the crowd he hung out with. But nobody can understand that kind of circumstance unless they were shipped off to fostered hell like Rez had been. Nobody knew how it felt to be so alone, to not have any blood relatives to comfort you, to understand why you look the way you do, to smile like you do, to laugh like you do.

And so Rez knew his strange blue eyes would forever glance out of the curtain of black hair, just waiting for that one random person to come out of the shadows and announce that they were related by blood. Who was he kidding, there're over eight million people in this city. Nobody ever did, and never would. Back to the hole in his heart he must lay, a deep gauge his writing used to be able to dig him out of. Without that, Rez would certainly drop again, but this time he'd let the wet black dirt cover him.

4

The sky indigo just before night, and the cold vegetation slithers into dens of dust and mildew; mice shuffle into the forest as owls scourge the air. It's just past nine so says the silver bracket clock nailed to her desk.

Delilah: girl with the long hair, blue-black hair dyed too many times now, backcombing the jungle into dreads before the mirror. Ghost-girl in the reflection, girl who doesn't reject the judgment staring back at her; girl who wants to get the fuck out of here. Her peripheral vision catches ragged piles of books piled high: a stack of National Geographic magazines shredded and thinned of their covers, their posters, all glued to the walls in a papier-mâché fashion. Heavy metal icons, industrial innovators and authors of the macabre are there too. A small shrine to William S. Burroughs gleams dully in the dark, pictures of cats and signature explosive spray paint portraits.

The room is lit by candles; the cool air is permeated with dreamy incense that smell of Hooka and burning desires. ART SAVES ALL OF ME! is slathered in bad paint on the ceiling, from Otep's *Sevas Tra* album. Blue starlight trails the edges of her room and brings on a psychedelic effect. But Delilah looks up and sees that it's only the rope light, brand new set she bought at the Sideshow Music Shop.

Ticket stubs are tacked across the walls, silver spheres like tiny disco balls, stubs from local shows. Bigger, nastier bands only tour the cities. Nine Inch Nails would never dream of stepping foot in Violet Hill, neither would Tool, Black Sabbath or Guns n' Roses; Otep and Glassjaw just aren't popular enough for the dark children of town.

The fishnet is tightly wrapped around her legs, and the lace is secured across her arms; the studded belt sits atop her pinpoint hips. Black upon blacker, Doc Martens on her feet; the scary pallor of her skin glows through the darkness, her eyes like twin campfires of blue

43

and silver. She is Lestat De Lioncourt, she is murder, mayhem. She is Delilah Dellinger.

She looks out the window and sees the twisted nightmares that live inside her head fill the sky with grey cloudy blankets, pregnant with rain. She imagines they will burst and the wet goblets will fall upon Violet Hill like placenta, drippy, filmy, and stinking like the inner lining of a swollen cavity that has just pushed out a child. But that was her dream talking again.

Then she hears the voices behind the door, annoying voices, knifing voices, voices she hates. A knock, and a couple of gentle turns jostle the doorknob. But no one can get in as there's a large stick between the door and adjacent wall, locking her safe inside. Whoever wants in will have to break the damn thing down. *As long as you live under my roof you will respect me!* Delilah's parents: ignorant to the fact that they'd raised their damaged little girl in a bubble, no matter how much they tried to deny it. They'd trained her to love complacency and to never ask questions. They wanted her to keep calm when deep inside she was spinning, spitting and screaming. She recalls their famous words.

Delilah, you have to remember that girls aren't supposed to fight. They're supposed to be pretty, be happy. Stop being consumed with all this self-loathing, it's very sad. Those scars on your arms and knuckles look calloused and ugly.

"Delilah, please, I don't want you to be upset," her mother says.

"Go away," Delilah hisses.

Not supposed to think for myself?

"Miss Dellinger, you've five seconds before I make my way in there," her father speaks of bad intentions.

Delilah turns the television on and *Tales from the Crypt* is still on repeat; *Masters of Horror* will be next. But for now Delilah can see the Crypt Keeper's face jumping up from his coffin in the mirror's reflection. She whistles the opening theme and realizes that she wants a puppet just like that, a puppet she can turn into a friend. She lights a Clove with her stick matches. *CAN YOU DO IT?* asks the cover: a sick man, obviously debilitated from smoking too much.

Smoking never results in a dignified death.

Everyone was telling you what to do these days; the television said you shouldn't smoke and shouldn't take drugs, that you should just be happy and shut up about it. What did they know anyway? She strikes the match and lets a small cinder fall upon her arm. It stings, creates a red blotch, and then finally fades. Fades like her nightmares eventually do, fades like she knows night will to the daylight of tomorrow, and at some point, her own life.

Nothing lasts forever.

"YOU'RE SMOKING IN MY HOUSE!" her father roars. "You have school tomorrow."

"Honey," mother returns, "you can't stay up all night and listen to that foul music, that music of evil."

"I'm going to drink myself into a coma, if you're that curious."

Television off now and Delilah hits the stereo. *Ghosts I-IV* comes sizzling out of the speakers. Symphonies, harmonies, percussion and synthesizers. Devoid of Trent's distinct vocal melodies, this CD is just as strong as any other Nine Inch Nails album. The instrumental of solitude is fine as wine. The piano soars into her blood, the electronics crackle like fireworks. She wants something to drink now, something to burn her belly. Absinthe comes to mind, but that was a liquor one could only find in big fancy cities, like New York or San Francisco, Miami and New Orleans. It's not an option. So she deals with the Jägermeister, the cloves, the bad weed and the boxed wine. Gods, it was a wonder how she functioned day to day.

"We didn't mean to spring it up on you like that."

The sounds are muffled through the door; she doesn't want to hear them anymore. Only music can save her before the pain becomes so bad she will rip it out of her chest, rip her heart straight out of her thorax and nail it to the wall beaten and bloody. The realization that her existence never belonged here makes Delilah dream of an exciting life, one filled with the filthy poetry of Burroughs, of song, guitars, and a sibling to stay side by side with, a partner in crime. If it is out there, it will be in New York.

"We just thought it was time. You're not a teenager anymore. You're a grown lady."

Grown lady, like she's some shriveled baby-boomer.

"It was time you knew, that's all honey," dad again, trying to be as nice as he can be.

"I can smell her cigarettes, even through all of that hoodoo herb crap she burns," mother says.

"They're called incense!"

"We still love you. You're our daughter. You're our life."

"Yeah fucking right."

Two parents more concerned that their daughter is raising hell than anything else; two parents breathing Barbie dolls and pink dresses down her throat. Delilah remembers how good it felt when she tore those dresses up, when she melted the faces of the Barbie dolls into plastic sludge over the stove.

Her DNA is the tainted strain, the crazy girl birthed in the dark scary city of New York. Rebellion and thinking for yourself is not for Pennsylvania girls; that's only for ratty city folk. And so Delilah manages to find a new damaged girl deep and wet and black inside of herself. The chrysalis of old skin sheds, lays open and vulnerable to the blade.

The piano crescendos; Delilah holds her ears, tugs the spiraled industrials. The swig of Jäger is like battery acid, and then the smoke goes rotten. She puts the stub out against her skin, skin she will tattoo, but not before she gives it up to the butterfly blade. She doesn't like to be filed into a statistical slot that says most girls suffer the terror and addiction of cutting, and that being a cutter is something most American girls think about at least once in their lives.

Delilah never thinks about it, she simply executes.

The butterfly knife has a shining green handle like the back of some exquisite beetle, some prehistoric insect caught unwillingly in a shell of tree sap. The blade itself is like the tip of a diamond, so sharp, indestructible. You don't even know it passes through your skin until you hear the blood drip and slap onto the floor.

But that's how it all begins to make sense: the physical pain like a vacation from the mental agony; the scab and the burn so distracting. Picking at the red and raw scabs is as close to redemption as it comes. She never feels the sorrow of nerve endings severed in the wake of her cutting. There is nothing to ever stop her, and Delilah thinks for a minute that she will never stop, will never be satisfied until her arm is a roadmap of scar tissue and useless, ugly skin. Skin to match the way she feels inside.

Truly, unrepentantly, indifferent.

Their worn shoes took Avenue A south toward St. Mark's place. The taste of pollution was strong, whispering a song of carbon monoxide inside everyone's mouth. Clive darted through these tight blocks, blocks he knew like the back of his hand. Rez rushed through them too, a stampede of hate falling from his pursed mouth. He'd forgotten his metro card, and they were already too many blocks from Stuyvesant Town to turn around. *THE MTA CAN SUCK THE BIG ONE!* Rez yelled.

Clive would buy Rez a metro card if he needed it, but that didn't stop him from thinking about how half the time trains were a joke anyway. Though they were the city's lifeblood, they were also the city's deep vein thrombosis. They were always broken, under repair, and just when you think it's safe to board again, the damn things skip stops and change routes.

"I'm starved," Clive said. "2 Bros. anyone?"

"I'm meeting with my dealer first," Rez pronounced. "Need some trees. Anyone putting in?"

"A twenty, for Lynk and I . . . right Lynk?"

Lynk straggled behind, his face bathing in the moonshine that shot down between the buildings. There was no tracery of age to be found in those sharp features, beneath those eyes like the color of honey. Clive had never seen him in direct sunlight; in fact Lynk had been working on his pallor long before Clive knew him.

"Cigarettes too," Rez said.

"I'll buy you a pack," Clive said. "No problem."

Lynk snorted snarkily, and Clive caught Rez wincing for one sharp second. These past few months Clive had been taking care of Rez since he was pulling in bank emptying the tap for hungry yuppies who didn't know how to close their wallets. Clive didn't mind at all; he loved big tips. But Rez had fucked up every job he had for the past few months, even fucked up the most lenient of places like his part-time job at *Evolution*, the science and art store in Soho. And with the current market employers knew his name, strictly avoiding him at all costs.

But Clive couldn't bring himself to care about these trivialities, not when he had such a fat wallet. Why not share the wealth? That was one of America's biggest problems: the poor on one sad side and the rich on the glorious other. Plus, Rez was suffering with writer's block, so Clive knew it was his duty to be there for him. He could not imagine living a life without art, without something to keep challenging him, so there must have been exquisite pain for Rez. And yet nothing ever truly soothed Rez's soul. Having the rent paid for him was no big deal because Rez didn't fear the streets; he'd welcome homelessness with open arms if he had to. For this reason Clive would never ask Rez for money, afraid he'd just go and never come back. Clive remembered something Rez said to him once.

I've lived here my entire life. I carry the scents of scum and finesse in the palm of my hand; I hold shame and dishonor in my heart; I breathe what others cannot bear; I've eaten what most people would consider horrifying. I am the city, and yet, I don't even know myself. I don't even feel like I fit in.

Rez was so fragile, so vulnerable to his fucked up emotions. Someone in the group had to be the glue. Plus, Rez was always there to support Clive with his work, his expeditions, even if it was just to help Clive's hunches with his talents. It was no small truth that things became very sour when Rez was around. Regular days turned into shit-shows—butterfingers dropping food, slipping and skinning his knee, or breaking glass antiques in shops around the city—and people even crossed the street when he walked in their direction; nothing he did was considered normal. Being with Rez was like being inside some aberrant reality, like the very air turned so thick and juicy you could either swim away or sleep forever.

Lynk remained weary of that kind of talent, afraid that the entire world's evil was ready to jump off Rez's shoulders, and infect everything it touched. *Rez is like a magnet for destruction. He'll tip the damn world into doomsday if we're not careful,* Lynk reflected. Clive called it bad luck, but Lynk was certain Rez was struck by a cavalcade of curses while still in his mother's womb. The truth was that Lynk thought Rez got in the way of his stream of conscious, his focus, but most importantly in the way of the ghost hunts.

Clive never found that to be true. All the voices and traveling ghosts that were attracted to Rez were a beacon of hope. How could Lynk not see that? This was how Clive was going to literally prove the existence of life beyond what we can see. It made the clock tick a little faster while waiting for some cold hand to strike them out of the blue; it was finally worth it to sit out in the rain and sleep in bushes. Rez wasn't psychic, or even a mystic, not that Clive knew, but his sixth sense was finer tuned than your regular person. Half the reason why Clive took Rez off the streets was because he wanted to study Rez, wanted to test the theory of orbs that surrounded a supposed haunted person.

Lynk brushed it off as rubbish, but then again Lynk brushed off anything Rez did as rubbish, and any girl Clive liked as well. There was Holly Brown, the punked-out East Village chick; Mary Levine, the Jew with the crazy died hair; and Henrietta, the goth from Long Island. Lynk got rid of them all quickly, as he always did in his own sneaky way. The damned kid had a problem with sharing. *Too fat and too ugly for you, Clive. Too clingy, too annoying, not interesting enough, not GOOD enough for you, Clive!*

But then there was Jennifer McDade. The Irish girl who dressed like Buffy the Vampire Slayer but listened to The Misfits like it was her destiny to be one of their poster girls. Lynk didn't approve of her either, her skinny legs, the corn silk hair that Clive had so very much loved smelling when he woke up next to her in the morning. She was interested in paranormal photography, interested in learning the machines and the lingo, but Lynk treated her like a vile dog, didn't want her part of their ghost hunting life, and so she took it to heart and found a new crowd to party with.

Clive could've had a relationship, could've paraded with her through the East Village, in all the dives and all the underground parties to stop the horrid gossip. Blithering gossip about his and Lynk's notorious hook up. But Lynk was never going to *have* Clive in that way again; Clive was never going to *fuck it up again*. Being constantly reminded of his mistake came in the shape of Lynk himself. He was like a ticking time bomb ready to blow at any second, jittering like some coke head. The entire ordeal had changed him. But Lynk was Clive's ghost hunting partner, so it was better to ignore it than add fuel to the fire.

Such is life. Without drama you wouldn't know what serenity is. Bisexuality was a common tradition amongst the stoners, the emos and the rock n' rollers, but not with the English. The English are tough and manly. They'd never slip like Clive did. Once was more than fucking enough. And with that thought, Clive let his mind relax, and thought about photography. He was on a mission after all.

Delilah jolted awake from another nightmare, sweat like syrup gliding down her forehead, dripping into her mouth tasting of salt and fear. A slick wind cooled her face; the radio was turned louder as if to block her thoughts; a shrill echoing of Jimmy's typical *shoot shoot shoot shoot shoot I'm gunna' come all over you!* could be heard.

A matted Kathe Koja novel was crumbled in her grip, the pages marked up like mad, the spine nearly broken her hands were gripping it so hard. The cover was spattered with blood, and when her eyes made sense of her surroundings, she realized that she'd been cutting herself again, cutting deep into the selfish pain, across the tattoos that she'd spent way too much money on.

Delilah wiped her arm clean with her shirt and bandaged it with cheap ACE gauze. She stretched, yawned and slid the butterfly blade into her pocket. Delilah brought her eyes back to the spellbinding words, but found that she couldn't focus anymore. Something kept writhing beneath her body like she was riding on the husk of a giant serpent. She slowly realized that she was in Jimmy's pickup speeding down Steeraway Street. Behind her the endless road shimmered; in front the trees hunched over as if forming a tunnel to their spider-branched world.

Soon, the dream voice told her. *You'll know.* The same nightmare over and over: a screaming woman in a dark, dark room lit only by the faint glow of fire, face concealed by long black hair. Her legs wrenched open, pale and bruised, slicked with hot wet gore; her mouth a bleeding chasm of meat, and a shadow looming above her, eyes like blue fire—like her own eyes. Hands wrenched her legs open, reached inside her swollen cavity and pulled out something large, something alive, bleeding . . . alive and crying . . .

Then Delilah heard the smash of glass and her soul rose out of the jagged landscape of nightmare land. She saw the night sky out there, too black sky, and saw Jimmy throwing empty bottles of Jägermeister out into the open, screaming about going to New York City. *Stop it, Jimmy*, she thought. *Animals live in those woods.* Then a memory began to lick the inside of her skull: Electric Orchid beating the shit out of Blood Hunt, the rival band at The Skeleton Grin's battle of the bands bonanza. Blood Hunt's sound of stringy guitar riffs, talentless drum beats and boring rip-off grunge vocals was a spiraling blend of teenage angst that any Seattle boy could muster up; it all echoed inside her like a string of broken instruments clashing together.

Now Delilah could see the floor of The Grin packed; it was all shadows and dark angles, phantasmal things that only she and Alex knew about. The Violet Hill kids were cheering for her; pillows of hair concealed their faces; dirty metal heads in torn Iron Maiden muscle shirts moshed madly. She saw two grunge kids who thought they were Kurt Cobain's godchildren, but who had Courtney Love's name secretly tattooed in a place that only intimacy could discover. Electric Orchid had brought the house down and were now on their way to the city that celebrates carnival all year round, a place they rightfully belonged.

THE ABSENCE OF LIGHT

The thought of walking on the land where bastard sperm met dark egg excited her. Delilah imagined the roads leading there would be swathed in arcs of deep yellow sodium light and flickering fluorescence, with the drool of monsters. It would be a lunacy of sights and organic smells, the city that never sleeps. She would get lost between the buildings, bathe in acid rain and kiss the sweet, mucky black top.

Delilah had never been anywhere outside of Violet Hill, not even to Philadelphia, and this realization saddened her. Some of her high school drinking buddies had been to New York; they said it was crazy, smelly and too expensive for the amount of garbage on the street. Alex and the rest of the band had been as far as Philly to cop salvia, but they had more money than her, had better jobs at the bars in town while she was stuck droning to the gods of laundry at the No Catch Dry Cleaners.

If Delilah seriously thought about it, her life was consumed by Violet Hill. Her lungs were polluted with so much anthracite dust she wondered how many lobes of cancer were currently eating her insides up. Her knuckles have skinned across these gravelly roads; her knees have scabbed over so much the scar tissue was bright and pink and gibbous. Her nails remained pitiful stumps broken off from one too many fights, painted over black to hide the shame.

"Fuck! I fell asleep," Delilah said.

"I know . . . you hate sleeping," Alex said, his face pale above hers, his eyes darting for her arm. "You cut yourself . . . in your sleep this time. I thought you were going to stop."

"I am," Delilah lied, lied like she always did, the permanent addict.

All of a sudden she wanted Zazo, her pet bat. Delilah had found him bare as a babe squealing from a branch on the oak tree by her balcony. He'd no family to love him, nobody to depend on. It was like looking in a mirror. That night she'd drank a bottle of Jägermeister Sheigh had stolen from the liquor store on Steeraway Street. The plan was to drink until she passed out, knowing that only Jäger could squash all of her awful dreams. But something made her stop sucking at the tip of the bottle: a tiny squeal outside her window, an animal that needed Delilah's help.

She took Zazo in with warm hands and he'd shown her immediate kindness. It was then she knew that love was out there in that big hopeless world somewhere, that she could aspire to be somebody, unlike so many of the complacent kids here. But would Manhattan would be that place? Would it drip dreams and nightmares?

Being that the nightmares were getting stronger these past few weeks, their messages clearer, Delilah thought perhaps her ticket was up and death was ready to claim her. For some reason it wasn't such a bad thought to die. Once it was said and done, you wouldn't have to think anymore. But Delilah tried not to take her dreams too seriously; they'd done a good enough job of scourging her mind. The past few dreams had brought visitors, and she'd read in *The Dreamer's Dictionary* that when a visitor comes you're in trouble, let alone when your own music is what attracts them to you. But how do you give up your first love to avoid your number one fear?

Unfair.

With her head was on Alex's lap she saw Gir holding a little pink piggy and lifting it for the world to see: Alex's Invader Zim T-shirt. His fingers were working through her black dreads and playing with the industrials in her ear. Then he stopped, thought for one moment and then began tracing his finger down the squiggling black line tattooed over the ridged razor scars on her forearm, over the fresh spongy scabs weaved throughout her skin like black veins: scrawled lyrics, G-clef musical notes, a bed of shimmering anthracite dust, and soaring bats like from the *House of Mystery* comic series.

"When we get to New York I don't want you to cut yourself anymore, D. I mean it this time. I want you to let your skin heal . . . set your soul free."

They were listening to Avenged Sevenfold: the perfect cruising band. *Cruising to New York, my home*, she thought. It was the place her parents swore was a breeding ground for disease, a place where murder was revered and AIDS was culture.

This shining city built of gold, a far cry from innocence.

"It's easier to deal with the pain this way, easier than all the mental stress."

"It's unnatural and unhealthy. I'm your friend, and I can't see you do this to yourself anymore."

"YOU USED TO DO IT!" Delilah scowled.

"Yeah, but only because I was tagging along with you. I haven't carried a razor since my seventeenth birthday. You should've followed my lead four years ago."

"If I followed your lead, I'd be dressed as a boy right now."

"Whatever."

Delilah grinned fantastically sharp. "Tommy left?"

"Lost him in The Grin," Alex said nonchalantly.

"Oh, you sound happy."

"He's a low-life horn-ball. He found someone else. Oh well."

"You liked him. *Admit it*."

"I did, but I'm over it."

5

ez ripped himself out of the daydream: a writer's life, a pen dripping blood-ink, a notebook with a thousand guttural words spread across. Tales of horror and glum, tales of misfortune, tales that tested the human soul to its fullest potential. His own tale? His own life? He'd never know, it seemed. For now he was on the hunt for some sweet Sour Diesel and a pack of cloves, but there was a critical choice to make. He was low on cash and had to choose one of the two: the cloves were only sold in smoke shops and the weed via his dealer. Fuck it, he didn't feel like taking the walk to 8th avenue, and he wasn't about to let Clive pay for everything. He had more pride than that!

The buildings in this part of town were uneven; the walls were collapsing and the paint was chipped, bitter; the people were secretive and drunk. It was the perfect place to hunt, to hear voices. A breeding ground. *Join us*, a voice said. *Always open*, another grunted. Rez constantly heard these kinds of invitations, but he wasn't about to fall into the temptation of *I SEE DEAD PEOPLE*, not about to sell his talents on the street like so many other hooligans did.

He was best suited selling his talents through words.

But Rez knew that if you looked hard enough at one of the buildings here you could get lost in your own gaze, perhaps spot the twinkling reflection of a lost apparition. If you stood long enough by a crack in the cement you could smell the rot of the underground, see the steam rising like the boiling plasma of hell. And if you found yourself stuck in the subways, you'd be bound to see Rudy Pasko, or the Midnight Meat Train.

Remember how many voices you heard when you saw Tool in Nassau Coliseum? You couldn't even focus on the music, couldn't even enjoy your favorite band.

"Here," Lynk's hand shot forward, his rings catching the moonlight. "A clove."

"Speak of the devil," Rez said.

Lynk's voice seemed to never rise above a whisper, but tonight it was practicing a more irritating decibel. Maybe it was the heat. The humidity was like a free sauna for the city to use, making people a smidge more irritable than usual. Summer was supposed to be shifting into autumn, and the leaves were supposed to be the disfiguring color of old fruit left on the wasted vine. But the most bearable weather of the year was now the most temperamental. Global warming in its prime.

When Lynk's voice got loud, it became quite frightening. These days it was getting louder, and always for the same reason: that fucked up night in The Continental, his unhealthy attraction to Clive. At least Clive didn't suffer from anything other than the guilt that ate him alive through gossip. But Rez hated knowing that Clive had to duck his head into his shirt when they went out, embarrassed that another person accused him of being gay, fully aware that the harrowing guilt of letting his hormones spiral into his brain and take control of his third leg was what made the kids in his crowd tick. Rez knew that he shouldn't have to feel inferior about that, but Clive was British, and so sometimes his opinion was still stuck in that tough English mind-set.

"Dago's throwing a huge pre-Halloween bash tonight," Lynk said. "We should go."

"I'm not going there so all those wankers can think that I'm dating you, Lynk. They get off to that shit. You and your big fucking mouth."

"I never said anything to those graveyard punks!"

Clive stopped. "Did so! All they do is talk about it. Dago, Frances, Ashlyn, Steve-o, everybody!"

"All the fringe fuckers, who cares."

Clive halted. "I mean, big fucking whoop, you slip up one time in a bar drunk off Jäger and all of a sudden you're a gay pimp."

"Here we go."

"I can't stand those androgynous fringe fuckers, always trying to tattoo their view of the world into someone's skin. They're probably getting off to the thought of my dick in your mouth as we speak."

"Omigod! How many times do I have to tell you to ignore them?"

"You shouldn't have told Dago anything. It wasn't any of his business. He's the biggest gossip queen ever."

"Look, one night we hung out, we got drunk, and I let it slip. It was an innocent mistake," said Lynk. "He's a very approachable guy."

"You let it slip like you let your mouth run whenever I hang out with girls. You gotta get the fuck over it."

Rez saw Lynk cringe, frown.

"The innocent mistake was letting my loneliness hypnotize my horniness into thinking I could be satisfied with a dude."

Lynk stopped now; Rez smiled, they were finally seeing the picture!

"Look Clive, I'm sorry," Lynk put his hand on that scrawny shoulder. "We all know Dago was born on planet DOOM, and that he loves gossip."

"Apology accepted."

Fuck, Rez thought. *Clive, you fucking prince charming. Always out to make friends.*

At the end the dark block Rez waited for his dealer. Clive and Lynk got back to their mission of hunting ghosts.

"Apparitions are known to haunt the same place over and over," Lynk said.

Rez knew the thought of apparitions was scary, and to actually see one, well, he didn't want to think about it much. He left that up to his dreams. *Soon*, he heard another voice say from an alleyway, small whispering voice made of dust and blood and gun powder. No one else heard it, of course, but when Rez turned he saw a long line of bums mumbling to themselves. It was there he met up with his shadowed dealer, a punk kid dressed in ragged scraps of leather and denim, with hair so tall and peacocked he could've taken an eye out. His labret ring was huge and he licked it maniacally. Rez and him made the pass and shared little words.

"Sour D's good this time around," the kid said.

Rez nodded and the dealer caught his unease, jumped back on his bike and took to the night. Rez couldn't bring himself to care that he just let the dealer go. It was in good culture to light your dealer up, let him smoke for free, but it didn't even cross Rez's mind at the moment. Oh well.

"Sour D reminds me of Dago's graveyard party," Rez said. "Now that was fun."

"An army of fringe fuckers cutting their wrists and bleeding into the punch bowl. What cunts," Clive said.

"You know there's a show tonight, right? Battle of the Bands kind of gig. Some band from town versus a new one from Pennsylvania."

"What good can come out of Pennsylvania?"

"Abso-fucking-lutely nothing," Rez said.

"Well look. We've a few choices. There's this building in Queens called 5Pointz. It's like a loaded gun worth of activity there. We can do this tonight, or the show."

"Let's at least check it out," Lynk said. "And you know we need you there Rez, you're like the catalyst; ghosts love you."

"Are you mocking me?"

"No."

"What's so good about that place besides the graffiti and the junk yards?"

"Old chap, it's haunted!"

"I hate when you call me old chap."

"The thing is, half of the joint burned down, and you know what that means. There's bound to be something lost, wandering inside there."

But then Rez stopped.

"LOOK! Down the alleyway."

"Heard something?"

"Yeah."

Lynk and Clive jetted between the buildings, their flashlights and cameras illuminating like small beams of hope in a dark, dark world. There was garbage everywhere, rats scampering over shoes; a bum's feet stuck out from his blanket of cardboard and fast food wrappers. Rez heard the crafted words of ghost hunters flying out of their mouths: the perfect angle, texture and gust of wind. They were a great team, no doubt about it. They had so much to live for. What did Rez have to live for anymore? He wasn't a writer, he wasn't a ghost hunter. He was a big fat nobody. Rez pulled on the clove until it was down to the filter, the spice burning his throat, and then sucked a little of that too.

"There was a hotspot there!" Clive said, overjoyed. "I bet I'm gunna get a camera full of orbs."

"Vortices . . . souls!"

Coming down St. Mark's Place the famous cube could be seen, the universal sign that you made it to St. Mark's. Radiant drag queens suffused in cheap evening gowns stood tall next to punks and yuppies. Along the streets were African men selling colored pipes and hookahs, and if you followed the street up Astor Place you could find a taste of the old world trapped between the new. Sounds, St.

Marks Comics, Search and Destroy, Trash & Vaudeville. Being inside one of those stores truly took a person away from the city, from the lights and maniacal mindset and left them in a small space worshiping the wall to wall shelves of records, toys, sketchy advertisements and the arid smell of settled dust. It brought you back to an era when punks ran free, when it was culture to wear leather jackets, ripped black jeans and dark makeup slathered all over your eyes.

DIE DIE DIE didn't mark the windows any more; the smell of spilled beer had faded thanks to chic restaurants and ice cream shops. Lynk hissed, ashamed of these blocks, and Rez actually agreed. If there was one thing all three could agree on, it was that this town needed to be saved. It had been shape shifting towards the new interests of the people for years. Rez saw the punks get kicked out, the druggies, club queens and dirty musicians asked to leave so the blocks could be bleached of its supposed disease. That hurt. The Asian eateries moved in and took over the old ghosts of this town.

They all ran down Astor and settled into 2 Bros. Pizza. Rez's senses swelled with hot cheese and sugary soda. He purchased a famous dollar slice and devoured it. Nothing like pizza in New York City. Clive stopped for a moment to idolize the block, aching to walk up the scraggy staircase occupied by a passed out punk with little lines of drool shimmering across his flaky leather jacket. He pulled out his Nikon camera to take a photo, suddenly inspired, but quickly gave up as Lynk pulled him away, saving his heart from being let down. At this sight Rez stumbled over his shoe laces and his pizza splat to the ground.

Clive looked over. "Bloody 'ell your luck keeps showing you that it's in charge."

"Fuck my life! Drink anyone? I got my last few bucks to burn and there's no better way to do it than beer," Rez offered.

They ran to the corner and turned, seeing the faint glimmer of The Continental. Rez knew Lynk hated the place, knew that this was where all of his problems began, but the insidious child inside Rez became happy knowing that fact. And so he marched along, with Clive tailing him, and Lynk as always tailing Clive.

Out of the four major roads to Delilah's house Jimmy took Worship Street, which also headed south toward Philly. It was the most deserted, the most eerie, and the most run down. Barns were flecked with gravelly cobwebs; stores had signs in the windows that read NO BUSINESS and CLOSED FOR GOOD!!! in cheap marker, stores that once sold pierogi, fresh honey and little shining pieces of anthracite fashioned into jewelry for the tourists that passed through. A lost boulevard of dreams this was, a boulevard that once thrived before the economy collapsed, before money became the way to smile. But now money only brought frowns there was so little of it.

Alex brought his mind back to the wind, to the Pennsylvania silence that shivered like wet cats through all those trees, echoing through the empty lots. Alex found Violet Hill in itself to be pretty lonely now that he was on his way to New York; so much space, and yet so full of constrictions. It was amazing how much a small town could ruin a person. Delilah would agree. He'd yet to explore who he truly was sexually. There wasn't a lot of acceptance by the crowds he hung out with. To kiss boys *and* girls confused his friends, though most of the kids didn't care; the only erotic overtone this town had was that of the crumbling Oasis Strip Club, and Alex wouldn't even step foot in there because the women were all haggard and always missing teeth.

"The trees," Delilah said. "I'll miss them. I've climbed many and they've shown me kindness."

"We'll miss and not miss a lot of things about this place. I won't miss the people. I won't miss the predictable pansies who hang out on Steeraway Street."

"What about The Grin?"

"I'll miss it the most."

Alex thought about the owner for a moment. Yosef Klurn had built The Grin from the ground up, engraving the freedom to *be who you want to be* into the very foundation. He wanted kids to have a safe haven where they could celebrate having an identity. Too many kids were told that being unique was a cry for attention, and that they should try to fit in rather than stand out. *It's about being yourself; not a cry for attention.* Yosef was ex-Amish, and so he understood this misconception; he vicariously lived through his youthful patrons, watching them carry out the life he could never dream of having raised in strict Amish society.

"You'll miss your parents won't you?" Alex grinned, knowing the answer.

"Miss who?"

"I thought you'd say that . . ."

"What about your grandparents?"

"They already accept my new fate. They want me to explore this side of my psyche."

"Ah, always the intelligent one, yet the most lush of us all, Alex."

"No, him," Alex pointed with his thin long finger, black ring reflecting moonlight. "What do we make of *that* lush?"

Billy was in a Jäger coma and a copper colored drizzle of sleep-spit moved across his makeup smeared cheek; he seemed at peace, resting for the next adventure. The night air was tinged with the smell of foliage and fallen tree leaves: the scent of journeys yet to be made. Sheigh was in the front with Jimmy lighting pieces of paper on fire, her hands flying out the window and violating the air by filling it with flame. Delilah dreamed about fire the other night, and Alex wondered if this moment was as cliché as some cheesy movie coincidence.

"We're probably going to get lost. Jimmy sucks with directions," Alex said, sipping a Sam Adams Oktoberfest.

"Like it matters anyway."

"Exactly. We don't have anymore rules to follow! We're rock stars!"

Leaving took money for gas and tolls and food, and lots of it. Alex wasn't worried. He'd saved all of his barback tips he earned at The Grin, and there was no better reason to use all that excess cash than this. Plus, in New York there was bound to be endless places that could supply them with work. They'd make a living without worry. Five paychecks combined would allow them to settle comfortably. Maybe, though he had his share of many lovers, he would find *the one*, as they say.

"I hope I'll find love in New York," Alex said.

"You, love?" Sheigh yelled from the front. "You don't know how to love. Only your PENIS loves," lazy elbow cocked out the window, huge in the rearview mirror.

"I *love* . . . I think."

"Uh huh."

"You're a whack-a-doo," and Alex went back to rubbing Delilah's head. "Hey, double D, what's wrong? Why so serious?"

"Like the movie?"

"I guess so."

"Oh, nothing, I just want to keep going . . . you know?" Delilah said hoarsely.

"Well . . . we are. So cheer up!"

"I'm just so fucking tired Alex. So tired of this place. This life! Perfect this, perfect that. Plastic Barbie dolls, conformity . . . all crap!" Delilah growled.

"Rest your voice! After that performance I don't know how you're even talking."

"Yeah, a real madwoman!" Billy mumbled half asleep. "The crowd went nuts! Especially when we let the *phantoms fly!*"

That was the code word for how their music wakes up the dead.

"And fuck, Delilah, take look at this thing."

Alex unfurled a stark-white roll of paper from his grip. It filled the back of the pickup like the Wicked Witch's Certificate of Death, like Jack Kerouac's Souls on the Road scroll. Endless pages of neatly scribed ink with dozens of straight lines and X's in bold to sign here and sign there to satisfy the business aspect of the music industry. Alex didn't know too much about that stuff, how to calculate profit percentages, how it was split between the band and their future manager. His mind was constantly on the thought of sex, drugs, and rock n' roll. *An unhealthy way of thinking*, his high school teachers constantly told him.

Oddly, Sheigh was a high school math whiz. She often talked about how if she didn't love music she would have went into research. But she'd sold her purple and black soul to rock n' roll in high school, and was much happier that way. It was the only world she fit into. It was no surprise after all. Anything is better than Violet Hill. A hellish town overrun by the unruly circle of gossip. It had plagued the conversations Alex heard most of his life. Stories of the Bavarians and their weird Dutch Country Magic, their vials of rooster's blood crafted by hexenmeisters (witch masters) that could cure influenza. The kind of people who had a deep faith in the omniscient god living in the blue space above our heads and who considered themselves the salt of the earth by ignoring everything that surrounded them. Delilah was the Queen of rebellion when it came to Violet Hill standards.

"You okay?" Alex asked from above. "You're spaced out."

"Yeah, I'm fine. Just want to rest my mind." Alex's cell phone light ignited Delilah's features like an x-ray.

"Then rest, D, because we'll be partying all night in New York."

"It's going to be a long ride," Alex said. "I'm going to read."

"Fuck that, I gotta get home and pack my shit. I gotta get Zazo! I gotta—"

"We'll bring you back, D. Don't worry. Stop being such a weirdo."

Delilah was pretty awkward when it came to simple situations. All that social introversion could only be blamed for the subjection of solitude she suffered as a child, from being given up at birth. Being deprived wrongfully of the first two people who are supposed to love you no matter the consequence can truly scar a person. Sometimes Alex wanted to dip his finger into the jelly of Delilah's brain and take it for a ride; it would be a rollercoaster that would rock n' roll him all the way to the chamber of her secretive mind. It would drive him mad.

But then the pickup fled off of Steeraway Street, the wind and the eerie lights of the Gheligg anthracite factory began to vanish, darkening his view of the world. He knew Delilah's house was only a couple more miles down, and she stirred beneath his touch as he thought this.

6

The bar was half empty. Tuesday nights are so fresh, but working The Continental on off nights let Hans catch up on his Chivas Regal habit. A few pale forms marked its insides; Hans knew half of them, knew their gossip and their complaints, their favorite drinks. Knobby faced Joey always drank Wild Turkey straight up; needle-boned Jaime always threw back car bombs, in love with the milky-sweet taste of Baileys, hoping that her drinking habits would put a few more pounds on her twiggy bones.

The Heavy Metal Kid drank only warm PBRs and Brooklyn Lager from the tap. They were all here tonight, their tips spread across the bar top like green tongues wet with the condensation of beer in cheap glasses. Their hands tapped their drinks soundly. Hans delivered and they were happy, then wiped the scratched black bar top clean in one vicious cloth swipe.

"Load me up on another, old man," Joey said.

"Same shit every Tuesday," Hans said.

"Hey, barkeep, you in a bad mood?"

"Nah. This one's on me."

Hans poured him Wild Turkey. The usual deal was *5 Shots for 10 Bucks*, but Hans was feeling generous tonight. When he watched Joey take two back with a pinched face, he imagined that the whiskey settled like hot molasses in his stomach. He never liked Wild Turkey; it made him sick to even smell it. He was more of an Old Number 7 kind of guy, but the occasional Jäger wasn't argued either. Joey slapped a dollar on the counter and Hans took it reluctantly, thinking about adding it to his tattoo fund. He wanted to get a giant fire with ghostly eyes peering from within its burning depths sleeved from shoulder to wrist, something to mark his life, a badge of surviving all these years with the same thoughts whirling in his brain over and over.

Something had to change soon or he was thinking of quitting this place—quitting this torturous memory of hanging all night with Arkham—and living in the park with the Beatniks. Magda would take care of him; Marty would certainly fill his ears up with stories of the good old days and make sure his belly was warm with the day's bottle of rotgut vodka. Hans realized then that he needed some fresh air, and with the turn out so low, he shot for the front door, passing the juke box that barely worked, its neon bones puttering, blasting Black Sabbath, perhaps Ministry . . . too distorted to tell. Three cloaked figures were pressing the bright buttons idiotically and mumbling to one another, three metal heads, three Screamers on the verge of trying to find the right sinister song to christen this joint for their inebriation.

Outside was a cloud of smoke; colorful tobacco pipes and clove cigarettes extended between long pale fingers. It was like being back in the days of his youth when time and money wasn't the enemy, when feelings were worn on the sleeves of torn leather jackets, ripped denim pant legs. Everything back then was so expendable, so *eternal*. Who would've thought that so much change could be thrust at you, exploding the bomb of reality on your doorstep? Alas, it had. The dog days were over.

To be so frighteningly aware of life, how infinitesimal it truly is compared to all those stars above our heads, all those ghosts waiting between the dimensions, was enough to drive a man mad. To be so painfully aware of your own heartbeat, the pH of your bloodstream and how it could all turn to poison or end in cardiac arrest at the mere changing of a dial on the clock, or from a simple shot of burning liquor, was sickly unfair. Life was short, indeed, and Hans knew then that he'd wasted enough of his life. It was time to live, time to change himself, change that would actually bring some positivity.

He decided it was time to go back to 5Pointz. *Inside 5Pointz*.

"Hey barkeep," Joey shouted, his face paler and longer than ever; Wild Turkey always tweaked his features. "We need another round!"

Hans stamped out his Marlboro and just as he was ready to turn back in he saw a strange looking trio turning off of Astor Place and onto 3rd avenue—a trio marked by the familiar scraggy signature clothing of artists. Two had sticker-scarred cameras on their necks, stickers of Black Sabbath and The Misfits—two youthful photographers that resembled two different universes. One was very tall and lanky, with mousy brown hair, sporting army green corduroy pants, a grey Misfits T-shirt and thief gloves that offset his fluttering British accent. The other was knife-like in his stance, completely draped in black; his hair was straight as a pin. Hans thought that if he brushed his hand against it that black and orange snakes would bite his fingers.

But it was the last kid that took his attention away. He had a great shock of dyed black hair streaked with a touch of red that drooped across his bird-like features, so quiet and complacent compared to the chattering photographers. Hans caught a glimmer of anger concealed within the twin webs of those fascinating eyes rimmed in black liner. It was a look he knew all too well, a face he knew as if Arkham were still alive. For a moment the three stopped and the vampire wannabe flipped his dark hair and screamed two simple words.

"THE CONTINENTAL!"

"Oh get in you blithering idiot!" The British one said.

Hans couldn't hold his emotions. There was something about that little quiet one. It made him feel sick. Change had come, and life was going to have its way. He felt his stomach slowly gurgle, moving nasty liquids up his esophagus. Hans let it all project out his mouth, a sickening puddle of whiskey tinged vomit, but nothing this sidewalk hadn't tasted already. He wiped his mouth clean and hoped that the three were ready to drink.

Night. Soft, dark, formidable. Pale black night cutting through the vista of crooked mountainside and glittering ribbon of highway. Riotous music, velvet wind thrashing against Delilah's hair, bottle of wine wetting her lips; nothing in the way but the open road and the ghosts of trees.

The sky was filled with huge glittering shapes like a puzzle up in the universe: big dippers and milky ways, the linear patterns that determine one's horoscope. Jimmy continued hammering the pickup down Worship Street, the boulevard of broken dreams. They passed Sideshow Music Shop, saw moonlight dappled across its crumbling awning, forming creepy shadows inside the window display of old heavy metal records, McFarlane toys and horror comics. Lacuna Lake twisted itself like a sensual snake in the distance, scintillating like a landfill of glass, and beyond it was an entire field of sunflowers standing tall amongst the dark. Delilah thought they looked like worshipers waiting for the crop circle to be written.

"Let's stop for a quickie," Sheigh laughed, pointing to the sad excuse for a liquor store. "A five finger discount on Jäger never hurt anybody."

"I'm down," Delilah said.

They were blasting Black Sabbath's "Children of the Grave" and Ozzy's melody vaporized like death in the Pennsylvania air; Tony Iommi's riffs beat the shit out of their ears. Sabbath was Alex's absolute favorite band, and he thought perhaps his own band was composed of graveyard children about to start a revolution. It was Black Sabbath that taught Alex music was a way of escape, escape that didn't encompass the unwilling blade to pale skin like Delilah practiced.

Jimmy stopped in front of the liquor store; Delilah kicked the back of the truck open, scooped up some dirt and let it settle into her pockets. Alex supposed that she didn't want to forget what this place smelled like in case she never came back. *Like coal ash and sadness.* That dirt would weigh her pockets down; much like this town weighed her down. Alex stopped thinking as Jimmy pushed through the glass doors and disappeared within the blooming neon light. A sad little bell rang like a tiny fairy.

"Store's closin' soon. Make it quick," the counter lady said.

"Not *quick* enough," Sheigh laughed.

The immediate stench of caulk and spilled red wine ran up Alex's nose. A sad display of boxed wine was ready to tip over; shelves of Sutter Home gleamed like big bowling balls, boxes of Franzia stacked high. Tonight the counter person was an overweight shrew with eyes like drug withdrawal and a stroke victim's drooping mouth; thin white hairs squiggled around her butt-chin. *LYDIA*, said her madly placed name tag, barely sticking to her flannel shirt. The trick was easy: buy something cheap and distract the sales person so Sheigh could lift the Jägermeister scott-free from the shelf. Most people here were too naïve to think their own neighbors would or could take from them. *What weak minds*, Alex thought.

Lydia paid no mind to Delilah as she slammed the box of Franzia and bottle of Sutter Home on the counter. Alex saw that her eyes were on him, and then Jimmy, who was picking at his duct taped converses stupidly and arguing with Sheigh about which bottle of Yellow Tail could fuck them up the most.

"You gunna buy that, girl, or what?" Lydia said, looking fiercely at Alex.

Girl, Alex smiled. "Yeah, I am."

Lydia's big ears bent inward. "Since when did they let the niggers and the faggots this far into Pennsylvania?"

"They let us in when they opened up the Burger King to feed your fat ass," Jimmy snapped back.

"Get the fuck out my store you monkey before I club your jungle swinging ass."

"Eat shit, lady," Alex spit.

Lydia snarled. "Boys who dress like girls get no respect from me. Pansy ass sissie."

"HEY!" Delilah screamed.

Out came her butterfly blade and she performed an exquisite hand trick called the Helix. With the flick of her wrist and the flow of her fingers, the green handle glowed deep as absinthe as it twirled and fluttered like real butterfly wings. Alex had seen this trick many times but never in this animalistic fashion. Delilah seemed to slice the very air itself, cut particles of dust in half she was so precise as she placed the blade an inch away from Lydia's turkey neck.

"Ring up my fucking wine."

Lydia froze for a moment, her eyes meeting Delilah's cold. There was nothing but silence laced with the dread of whose words would pull the fight's trigger.

"Put that thing down, girl. It's no good fighting your own kind."

"I said ring up the wine, you toad bitch!"

"Looks like you use that thing more on yourself. Strange little girl," Lydia said about Delilah's scars.

"I'm not your kind!" Delilah gritted her teeth.

Alex heard Sheigh begin to giggle, heard the cling of her rings and the slide of glass on linen as she scooped up the Jäger into her hands, then into her messenger bag. But her eyes didn't leave Lydia.

"Six dollars, you snaky haired little witch."

"You ungrateful cunt," Delilah growled.

Everyone bolted, spitting laughter, knocking into shelves and tipping boxes of freshly delivered liquor to the floor. A flood of red wine and vodka wet their shoes. Jimmy was the last one to leave, and Alex heard him cursing out the lady and throwing around a couple of bottles. But not in vain, because he'd come out with two extra bottles of Jäger, something that would surely bring more fun to their wicked world.

"For luck," he said.

7

The trio of trouble sat wearily across the bar; the vampire looking kid was jittery and complained in an annoyingly soft voice, laryngitis voice that needed to either suck it up or shut up. Nobody can resist the deal of five shots for ten dollars. But to Hans these kids weren't just trouble, they were *answers*. Old ghosts opened their eyes inside his head; their mouths grinned and began to gnaw his brain.

"Hey barkeep, a round of Jäger for us. Chilled."

"Chilled for a Brit?" Hans said, lightening the moment.

Hans spun the Jäger in his hand a few times. He loved the dark green bottle, loved the cough medicine burn when he drank it. The top popped open with ease and he threw a series of shot glasses at the crew, pouring the delicious liquor until full. The kids pounded them down and began to whisper amongst themselves, the talk of youth, of happily wasted years, of eternity. There came the flash of his old life again, of him and Arkham taking back shots in the very same seats, two happy teenagers in a world against them.

"You guys tourists or something?" Hans asked.

They all cackled. "Tourists?" the crow haired one said. "Natives, except this British lush."

"Oh, sorry. I mistook the cameras as something else."

Silence for a moment. Three pairs of eyes stared him down.

"You wouldn't want to know what we do with these cameras, old man," the British one said.

"Probably nothing I haven't heard before," Hans said as he poured.

"Oh, really? Then what do you know about *Them?*"

The British kid showed Hans a small LED screen, and there he saw a jumble of bright round lights.

Hans sucked in his breath. "Orbs."

"WEEEEE GOT A WINNER!" the vampire kid yelled.

"I'm not just some naïve old bartender."

"But these cameras aren't just any lot; these are the keys to unlocking worlds."

Worlds, Hans thought. Worlds like Arkham wanted to open. Could this be happening? Could such coincidence fall upon his feet when he was just about ready to fucking give up? It was a wonder how the yins and yangs of life worked, how karma functioned, showing its face when you're damned near ready to let go of old grudges, old haunts. But fuck it now; he had nothing left to lose anyway. Plus, the one damn kid looked too familiar. Hans knew the curves of that face, the thickness of that black hair, that sneaky smile.

"We're ghost hunters," the British one said. "I know that sounds weird—"

"Doesn't sound weird at all."

"You mean you believe?" the vampire kid said.

"I used to . . ."

"No fucking way!"

"Way. The name's Hans. Juice Box when you get to know me better."

"I'm Clive, this bozo is Lynk, and the quiet one is Rez."

Rez poked his eyes up from his William S. Burroughs novel. Hans caught their sapphire glimmer through the tangle of hair, saw the redness flushed in his cheeks. All their cheeks were red; the Jäger was working, and so Hans gave them another round just to play it safe, just to make sure that if he slipped up with his words, they wouldn't run away like mice from an angry boot.

"We've been hunting for a long time, Lynk and I. Rez here, well, let's just say he's like the roadmap most desired. He hears things others cannot."

"Hears them? Oh, those words . . ." Hans' hands began to tremble.

"Don't be scared barkeep. Rather, tell me more about when you believed," Clive said. "I'm always looking for people who understand my kind of craft."

"I don't *believe* anymore," hand wiping down the bar awkwardly. "That life betrayed me."

"Betrayed you? It's the most exciting life I can think of."

"Yeah . . . until you lose everything that's ever meant something to you . . ."

"Deep barkeep, too deep," Clive said.

"I have to say," Lynk interrupted, "this lifestyle is highly unpredictable. You never know what you're going to disturb, and how it will react."

"Exactly!" Hans said, clapping.

"Well look, we're on our way to Long Island City. A place called 5Pointz. Haunted as hell, a fucking breeding ground for ghosts. Ever hear of it?"

Hans slammed his hand. "Long Island City . . . now that's a town I know too well."

"So you know?"

"Yeah . . . alright! You shouldn't be snooping in there. Especially *uninvited*."

"Why not?"

"Ever walk into a house that doesn't belong to you?"

"No we—"

"That's Arkham's place. It's where he—"

"Who?" Clive said, leaning in closer.

Hans' eyes shifted. "The man who looks just like Rez here."

Rez's face shot to Hans. "I've never been told I look looked like anyone in my life."

"Quiet Rez. Don't change the subject barkeep!"

The word vomit was as sour as he expected. Not just sour, but it had ruined the entire conversation. Clive's face dropped; Lynk stepped away from the bar and went stumbling outside. Rez simply stared into his Jäger shot, rimmed the tip of the glass with his finger and then gulped it down.

"I don't need a damn lecture from someone I don't know."

" . . . I didn't mean it that way. It's for your own good"

"Can it old man. I left England to get away from overbearing parents. And I don't need my art to be insulted on top of it. Wanker."

And just like that they were gone. The youth are so impossible.

Alex and Delilah drank the Sutter Home as he thumbed through his dog-eared copy of *The Cipher* by Kathe Koja. The nifty book light made his skin glow pale as bone, teeth sharp and lips ghostly, just like the shimmering cover: scaly hand full of razor teeth. *The Funhole*, Delilah thought, *I need to find it and never return! Or at least dip my face inside and come back distorted.*

"Can you believe that fat bitch?" Jimmy yelled. "Calling me a nigger when I hardly look like my mom."

"Fuck her. She needs to get laid," Sheigh yelled, giving Jimmy a noogie.

At the tip of Worship Street Delilah saw her high school fading and black against the dark vista. She recalled all the wasted years spent there through a foggy memory lost inside her head, perhaps killed off by the hair dye. Delilah never found school work to be fun or inspiring; it was laborious and wholly evil. She attended by pure force of law, lazing around with her heart barely beating and lyrics thrashing inside her head: a dark carnival of lonely music. Some of the lyrics to "My Personal Hell" spoke to her.

Emptiness speaks eloquence . . .
In this nest of hate where I thrive
Cannon tongues and crooked lungs . . .
Grind me down to wet dusty strife

Most of the kids were complacent and plain; the teachers were banal and uninspiring. Their job was to just show up. The goonies, punks, metal heads, geeks and funzies were alright; she always felt a tiny bit of place within their jagged social circles. But that was a small minority. Everyone else was satisfied with the fact that being the same was the best way to fit in. If Delilah lived her life that way she would've ran the jaded knife into her heart years ago. There's more to life than hiding the rotten feeling inside one's heart just to pass as normal. Sometimes it's good to feel bad.

But school meant hanging out with Alex, so she attended with half a heart. Besides Alex, the only other good thing that came out of her dreaded high school years was meeting the rest of the band. It was Jimmy who noticed the way she hummed her lonely melodies. *Sibilant as a snake*, he said. Delilah remembered sitting on the morgue-cold tiles in the corner of that famous lunchroom, knees pressed up to her chest, army green UFO pants swarming her skinny legs, when a scrappy looking kid with a Fender on his back and wiry yellow hair placed a Vector microphone in her hand and told her to sing for him. It looked like the kind of microphone that hangs from the ceiling at boxing matches.

At seventeen Jimmy was already a wizard with the guitar and he was looking for a singer to compliment his style. He asked Delilah to let her voice rip against his riffs, and when she did it was like a galvanizing flood. They bonded immediately. In the basement of

Sideshow Music Shop they spent hours writing and recording, backs arched, beer everywhere, notebooks bulging with words and musical notes. There, Delilah learned about chords, levels, the importance of certain microphones, falsetto and vocal melodies.

Billy and Sheigh were Jimmy's goonies already, and they welcomed Delilah with crooked smiles and lots of beer. Soon they pieced together their first song called "28 Days." With Delilah's words they said they'd won their ticket to salvation, so she couldn't say no when they asked her to be their permanent singer, but only if Alex could join too, that he'd bring his piano skills and round the band out. They didn't refuse. When they began stringing songs together everything clicked easy as a padlock. Delilah's lyrics evolved into evil melodies; the music rushed into it like a bull at a red flag. Their days melted into nights, into obscured neon blurs of sweating beer cans and surging musical notes. The band had made a bond by music, forever, drawing itself out like the blurry map to the rest of their lives.

Music took focus away from the hardships of the real world. It was the only way one could express themselves about the angst of not fitting in with the majority. Makeup was how kids concealed their inner demons; black clothing made them brave enough to stand against the brain wash of mainstream beauty that said they were too ugly to live, too stupid to thrive, too misfortunate to be loved.

"Don't let that contract fly out of here! You know Jimmy and his crazy-ass driving!" Delilah said.

"TELL THE BOY TO HOLD IT!" Sheigh yelled.

Alex turned his head. "It's not funny. Delilah, tell her it's not funny."

Delilah always protected Alex. She took him on as the sibling she always wanted being that he was a year younger, though an equally experienced musician. But Alex could be very adolescent; being raised by his grandparents harbored that in him. He was their prize possession in a sack of skin and bone, especially since their daughter had died while in labor. Rumor had it a great red gout of blood had slicked the birthing room. People in town loved to talk, and Delilah figured that if they got off to such a horrid rumor as death by giving the gift of life, she had no reason at all to give a fuck about leaving this place.

"It's not funny, Sheigh. *He's* sensitive."

"*HE?*"

"Kidding! *Alex* is sensitive."

"This'll make you feel better, buddy," Billy said.

He took out a silver paint marker and attacked Sheigh's face, making a sloppy silver moustache across her cheek.

"You son of a whore!" she yelled.

But then Jimmy was turning into a familiar field; Delilah knew the musty smell, the feel of the wind here. The trees became sparser; the ground morphed into checkerboards of dead and alive grass; the houses were old and Victorian with their small balconies and peaked roofs. The outskirts of town, her part of the town: Delilah's house.

"Get your shit and make it quick," Jimmy said from the driver's seat, chewing bubble gum rapidly.

"Hey, double D, your keys," Sheigh passed the set back, keychain of a man wrapped in chains heavier than Delilah remembered.

She jumped out of the truck and ran up her porch; the boards shifted beneath her feet, opening like an embrace but closing like a mouth full of sharp teeth as if to trap her forever in boondock torture. She focused her attention on the sound of the pickup's grunting muffler, focused on her own breathing, her senses, not the antimagic of Violet Hill that killed the dreams of countless people.

When Delilah opened the front door the living room bathed her in smooth yellow light. She was quickly assaulted by the angered stares of her parents sitting patiently on the blue velour couch, the *family talk* couch. Quiet and undisturbed, naturally, while Delilah was screaming inside, her fist in the air. Typical. Delilah pretended to not see them, dashing for the stairs to her room.

"Delilah! Talk to me," mom said, standing to follow.

The stairs felt endless, like trying to climb a mountain of quicksand, but finally she got to her room and threw a stick down between the bottom of the door and near wall so no one could open it. Her mother was right behind, hammering softly with the hands that used to caress Delilah's face as if trying to find the start of her daughter's corrupted mind so she could crush it.

"Listen to your mother, Delilah," father demanded.

Fuck you . . . you insecure piece of shit.

She didn't hear them, couldn't hear them. They were living, breathing rejections that she should have realized sooner. They weren't her blood. New York was her blood.

"YOU TOOK TOO LONG TO TELL ME!" Delilah yelled.

"Honey, please," mother said.

"I knew I never belonged in this shit-hole town," she growled.

"DELILAH!"

"Watch that filthy mouth of yours."

Ever since her mother finally confessed that Delilah had been adopted, the repeated longing began to make sense, the yearning for a past became clear; the unjustified need to escape boondock hell had real meaning. Twenty-two years of questions and nightmares had answers now, and mother had the gall to insinuate that she knew how it was to be Delilah, knew what *dead inside* truly meant.

Mother used the glorious excuse that she had been rendered infertile after a few bloody miscarriages—such is why she was left to adopt—which equaled to the emptiness inside her daughter. If losing the ability to carry a spermy blob of meat inside your belly equaled Delilah's emptiness, then why didn't mother try losing an entire existence?

"OPEN UP DELILAH!"

Through the flicker of votive candles she saw her notebook lying upon her desk, saw Zazo darting in his cage happy to see mommy. That notebook held all her lyrics. "My Personal Hell" was the first page. She remembered writing those words when she drank boxed wine with Alex, wondering what lived between the shadows, and how she was going to one day get out of town.

Her personal hell, she remembered, was not having a real past, which came back to haunt her in her dreams, a deep-dark and wet place. *My weight, my face, my height, my race, I'm a mistake.* This made her sing like mad, made her voice stretch into octaves that she never knew she could squeeze out, vocal chords ripping like razors inside her throat. She knew most singers could bend the rules of the voice box, but when Delilah sung "My Personal Hell" it always left a creamy warmth over her tongue, the taste of blood on her palate.

But what did all of this matter? Delilah didn't plan to come back, ever. Yet this little square room knew all of her foul secrets, and it was something that she was more attached to than she remembered, especially now that she was leaving it. This was where she wrote her best lyrics drunk on Jägermeister. This room was where she found her addiction to cutting. This dark velour bed was where she taught herself to hum; this wall with the glued pictures of bats and National Geographic cut outs of extinct creatures was where she learned that animals were to be her best friends.

She touched Zazo's cage and he zipped back and forth; his small fangs bit the thin metal bars. Lost souls together, Delilah couldn't recall one night when Zazo wasn't there to listen to her complaints with beady and curious black eyes, his little pink nose ruffling at the smell of her cigarette breath. But then something brushed against her face: rope light. It sagged like a bright green noose from the ceiling, imploring her to stay . . . in death. No, she wouldn't oblige.

Above the tattered desk was her dream catcher, its webs of black strings intertwined, creating an intricate hex that dangled powerfully from the edge of the loop. Too bad it never worked. Her nightmares were too vicious, telling her that things were coming, the missing pieces to some phantasmal puzzle.

Nevermind. This was it.

Delilah grabbed her messenger bag and threw in all the things she'd need the rest of her life: CDs, her Vector microphone, dream catcher, a pen, beat up notebook, and some ragged paper backs. She found the original sketch that she drew when she started the ink on her biceps: bats, the map of Steeraway Street, musical notes drawn jagged and tawdry in pencil.

What's in this bag represents me, she thought.

Delilah thought quickly for an escape plan. There was no way she was going back out the front door; the window was the only way out. For the last and final time this window would free her, and she didn't even have the courage to take a look back, for it was too eerily tempting to stay if she did.

A part of Delilah wished the darkness would steal her soul.

Then the branch banged against the glass, its great withered leaves swooping around like a thousand brittle hands grabbing for her. She took one last panoramic view of her room, rope light frowning and the band posters wilting: Nine Inch Nails, Otep and Black Sabbath. She wondered what they were thinking. But then Delilah was on the balcony holding for balance, and down, down, down the dark green lattice she went.

Her feet moved so fast for Jimmy's pickup that she almost left her boots behind.

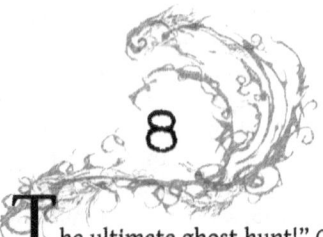

8

The ultimate ghost hunt!" Clive said, stepping off the 7 train. "Surreal, if we can even say that."

45th Road and Courthouse Square, nothing here but timeworn brownstones disappearing to new money and trends, to the illusion that you could wipe away a town's scummy reputation and sordid population with higher rent and sandblasted brick. This place was just another shit hole being renovated, but to Rez it was something deeper. He'd lived in this city his entire life, didn't know if he was born here, but one thing he knew was that home is where the heart is—if he still had one.

"Rez, what's the word on the street?"

Rez felt something strange, special, and ephemeral. Was Hans right about 5Pointz, that it was dangerous? If Rez listened hard enough there would be a whole new conversation radiating here beside the loud chatter about film cameras, geigers, infrared motion exchangers and EVP recorders. It would be a conversation that he could only hear, not the typical conversation between ghost hunters.

"Huh?" Rez said, prying his eyes away from the nameless paperback he was destroying with his mind. "Nothing. Nothing yet."

Down the stairs and out the exit, glass prism stained with long dried stripes of mucus like worms. The streets were barren and wide, generous. 5Pointz was in his view now, a building colored by whorls of graffiti art, swirls, light bulbs with bulging tongues and crooked smiles missing teeth: the angry expressions of today's hard life, all foreshadowed by each artist's tag. *FUMES* was painted in white bubble letters and marked the corner edifice. *PRESS* was yellow and gaudy; *MERES* was surrounded by a chain of screaming light bulbs.

Lynk controlled these streets madly; the way he dragged his gear and juggled Clive and Rez around was of someone with a prior knowledge of this town. He hissed at the passing yuppies who frowned at their conversation: the cynical problems of three skinny white boys in makeup and tight black clothes talking about ghosts, echoes, and specters. They were a lost tribe amongst the new money here. Lynk was from a run down Queens neighborhood currently being gutted, resold and gentrified; a slow genocide much like the Lower East Side. Kids like him—smart and artistically inclined—were outnumbered.

Depressed as anyone else who hates their reflection in the mirror, Lynk's greatest strength was his cunning intelligence. He could outtalk anybody and teach them something in the end. But something evil bubbled in his brain. He was uncontrollable once he was double-crossed. Lynk recalled how he stabbed a classmate in the hand with a needle compass because the kid had sat in a seat Lynk claimed was only for him; his name was carved on the desk in angry script.

"How're we going to get in?" Clive said, licking his fingers and testing the air.

"Let's ask if we can have a tour. They offer them to the community," Lynk said.

"Fuck the community. They sold out years ago."

"How about we just shoot with the full spectrum? We're bound to get some great light sources recorded."

"No. If we're not inside I don't want to waste the battery power."

Clive stopped on the corner of Jackson Avenue, looked both ways and crossed the street. That's when Rez felt something dangerously close. He could sense it in the wind, in the way the 7 train roared in his ears, the way the voices started coming to him. He'd never felt so much nostalgia in his life. In his head he saw a great fire, saw a man in leather, sad and crying and sprawled upon a bed of concrete before running back into a long black hallway.

"But I mean, I feel something about this place, this town," Lynk said. "It's special. Has that touch we've been looking to catch in our work."

"It's a dead city, like the barkeep said."

The lights from the train tracks threw blankets of shadow down to the concrete, so dark in some spots, so silent and calm. A dangerous mix. The corner bar was packed with patrons, its window a sad display of neon and cherry wood. It was a dark and heedful place with dead lights strung like up bad fruit, tinkling as if a waning heart beat. It might've once been an antique shop of some sort, or maybe a thrift shop that sold dusky typewriters and quills, sealing wax and stamping rings to mark them final. The soul of its former self could be seen across the walls: photonegatives of whiskey patrons in top hats and long trench coats, yellowed teeth from the constant cigar in between their lips. Rez thought about how quickly things can change in New York. He hoped some of that change would come to him soon.

There Rez saw the menu. PBRs for a dollar; Brooklyn Lager on tap for two, various craft beers for four: Flying Dog, Magic Hat, Dog Fish Head, all the ales of autumn, pumpkin and bitter hops, stout like a mouthful of lethal tar. He very much wanted a drink. But they were already scuttling down Davis Street, passing strange garage shutters, pools of broken glass, and were soon at the entrance. Rez saw that a full day's work was coming to an end: construction projects spitting dirt and aerosol artists throwing paint into the air, running into their eyes and faces.

It was then the hand shot out from the deep recess of shadow, grabbing onto Rez's shoulder and pulling him back; a flash of silver caught his eyes. The face that met his was pale and older, lined with stress marks. A cigarette hung lazily between his lips; white feathery hair fell over his tired eyes. Rez saw a dusty leather jacket and impossibly black jeans painted on skinny legs.

"Don't do it!" the man said.

Clear blue eyes caught Rez. The man's eyeliner seemed permanently tattooed it was so dark; his sullen look spoke of *get the fuck out of my way*.

"BARKEEP!" Clive yelled. "Did you follow us?"

"I . . . can't let you do it . . . please believe me when I tell you this."

Clive stepped between Hans and Rez. He moved his hand off Rez's shoulder, always there to be big brother the protector, and Hans flinched as if he was sorry.

"Oh, boy, you're tall!" Hans said.

"And you're a drunk fuck!"

"Eh, eh, oh. I don't mean any trouble."

"What's it you want?"

"I don't want you to ruin yourself like Arkham did . . ."

"Here we go with that name again."

Hans turned to Rez. "You, young man. You look just like him! That dark wiry hair, those sapphire eyes. You're his spitting image."

"Who?"

"ARKHAM!"

"Like the asylum?" Lynk, Rez and Clive said in unison.

"YEAH!" Hans shook like a leaf. "He lived here . . . long time ago. I held his kids in my arms; I know what they would look like! I swear it!"

"Now he's getting whacky."

"I held *you* in my arms once . . . I swear it, young man. I swear it . . ."

Clive and Lynk walked away, completely unamused by Hans. You get used to freaky people talking about prophecy in New York; your mind becomes wholly numb to them.

"Trust me, young man. I don't know how I know . . . but I do . . . you're him. I got nothing left . . . nothing to lose."

"I don't know what to say . . ."

Clive and Lynk stamped back to Rez, pissed off.

"Well, we can't get into 5Pointz . . . *for now*. Might as well go. I've a lot of work to catch up on anyway. Lynk, you coming?"

"LET'S GO!"

Clive and Lynk headed back to the 7, but Rez didn't follow. He couldn't, not when someone was claiming that he had real roots in New York, not when someone was so convinced that he looked like this character named Arkham. Rez knew about the loonies of the city, but this guy was serious, drunk but serious, and he just couldn't resist the temptation. What else was there to do anyway?

There was a weird silence between them now. Rez felt a sudden strange psychedelic presence. It brushed his soul with the power of the '80s, challenging his own bizarre aura. It brought out a natural respect for the old guy, like being perpetually drunk. He wanted to know more about this Arkham, and why he looked like him. This was the closest he felt to actually having blood ties in the city. There was simply nothing to lose anymore.

"I'm gunna stay with Hans here," Rez said.

"Suit yourself," Lynk said, and they were gone.

Billy tapped the amps and chords to the radio as Jimmy sped back onto the yawning road. His thin curly hair bounced in the wind, held back by a crossbones bandana. Trent Reznor's voice through Jimmy's terrible speakers sounded like a blend of hypnosis and someone puking from a bad night of drinking. But Delilah could still make out the pain, the reluctance, the suffering sounds of Trent's screams, much like herself.

Some of the only words that have ever made sense to me, she thought.

Sheigh passed around the Jäger after she got done swigging it like chocolate milk. They could never have enough Jäger. Delilah remembered the first time she drank it. She'd stolen the bottle with Sheigh on a grueling winter night and scrambled to Sheigh's backyard watching the bottle gleam with moonlight and mocking the faces of the tricked liquor store employees.

"Tits get all the men crazy. Lucky you have a pair, Delilah!"

"Yeah, yeah. Let's get to drinking."

"Open it then, wussie," Sheigh said.

"Fine!"

Delilah liked a challenge. Her hand snapped the top off, and Sheigh dared her to take a few chugs. Delilah did, and the chilled brown drink spread an embalming heaviness down her esophagus, swirling through her veins and zapping her brain. Delilah felt the liquor coat her soul a thick dark brown, staining her liver, pickling her intestines. The taste was of cinnamon and licorice, like liquid candy. It was heaven. Jäger was the only liquor that let Delilah sleep free of phantoms, of demons, free of a wasted, fake life.

"Lay on my lap, Delilah," Alex said. "I'll rub your head."

She obeyed. Only Alex could calm her and so she leaned her head against Alex's bony knee and savored the music, the graceful silver shower of stars, half sliver of moon. Every star was close enough to touch, winking, each one filled with the millions of wishes of dreaming kids looking to get out of the hell that was their home, the inferno that was their lives. One night Delilah stayed up all night staring at a hot orange dot in the sky through her window, but the newspapers let her know that it was only Mars. She wished it to be an alien light of some sort, one that could lift her body into its ship with a Halloween colored beam, never for her to return.

It seemed everything was about travel right now. It was natural to christen her first major travel expedition in the city of her birth. Delilah watched the road spin away like film cut from a cassette tape. It was a cracked mass of black varicose veins and pot holes like liver spots. Then the pickup fumbled; something small and dark jetted across, something that obviously didn't realize that there were four speeding wheels on their way to crush it to death.

Delilah's tiny body swerved, the wind whipped; she closed her eyes, grabbed onto glittering guitar chords, Alex's leg, and hoped that Jimmy wasn't stupid enough to squash any poor animals. Alex held the equipment down for fear it would all fly right off the truck, but Jimmy cocked his baby back into a normal gear with ease and it was then they all saw the bright yellow *XING* signs that warned drivers of wild animals.

For a moment, with her eyes closed, Delilah felt sleep crawl free from the depthless core in the middle of her brain to try and grab her, felt the feverish hand of dream caress her heart. She hadn't slept in a good two days, but she could last another two, she knew. When her eyes bolted open she stared at everything around her. The trunk was littered with too much shit. She saw peeling band stickers, markers rolling back and forth, beer cans way past the expiration date clinking together. But then she saw what she wanted, the bottle of classic Sutter Home. Delilah sucked at the tip of the wine bottle, tasted sour pale grapes, and let the music get into her head.

As it settled into her stomach, warming her face and forcing a grin upon the usual frown, she stuck her hand beneath the Catwoman pillowcase that covered Zazo's cage. Just like any pet bird, you don't keep bats in a place with a draft or cold spell. Zazo's stomach was soft with raised brown hairs like frightened peach fuzz; tiny needles with felt tips. Delilah put one finger out so his teeny claws could attach on, his little mouth nibbling her finger gently. She could feel his itsy bitsy tongue sliming her finger tip looking for a meal worm or spider. Then she wrapped her hand around his entire little body like a mother's embrace.

It made Delilah wonder if her parents were still banging on her door demanding that she talk to them now, now, now! Did they not think that she'd just escape through the window and down the balcony? She imagined their pale grim faces and their wannabe Beaver Cleaver attitudes, thinking of new ways to try and talk sense into their strange daughter.

And so Delilah thought long and hard about her own procreation: the darkly-slimed ovum, the raging zygote jellied within umbilical residue ready to rule the world. Life begins when you're no bigger than a pebble; a scrubby glob of meat stretches itself to become a man, a woman, a shadow, a terrorist, an *artist*. But enough was enough. She needed to shake these thoughts from her system if she was going to live happily in the place where her bloodline was born and would not, it seemed, come to an end.

They took a shortcut back to Alphabet City, sketchy walking tour, a little more muck here, a little less posh. They entered Clive's building and zipped up the stairs. Clive was not happy; Lynk stared at him in wonder, his eyes shifting, his hands gripping his shirt tightly. But being angry made you see things in a clearer perspective. It was how a photographer could fit the puzzle pieces of texture, angles and light together. Enough thinking, it was time to work.

"The Gallery . . . the Gallery!" Clive said.

"Is this all you think about?" Lynk asked.

"YES! We gotta win the hearts of those wankers so we get some good street cred."

Clive remembered Dago's first gallery opening in Chelsea. A night of mysticism and photography and art. The artists showcased their work loud and proud, all with great explanations as to how they captured spirits on camera. Dago would have you think differently about all the realities around you; that was part of his nefarious charm, and it's what attracted people to him. But now it was finally Clive's turn to rule the world of underground art.

Into the darkroom he went with Lynk, black door like his own personal portal into the heart of art, small square room the island of one's dark fantasy. Lynk cleaned up the silver halide that he'd spilled earlier, trashing the film negatives, and started a new batch. Clive watched him carefully, the pink and yellow lava lamp spinning liquid goops around and around, trippy mix of colors casting liquid candy-colored shadows against the walls, against Lynk's sharp face.

The ceiling was tacked with creepy photos. The local haunts stared back down at them as if peering eyes: outer borough graveyards, abandoned buildings, the lonely midnight train tracks of endless subway lines. Those were some of the best shots. Lynk hung last night's work across clotheslines, black and whites: statues, mausoleums and Rez a caricature, bird's smile, eyes like blue flame.

It made Clive think of when he met Rez at the Limelight club on the night of 666. What better place to throw a party than in an Episcopal church morphed into a raging night club full of neon fingernails, tongue piercings and decadent drinks? He remembered Rez had told him that he had been nursing the same beer for over two hours as the local blotter acid played with his head. The lights around him grew tall and scary, the dreary colors slithered, mingling into a concentrated madness. The walls were suddenly the enemy, taking shape into monsters. It was like Rez was stuck in his own fucked up psychedelic dream.

But that's why Clive noticed him: whimsical bony form dancing between riotous bodies slathered in neon, face deeply scarred by some unmarked shame, scared little puppy learning how to grow up into a vicious canine. Clive was twenty-one and Rez was only seventeen, sneaking into rock clubs four years below the legal age limit, but all you needed was an I.D. with your birth date tainted by a sharp pen to make you legal.

Rez called him a hipster but Clive said that was American-English trash; he preferred punk. But that was all beside the point. Clive simply wished to photograph Rez, eager to know what was going on behind Rez's sapphire eyes; perhaps there would lay the weirdest thoughts in the world. He was half right. They shared some words, dropped a tab, did a shot, and all of a sudden conversation started.

That was the same year Clive had come to New York on a photography scholarship from South London, fully paid by NYU. But soon after docking in New York, he found that the Midwestern ideals of the student body and the formality that his teachers pushed down his throat were unjust, sickly; unfair. Clive had fallen in love with the real New York, the muck and grime and gunshots, not the crap they show you in fancy photography magazines. There was always something amazing to be seen: a robbery, abandoned construction sites, a peddler with deformities that only horror stories could tell. Plus, no one ever saw eye to eye with his quest to unravel life after death.

All his photos came back with something extra. Clive referred to the orbs as *Them* or *They*. It was then that he gave up school, afraid some snarky jerk of a teacher obsessed with form and order would try to reshape his whimsical visions. He didn't read the photography magazines recommended to him, didn't want to know what everyone else was doing. Clive only wanted to do his own thing. What was the need of some dreadful piece of paper saying you completed four years of bureaucracy when Clive was perfectly polished on his own? No big shot university could teach Clive what he couldn't learn three freaky square miles from his own apartment. To Clive photography was the way one held the camera, where sight turned to smell, hearing to taste, taste to touch: a culmination of the senses. It was about letting go, not thinking. That kind of concentration usually ruined a picture.

Lynk snapped his fingers and put a smock in Clive's hand. The black curtain across the window blocked all of the dreamy moonlight. He looked at the photos slung up from St. John's Cemetery, saw some that offered evidence, though most were duds. *Fuck*, he thought. *I've lost my touch.* He knew that the bright smears of light were simply his own finger prints, knew that the sounds replaying from the EVP recorder only spit back the drunken conversation between three friends. But it was in Rez's photos that he noticed the change, been noticing it for years. After looking for that one clue that life after death truly existed, was truly part of the cosmos, Clive had nailed it with Rez. The orbs this time were real, not dust or water vapor like so many times before. They were in all of Rez's photos. Must've been from that aura that nobody could explain.

Clive hit the switch for the safe light and a wave darkness splashed like spilled red wine. Nice. A *Hustler* centerfold stared down at him, the cover girl stretching herself wide like twin pink rubber bands, her eyes smiling at Clive. He let the thought go as soon as the blood rushed to his crotch, didn't want Lynk to get any bad ideas. Scissor in hand, dried photos in the other, edges cut and Lynk assorting them, whispering a whole lot of nothing to himself, sneering at the girl above their heads, and they both began to assemble the portfolio of macabre.

"Please stop it," Clive said.

"Stop what?"

"That moronic whispering. I can't take it."

"Then I'll have to rip out my voice box . . ."

"No man, just get the fuck over it. I mean, you told enough people, now they want to know why. I told you that it was one silly time."

Lynk froze as if an ice sculpture. "I know . . . I know . . ."

"So then? We're good?"

"What?"

"Good, as in G-O-O-D."

"Yeah, smart ass. We're G-O-O-D."

"Then back to the photos. We gotta kill it at the gallery."

Clive's English accent came out strong when he was annoyed or drunk, and he wished the latter right about now. But when he calmed down he felt the old country slip from his tongue and the American vernacular slide down his throat like a slug. Lynk looked at him for a couple more seconds, those insouciant eyes begging for Clive to quit reminding him of that night, but Clive couldn't help himself. He had to let Lynk know where they both stood at all times so he'd never slip up again.

"Hit the stereo."

They always developed photos to music and the room swelled with a song: "Scream" by The Misfits. This was a great way to relax them both, to get into the developing mode, especially for Clive since he loved punk, and horror. What better way to get both?

"Hmm," said Lynk looking back at the photos.

"What is it?"

"The thought of *actual* evidence," Lynk said slowly.

"Yeah, well, duh."

"Have you ever broken down our passions into little pieces? Have you ever really *thought* about what we actually do?"

"All the time, Lynk. All the bloody time."

"So then you understand the fact that when you take pictures of ghosts, you aren't capturing their existence . . ."

"What?" Clive said, curious.

"Listen: these photos don't *prove* evidence of the afterlife, but rather they show that ghosts allow you to see them. It's a paranormal law."

"Never thought about it that way."

"Well come see this then."

Lynk pulled a photo close. Clive got a whiff of chemical baths and liquid silver as Lynk pointed to little curious things with his one sharp pinky nail, swigging a small silver flask. Clive saw everything right away: dust mites with iridescent wings, drops of water stuck to the shutter of the lens in the shape of obscured faces, glowing a million reflections on blue mirrors.

Only Rez's photos.

"I remember we learned about smudges and water vapors . . ."

"But this is real. This is . . . very intricate. Look at the faces here, and the wings, fedora hats in the background of this one. He's haunted. Maybe we're haunted. Who knows?"

Sanity's Abyss, and it was to be Clive's breakthrough. One thing Clive knew was that ghosts come around when there is a weak link to latch onto, or something that they can channel through, namely Rez. So they both examined more photos, seeing bright roundabouts covering Rez's face and mouth as he leaned against a tall oak tree and stared into the sky, chin soft and round, piercings glittering, eyes dark and lovely in the night. The little dots reminded Clive of huge colorless fireflies. They could drive a person nuts if they looked at them long enough. Then Clive's peripheral vision flashed momentously, but when he turned to look nothing was there. Clive stared blankly at the spot where he saw the flash, nothing but a dog-eared Misfits poster and *EAT ME* written in scrappy magic marker across the wall.

"What the hell are you looking at?"

"Nothing . . . so anyway, talking more about the orbs."

"This is paranormal; paraphysical."

"Mhmm."

"But listen, these things shift from realm to realm; ectoplasms, spirits," Lynk's face darkened, his mouth turned into a black hole. "We may not capture them again, that is . . . unless they're attracted to Rez."

"Dago's going to be stoked!"

"Well, let's tell him now! We can't just depend on our own eyes anymore . . . or Rez."

"You better not make him think . . . well you know."

"He forgot about it already, Clive."

"Fine. Dago will know exactly what to do."

9

The pickup swerved. Gravel, dust and rabid music polluted the throes of night. Jimmy slapped the jittery FM radio when the signal cut out, and with so much silence engulfing them everyone heard Delilah's new demand: that she be taken to Alex's house before the road to New York, and that everyone shut up about it. When Delilah said her piece, they all listened. It wasn't that she was a tough bitch; she was their leader, their mentor.

On the ride there Delilah saw motes on either side of the road, motes that you could stuff a dead body into if need be. The pine branches bowed so close to the road they could sweep the fallen leaves; across the street a slew of Amish were selling homemade fireplaces, fresh pierogi, pies, and jams that smelled of every fruit of the world. Further down the usual old hicks were throwing apples at one another; kids in black gathered like dirty geese at the foot of an oily ocean, selling lemonade for a dollar. Delilah smiled remembering how she used to do the same thing, though her lemonade came straight from her bladder versus the sugary shit the other kids vended.

At the foot of the driveway now, and Delilah looked upon Alex's house, cabin-like structure, badly chipped front porch; no windows lit. It was so dark here. She jumped out the trunk and let her body fall into the old metal swing set, listening to it squeak as she lolled like the tide, watching the dark through the net of tree branches. Before she knew it Alex was storming up the driveway and through the front door. She followed.

The living room smelled of carrots, fried onion and was full of the presence of humdrum. Nothing was out of the ordinary. Nothing could make this place physically seem eerie. But truth in the matter was that it was. Through normality lies distinct fear, madness. You can't hide it, can't cover it up like some bruise you don't want people to see. This was the house that bore their music; this was the house that told Delilah the poetry she wrote could be turned into lyrics, could mean something to other people. She couldn't imagine not coming here on Saturday mornings anymore, couldn't imagine not eating Alex's grandmother's chocolate porridge and drinking ancient Chinese green tea down to its last bitter drop. It was unthinkable that she wouldn't watch Alex tend to the orchids.

Orchids are like landmines. One wrong move and BOOM!

Death.

Life's eerie scale tipped ever so gently the day she met Alex in ninth grade. It was in the handball court; Alex was jumping like Wolverine, winning game after game and screaming about it too. His wild growing hair was netted across his face; mascara marked his gem green eyes. She couldn't tell if he was a boy or a girl his features were so soft, his face so peaked. Later, Alex would tell her that he preferred to leave people to their guesses because the world loves to slot people into boxes and label them unfairly. He felt very out of the box.

Alex was the most fabulous shapeshifter Delilah had ever met. He wore girl's jeans with guy's shirts; he painted his eyes and his nails, and dyed his hair crazily. Alex never listened to what any teacher told him, never learned life's lessons from detention or suspension, and never followed any specific trend. That made him interesting, dark, unique. You never knew what he was going to say, wear or do next. He even had the balls to smoke cloves in the lunchroom and wrote the numbers to a lot of the hated teachers in pink magic marker across his converses while they yelled at him. *FREE BLOWJOBS! CHEAP! CHEAP! CHEAP!*

Delilah didn't know what had gotten into her head that day, but she challenged Alex to a match and it changed her life forever. Delilah wound up getting her ass beat, leaving her legs sore, shoulders and the palm of her hand feeling like they were on fire. But Alex was a graceful winner, offering Delilah a dime bag as a token of her challenge, and they became fast, inseparable friends. Delilah felt something different about Alex instantly, something strong and incandescent. Later, when she got to know him better, she realized that same shrill aura came off his fingers when he aggressively played the piano.

When Alex was around it was okay to feel fucked up inside; you knew that you had a friend to support you. But it took work to get through Delilah. She was a shy flower full of secret wants and needs, ready to burst the finest nectar if teased the right way. And Alex tested her limits. He threw paint in her hair and spit food in her face, just waiting for Delilah to respond in some way (some psycho-violent way, truthfully), but she was dead inside. Delilah would just look down at the floor, pretending to be invisible, nothing, ash.

But it was the day when Alex had pulled the ultimate prank that changed everything. Delilah was publicly known for loving animals more than people (what other girl in Pennsylvania owned a pet bat?) and Alex used this to his advantage. He'd placed a dead mouse in her locker and when Delilah opened it up the damn thing plopped atop her head, sliming her face with goo and made her stink for a week because she didn't give a fuck about washing her hair. Though Delilah couldn't recall exactly what happened in that moment when she felt the electric snap in her brain, Alex said she nearly choked him to death.

But that's when the friendship took off. Delilah had found the key to her true rage, her passions and maledictions. She realized that combining them was another form of expression; it was art. From then on they never separated. Her parents never allowed a boy to sleep over, even if he looked like a girl; they believed in marriage before sex. Too bad they didn't understand that boys and girls could be friends and not be intimate. So there came the nights (Alex tapping softly at her balcony window like a vampire; Delilah even thought he sort of looked like one) when they walked the cold streets of Violet Hill; nights spent drinking wine lazily on the branch of the giant oak tree and watching bats take to the night sky, watching the owls and their yellow eyes scan the field for mice. The spiders spun exquisite webs and Delilah often threw insects into the silvery hex to see them become drained of their life.

Those were the years they they'd watch the clock tick its phantom seconds away like betrayal during the most solemn hours after the sun gave up its place to the moon. Night was where life truly lived in Delilah's heart; night meant day was close, that she didn't have to worry about sleep. In Delilah's room, as if they'd taken scraps of night in with them, a deadstill dark coagulated above their heads, pricked by the daggered points of candles. It was well known that something was alive (something that lacked vital signs), but it was left very much unsaid. Instead of questioning the dark, they became inspired by it. They wrote their asses off; powerful, youthful music that resonated not only with them, but with a lot of the kids in town. They hit nerves that hadn't been groped in years; they claimed ears that were supposedly tone-deaf to the world. They became popular fast.

That was when Delilah came out with her big secret: that she could project her own body through dreams. It was why she hated sleeping; the ghosts in her head tempted her too often to escape life and come visit them, and those ghosts brought the most unwanted memories. Sleeping meant pain, over and over. But she could sleep soundly with Alex, could trust that he'd watch over her body and would wake her if she was in danger. Delilah once tried to get out of Violet Hill via dream, but the physical body is always stronger than the ectoplasmic one, which meant that if she wanted to escape, she'd have to do it the old fashion way.

Remember Sabbath's "Behind the Wall of Sleep"? You know the band was addicted to Lovecraft, and that Geezer's lyrics correspond to Lovecraft's ideas that humans are energy beings when released by sleep, unshackled from our tumid flesh! It's the most personal way to transcend. Sabbath knew about the soul leaving the physical body mischievously before we were born!

In dreamland every sound was a song; every voice was a melody from deep space. *Astral projection.* To Alex, the thought of witnessing a true outer body experience possessed him to sharpen Delilah's talent. *We as humans are shackled by flesh; you're the only person who can break the laws of physics.* They practiced this night after night, and before she knew it Delilah was able to not only project herself, but take things with her into dreamland. A pen exploded in her grip; a candle melted into a blob forming a cavernous face. Anything that touched the viscous miasma of nightmare came back faintly changed, mutated.

Let's not force it. There're rules that can be broken.

But then something else happened. Delilah and Alex were still teenagers when they began sewing their creative ideas together, just beginning to hone their talents when they'd begun writing a tune called "My Personal Hell"—Alex sweating heavily behind the grand piano, the music shimmering like dragon scales; notebooks swelling with Delilah's venomous poetry—and began making *real* music. They left their vagabond inspirations behind, abandoned their tedious melodies.

It was time to put creativity to the test.

They strung the song together within a few grueling practice sessions. As they played it loud and fierce in Alex's living room, something awoke. It was ectoplasmic, and it came crawling, dripping and slimy from Alex's basement, something that was looking for a final resting place, or to spill a secret long forgotten. It freaked Alex and Delilah into silence. She remembered what she saw the minute his fingers touched the piano: eyes rolling wetly in dead sockets.

Since then, Electric Orchid's tunes had a slight effect on the afterlife, something like a siren, as if all the macabre of the world was *attracted* to the music. It was a hallucinatory power they didn't create on purpose; it was the magic of five minds weaving together five different trains of thought into vile poetry and scabrous sounds. When people came to see their shows, they came to see the thrilling sights, the smell of decay, but ultimately for the music.

"Look, D. Our relic."

Delilah realized that she'd been thinking for a good half hour, that Jimmy was beeping outside, and that her palms were sweating. Alex wiped them dry with his Invader Zim T-shirt, kissed her cheek and smiled. She could smell his familiar scent of clove cigarettes and spicy liquor. It put her at ease, at least for the moment. Alex would always be the one to keep her thoughts in check, wouldn't he?

She looked into the blanket of darkness of the living room and saw it: the grand piano, matte black surface gleaming beneath the moonlight. The keys were sharp as teeth in a freakishly huge smile and the legs wavered like cloven hooves. Alex slowly dragged his finger across the keys and sent a shockwave down the nubs of Delilah's spine. It made her think of "Something I can Never Have" by Nine Inch Nails. Everything she first came to learn about putting tunes together was from this place; every promise her and Alex made to be friends forever began here. This was the place where "My Personal Hell" woke the strange demon in Alex's basement.

"Fucking creepy in here at night," Alex said.

"Yup," Delilah began to light a cigarette.

"Don't!" Alex yelled. "My grandparents don't allow smoke in the house."

"Fine. Are you taking anything?"

"Some books, CDs, tape decks, my lucky flower necklace."

"The one you bought at the flea market?"

"Yup. The silver orchid. Can't live without feeling that exquisite metal flushed up against my skin."

"It's a cheap Hot Topic piece of shit."

"TO YOU! But to me it's fine as wine."

"Whatever," Delilah said.

Alex bolted up the stairs and left Delilah alone in this huge lonely space. She stared the basement door down; it stood tall and proud as a sentinel, the knob like the eye of a withering Cyclops. Delilah's head filled with her teenage nightmare, of Alex's ripping piano scales and her grueling melodies. She remembered this door opening by a phantom hand; she saw the closet in the basement shaking madly. Who knew what the hell really lived in this house, what kind of land this house was built upon? The colonists massacred the Indians all those centuries ago, scared of the brown demons covered in chicken feathers and war paint. If you didn't conform, you died. It seemed not much had changed. So maybe Alex's house was built upon a massive unholy grave.

"It's not her spirit," Alex said walking slowly to the door.

Alex was adamant that the thing in the basement was not the ghost of his mother, but Delilah disagreed. It couldn't have been anyone else. That basement closet was where she was punished as a little girl, that closet was where his mother had learned that the piano could be an outlet that didn't involve drink or drugs. Delilah *saw it* with her own eyes.

"For real. I don't wanna even think about it."

Delilah saw his hands grab the silver orchid necklace. It sat uneasily between the black tattoos that twined his collar bones and it made her want a necklace of her own, want to get more tattoos.

"Love that pendant on you, Alex."

"Funny, I love it on me too."

"Feels like we're sixteen again."

"Liquor in flasks and cigarettes in our pockets; all illegal of course. Oh, and there's this," Alex pulled out a small wooden box from beneath a secret compartment in the piano, sticker-scarred and scratched with badly drawn musical scales.

"What is it?"

"Just a little something," and Alex opened the box, revealing thin membranous sheets cut into tiny little squares. "Put it on your tongue and let it dissolve, slowly. It might taste bitter. Acid always is the first time."

"Acid . . . like we're rock stars already."

Delilah assumed there was tons of acid in New York, so why not get used to it now. The tab was a blotter Alex scored through Jimmy's Philly hook-up called *Rat Salad*. It was a small square, flimsy . . . filmy, and had a wide-eyed skull imprinted on its surface. She thought it might melt in her hand, might wilt like an orchid petal. So she placed the drug on her tongue and let it sizzle away. It tasted faintly sweet, faintly rotted. The only time Delilah ever hallucinated wasn't even from a hallucinogenic. It was a shit-load of Ambien that she managed to get her hands on, and the dose jellied her brain into a stupor for five hours straight. She learned her lesson and stayed away from the stuff, afraid of all those twisted worlds puckering like red lips before her eyes.

"It'll bring the orchids to life," Alex whispered.

Down they went and the basement was cold as ever. The floor was damp, lousy rose colored carpet and faded brown tile, mold growing up the walls like little monsters. Delilah scanned the darkness, made her eyes become one with the absence of light. It congealed before her, made the room smaller, made Alex's hand get colder as he held her tighter. The acid had kicked in. She felt nearly weightless. She thought she could fly.

"Nothing's changed," Delilah said.

"Why would it? You were just here last week."

"I don't know. I'm . . ."

"Tripping?"

"Don't be dramatic," Delilah stuck out her tongue.

Alex cranked the basement's stereo and Otep's "Ghostflowers" came rumbling out of the speakers. Delilah felt really high now, felt herself fall into the nightmarish thick of the hallucinogenic. She could see Alex's orchids glowing like a vortex through his homemade tent. Timed plant lights shut off at certain hours; a misting system sprayed the orchids like you see in the vegetable aisles in big supermarkets. But it was the music that had twisted Delilah's head.

Alex headbanged for a moment. Otep's crazy grinding voice was haunting. Delilah often cited Otep as one of her inspirations. A queen of poetry. Then she and Alex walked into the makeshift tent and the rainbow of sights pulled them in with verve. The colors, the spirals, the shape shifting orchids! They were tragic, fragile, perfect! All of the petals wavered, swarmed; they grew tiny little faces that screamed with no mouths.

Alex picked up a big orchid labeled *Phalaenopsis electricidae*, the genus named after the petal's appearance of a great moth taking to the sky. The flower was sun-yellow with whorls of red running through the center, moving outward toward the end of the leaf in gentle arcs. The colors formed a downward spiral before Delilah's eyes, the most beautiful orchid she'd ever seen. She was proud that her band name was honored after it.

"This is the one. My baby," Alex said, plucking off a few petals. "The band name. My tattoo. Beautiful ain't she?"

"Gorgeous. But what happened to the jar?"

"Up there."

Dust above the armoire; Alex reached over and brought the jar down. When he opened it Delilah caught no smells, no pompous flower power; it was just the negative stink of Pennsylvania. But yet these were the petals that refused to wilt and die even after being ripped from their motherly stem. They were resilient, tough, and Delilah wanted to be just as tough.

"They don't have a scent, Delilah. Orchids are simply beautiful. They don't need to show off with their exquisite smells like lilacs or funeral lilies. It's why I love them. Subtle and unique. They can't be categorized."

"Just like you, Alex."

"I kept the original petals in the jar because I thought once I picked her free of them, they'd never grow back. But they did. She's a wondrous plant."

"I wish we could bring them all. Orchids are your life besides music. I'd hate to see you lose your green thumb. Only you can care for them without sudden death."

"I made a choice. Music it is. But I know what we can do to salvage the memories."

Alex ripped the rest of the tent away, revealing a jungle of orchids and their myriad varieties. There were white petals and color-spiraled petals, twin plants and single bulbs, seedlings in rows of fresh dirt. The stalks bowed into one another, families of rich green life keeping secrets and sharing stories of Alex the careful botanist, and the ghosts in the basement. The lights made the flowers throw twisted shadows upon the walls, made them waver like a sinful dance.

"Take some," Alex said.

The last of the lyrics burned through Delilah's veins and then she saw Alex begin picking petals and stuffing them into his jacket pockets and another mason jar. When she touched a petal on one the plants, it instantly wilted and died. Alex grinned, that maddening sharp grin, but kept stuffing his pockets with petals and bulbs to plant in New York. Delilah hadn't a green thumb at all; her talents besides music laid with the caring for animals. It was why Zazo hadn't died when he was just a pink little baby, and never tried to fly away as an adult.

"Well . . . think we have enough?"

"Yeah. Now let's get on the road."

10

Lights innervated the night sky like Mardi Gras. Hans and Rez were on the move, picking up the pieces of their conversation. One quick stop for a drink at The Continental, and then their shadows flashed across the bare bone plaza that separates Greenwich from the East Village, the cube like a huge space rock: take us to space, a forever getaway. Then all aboard the number 6 to Chinatown, rocking and rolling to Canal Street.

Out the train doors and up grimy stairs, old cobblestone mess of streets, languid corners bathed in rot and shimmering gold-red of the Orient. Their mouths gawked at all the filthy windows lined with roasting Peking duck, the shelves of fetid fruit that formed clouds of black flies and the pork belly slivers slimed in sour red barbeque sauce hanging from chains, wriggling as if alive. It was a wonder what kind of mutated rodents lived here, how many ducks had to die for the carnivore palate this side of town. Not just ducks, but frogs, squid, shell fish and even a rat or two.

From Canal Street they skittered south to Bowery and crossed over Chatham Square where the valiant onyx statue of Lin Zexu watched them with stone-grey eyes, pioneer of the war against opium that scarred China in the 1830's. Hans was leading them not to any bar or nightclub, or anyone's shabby apartment, but an arcade, the last of its kind: Chinatown Fair.

That was the permanent kid in Hans' mind; he didn't much like the new kinds of electric entertainment, but he indulged in the old. Turning right on Mott Street, grim and deserted, Chinatown Fair Arcade snuck up on them. There came the sounds of huddled voices, a young crowd, and the metal cling of coins hitting the pavement. Number 8 said the sign, lusty purple shroud.

"This will help clear our heads. A few games and a good talk," Hans said.

"What do you play?"

THE ABSENCE OF LIGHT

"Asteroids! Point and shoot and BOOM!"

"I like Ghosts and Goblins."

"You would, kid."

They walked in and squeezed through the bodies glued to the anachronism of gaming systems. Tetris, Rampage, the entire Pac Man family, Dance Dance Revolution, Street Fighter, Super Mario Bros., Ghosts and Goblins, all ringing to life. It was like being in a slowly popping bubble of the past. But soon this culture would die like everything else to the modern mind-set.

Rez heard a building come tumbling down like some 9/11 ghost, and the roar of King Kong, but saw that it was the game Rampage, and that a scruffy looking kid was yelling about making it to the next level. Then he saw another kid playing Ghosts and Goblins; a fat demon was flying around while the thin fingered youth beat at the buttons, battling to the death with flying axes. Rez wondered when the ghost of his past would come claim him; there was no hiding from it. Right now he felt it closer than ever.

The voices were awakening.

These were the sounds of his past, present and future. They were the sounds of his rugged love life, his sexless desires. Rez thought about all the guys he'd slept with. Sadly, he could count them on one hand. Where was his libido these days? Lost in the disastrous puddle of writer's block? The last lover Rez even remembered was a kid that had given him the "look" at Santos Party House. A kid with a pin pricked face and wild hair, luscious lips and the tightest black clothing Rez had ever seen.

All he remembered was sitting by the bar drinking BOMB craft beer and drowning out the sounds of the horrible band on stage. He was trying to not look suspiciously nervous, trying not to take notice of those clear eyes marking him, those insidious fingers clutching the studded belt, the swollen penis sticking up through the black jeans. Sex was what some people lived for, and Rez didn't know if that was part of his disposition, but it always seemed to cross his mind.

Everything else was a blur. There were warm hands sifting through his hair, a tongue running across his neck and collar bones. The smell of cigarettes and sweat and dirty feet was like heaven. Something in a way a man smelled turned Rez on madly, perversely; something in the way they took control of him turned him on too. He very much liked to be submissive, especially in bed. And that kid took full advantage, slapping Rez's pale skin until it flushed red, tugging Rez's hair until it nearly pulled free from the root. The kid bit and sucked every orifice he could find; every finger and toe that was available.

But that was the end of it. Rez woke up the next day severely hung over on a strange bed; the sheets were entangled into a huge knot across his torso, the pillows were on the floor and a sopping stain of sweat surrounded him. There was no warm body next to his, no feet to entangle with his own, no lips to kiss. Alone again. All that was left was a hand written note that said THANKS, and that he should lock the door on the way out. If that's what love was all about, then he wanted none of it. Were the one night stands ever going to stay?

"Hey, kid!" Hans waved his hand.

Rez realized that he'd worked himself into a minor sweat. So much for memories. They both found flimsy chairs in the back of the arcade. It was a whole new world here, one where there was no end, and ultimately no beginning. Everything all of a sudden grew huge, kaleidoscope vision, and Rez began seeing the world under a different light, tumbling through numberless angles, hues of blacks and grays. The blood-red walls flashed darkly; the lightning strike of video game lights didn't illuminate back here.

"It's safe," Hans said. "From *them*."

"Safe how?"

"All these worlds: the claw, the fortune teller, the arcade games, they never change. When you come in you know what you're going to get. Here you're safe from change, from being hurt."

"You're right."

"I see how you look at things, Rez. You ache for your *story*."

The words settled deep and scalding into Rez's mind. The shadows living in his head began to writhe; the whirring voices became louder. Hans told the story. A man with exquisite photography skills who opened a door of some kind—a door not to another gateway, but one in real time that let *other* things in—with the flash of his camera. Of murder. Mayhem. Betrayal. Rez dreamed of this: a pale beautiful woman screaming for all that is mercy at the top of her lungs, black hair fanned out and crazed, concealing a swollen bloody mass for a face.

Too hot inside now, heartbeat racing, and Rez removed his button up shirt, down to fishnet, black net against his pale jutting torso, and rubbed one finger across his arm. The raised pink scar tissue was like a small carnival fun house there were so many grooves, so many mirrors reflecting his old life back into eyes. All of a sudden Rez's brain convulsed and the voices were diesel trucks now. Every time the lights hit a new object, shadow forming like some dark twin, another voice joined the melee.

Still here!

"Your father," Hans said, opening a flask from his beat up messenger bag with a shaking hand, "was a very gifted man."

Hans pulled some photos out of his velvet-lined jacket pocket. Rez saw a young boy dressed in black who looked just like himself: same sharp features, black shock of hair, bird smile and blue flames for eyes. There was a woman there as well, pregnant woman in a black silk dress, long legs drawn up over her lover's lap. Mom and dad! Rez swigged from Hans' flask, the burn of whiskey riding down the tunnel of his throat, flushing away the taste of the dusted air, and the voices finally stopped.

"What else you got hidden in there?" Rez laughed.

"Something special. This."

He opened his jacket and out came a very old, but awesome looking camera and some beat up notebooks with glued pieces of paper scattered all over the covers and sticking out from the inside. The camera had the letters T70 etched in fading gold above the foggy lens. There were so many buttons, controls and numbers that Rez knew nothing about, but Clive would. Hans passed it to Rez, and the moment he touched it he felt a small electric current run through his fingers.

"Arkham's."

Hans was a genuine soul, and Rez could tell this as he went into a deep sob. He cared for his old buddy, *my father*, Rez thought, *a fucking photographer. Great.* Rez tried to keep calm, tried to focus on music, the video games, anything other than this distorted reality. But it was useless.

"Rez, you okay?"

"I'm fine. I just . . . don't want to hear *them* anymore."

Hans' eyes widened. "Arkham heard them, he always said this. He heard them!"

"Make them stop! My fucking head's pounding!"

4 . . . 5 . . . still alive!

"Your father was a very driven man who sometimes took his work too much to heart. I can tell you have a lot of that in you the way you talk about your writing. You have his gift."

"His what?"

"The gift. It's something people are born with."

"Born with *what?*"

"Art. An *identity.*"

Rez thought about that for a moment. *An identity. An identity.*

"I feel nauseous."

"How is it you hear *Them?*"

"Whispers, jumbled words, you name it. Depends on what they want."

"Ever try predicting the future?"

"No."

"Why not?"

"Because psychics predict the future."

"Well, Arkham tried to predict the future in his own weird way . . . with cut-ups. Open that book."

Rez opened to the first page he saw scratchy black handwriting that was similar to his own, passages from novels cut out and jumbled next to one another, creating a collage of words, montages of the human mind.

Why is it dark? That startling thought came, gurgling little laugh, which caused photography to be held above all other considerations.

"Cut-ups come together like a painting. And when you experiment with them over a period of time, you find that the rearranged texts predict future events."

"You're quoting Burroughs himself."

"Yes I am. This technique has been used by a lot of great musicians too. Kurt Cobain, David Bowie, Thom Yorke and the list goes on. They all utilized cut-ups in their lyric writing . . . some of their deepest and saddest songs."

"So you mean Arkham was using the system to predict his photography? His doom?"

Hans' eyes flashed. "Sometimes the things we want or need to be explained come to us slowly, and when they come it's when we least expect it. This is fate Rez, it brought us together."

"I don't believe in hocus pocus like that."

"Well, believe it! It's funny because cut-ups are so innocently fabricated. You simply cut two forms of linear texts, such as a newspaper, a book of poetry or a novel, and jumble them around, then place them back together. The results are amazing."

Rez looked away and read some more tethered passages.

I can only hope that my account will not arouse greater curiosity.

Journeys end in lovers meeting, and his hands clamped into tight fists.

Then Hans told the last of the story. It flew out his mouth like it all had happened yesterday. *Sister. Twin sister.* It made Rez's lungs nearly give out. The room lilted; posters twisted into fathomless black shapes, ravenous, his stomach in knots.

"I know it's a lot, Rez."

Horns blared outside, followed by a huge crash of metal and glass. Someone blew the light. Rez's hand took on a tremor, fingers barely able to grip the flask, black nails clicking against the metal. But he opened the notebook again to read another passage.

Their shapes were only dark silhouettes in the glow of the night light.

Ghosts?

Twins!

Silence, momentous and still. Was this why he sometimes felt a mysterious pain every now and again, from her?

"We have to find her!" Rez stood.

"We will."

"But there are like seven billion people on this fucking planet. She could be anywhere."

"I held you guys in my arms once. I remember your faces like the back of my hands. I imagine she looks much like you."

Rez's eyes widened.

"But first thing's first, we go see the show."

"I'm not in the mood to party after all this."

But Hans put headphones over Rez's ears and a frilly keyboard blasted out of the speakers, followed by a clang of guitars mangling one another over a quick and crunchy bass line. Rez felt the music seep into his skin as if a thousand little shimmering notes lifted from the CD and shot like stars. The lead singer had a rough, raspy voice. It suited the music behind him, caressing the air.

"This band is Bone Crushers. The last of their kind in these parts. They're up for a contract come tonight."

Hans moved to the music, his piercings catching the light. He licked his lips until they were rimmed red and dry and cracked as if a cold sore was coming, or a bad case of eczema.

"Let's go to the show and talk after," and then Rez smiled like there was only one thing worth smiling for: music.

The last glint of Violet Hill behind them; the arid Amish forts far and few, the Dutch faith of a crazed Anabaptist God growing weaker. Farm windows lit by kerosene lamps; carriages lined in rows ready for the morning's corn picking.

The makeup smear in Alex's eye made the ragged lights of The Skeleton Grin run messily, twinkling. It reminded him of the one time he went to Philadelphia. He'd gotten so drunk everything looked skewed and stretched like taffy. He half wished that Tommy was with him, oppressed by some pitiful woe-is-me feeling. He was in need of another body to call his own, another mouth to kiss, another sweet sex between the legs to claim. It was no secret Alex's hormones were always spinning out of this world, and that he was always in need of a lover. Too bad none of his flimsies ever wanted to commit. It was the curse of a small town. Too many people talked, too many people wanted to be single so they could taste everyone else's spit, everyone else's come.

The thoughts lingered in his brain, then spiraled into his penis. Alex half touched himself underneath his big black coat. His penis felt good, but it would feel better if another's hot embrace were here. If Tommy were here he would put his mouth right over his shaft, push it down until his smoky throat gagged in return. But he couldn't let himself fall into the glue trap of lust, not yet anyhow. There was a show to play; his band depended on his keyboard skills. It was time to start thinking about the whole picture instead of his own emotions.

"What's the first thing you're gunna do when you get there?" Alex asked Delilah.

He had to move his mind away from sex or he was going to explode. He grabbed his copy of *The Cipher* tight and applied rouge lipstick to his thin lips. He felt as if he was still tripping a bit, but the wicked throes of acid had long since faded from Alex's vision. Left only was the hole in his heart for true love.

"I don't know yet. Probably get a hot dog."

"Oh, D. That's the white trash in you. You can't get a *good* hot dog in New York anymore."

"Says who?"

"Says anyone who's ever been there."

"And you have, Alex?"

"No, but my friends have!"

"Who?" Delilah felt all of a sudden annoyed.

"Tommy."

"The coke head?"

"That's closer than anyone you've ever known that's been to New York."

"The city is my blood."

"City?" Alex questioned, stealing the wine bottle from Delilah's grip.

"Yeah, it's what people who live there call it."

"But you don't live there yet, double D."

"Will you shut the fuck up already, you smart ass."

"Whatever," and Alex swigged the bottle messily.

"So, smarty pants, why do they call them dirty water dogs?" Delilah snatched the bottle back.

"Because the vendors never change the water!"

"I hope there's an awesome music shop in the village, a bookstore too."

"I hope there're boys who wear dirty jeans, flannel shirts and skater shoes . . ."

"If you keep putting these standards up you'll never find anyone to love you."

The wind roared, grew cold as a zombie tongue, and then warmed up again.

"I can dream, can't I?"

"Hey! You two!" Sheigh's head was sticking out the back window of the pickup, her dark brown hair moving in little waves across her face. "Want a hit of this or what?"

"Pass it over," Alex said.

Delilah watched him cup his hand over the tie-dye bowl piece. The dark sticky resin lit like stars against the dollar store lighter. Alex pulled in the strange smelling smoke, sweet smelling smoke; Delilah next. It tasted faintly dark, like incense and tobacco. A wildfire spread into his lungs, vacuuming his mind out of his head and threw it into the trees and the aching grasslands. His heart beat so fast he thought it might explode; his head filled with new ideas fast.

"Salvia," Sheigh said. "It's a little taste of New York."

Who the hell had access to salvia in Violet Hill? That kind of drug could only come out of exotic cities, gritty cities, and Violet Hill wasn't one of them. The thought confounded Alex, but—to his pleasure—it was just part of their new rockstar lifestyle.

"You're supposed to smoke salvia with a butane lighter. But fuck it," Sheigh said.

"Tastes sweet," Delilah said,

"I love you SWEET LEAF . . . though you can't hear!" Alex sung wildly. "OH YEAH BABYYYYYY!"

"Hey Alex, do you remember that boy at school that used to always . . . well, who tried to *be* you?" Delilah asked.

"Carl? That little fucking pansy?"

"I guess so, I don't remember his name. Maybe it was even Tommy, your little twink lover."

"That little fuck was such a poser. Good in bed, but such a poser. Gods, the way he blew me, the way he touched my face, how he worshipped me!"

"Alright stud, enough."

"Well, Delilah, if you ever decided to *get any*, you'd know what I mean."

"Fuck you. Fuck you long and hard!"

"Thank you."

"And your little dog too . . . bastard."

"The human body is a puzzle of flesh, Delilah. Try to make the pieces fit. You might surprise yourself."

"I don't want to figure out any puzzle."

"Of course you don't, Delilah. Too tough for your own good."

"Too smart for my own good."

Alex rolled his eyes. "Anyway . . . look what Carl the blow-job-god gave me!"

Alex pulled out a silver cigarette case. It was scribbled with dark red nail polish and when the moon's light scampered across the silver surface it was clear to Alex how much Carl had liked the band. He'd drawn the words *ELECTRIC ORCHID* on it, and had painted a terribly poor version of an orchid flower. Inside was a row of cloves and beneath it were some dried orchid petals.

"Neat huh?"

"Whatever."

"He liked our band a lot!" Alex grinned.

Delilah ignored him for a moment, her hands covering her eyes, fingernails raking across her bright green labret hoop, the gauges in her ears. She could almost get her middle finger through. Alex felt himself getting fucked up again. Drinking put him into a quiet zone, a lonely little place where all heartache and sorrow was to be spread on a table and stared at like a dunce in the classroom. But one smoke of something sweet and spicy and he was on his way to the high land.

It was time to dance.

Alex stood up and lifted his arms into the air, his black trench coat whipping open and the moon shown upon the patch of hair leading down to his crotch for everyone to see. But then a million orchid petals ascended into the night like huge moths. Alex saw them litter the ground as if a funeral procession. Jimmy swerved the pickup, jolting Alex to sit back down again.

"THE ORCHIDS!" Delilah yelled. "You're wasting them! What would Robert Mapplethorpe think?"

"He'd take a snapshot and make them look like monsters."

"You're right! Gimme some!" Delilah snarled.

Alex fished his hand into his jacket pocket and brought up a handful of dark yellow petals swirled with lavender stripes. He noticed Delilah's jealousy flare at how vibrant the petals remained in his grip, but the second he dropped them off in her hand, they began to wither and lose their color.

"Fuck, they're dying! I can't handle the petals like you."

"Just toss them!" Alex yelled. It's how we leave our mark."

"Hey fags!" Jimmy interrupted. "I heard you guys talking about sweet things, and I like pussy sweet. I want wild, dirty, city cunt from now on."

Alex slowly realized that the bulk of their conversations were about pure bullshit unless it came down to art. When they all worked together it was a match made in heaven, but other than that they were all regular kids out to cause debauchery. This was the William S. Burroughs influence on the band. They all loved his books, unlike the other kids in town who were glued to television screens and video games.

Needle drugs, ancient hallucinogens, and the beat generation was something they wanted to mirror. Timeless stories about the unacceptable culture of that era: gay men shooting great globs of milky jism over the moon, being a junkie, people turning into red faced mutants by the simple human act of fornication. Literature pushing a greater cause and mocking conservative beliefs before it was cool to do so. Literature that made you think, challenged you. They didn't want their vampires to sparkle or to be at war with a southern town and it's stupid, close-minded populace. They didn't want to read about indolent werewolves or the endless, pointless problems they faced. That would make them sheep, and they were the herders.

The mix of influences affected their music too. Heavy metal was the cornerstone of Jimmy's guitar riffs; Sheigh and Billy practiced erratic time signatures; Alex's keyboarding was pure black magic. But it was Delilah who stood out the most. Her melodies seemed to rise from some mystical place in her gut where little gnomes spent their nights brewing acidic potions in huge cauldrons that boiled out of her mouth to sound so fucking perfectly destructive. Her lyrics were black venom that controlled the crowds she sung to. And it made them beg for more.

But the road twisted away now. Alex saw a dilapidated sign for Interstate 95 North and the pickup was heading straight for it. His eyes could only focus on the mountains, just black and blacker, fading. They were same color as the young night, mysteriously dark. If he looked hard enough, Alex could see a thin sheen of snow at the peaks, glowing like a T-shirt under a black light. He was surprised it was not polluted from the anthracite. Then he saw Delilah waving, imagined that she was kissing this old life goodbye and accepting the new one head on.

11

The party filled two rooftops in the East Village at sunset with a specific dress code: heavy metal-industrial-punk-fetish-creative attire, or an all black minimum. *THIS FLESH A TOMB!* said the painted banner across the small doorway as Clive and Lynk followed thumping bass and hypnotizing melodies onto the rooftop. System, from the *Queen of the Damned* soundtrack was playing.

The sky above was black slate; the city below was like melting ice cream with too many sprinkles. Kids were sprawled everywhere, making out and slipping their hands beneath tight clothing. The music cut conversations in half, indie bands fronted by Brooklyn hipsters this time around. Two huge tables with kegs and punch bowls were set up; a Joan Jett looking girl drank straight from one of the spouts until a yellow cloud of foam dribbled down her chin. Lynk saw the girl eye Clive, and that Clive's face had begun to lighten up, but Lynk pulled him away. No time for that shit.

"Drink and relax," Lynk said as he filled two cups with punch.

"I can't, mate, I'm too worried. I know he's going to do something stupid without me."

"He's with the old man. Did you forget that?"

"Right . . . you're right."

The punch went down like green gasoline with a hint of licorice. But it didn't stop Clive's nervous jostling, the tapping of his foot, the rubbing of his hips with his fingers, and biting his nails down to bone. But then a huge batty form came swooping through the bodies toward Lynk and Clive. Its eyes marked them, and for a second Lynk thought that it was going to eat him alive, that he'd pissed off the wrong ghost.

"Yo man, what's good?" Dago said.

"Hey, what's up, Evil D?"

"Been drunk all day."

"Good. Clive and I are in need of release."

"Oh . . . *hey Clive,*" Dago winked.

Clive spit out his drink. "Don't say it like that."

Dago smiled heinously; his demon face sharpened and his thick black eyebrows scrunched. He was clad in his usual black on black clothing, the leader of the fringe kids who hated the world, who channeled their rage through art and the macabre. Dago also played a wicked bass and knew every musical scale the books offered, could bend music to his will, his skills were so sharp.

Lynk thought about the last time he partied with Dago. It was in a Brooklyn graveyard where the sloping hills, crooked trees and lonely grass paths were filled back-to-back with shadowed kids who'd gotten so wasted that by the time the sun rose there was no recollection of the destruction they'd caused, of the tearing funeral flowers to shreds, of defacing the tombs. But if Dago wasn't fucking with the dead, he simply wasn't happy. He was also a ghost hunter, and Lynk thought maybe Dago would let him borrow his fancy equipment . . . and maybe he could get Clive drunk enough tonight for a kiss—

No, he mustn't think that way.

Friends only.

"Oh, stick up the ass today?" Dago said lightly. "No pun intended."

Clive took a step forward. "Don't fuck with me."

Lynk grinned nervously, aware of Clive's heightening temper. "Drink some more, you'll lighten up for sure."

"It's horrid."

"Couple more sips and you'll forget you even have it, well, if you don't pass out first," and Dago rubbed his tongue across the filagree of safety pins attached to his wrists.

"Right."

"Killer party," Lynk interrupted.

"Isn't it? I don't do clubs. I do the open air. Plus, you can't smoke inside. But out here," Dago pointed to the black horizon, pricked with tiny lights, "you can smoke whatever you want."

He opened a cigarette pack and gave out joints to anyone passing, Sour Diesel straight from the city, with fingers that were heavily calloused and torn, nails chipped: the sign of a musician.

"The Cabal Gallery opens in a few days. I want you guys there. I got people lined up who are going to spit fire; I got an old silver section of photos, my paintings, sculptures. *Everything.*"

"We'll be there!" Lynk said.

"Clive, you still have a portfolio to show, right?"

"Well—"

"No talking, only showing," Dago winked. "You'll be able to meet kids from New Brunswick, New England, Philadelphia, Athens and all. They claim to have pictures of ghosts. Should be interesting."

Suddenly crazy laughter up roared from the back of the party; a shrill voice demanded that her minions worship her.

"They're playing Nightmare," Dago grinned. "Remember that game?"

"MEA CULPA, ANN! Who could forget it? We're 90's children," Lynk joked.

"The best damned role playing game I've ever played."

Then Dago moved like liquid shadow to another part of the party and Lynk followed, dragging Clive. His head was beginning to throb; his heart was starting to race. The punch was *that* good. His vision blurred, became overrun with the image of Clive's frilly hair against his face, the heat inside a small room growing, his long thing legs spread as he unzipped his fly . . .

Fuck my life, he thought.

Lynk couldn't help but to be plagued by that night: The Continental, Clive's big strong hands on his bony shoulders, their eyes meeting each time they sung another Misfits tune. It was a match made in heaven, wasn't it? Yes, Lynk was lonely. Yes, Lynk wanted a lover. But who didn't? Lynk noticed that most of the people he saw on the street walked alone, lived alone, ate alone. It was a normal part of life. Lynk was okay with the fact that he would die alone, so long as he was by Clive's side. It was the perpetual price he had to pay the moment he ran away from home: that he'd have to get used to the reality of solitude.

But now it was different.

Clive had to have known what he was doing that night. Lynk had never been with a girl, never dreamed of them, their piny scent, their monthly attitudes. No. Lynk only had feelings for guys, whether it was accepted or not. Clive always accepted it, always made Lynk feel like his buddy, like his *best friend*. So why would Clive fuck it up like he did? Was he seriously one of those macho freaks that thrive off of the desire of being wanted, whether by a boy or a girl? If so why would he get mad when Lynk tried to talk about it? After all, Clive was the one who took Lynk's hand and put it between his legs; Clive was the one who'd led them down those dark smoky stairs and into the bathroom; Clive was the one who made Lynk kneel on the mucky tiles, unzipping his black jeans and letting that big white serpent out to flood his mouth with salty, molten ejaculate. Lynk only did what he was told, as any good friend would.

But that didn't mean that he had to let it go.

But then Dago kicked a beat-up pillow away from a couch that smelled like wasted meat and brought Lynk back to his senses. They all sat down to enjoy drinks and smokes, listening to the music and watching the kids continue playing Nightmare. They talked for a matter of minutes about music and ghost hunting before something stole Lynk's attention.

They came out of nowhere, perhaps from the darkness in which they lived: sharp-faced figures who formed a circle . . . no, a pentagram. They all began sniffing one another like animals, feeling each other's clothing until their fingers were traveling beneath lace and lycra, tracing eloquent blood vessels throughout their limbs and necks, the blood so rich and hot below. They offered their wrists to one another, pale flesh exposed to moonlight, whitest white that can be, the color of cotton. And then he saw the tiny razors slashing across highways of veins, *across the stream,* and their thin lips wet with all that blood, glittering red like melted rubies.

"What the fuck are they doing?" Lynk asked.

Dago didn't answer. He was too busy watching the show, the music droning like possession. Lynk saw that Dago was touching himself too, his hand wrapped so tight around his boner that each time he stroked it a small spatter of blood ejected from the red-raw tip. The girls surrounded the boys now, licking their lips thirstily, dipping their fingers into the wrists, revealing swollen breasts and perfect pink nipples for the boys to bite until their tongues were stained red. Lynk heard them howl in pleasure and pain as they touched themselves, thin bloodied fingers like a decadent lubricant for this sinister spectacle.

"Dago, what the fuck is this shit?"

"Mmmm, Dago licked his lips again. "Bloodletters."

"What do you think you are? A splatterpunk?"

"All this time you spend judging and you've yet to even look in the mirror. Afraid of that reflection? Would there even be one? These kids would worship you if you let them."

"Fuck you."

"The fringe scene is still thriving, no matter what this gentrifying city does to destroy it. I'm the one keeping it alive!"

"I'm a ghost hunter, not a vampire," Lynk clenched his fists. "And I *hate* my reflection."

"Silas and Jacob used to hang out up here . . . but," Dago moved his finger across his fine throat in a slicing manner. "They jumped off the side, sick of life."

"I'm leaving," Lynk growled.

But then the shit hit the fan. One girl roared with all her might, squeezing the face of another, sharp nails ripping furrows into that pallid skin, digging into her eyes like bad fruit. Lynk heard the squish of meat, felt her agony as she shrieked and begged for them to stop. Lynk could see all the makeup and meat meshing together, the jellied blood clotting and glistening beneath the moon. Everyone cleared the roof to let them fight. Vicious brawl, so close to the edge; they could fall over with one wrong move.

"Stop this shit!" Lynk said.

"Let them get their kicks."

Dago was beating off to the scene now, pants down to his ankles, his long legs covered in golden hair and his penis a bleeding chasm. Then the unthinkable happened. The girl was lifting a knife, skinny blade made for filleting fish, and drove it into the other girl's stomach, then her chest, dragging it down until her corset was ripped open like a red-wet bag of chips. Dago spurt sickly looking semen at the sound of the knife sucking back against the flesh. Then all at once the fiends pulled the girl into a dark corner; dozens of eyes marked their meal, dozens of fingers clutched limbs to drink, and disappeared into the night.

"What the fuck's in this drink?" Clive said.

"Jägermeister and Absinthe," Dago replied. "What . . . never drank such a deadly combination?"

"I just saw . . . saw . . ."

But when Lynk turned he saw nothing. Peace, simple party goers. Kids were talking, smoking, making out and playing Nightmare. He'd imagined it all: murder.

"You lightweights never have! Real absinthe makes you see the things you refuse to believe. It's the wormwood effect. Sometimes it brings out the worst in people. Sometimes it brings out the best. Depends on the person."

Murder, Lynk thought. *I saw death.*

"So . . . what did you *really* come for?"

"Your equipment," Lynk said.

"Ah. Follow me."

Dago moved from the couch and back through the fire escape and into the stairway. There were hardly any lights, but when he took out a softball sized sphere, glowing like chartreuse, like mist hanging over a swamp, they needn't any light. The ball threw deep green tinsel all over their faces, making their noses itch.

"It has a funny smell," Clive said.

"You know the rules, Lynk."

"I believe in it this time."

Dago's eyebrows fell into a huge V. "I hope so. Don't embarrass me again."

"What did he do to embarrass the great and powerful Dago?" Clive asked.

"He wanted something, and when I told him the answer, he didn't believe in it. Hence, he never found what he wanted." Dago's face trailed to Lynk.

"What was it that he wanted?"

"A book of magick."

Dago lit his joint with a cheap lighter, creating weird shadows across his face, leaking into the hollows of his eyes.

"We just need your *hunting* stuff. The advanced Geiger counter and digital EVP recorder. We're going on the ultimate hunt in—"

"Shhhh, listen here, it's telling me something."

Dago's face was blank; his small dark eyes rolled into the back of his head revealing the whites. Lynk could only think about what he saw before, that murder scene, the teasing of sex. He hoped that didn't mean he would do that to somebody.

"Bad times. Bad times are coming."

"Wut?" Clive said.

"Bad . . . times . . . are coming. That's all I'm getting as a read."

"Forget it," Lynk began to pull Clive away. "Thanks Evil D."

"Oh, fucking shit you're doing it again Lynk!"

"Doing what?"

"Running away."

"If you're not going to help us, you're wasting our time."

Dago let out a grueling, but serious sigh. Awkward silence following an awkward moment. Then he passed a small beat up suitcase sparkling and jingling with a filigree of safety pins. Dago opened it and showed them the contents: small silver EVP recorder, the soul detector which resembled an awesome distortion pedal, and a strange looking board.

"The spirit board. Use it with *extreme* caution."

"You mean Ouija," Lynk corrected him.

The board had gothic numbers and letters juxtaposing a dastard skull with bat's wings for ears while it swooped over a grinning moon and sinful sun. Lynk grabbed it and ripped off the glass heart-shaped planchette, twirled it.

"Lynk, listen. You go trying to contact these things and they *will* take advantage. I promise you that. Spirits are like leeches: they latch on and suck you dry."

But Lynk waved Dago off, thanking him, and watched Clive finish his cup of the absinthe and Jäger mix. Would it morph his mind too? Lynk never said how he'd just seen the *bad times*, but how *good* they felt. It was as if something pleasurably terrible was lurking inside of him ready to take control at any moment.

It was real.

It was cold.

It was scary.

12

Dawn churning in the sky, dawn on a road corkscrewing to a new life. The death of the moon was upon them; the curse of the morning was rejected. Bottles flew from the trunk and cigarette butts were thrown from the windows as the unease of impatience settled into the blood.

Jimmy's beer goggles took them too far north, or south. Nobody knew. The subsequent roads were barren, dusty, and bumpy. There were no sights to be seen. Surely this couldn't have been the way to New York City. There had to be another route, another street to enliven the road trip of a lifetime. Then Jimmy took a sharp turn and the pickup was rummaging along a strange gravelly road sideswiped by crumbling factories and timeworn mills dripping yesterday's water. The one burned down mill spoke to Delilah.

Fire, she thought, *I keep thinking of fire.*

They collectively prayed that some ancient monster from the Lovecraft mythos with slimed tentacles and rows of razor teeth was waiting to rise and rule the world. *Cthulu here we come!* By the time they found blacktop road again, there was a sign that said Philly was not even a mile away, and so it was only right to stop there. Everyone was considerably groggy, too high for their own good, hungry and running low on booze. They needed refills and rest.

"PHILLY!" Delilah yelled.

"No fucking way! We're lost enough as it is!" Jimmy roared.

"Fuck you then. I never get to see anything cool."

"You will, D," Alex interrupted, smiling. "You'll see New York."

All of a sudden the pickup puttered, the tires shook and Jimmy started to curse his ass off in some extravagant car language that sounded drunk. Something in the engine had blown; a billow of steam shot from the hood and brought them to a stall. Jimmy shuffled to the front of the pickup and began kicking the bumper. Delilah saw his converses lift and slam, lift and slam again.

"The whore's betrayed me!"

Luckily the town they were in had beer and food. Jimmy ran to a crowd of bikers smoking in front of a bar and began talking to the guys. The dry stench of gin trailed into Delilah's senses. It made her hungry. When Jimmy came back he was sweating and annoyed, said that the engine needed to cool down. After that they tried to hang out in the biker bar, but the very unwelcoming bouncer with the fat red face and huge black sunglasses didn't like the sight of the five freaks that looked way underage. No one had proper identification, and with no proof of age you might as well be a ghost.

So they headed for the patch of woods, nothing but simple oak trees and large dumpsters filled with wasted food. *Good compost*, Delilah thought. The smell of methane and rotten bananas wafted as she collected maggots and worms from the hot wet center, jarring them for Zazo; pulsing invertebrates jumbled atop one another, searching for a way out. They'd be dinner soon.

Inside another cabin-looking establishment was a food joint. Delilah found a map of New York State, Rhode Island and Maine; she supposed this spot was a frequent stop for hitchhikers traveling north. Delilah opened one and saw how rural upstate was, barren. Aliens had to have lived there; there would be so many places to hide. Maybe she could hide herself there.

When she looked over to her right, she saw Alex sitting in a booth working his game on a cute little blonde boy whose face kept going pink every time Alex touched his leg. Leave it to Alex to find lust in the middle of nowhere. She watched them for a moment, making sure the boy or anyone else wouldn't do anything stupid. You couldn't be careful enough; the gays are still hated no matter where you go. But this empty place screamed nonchalance, and so Delilah left Alex to his desires.

Her mind was on food, on the greasy stench of French fries and salty goodness of ketchup. She fished in her pockets and brought up a few coins, a crumbled dollar bill. Not enough for a decent meal. But Sheigh had stolen her father's credit card and so she ordered a carton of honey maple pancakes, burnt home fries and too many bottles of ketchup; the coffee rounds seemed to never end, something to wake up their drug-pricked minds. They ate rambunctiously, stupidly, messily, smearing their hands across the gravel and the pickup, using their clothes as napkins, and using one another's faces as tables.

"The waitress asked me if I was a rock star," Sheigh said.

It's already begun, Delilah thought. All they could do was laugh.

"Ugh. I can't eat; I'm fiending," Billy said.

"I've some hash."

"Nah. Don't feel like smoking. I want something easy."

"What about some Dilaudid? You remember Saul? His mother steals it from her job. She's a nurse, and they both sell it, making a fortune. Why couldn't my parents be nurses! I'd never have to leave home AGAIN!"

"Dilaudid helps me sleep, makes me nice and numb."

"Keep that shit out of my face," Delilah demanded.

"I know. You don't sleep. But that doesn't mean the rest of us can't."

Jimmy fed Billy his pill and they all rested, their limbs hanging off the side of the truck lazily; squirrels picked at the garbage they left open and wet. They talked about dreams and nightmares, of living in the city and getting odd jobs. Sheigh wanted to try stripping; Jimmy wanted to work on motorcycles and cars. The rest wanted to sell comics and old school records.

"I'm horny," Sheigh complained. "Horny as a virgin at a prison rodeo!"

"Oh yeah?" Jimmy said.

"Take care of me," finger pointing to a large expanse of forest.

"I don't have any condoms."

"Then pull out!" Sheigh snapped. "I gotta get mine!"

Jimmy ripped off his Guns n' Roses T-shirt in a flash, half naked babe, torso bones like sticks. Sheigh pulled herself up and nearly jumped on Jimmy she was so ready, fishnet leggings ripped, her tight purple and black shirt too. Delilah watched them run into the far end of the woods, two bodies hungry for one another, two sets of hands gripping pale flesh, mouths wet like drooling children.

For Billy, Delilah and Alex it was time to think. Delilah pulled out the lucky bottle of Jäger, the sun beating off its dark green surface like a gem, and fed herself a liquid snack. Hours passed, good time for contemplation, for the rebuilding of energy. Her head bloated with excitement for New York, sharp as static combing across body hair. Billy was all of a sudden sleeping, high as a kite, echoing snores and farts; Jimmy and Sheigh were done fucking, a pile of limbs in the far distance. They were all asleep.

But not Delilah.

Too afraid to sleep, didn't want her one way pass into dreamland; she wanted the city. So she sat awake with Alex, slashing lyrics with a ball point pen across her notebook. *WORDS REMAIN MY ONLY ESCAPE* was written a thousand heartbreaking times on the cover. Alex read the prose out loud and agreed that Delilah's darkest secrets were best told through music.

"I love your notebook. Loved it for years."

"Moreso *our* notebook. We wrote 'My Personal Hell' in it." Delilah opened up to the page. "Look!"

Two signatures slashed across the page, pale brown, the color of dead blood. Alex laughed, took the pen from Delilah and began to sketch a piano scale over the words, blending the picture into one hectic portrait. It amazed Delilah how much their minds clicked. They barely had to talk; they had a mutual, telekinetic understanding of one another.

"It's a strange world how fast things come and go," Alex said.

"Come lay by me. Let's watch the sun go down together. Best part of the day."

"Got a light?" Alex said, flashing the joint.

"Salvia again?"

"Yup."

It was a spot beneath the oak trees, where pine cones crunched beneath their shoes, where evergreens shed their sharp needles like growing green carpets. *True nature before the storm of smog and jungle of buildings.* Delilah took Zazo from his cage and let him lay on her shoulder; Alex had his head on her lap, his dark splay of hair tickling her soft skin through the fishnet. He lit the joint and put spirals of smoke into the air.

"I won't sleep a wink until we get to New York."

"To sleep, perchance to dream!" Alex said

"Overrated! Why sleep when life's so short?"

"Because it rests our brains so we can think."

"I don't want to fucking think anymore."

"How you gunna write those haunting lyrics if you don't think?"

"I just want to drink, and . . ."

"Don't say it. Don't say it like that. You're not cutting yourself again."

"What if I just don't care?"

"Why do girls always think that tearing into flesh takes away the pain? It doesn't."

"Mhmm . . ."

"Suicide is the only way out . . ." Alex said, afraid.

"It's not about suicide; it's about getting through the worst of your fears, your failures."

"And what are yours?"

"My empty existence. My insubstantial life."

"Come on . . ."

"My skin itches like a motherfucker until I put the blade to it. End of story."

"Talk to me. Tell me about it."

"Why do you always want to fucking talk?"

"Talking about things helps people get over their issues. Holding it all in is useless and crass. It winds up killing people."

"Not a bad idea if you ask me . . ."

"Ah, typical Delilah. Always out to bring herself down."

Delilah grabbed a handful of Alex's hair, gritting her teeth. "Typical Alex, always trying to contradict me."

"Whatever, D. Can you at least rub my head instead of pulling on my hair? Though, if you were anyone else . . . I'd ask you to do it *harder*."

Her fingers sailed into that black mop, the softest hair that she'd ever felt on a boy. Not like she had many boyfriends. Delilah wasn't the loving type. She much preferred to protect, to stand guard. She didn't believe in wasting time on her own feelings when all they did was fuck with her mind in the first place. If someone else's heart was at stake, she'd be there to make sure it didn't get broken. Her own heart? Fuck that little black apex shaped thing.

"But it's a whole new life in New York. A fresh start, D. A fresh fucking start . . . finally!"

"Fresh for whom? I still don't know who the fuck I am, or where the fuck I come from."

Alex's green eyes shot right through Delilah. "You know enough. You're Delilah Dellinger, singer, sorceress of music, tough bitch—and a beautiful one at that."

Delilah felt her face go red.

"See, you're blushing. My blushing beauty!"

"Yeah . . . I guess."

"My own story isn't as fluffy as you make it seem. I don't have parents; I have tiny old midgets who take care of me!"

"Still, they're your *blood*."

Alex rolled his eyes. "Look, no matter what, there's music. It's saved us when we needed it the most; it's saved *you* especially."

"Yeah, and it also—"

"Shhhh. Don't bring that up. We all know what our music does. Point is we're never going to lose this bond. We're meant to be together forever."

"I hope so. I love you, Alex. More than I can say for anyone else . . . well, except Zazo."

Zazo pointed his head to Delilah now. A single beam of sun cascaded down his face, making his eyes gleam wetly, making his little fangs glow.

"Love that little fucker!"

Alex kissed Zazo on the head, opened his arms and took Delilah into his embrace. The smell of clove cigarettes, liquor and dirt swelled in her senses. He was the best friend anyone could ask for.

"All of a sudden I'm so tired."

"Twilight and salvia. Great combination."

Delilah looked through the trees, through the silvery nets of spider webs. She felt a moment of serenity at hand. It was pure nature. Twilight threw violet scarves of light across the land; the birds moved into their nests and the field mice were scampering away. A long trail of black ants was piling atop the corpse of a hornet, chewing through the husk of flaky wings and desiccated legs. Delilah fished her hand into the pile, letting all the tiny black workers run across her pale arm crazily, through the grooves of razor scar and glowing tattoo work, down her chest, her navel, and up her neck. It was a pleasant take over. She scooped a few dozen off her collar bone and crushed them in her grip, handing the goop to Zazo who ate it in two quick gulps and then closed his tiny eyes.

"Animals are nature's innocence," she said.

No reply from Alex. He was admiring the natural light.

Fuck my life, she thought. *I'm tired.*

The Jäger had made bed in her bloodstream, a big huge wave of licorice-laced dream, sweet smelling things, safety. Delilah couldn't hold it any longer, not with Alex here, not with Zazo sleeping on her shoulder like an infant. She had to let go, and so she did, holding Alex's hand ever so tightly before her eyes gave out.

Sleep came easy.

The kid was flimsy, flirty and called himself Joey. Alex noticed him the minute he entered the diner, noticed that cornsilk hair, imagined rubbing his fingers through the soft mesh and playing with each strand like he did the piano. The exchange of names was easy, and so was the confirmation of attraction. Joey was a shy boy who lived a mile down the road from this no name town; a town much like Violet Hill.

"I didn't know if you were a boy or a girl," Joey said.

"Thank you."

"That's a compliment?"

"Yeah. Now take this."

Alex dropped a tab of Rat Salad onto Joey's tongue. Joey sucked on Alex's finger for a good couple of seconds. Alex thought his tongue felt like hot spongy velvet. In no time Joey was tripping, laughing his ass off, and licking his lips. He couldn't keep his hands off of Alex, but neither could Alex.

He turned around to make sure Delilah was okay. She was lying in a pool of moonshine that made her tattoos and piercings glint like grey neon. Her lungs made awful choking noises; her lips curled angrily and her hands gripped the bottle of Jäger like rigor mortis. Alex wondered if she was slipping into the dreamlands, if her soul-body was rising up and watching him she was in such a terrifyingly heavy sleep; the sleep of a person who needed to catch up on a couple of years' worth.

"Who's the girl? Is it a girl?" Joey said.

Alex smiled. "Yeah, it's a girl. My best friend."

"Her name?"

"Delilah."

"She's beautiful."

"She is, but don't tell her that."

"Why?"

"She'd probably punch you in the face."

They walked to the loneliest spot they could find, arm in arm. Joey stared at Alex with one big brown eye, the other covered by his longish blonde hair in a grand emo fashion. *What a twink*, Alex thought. Then Joey moved his fingers like spiders into Alex's big coat, underneath his Invader Zim T-shirt, and raked them down Alex's ribs. Alex didn't suspect that Joey had long nails; he'd mentioned a bad habit of scratching the wooden desk in his room, a habit brought upon his by an alcoholic father and a demeaning mother.

"How did you know?" Joey asked.

"Know what?"

"You know what I mean!"

"I just know. What're you afraid to say that you're the G-word?"

"No. It's just not appropriate to say out loud."

"Oh, bite me."

"No, kiss me!"

They kissed for a long time. Joey was well experienced for such a prude looking boy. He had that Bible belt look without the accent and the perfectly combed hair; but his knowledge of pleasure was far from rookie status. He moved his tongue through Alex's mouth in ways that he never thought were possible. Alex tasted Rat Salad, the ketchup Joey ate with his French fries and the amber flow of malt from the Colt 45 they shared. Joey's ballsy approach was almost intimidating, but Alex found this moment to be nice, one to forget the chaos and fill the terrible horny void in his heart.

"Keep kissing me, Alex. I hate this place. I hate this life."

"Do you want to come to New York with me?"

"New York? I don't know . . ."

"Think about it."

"I . . ."

"*Think.*"

"All moving so fast . . ."

Joey was tripping good now; his words were slow, his pupils were fully dilated. Alex couldn't hold himself any longer. He unzipped his black jeans, ripped his cock from his underwear and Joey's eyes sparkled beneath the moon. His mouth opened wide and he took Alex in as far as he could; Alex pushed his head down until he heard Joey gag, until the sweet relinquishing pulse of orgasm filled Joey's throat and electrified Alex from his groin to his toes.

"New York. Do you want to come with me there? I play piano for my band, Electric Orchid . . ."

Joey looked about the trees, licked some residue from his lips. "Orchid like this flower pendant?"

"Yes. So what do you say?"

"You mean you want me to tag along like a groupie?"

"No, like whatever you want."

" . . . I just can't. This is all I know. Big cities aren't for me. Look around you."

"Why not? Take a risk in life. You only live once."

"Easier said than done. I'm not the settling type."

"In life there's no such thing as settling."

Figures. I always bag the flimsy ones. When will I find a lover who will never leave . . . never cheat?

"I'm sorry, I—"

"Well, fuck you then. It's been nice."

"WAIT! Can I get your number?"

"I don't have one."

Alex climbed through a thicket of bushes, quiet as can be, afraid to wake Delilah. But it was no use. She was already staring him down, assessing his messy hair and his satisfied glare. He knew the lines within that face, how her lips curled into anger and shame. And now eyes were upon him, shrouded by big dark sleepy bags, and hands were ripping at fishnet leggings, coming for his throat.

"Where were you? Fucking that twink?"

"Yeah, but it wasn't worth it."

"You left me alone. You left Zazo unattended. I had a fucking nightmare!"

Alex felt horrible. He'd never let his own hormones get in the way before, but he was desperate.

"Shit, D. I'm sorry. You know how it is for us boys."

"NO, I DON'T KNOW! I DON'T WANT TO KNOW!"

Delilah grabbed a handful of Alex's coat and pulled him close. Delilah was much tougher than he, and had a good pound or two more to take him down, so he knew he could get an ass whooping easily.

"I'm sorry," Alex said.

She let him go reluctantly. "You make me want to bash your *BRAINS* in all the time Alex. Why I trust you with all of my secrets is beyond me."

Delilah woke up the crew. They scrambled to clean the crusted spit from their mouths and pretended to brush their teeth. Nobody honestly gave a damn. Being dirty was a badge of honor. When Jimmy sped back onto the road Alex felt the first wave of city air spiral into his lungs: damp and mucky, weighted with smog. A sensual blend tinged with insanity. They pumped up their own CD. and Alex watched the road beneath the tires turn into a foul, fissured stretch of dark highway. He saw pot holes and cracks that gave way to watching eyes, puddles of finite darkness.

Like living black!

Alex laid his head back, sucking smoke through his mouth from a clove cigarette; the stud in his nose caught the passing lights, the silver orchid glowered upon his neck. The pickup seemed to defy time and space as the George Washington Bridge swallowed them whole. Would love be on the other side? Would happiness be? It was only a matter of minutes now.

13

This side of town mottled like the strange hallucinations of psilocybin mushrooms, the air thick and wet as a kiss, echoing noises of a squalid kind. Everything seemed to have been built before World War I, a time when the industrial rush had made landfall in America, a time when great iron machinery stole jobs from peasants, paving the way into a sterile economy.

Hans and Rez were penetrating its molten iridescent core.

This surely must have been hell.

The sky was starless and the streets were darker than black; neon puddled like toxic waste. Rez gazed into the twiddling street lights, seeing a woman stand beneath the intermittent flicker; her hair was like dried twigs, her legs were slimed in blood. But she was gone at the sound of his whisper; left only was the perversity of midnight.

OuT oF BuSiNeSs and *Do NoT EnTeR!!!* was scratched into huge plate glass windows. *NEVER COMING BACK!* and *CaN YoU SaVe ThE ToWn?* was written in bane magic marker across raided storefronts. The hope for a better tomorrow was shriveled; left only were the slippery spirits of a dark past.

A huge color-spiraled carrion plant sat alone inside a hallway, vicious, beautiful. *Carrion, blood, cordite. Death smells.* A fluted candelabrum dripped jagged wax onto a window ledge, dangling like striped candy. The deep alleyways were filled with reeking garbage—the painful rusty smiles of syringes, fast food wrappers collecting mold, shining cockroach families and newspaper clippings swooping. But despite all the filth Rez caught the small gleam of something he knew very well: a lucky coin scarred by time. He wanted to throw it in the fountain in Oval Park, but as he bent down to pick it up he felt a cold trickle run down his spine, saw his hand lost in shadow.

Let's dance, a voice said. Rez quickly drew his hand away.

"Look!" Hans said.

THE ABSENCE OF LIGHT

The club was a smog-scarred building, tall dark structure of senescent brick that buried the hopeless wails of person after person let down by society. A crowd hung around, slicked in orange street light: aberrant kids careening amongst a city of sheep. They were community college dropouts and high school seniors, neo-Nazis, punks, hipsters, metal heads, goonies, bums, hooligans, whippersnappers, beatniks and posers. Their clothes were torn and dark as all the shades of night; their features were skewed, sharp; their tiny lipstick covered lips babbled on about music, wine and weed. Their fine features and pinwheeling hair screamed prepubescence. They were all beautiful.

Dealers in battered leather vests sold the night's delicacy in colorful baggies for chump change. Their fingernails were filed to points, colored all the shades of autumn. Though age had clearly caught up to them with their salt and pepper hair, they had no wrinkles on their moonfaces. Hans had many wrinkles that he outwardly hated, and thinning hair too, but two decades of regret does that to a person. Feelings are easily worn on skin, deep sad lines sculpted beneath eyes; long indentations in cheeks.

Hans looked happy to see the new scene mixed with the old. Thankfully not everybody in the world was balled up in a corner living life by I-phones, video games and their own mutated, irrelevant gossip. Rez took Hans' flask full of pepper vodka and nearly drank the entire thing in one huge gulp, trying to wash away the emotional unease that had transferred from his heart to his messy hair, his tired eyes.

"Enjoy yourself tonight, Rez."

"I will, with liquid encouragement. Do you mind?" Rez held the tiny flask up.

"No, by all means go ahead."

Rez finished the flask and the burn was wonderful in his chest. He walked into the middle of the crowd, avoiding all of their googly eyes, their cigarettes burning the air, and found some beatniks he knew. They were the original rebellious kids from the '50's and '60's on their way to grave, but had pickled their organs with enough needle drugs and Irish whiskey to allow them another decade of party. He remembered how he used to wish one of them would just reach down with a wide embrace and take him under their wing as a son, a companion, but they never did. All of them had plans for Rez, said his life was not to be doomed to the park like theirs.

They filled his head with stories of William S. Burroughs, his drugged psychosexual worlds, of jism leaking over the moon and ancient pharos fucking with ancient phalluses. Magda, the veteran bum of Alphabet City, was rambling about prophecies with a gummy mouth, her long Medusa hair jumbled like tumbleweeds and her teeth lost somewhere in Tompkins Square Park. She always smelled of some ancient spice.

Magda was the only person to care for Rez when he first came to the streets in the middle of winter, alone and hungry, shivering because he'd forgotten to take a jacket. She'd shown him kindness, finding ways to cure his insomnia with her array of herbs boiled down to gooey drinks, thick rubs for his chest and back when he was sick, or a potion made of liquor laced with strange spices he couldn't pronounce. Her recipes never came out of a book and were never written down; her memories were made up of a phantasmal spells and curses.

And nothing had changed.

Tonight Magda was tossed upon a black velvet blanket, invisible against the cobble; moth-eaten rags were her clothes. She tinged the air around her with weirdness. Incense were burning; thin trails of loopy smoke smelled of lavender, herbs and fresh potpourri. The depressed kids watched her like some freak show of ageless wisdom. She had an assortment of little clear bags around filled with strange leaves called asafoetida, smelly ones called red currant, cinquefoil and boneset. There were clay bowls filled with green goo and air-tight jars ready to be sold. Exotic smelling tea was made fresh in tiny black kettles. The people in the park always came to Magda to tickle their darkest fancy, to see if she was the real deal. Rez knew she was.

"Glass coffin," Rez said.

"And who sleeps behind it?" Magda cackled.

"The WITCH of course!"

Magda stood and hobbled to Rez, embracing him with all her strength. "I remember the first time you read Dandelion Wine. You almost cried."

"Green Town is the best town ever."

Echoing a few feet away was Marty, another beatnik, preaching about his love of being free, willing to sit anyone down and share a good tale over a drink, though watch out because he'd chew your ear off. Then there was Gene, crazy eyed and very loud, partying without an invitation, the shakes never quite relaxed until he was a few drinks in; he had a whiskey snack every hour.

"We gotta get inside and get a good place by the stage. I can hear the sound check already."

Rez turned. "So many people . . . faces young and old."

"That can't be good-ol' Juice Box, is it?" Marty said.

He came around and embraced Hans, the smell of human dirt and garbage was curdling and Hans had to immediately lift his nose.

"It is, Marty."

"Why, you haven't changed a day!"

"Thanks."

"My old ass changes skin everyday I wake up. I constantly find myself wondering who that old man wearing my bones is."

"You've been saying that since '85."

"I've been old since '85!" Marty's eyes went wild.

Then Hans was tugging Rez toward the front, through the mountain of bodies pushing to get inside. The lone bouncer with the eye patch and turkey neck was a friend of Hans' and he let them go first. They passed the heavy door and Rez stopped to read the insignia burned into the wood. *DrEaM CaTcHeRs: We MaKe ThEm rEaLiTy!* Inside there was no gaudy sign about the show, no poster introducing the names of the bands. It was as if this crowd just knew to come and dance and drink the tunes.

The immediate smell down the spiraling stairs was of sea water trapped inside a shell and warmed by the sun. Rez felt like he was in a huge magical castle from some fucked up fairy tale. They coiled down fast into a space swollen with heavy green light and black smoke, so deep underground this place could keep you safe from the skin eating bomb. When he hit leveled ground, the floor made Rez feel like he was surfing; everything lilted as if the earth's core was as soft and disfigured as warped floor boarding after a flood.

Band paraphernalia was everywhere: homemade iron on patches, pins scribbled with dual colored markers and stickers made from the local printing press; the walls seemed to get more and more compact. The bar area was flooded dark blue, making teeth and eyes glow like the plague. *Fulci's zombis,* Rez thought. The bartender was a pissed off girl with eyes so clear you could see into her brain; the other was a knobby limbed boy, skinny as rails but with a defiant look in his eyes to not fuck with him. He was not old enough to be inside this place, let alone work here. But the reality was that no matter where you went, kids had a fake ID to trick idiot bartenders and bouncers. At sixteen you were already twenty-one; Rez had done it so many times.

The taps were all craft beer: Magic Hat Blind Faith, Harpoon Baltic Porter, Middle Ages Dragonslayer, Six Point SMP and more. Liquor was served in plastic cups. Rez ordered Hans a Magic Hat and himself a Death in the Afternoon cocktail: absinthe and champagne.

"What a stupid name for a drink," Rez said. "But it's fucking strong, tastes almost like licorice."

"Absinthe! Ever drank it before?"

"Yeah . . . I think."

"Luckily the version you drink isn't the kind that makes people act like psychos. Manufacturers took out thujone because some people got a little crazy. Picture drinking LSD with the side effects of whiskey. A deadly combination."

Then feedback pushed through the walls with a static force, claiming the atmosphere around it with electric: sound check. Behind Rez, two huge stages lit by tiny pink lights faced one another like a duel; a cadre of hairy roadies set up the towering amps, testing the PA system and unwound snakeskin chords around the stages. Rez stood reading all of the glowing ballpoint graffiti on the walls, wondering who wrote these cryptic messages, who drew the drab skulls and knives in sharpie marker across the tables. But he sipped his drink again, green liquor singing his throat, the taste of wormwood like bitter herbs over his tongue.

"I used to drink this terrible drink when I was younger . . . it was a dash from every bottle in the liquor cabinet: blackberry brandy, dry gin, Wild Turkey, Stolichnaya and more. I called it Sonic Brew, named after—"

"The Black Label Society album," Hans said fast.

The club was full now and Rez took a seat in the back where the floor was elevated for a good view. Hans talked more about the cutups, the coincidences, the T70 and how it could hold the answers. A drunk man's words are a sober man's thoughts. Then the lights clicked out, signaling the two bands about to emerge.

Sweet candyscape of dead sodium light and dark spires towering over her head. At last Delilah was in the city! Each building was different from the next, representing decades past, dimensions that don't exist. She could see inside each crumbling tenement, the ghastly eyes peering out each window and marking the loud truck violating their block. Delilah had never seen streets so narrow, blocks so dirty. The avenues seemed endless; the florescence kept the sky bright, but a strong darkness clung to you like miasma, a color she was already familiar with: the absence of light.

The pickup passed the foot of the club. Delilah smelled wine and beer as fresh and green as Bradbury's Byzantium. It was a smell of relief. *Her city. The Lower East Side.* Only in New York could the liquor flow free into good days. The Sutter Home would finally taste like heaven; worrying about the sun rising wouldn't haunt her anymore. Who needed a bed time when you finally have come home? Delancey, Bowery and Astor, these were her blocks now. Avenue A, 14th Street and Rivington, new avenues and streets for her to conquer. Delilah had never felt more alive.

She remembered that moment before the pickup was swallowed by the George Washington Bridge, the huge artery of steel and concrete that pumped people in and out of the heart of the city as if blood. The Hudson River was green and slow against the moon, and the primordial stench of low tide cleansed her senses. It was then first saw the silhouette lights, enchanting, sepulchral.

But the Lower East Side was strange. The smell of the Hudson was gone, replaced by the stench of the East River, pollution and spicy weed smoke. What kind of people roamed these dark narrow streets? What kinds of things lurked between the buildings, beneath the cracks of the cobblestone just waiting to pull you down to hell? Alex and Delilah once watched a news report about Mole People: families of mutant people living in the sewers and subway systems. There were monsters everywhere, but New York certainly bore the worst kind.

And how does one begin the journey into the city, into the crowded puzzle of streets, sweet shops and dark cafes to drink exotic coffee, into the dive bars to get a taste of craft beer? New York was famous for all of those things. Pizza, hot dogs and sugared peanuts were way up on her list too. Tonight was THE night. A night for chance, for change, to savor the sweet black air, the liquor burn in her belly, and the ultimate defeat of the rival band! It was New York City for fuck's sake!

THE EMPIRE OF DARKNESS!

Jimmy parked illegally and slipped through a door clothed by a huge black velvet curtain, drawn out tongue like some unearthly creature. Inside the sounds of screaming instruments christened her ears to the city's mental agony. Delilah saw kids drawing putrid shapes on one another's skin with ballpoint pens, the skeleton of tomorrow's tattoo.

When her boots met the pavement, downtown seemed to reach from below and inject electricity into her blood. *First footsteps in my city of birth*, she thought. *Where was the exact place that cradled my new-born body, all slimed and crying and red? Where was the apartment that conceived me?* The streets all of a sudden felt familiar; the bars bolted into the windows didn't frighten her, the peddlers and their dripping carts of fermented cans only excited her.

Everything felt real, felt safe, like someone had walked down these moon-dappled streets in a past life, a wonderful past life of parties and friends and love. But most of all a past life of security, of never questioning your roots. She wondered what it would be like to stay here forever. What would the mom and pop shops smell like? Where were the antiquities sold? Where were the smoke shops and the liquor stores?

Then she was on the move. A bodyguard smiled drunkenly at Delilah as she marched in with Zazo, bulleting back and forth in his cage; the rest of the band followed, dragging personal gear and mummified stage props in hand. She wondered what the rival band was going to bring. Bone Crushers was their name, and they were a local legend here. They had hard working experience on their side while Electric Orchid simply had their rookie goals and unpolished natural talents.

"Five whole minutes until stage time," a man shouted sipping from a goblet.

Check here, check one, two, threeeeeee, check.

The voiced wiggled through the PA system Delilah would soon sing into. Then Jimmy and Sheigh giggled, sharing a beer called Dogfish Head Punkin Chunkin. It had a strong pumpkin spice and brown sugar after taste. Sweet to the last drop. There were no such treats like craft beer in the boondocks, so that made getting used to New York even sweeter.

"Okay, let's see. Electric Orchard, right? That's a street here," said a man with a long checklist in hand.

"Orchid!" Alex screamed, smudging grey onto his lips.

"Well, band people—we're all ready. You guys are on stage left. Right through there."

"You're quiet tonight, Delilah," Jimmy said.

"She's always quiet before a show. She saves her voice. Her instrument is made up of meat and tissue and blood while ours are wood and metal," Alex winked.

Delilah stared into the walls as she drank her cup of Jägermeister down fast. The liquor coated her throat like honey, cauterizing her vocal chords. She was ready. No more wasted life, no more staring at the dream catcher on her wall and hoping for it to actually work, no more parents and no more responsibility! Then the black velvet curtain opened; hands pushed her out and the faces surrounding the stages were all gazing, radiating beneath the stroboscopic lights. The bands were cued to play.

Back to nightmare land.

14

Dual stages dimming, and Rez could see faint figures moving in the background: checking lists, swigging beers and swapping ale in one another's mouth. Rez wished he had someone to do that with. Then the lights collided and Bone Crushers' entrance music began to play: a schizophrenic mash up of horror movie soundtracks. First, *Masters of Horror*.

Rez heard the squeal of piano keys, saw shimmering scarlet blood droplets flowing from an open wound starring a pristine white cloth. Then the music morphed into The Exorcist soundtrack, reverb vibrating the floor, and Rez thought of Linda Blair twisting her scarred face, bearing rotted teeth, gnarled fingers, but as soon as that thought came to him he heard the wretched anthem for Halloween. The image of John Carpenter's original mad man came to life in his head, but soon stopped as the music halted and a maddened video shot onto the screen: Fulci's zombis were attacking the camera; fountains of blood poured from wasted mouths. And then everything was cut short as the ghastly, crooked limbed Nosferatu claimed everything in his path with spidery hands and jagged ivory teeth.

It reminded Rez of Lynk.

The curtains parted and Bone Crushers emerged on Rez's right, all shadows and white-rodent faces. Their stage props were aged much like the singer's hair, twisted salt and pepper mop, bad ink slashed on two rat-like arms. Gargoyles sat high above with bulging eyes and tongues like someone had crushed its balls with a brick; chimeras and skulls cracked in two revealed succulent gooey brains. A hand clenched a dead heart bejeweled in viscera.

The T70 on his neck felt all of a sudden heavier. *Pick me up! Use me!* Rez tried the buttons, but to no avail. It was dead. No matter, music would take him out of reality tonight. A mental vacation soothed the soul; if not for that Rez would surely smash his reality with a hammer, would make it crackle like the sound of music.

The sea of faces made a noise like that of a monster, screaming their little hearts out as an Elvira looking chick put her hands in the devil's horns position in the spirit of Dio; her black corset pushed her breasts up tight, buttermilk white, milk you could suck up from a straw. Her silver pentagram charm bracelets bounced light like a disco ball. Rez couldn't help but to think about Screamers going *EEAAYYOOWWW!!!* John Skipp and Craig Specter really knew how to write about Rock n' Roll.

She sat behind an Addams Family style keyboard that was attached to an advanced electronic system by a bad duct tape job. Rez imagined Lurch and his forever furious grin playing all night long. The rest of the band was waiting on her cue, and when her fingers touched the keys everyone went silent. Her vocals came out of left field over the dismantling tunes, something between girly and wet and grinding. The twin guitarists began to play a fast scale over the synthesizers; a rip tide of music shattered bones from two screaming guitars.

"Beware of those bombs, you own them too," she harmonized. "They're in the shape of your mouth."

Then the strung out lead singer began a separate, creepy melody, and the twin voices coiled into one strong, violent harmony. Rez closed his eyes, reliving a familiar past. It was then Rez heard the click of a straight razor. The singer showed it to the crowd before he ambled it across his jacket, opening a glorious flow of blood and passion that roped down his arm. The singer wet the crowd and the kids opened their own razors. But Rez wasn't impressed by the stage antics.

This wasn't a fictitious world; rock n' roll wasn't the devil's music anymore, and it didn't hypnotize youth to cut themselves, or to take drugs and become useless citizens of society. This couldn't have been the same band that Hans introduced him too earlier. That music was a band with power, with a style worth talking about. What he was hearing now was some industrial rip-off of the sinful sexuality of Nine Inch Nails; the guttural riffs of Ministry. It saddened him that Hans put so much hope into this band and their stage show, their expensive banners and perfect makeup.

Rez drank the rest of his Death in the Afternoon and wanted to know if there was a cocktail for night. The absinthe tasted like everything he'd read in books: herbally with a hint of anise. But as the champagne fizzled over his tongue and crashed into his stomach, he was able to separate the distinct flavors of grapes and herbs, and found that he'd grown a taste for the absinthe; he wanted to buy a bottle. When the searing sensation settled, the faces around him suddenly looked as crazy as the music. Their eyes were watery neon red like when blood drips into a cup of water; their heads were covered in fedora hats, a lone white feather flashed before him.

His face felt hot and sticky.

They're here, he thought, or the absinthe was living up to its name. But then he looked at the stage and saw the singer throwing his wrist in the air again, dribbles of blood coming straight for Rez, splashing him in the eyes, filming his vision wet and red.

"Die with the enemy! Bury yourself with the criminals. I'm the one who claims your soul!"

The singer growled the last part and it made the dance floor clear a circle. Fists began to fly; nails turned to razors swinging for supple flesh; hair slashed the air. The mosh pit was huge, raging. The song ended with a long tissue-tearing scream and a loud thank you. The crowd jittered and cheered. The kids in the front of the stage were soaked to the bone with sweat and fake blood; their hands were waving white banners; their nails were ink blots on canvas.

But the cheer quickly died when the other band came to the stage. No one knew what to expect. Their banner was not glitzy at all, just cheap black tarp with a huge tree drawn onto it with wormy branches as if from A Perfect Circle's *Thirteenth Step* album. Dried arrangements of dark orchids, swirled red and furious, were looped across a garland with funeral lilies; rubber hands clutched the corners for a horrific effect.

Then three shadowy figures stumbled onto the stage with no sound; the guitarist picked up his devilish Warlock and kept his head low covered by a cushion of yellow hair; the bassist came around and slithered to her instrument, a purple and black goddess with big skull earrings and a Marlboro hanging from her lips in a Joan Jett fashion. The drummer looked like a hick with the tight bandana keeping his wild curly hair under control; his bones jabbed his skin at painful angles. They brought out with them the smell of cough syrup, like Jägermeister, Rez knew.

Then the last two emerged, their faces scarred by the green stage lights, but as they moved closer Rez had to rub his eyes to make sure he saw what he saw. One was razor-faced with streaming black hair tied into a pony tail exposing a heartbreaking mix of bright colors like Mardi gras beads. His eyes were illuminatingly green; his aquiline nose was pierced with a silver stud that glittered beneath the strobe lights. He was the most beautiful boy Rez had ever seen, if what he was looking at was a boy.

He sat behind a Juno keyboard system and dragged his spindly fingers across the bone-white keys. The v-neck Invader Zim T-shirt he wore showed off a mosaic of beautiful tattoo work across his sharp collar bones, his biceps and forearms. A silver pendant graced his long neck. Rez watched him tape the set list to the floor, a plain white piece of paper scribbled with terrible handwriting. Then his mind took his eyes over to the lead singer, a girl with small hands wrapped around the Vector microphone, whose nail polish gleamed black and orange. Her dreadlocked hair was half untangled and Rez saw a touch of pink lightning through the brittle black. She stood sentinel in a tight pleather skirt, fishnet hugging her arrow legs, beat up black boots on her small feet.

Rez looked at her arms, sleeved with dark maniacal tattoos, hiding something as infinitesimal as a birthmark, or something as tragic as razor scars. And for a moment he thought his own burned. But then he realized that her small eyes had caught onto his, sapphire fire blotted with kohl like storm clouds. They marked him. It wasn't affection or hatred or fuck off. It was interest, curiosity.

Black silhouettes, he remembered.

Could it be? No, Rez didn't have luck of this sort, and he wasn't about to get his hopes up now. *Twin sister.* Then the crowd hushed, pin drop quiet, but all Rez could think through his absinthe haze was sister, sister . . . twin sister. Deep in his pocket he thought he felt Arkham's book *move*. And when he looked up at her sharp face again, a sarcastic grin stretched across it like some exotic bird; her eyes hadn't yet left him. That kind of smile meant she was mischievous, cunning, and sleek, just like him. He knew it now.

It was her!

Delilah stumbled onto the stage. Finally, she wasn't going to think anymore, she was simply going to play. Jimmy tuned his Warlock in a rush; Sheigh stood sentinel ready to rock, and Billy was twisting his drum sticks like lightning between his fingers. Alex gave her his familiar look of appraisal, the look of being at peace. Tonight they were going to bring down the house. Tonight it was time to fly.

"This is . . . *My Personal Hell*," Delilah said, sotto voce voice soft as baby's hair.

Delilah made herself look out at the crowd, at the rhythmic ocean of faces, trying to find a connection to them. Their eyes were white marbles; the light collided with their fine features like an X-ray. Their banter was magical; feral voices stitched themselves into her skin. Her heart froze, throat in protest. Would the kids cheer her on like they did in Violet Hill, would she WOW them? Would the man with the fedora hat come watch her from the crowd? William S. Burroughs wore fedora hats, so maybe it was a good thing.

When Alex taped the set list near her feet, she caught the sapphire glimmer of eyes way in the back, scarred by a familiar darkness, eyes that matched her own. She'd never seen a face with so much clarity, a face that belonged to a boy but could easily fit between her shoulders without anyone turning their heads. Who was this creature that looked like her? What did he want?

But it was too late. It was time to play.

The keyboards rang out, a sublime original sound that could only be conjured by natural born talent. The notes slicked the ceiling, running through the parched anatomy of lace, leather and glitter, unfurling a hidden magic that spread like wild fire. Delilah harmonized along with Alex, building up anger and focus, hot like magma.

"Emptiness speaks eloquence in this nest of hate where I thrive . . ."

Delilah saw the crowd swaying their arms, amazed, flabbergasted. Their lips were trying to mumble along with her lyrics, their minds in heaven, like that of a person receiving a great pleasure. Would they be this amazed within the next few seconds? It was time to find out.

Brought up in the excess of fake
With nothing but my identity at stake.
But I'll free myself, let the phantoms fly . . .
A living ecstasy for this tragedy . . .
Now watch me live to tell that this is My Personal Hell!

Delilah continued her melody. Her voice skulked over the warbling musical scale, dream-like, ferocious as much as it was welcoming, mystical as an intravenous of gold running into your veins. *Watch me live to tell that this is My Personal Hell.* She was nearly hypnotized as her mind, body and soul ran through the jungle of lyrics and twisted melodies. It was time to release the phantoms.

"Music is the key to souls, as souls are the key to the heart and the heart is the key to the mind."

Time to fly.

The singer's words conducted through the crowd like a copper wire struck by lightning. Rez closed his eyes. He saw musical scales tear apart and weave back together in obscure phantom shapes; he felt his own tightly sewn clothing rip from his skin. Her lyrics were the spiraling song of his life and the guitar's jangle was a freakish time signature against the other instruments. It was an ambient, ferocious sound. Each note was a thread of darkness, a fragment of pain.

A calling.

The crowd finally began to feel the music, opening the floor to mosh for blood and glory, for the love of music. A headache gripped Rez then, and he began to hear extra voices, sharp whispering. Behind the singer a shadow grew, swirled about like a mist, like the breath of some dark strange angel, and lifted her off her feet. A scarecrow shadow thrived to this music, to this sorceress of melodies. She ended the song with a throat-ripping scream and the phantom simply vanished. *It liked her*, Rez thought. He could see it in her eyes that she was in pain. Was that Arkham? He couldn't focus; her words had matched his entire existence: he'd lived a fake life, and it pissed him off to remember that.

Could I be so lucky? Rez thought. *Could it be her?*

"Juicy!" Rez yelled, but Juice Box didn't hear him.

It was as if the old man saw her the same way Rez did. After all, he did hold her once in his arms, and he never forgot their faces. But such luck could only be met with a bitter end, not pull the pieces of the puzzle closer together. And yet the battling music raged on, shrieking guitars and wavering keyboards over salient vocals. Song beating into cynical song. It was clear from the start who the winner was going to be.

His mind screamed at his heart. DON'T LET HER LEAVE WITHOUT MAKING SURE! Then boy with the razor face was throwing flower petals into the crowd, orchid petals, Rez knew. He watched the silver orchid pendant swing across his throat, and Rez all of a sudden wanted to kiss that throat. He collected some petals as he pushed himself to the front, reaching over the metal rail to snatch the set list. The lead singer looked down at him then, made eye contact with those impossibly blue eyes, and poured some beer on his head, smiling. Then Hans grabbed his arm and they moved out of the club. Rez heard the bands cue up again, their songs growing longer and angrier. They waited by the back door, discussing what they'd have to do to figure out if she was the one.

15

Down in the bowels of a city where the night air clings to you like goo, where discovery can lead to promise, and promise to a family. In another week it'll be Halloween and pumpkins will be carved with evil sneering faces, flickering votive light washing orange smells over the sidewalks, fresh as the death of summer. But these squalid streets are still alive at this hour; they teem with a dark glittering populace, nothing to light their way but the flare of cigarettes and the oily sheen of sputtering black lights.

Delilah was sharing a conversation outside of the club. The boy with the sapphire eyes was going on and on about her lyrics, her singing; the sweet old guy with crazy white-blonde hair was practically bowing at her feet. They called themselves Rez and Juice Box. Sweet names, odd names, good introduction to the city. They were celebrating with a complimentary bottle of Jägermeister.

"D, we're heading to the hotel," Sheigh said. "Down on Rivington Street."

"You go ahead. I'll find my way there."

"Who're your little posse?"

"This is Rez, and this is Juice Box."

They all nodded and shook hands.

Sheigh's girly face scrunched into inquisition. "Awesome names. I'm Sheigh. Did you like the show?"

The boy Rez looked up. "It was amazing! You guys are way too good . . . for your own good!"

Something hit Sheigh's brain and it shown in her deep brown eyes. "There's . . . something about you Rez, I can't place it. And, well, thanks I guess, for the compliment . . . yeah."

"Alright, go Sheigh!" Delilah demanded.

"Do you want me to take Zazo?"

"Hell fucking no."

Then Jimmy pulled around the bend and slapped the side of the pickup. He was midway in a frilly argument about the punky street names and liquor stores with Billy. But Alex was already in her ear, talking about how cute Rez was, and that it wasn't a bad idea to have a fan base in Manhattan. Alex was always thinking with his dick.

"Catch you later alligators!" Sheigh yelled as the pickup sped away into the river of night.

"Sorry about that," Delilah said hoarsely, scraping her boots into the concrete. "My band likes to stick together. We only have each other."

Her mind wouldn't stop moving. She took a moment to study her new friends. Rez had soft features, and his hair came over his eyes in waves of blue-black; his skeptic smile was cunning as a blade. Hans, or Juice Box, was an old gentleman with a serious face punctured by a lot of piercings. He wore a sheep skin hat over his thinning blonde hair, as well as vintage leather from boots to jacket. *Two New York Punks, score!* She thought.

New fans and a possible family.

Was this happiness? But to show emotion on the outside was sort of like squeezing blood from a healing wound for Delilah; that or she'd end up like her friends back home. Like Gary who had stayed indoors for months skipping meals and refusing to go out in daylight because he said the world was too evil when his Labradoodle was run over; something had snapped in him, and he was never the same.

Or like how Electric Orchid's cheesiest fan, Steely, had reacted when Layne Staley was found dead nearly a decade ago. She caked her face in so much funeral makeup she wound up looking like a corpse, deciding that her life was no longer of importance. She took it in her own hands with a bottle of Tylenol and cheap wine. When she woke up there was a tube down her throat pumping it all out, a paramedic shaking his head in shame and her mother's tear drops wetting her face. She never touched a drink again after that.

Looking at the peculiar boy Rez standing against the brick wall, Delilah thought she saw a thin tendril of shadow trail against the fine bones of his face; she blinked and it was gone. Then all of a sudden the kids from the club were coming at her, crooked hands and pale faces like mole people; all of those eyes stared at her, all of those hearts felt her pain, all those ghosts gnawed her soul.

Then they were gone, a scintilla of memory.

"You okay?" Delilah asked Rez.

"Yeah, it's just so noisy here."

Delilah didn't hear a thing, but Rez's hands were pulling at his black shock of hair; thumbs were at his temples rubbing the pain away. "It's eerily quiet," Delilah said.

I hear Them.

She thought she heard Rez whisper those words. *Them?* Was he referring to Delilah's ghosts, about her talent to walk through dreams? Then Alex was trying to get her attention again, but it was all about Rez now. Those eyes . . . they were identical to hers: tiny specks of sapphire light lost inside the dark pool of makeup. *Bonded by blood and not music?* It was a frightening reality; she was too used to constantly yearning. What would life be like if all her problems were solved? Would she be happy? It was a thought she couldn't handle. A person gets so used to being lonely, hanging with that hollow friend sitting atop their heart, that they soon find themselves liking it.

"Rez, did you see anything strange while we were playing? Like . . . well, I don't know how to say it . . ."

"A ghost . . . a bursting phantom."

"Was it that obvious?"

Rez nodded.

"I don't know how we do it, but our music has been waking them up. One time Alex and I—"

"Delilah! I don't want to talk about it . . ."

Rez's eyes snapped toward Alex, then back at Delilah. "At least you don't think that we're nuts for approaching you," hand resting his head onto the near brick wall stinking of fresh aerosol.

Then Hans talked some more, always fucking talking at this point, and his unease shook his strange assortment of piercings along his face. When he calmed down he took deep drags off of his Pall Mall and sipped the bottle of Jäger. He said that Delilah was the striking image of her mother. A real parent? No, Delilah didn't have real parents. Sometimes she believed she wasn't even conceived by humans, but simply washed ashore as some mutant whale baby.

"What's the bat's name?" Rez asked.

Alex's head snapped up. "Zazo. And I'm Alex Zweig, Delilah's bestest friend."

"Nice to meet you, Alex. Do you mind me asking . . . um . . . are you a girl or a boy?"

"None of the above."

"What?" Rez's face fell into flat confusion.

"I don't agree with being marked by a gender. My name fits me perfectly."

Oh, gods Alex. Don't scare them away with this crap.

"No labels?"

"Exactly!"

"You know, I've never heard of a pet bat. I see them in the parks sometimes, wild and free . . ."

Zazo squealed, flapping little wings, black eyes flickering back and forth.

"His genus is *Myotis*, or mouse-eared bat. Very rare, endangered since 1967. We humans have disturbed their colonies for way too long, killing them during their much needed hibernation," Delilah said, gliding a finger across Zazo's belly.

"What does he eat?"

"My little baby only eats the finest insects that the soil of this cursed earth has to offer."

Delilah pulled a jar out of her pink and black messenger bag. Insects throbbed, leggy things crawled, pincers sliced the air and thousands of legs stumbled over one another. Suddenly Zazo began to squeal.

"He loves worms and spiders the most."

"Can I try?"

"Sure."

Rez stuck his hand into the jar as if not caring what would bite him or crawl up his arm. Delilah watched his small white fingers shoot down, searching the alien contents like the claw claiming a prize in an arcade machine. *Hands like my own.* And then he was pulling up something long and wiry and bright pink: an earthworm. Its body writhed and protested against Rez's grip. Zazo's eyes zoomed in on his looming dinner and Rez offered it to him; teeny vampiric teeth clamped down, leaving nothing but sticky goop in Rez's palm.

"He likes you," Delilah said.

"I hope so. I like him," Rez's eyes wandered to Alex. "Maybe I'm a natural with animals," Rez quickly changed the subject.

"You better . . . if you're to be my brother," Delilah smiled evilly. "Humans are the breeders of destruction, while animals have to sit and wait for their expedited doom. It's an unfair, unnatural fate."

Then Alex swung his silky hair away from his face and the smell of clove cigarettes wafted to her. Delilah wanted to touch it for some reason, to feel it brush across her palm like water trickling from an ancient fountain. She wanted to do this because a stinging thought came to her mind: that she could lose her best friend to the plight of her new relationship with her twin brother. Delilah knew it wouldn't be a surprise for her to abandon everything for a new life. It was part of the problem of an adopted child: constantly seeking a new identity.

Delilah hoped Alex wouldn't be jealous now that she was going to focus her attention elsewhere. But Alex's attention was solely on Rez, and not out of jealousy, but spur of the moment lust. Rez seemed to be doing the same thing, taken back by Alex's youthful aura, twisting his hair in front of his face into homemade braids.

"Anybody got trees?" Juice Box asked.

Delilah pulled out Jimmy's baggy of salvia and offered it to Juice Box, who put it in his zombie-hand pipe and lit it with Rez's green flame jet lighter and made himself a happy man.

"Whoa! Heavy shit," he said, coughing the berry flavored smoke out of his system.

"Salvia. What were you expecting,—Sour D?" Alex interjected.

"How do you know that?"

"It's famous, I guess," Alex said.

"Let me try some," Rez said.

But Alex grabbed his hand instead. "No, wait!"

It was like an androgynous predator coming for his blood. His smell was that of clove cigarettes and alcohol sweat; his smile was sweet as candy. Rez couldn't fathom that such a devilish boy would come for him, or that he would feel such a strong and strange attraction. He dealt with his emotions much better alone.

But when Alex lit the green flame jet lighter and took a deep drag off of Hans' pipe, Rez couldn't help but to lick his lips, couldn't help but to stand still and wait for this sharp faced lithe beauty in black to come for him, to hold him and stroke his face with a child's curiosity. Rez couldn't bare the thought of not feeling Alex's long dark hair brush against his face, those mineral green eyes not glaring into his own, their bones not grinding together. He hadn't hooked up in so long he was certainly rusty. But he figured to just go with the flow.

Rez felt everything in his body get all hot and tingly—his crotch, his aching balls, even his feet. He knew then what lust was, and what love would be. Then Alex took two steps forward and opened his long coat, the toe of his boots touching Rez's skate shoes and his ice-white hands on Rez's hips, pulling them closer together by their studded belts, and parted his lips just enough for the spicy smoke to spiral out his mouth. Rez could not resist him. The silver orchid necklace glittered madly.

Their lips met, tongues invading, searching cheekflesh and teeth, tonsils and gums. Rez wanted to dive deep into Alex's mouth; his throat would be like wet incense, would be a place free of pain; his esophagus would be laced with liquor. This boy was a puzzle of flesh, and Rez wanted to make the pieces fit. He could not imagine a better lover, though he'd never had a true lover to even compare too. When Rez let go his face contorted into the glow of fascination.

The voices died down for a moment.

"You're eatable," Alex said.

Rez couldn't speak; his throat was on fire. All he could do was quickly shove his hands in his pockets, embarrassed, his teal musical scale and black quill tattoos a streak of neon in the night. Delilah looked square at his arms, as if sensing the razor scars beneath the ink, the universal sign of being sick of life, as if the suicide ghosts were coming back to haunt her.

But Alex didn't wait a second to take advantage of Rez again, burrowing his face into Rez's collarbone, licking his neck, biting the skin just before drawing blood, hands spidering beneath Rez's black and red flannel shirt, dipping his finger down his crotch. Rez froze, awkward. He didn't know what to do, didn't *understand* what to do. This suave character touching him with practiced hands had done it so many times before; this pale angel had experience on his side while Rez was a lowly rookie. Surely Alex would find out and laugh at him. Surely Alex would not want to break in a newbie.

"Don't resist me," Alex whispered. "It's okay."

"I . . . I don't . . ."

"Break it up fellas," Delilah said. "I gotta give these guys some patches, and a CD."

Delilah let them glow beneath a street light: jagged rocks scintillating like dragon scales, bats flying high over a cold Pennsylvania moon. It was a lonely sketch spawned from a lonely world. The patches were small and cylindrical, crisscrossed with a pink and black spider web as if some sort of hex.

"Electric Orchid was built upon the ruins of boredom and the fury of not fitting in anywhere: the finest ingredients for writing songs."

"Did you stitch these patches?" Hans asked.

"Yeah, not bad huh? The purple and pink interlacing was a challenge but I was able to pull it off."

"Your mother could sew very well. She made her own clothes, lace and fishnets, even leather skirts."

While Juice Box talked, Rez fought with his heart and mind to enjoy himself. He was frightened that his bad luck was going to come out of hiding and ruin the moment. But fuck it; he couldn't let it win, at least not right now. So he explored new territory on human flesh, grinding his bones into Alex. His skin was smooth as marble, inked up arms thin as daggers, and just as sharp. Rez did not know how long this was going to last, but he liked to hope that this moment of peace wouldn't stop. In wonderland, Alice is the Queen.

And then there were the heavy footstep; a Snapple bottle smashed against the wall near Alex and Rez's head. The shower of glass nearly cut them. All of his qualms came true.

"What do we have here, couple of fags and their leather daddy?"

Two thugged-out guys, their grins speaking of bad intentions. Insolent lurkers. One wore a backwards basketball cap on with a pissed off scrunch to his eyes. The other was swinging a huge gold crucifix around his neck for the sake of being macho, barely able to keep his pants on his hips. They were taller than all of them, cracking their chapped knuckles like schoolyard bullies.

"Fuck off!" Alex spit.

"Get out of here. We aren't doing anything to you," Hans said.

"Fuck you, pervert. Right Lonny?"

"Yeah, Terry," Lonny's nostrils flared wide. "You fags take up enough space in Chelsea and Tribeca."

Zazo screeched and took to the air, flying around violently. Lonny's eyes beamed upward.

"If that thing touches me I'll crush it."

"Touch him and I'll rip your eyes right the fuck out your face," Delilah growled.

"How 'bout we see you try, freak bitch."

This is her first night home, Rez thought. *And this is how you repay her, New York? Fuck you.*

Lonny took a step closer to Delilah and Zazo swooped down making an awful noise. He latched his claws onto Lonny's hair, tugging and biting crazily. Lonny tried swiping Zazo away, but Delilah jabbed Lonny in the throat with her elbow, sending him back, coughing. Lonny's reflex made him pull the string hard and Zazo came crashing to the ground. Alex scooped him up quickly and placed him safely in the cage.

"You piece of flaming shit!" Delilah screamed.

"Fucking thing bit my head!"

"Small mouthed Jesus lover," Delilah said.

"And you got a big mouth for a carpet munchin' dyke. How about I stick my dick in it?" Lonny said.

"She ain't doin' shit, Lon. Look at her arm. Pathetic little bitch is one them girls who chop at their own flesh."

"Fuck off."

"What you gunna do, take out your little blade and scratch me with it?"

"Nope. I'm gunna cut your dick off and make you EAT it."

"You DISREPESCTIN' ME? How 'bout you suck on this gat?"

Lonny pulled out a gun and pointed it to Delilah's forehead. A dread fell down and completely blocked one of her eyes, hitting against the cold black surface of the barrel. Terry laughed like a child and licked his lips over and over again. They were fucked up. Coke or E, Rez didn't know. But it didn't even matter. Someone was bound to get seriously hurt.

"Scared now, weird bitch?"

"You think I'm scared of a gun, you pussy?"

"You wanna talk like a man, then why don't I fuck you like a man?"

"No. How about you grow some balls and SHOOT ME!" Delilah roared. "MOTHER FUCKER SHOOT ME!"

Rez saw Delilah's green piercings glowing psychotically, saw her long dreads concealing her outer anger. Lonny's eyes were rolling now, and the sweat came down his face like clear bullets. In a flash Delilah smacked the gun from his hand and it scattered to the concrete. Lonny tried to punch Delilah's breast, but he wasn't quick enough. Her eyes filled with blue fire; her body tensed with a hidden rage. She grabbed Lonny's wrist in mid-strike, twisting it upward and slammed her elbow into his ulna using all the weight of her torso. Rez felt the bone crack beneath the skin as much as he heard it. The boy screamed for dear mercy falling to his knees; the sounds of agony echoed into the night.

Delilah grabbed a hand full of his wiry hair and brought her knee into his nose in a wet meaty smack; his blood was a black fountain that slicked her leg. Terry came around and rammed Hans with his shoulder. Rez saw his poor old head smack against the wall hard enough to stun him and ran to his aide as Alex jumped, kicking the gun far down the block before Terry could grab it, and then ran to help Delilah, vampire speed, fierce as a mountain lion.

He called out Delilah's name, threw a dark green bullet towards her and pulled on Terry's long gold chain. Their synchronicity was well practiced, tight as their own music. Delilah caught the object and it seemed to come alive between her delicate fingers, seemed to flutter with the sound of a hundred clamping scissors. That's when Rez realized that it was a butterfly blade, an extremely dangerous weapon. Delilah slashed the first chance she got, and Rez saw the ribbons of blood before he could see what Delilah had done: she'd sliced Terry's fingers down to the bone.

He stumbled back shrieking. Lonny's big hands were coming for Delilah again, but she did a pirouette, zipping the blade back and forth like it was a living thing, but this time with precise aim. For a second Rez saw the wound spread messy and wide like crushing an orange for all its pulp; then he realized that the terrible glittering thing was Lonny's hand meat roped with blood. Alex pulled a brick out of a decaying wall and smashed Lonny in the back of the head before he could try to attack again. He fell with a wet plop to the ground. Rez was stiff with shock, watching bemusedly.

"Anything left to say, you pussy?" Delilah asked.

"CUNT!" Terry yelled.

He bowed his head and went to spear Delilah into the near wall, but not before Rez's adrenaline peaked, spreading fire through his system. He saw Delilah's sweet face smiling, her spidery hair whipping back and forth as he moved like a bat out of hell, kicking his shoe skyward and making it meet Terry's mouth. Rez's shoe came back with spit and blood, with Terry's front teeth. They sprinkled to the ground like marbles as Terry plopped to the cement, down for the count.

"Fucking pansies!" Delilah roared.

"Everyone okay?" Alex asked.

"Let's go. Someone's bound to call the police," Delilah hissed.

"You guys, I'm SORRY!" Rez yelled. "It's my bad luck again . . ."

"No, it's alright," Hans groaned. "People fight. It's the way of the land."

"I bet they didn't think a girl from the boondocks could protect herself!"

Delilah's eyes remained in shadow; her racing thoughts seemed a mask molded across her face. Rez touched her arm, then brought her close to him, held her tight: making up for the two decade gap between their lives. She accepted his embrace.

"Why now?" Delilah asked.

"Chance, dear, chance is a marvelous entity and it allowed us to meet. Question it not once more. Now move."

Purple rain ran down Delilah's cheeks. Rez knew exactly what those tears would taste like, salty crayon flavor; he'd had many of his own. Somewhere in his head Rez heard the lyrical ghosts of "My Personal Hell."

Watch me live to tell . . . this is My Personal Hell.

"Rez, what is it?" Delilah said, seeing how nervous and pale he looked.

"Let's go back to my apartment."

They moved away from the club and began touring the outskirts of the town. *WeAr ThE GrUdGe LiKe A CrOwN* marked the bashed windows; *HoLe In ThE SkY!!!* and *NO RENT!* was painted on the walls inside. Delilah had never seen buildings so badly in shape. They grew older and more decayed as the streets went on; front doors were open and bodies piled high inside, filthy limbs crisscrossing one another for warmth. Such squalor didn't really exist in Violet Hill, but it did have a run down section; bad parts where people lived in stone houses and used left over anthracite to burn for heat, a place where people were raped and beat up for crossing the wrong side of the street.

It was a part of Violet Hill where drug lords made a fortune off of the depressed kids in town, where one could be sucked away into the woods and never return. Delilah could still hear the complaints from the two thugs, but it was a fading, worthless sound. There's no getting in the way of the ones she loves. Those goons will better think next time before trying to bully someone else. And then she couldn't stop wondering about her new life . . . if her music could call the past to her.

16

Delilah gawked at all the delirious sights as they scuttled through the blocks. Crooked stoops, buildings with aberrant names and even stranger people if that was possible; she noted in her mind how neighborhoods changed so much when moving north, and how the air tasted different going toward the water. It lost the grime and was replaced by a more briny flavor, strange when she had just become accustomed to the smog lingering in the back of her throat.

Constant change seemed to be the driving force of New York. And once again she wondered if inside any of these shabby apartment buildings was where she was conceived, her parents drunk and having too much fun. New York was a safe haven for all the freaks, the faggots and the dissident devils. She wanted to spend the rest of her life here.

The door to Clive's apartment was slightly ajar when they arrived. Not just ajar but *crooked*. A psychedelic pentagram sticker was cut through the center and the wood was slicked with a murky substance like cold sweat. Inside it was pitch black, a soft, permeable kind of darkness, a nightmare you could ball up and stuff inside pillows.

There was the immediate smell of burning rubber, bile and sour beer. Delilah found the smells familiar, enlightening; she'd had many mornings where she woke up on the wrong side of the bed drenched in liquor, the cigarette burns like black pimples along the sheets.

Rez played with the light switch until the pitiful bulb puttered to life. There Delilah saw cryptic drawings on the wall, magazine cut outs and a lot of beer cans. A kitchenette and a gaudy countertop, small living room with not enough windows. No space, cramped, Manhattan itself condensed to an apartment. She touched the dirty counter, swirled her small fingers through the wet smear of coffee and beer, and brought it to her lips. It made her happy. She noticed then one hand had a trace of dried blood on it, the mark of her first night in the city.

"I like these. Vintage," Delilah said, brushing her hand along the curtains.

"Salvation Army," Rez returned.

"What?"

"One day I'll show you . . ."

"Sun's about to come up."

"I can see that. *Damn it.* I hate sunrise, means I have to think about sleep."

"Me too."

Delilah and Rez made their first real connection: the love of night. A tepid wind blew from the window, and for the first time she could recall, Delilah wanted daylight so to brighten this small apartment. She needed some fucking light to see! So she opened the curtains fully and a slice of yellow light flooded the room.

Now the strange smells and destruction was clear.

Beer cans were ripped in two on the table; the couch cushions were upturned, and the posters on the walls were torn. Dog-eared Maynard James Keenan painted in blue; Trent Reznor in fishnet split like lips; Ozzy's "Bark at the Moon" shredded. It was the aftermath of a keg party gone mad, or a robbery. Anything was possible.

The bookshelf remained intact, and Delilah nearly fell back when she saw all the William S. Burroughs titles. Alex screamed with a red hot fervor when he saw a line of Kathe Koja novels, especially the first edition copy of *The Cipher*. The cover scintillated in Alex's grip: Nicholas' hand plagued by the Funhole, a black esophagus bearing sharp teeth. Delilah wondered what it would be like if there were a Funhole in the storage room of this building. Would it throw up dear old dad? Would her dreams come to life?

"Burroughs!" Delilah yelled. "And Nine Inch Nails . . ."

"Koja! All her books!" Alex said.

Then Zazo began to fly; she was happy that his little dive to the concrete didn't hurt him. The mothy wings fluttered, stretching toward the dark room. It made Delilah think of a stream of black flying pests bursting through this window like in the Bat Cave.

"I'm really impressed by Zazo's loyalty," Rez said.

"That's why I love him so," Delilah returned. "A graceful pet. So where's your roommate?"

"Clive!" Rez shouted. "There might also be a rat named Lynk here too."

"A REAL RAT? It'll be Zazo's dinner!"

That's when Delilah heard beeping, a string of hectic sounds coming from strange looking machines. Rez called it ghost hunting equipment. Delilah looked at the small devices on the table. One looked like a distortion pedal, the needle inside the glass jumping like a crazy earthquake reader, and the other was making a small pitchy sound. The third machine was burnt to a crisp; a big Ouija board with a glass marker was set on the word NO.

"You're a ghost hunter?"

"No, my friends are."

"That's fucking awesome. I bet you help them with . . . well you know, your talent."

"Sometimes . . . if I feel like it."

The Ouija board latched onto Delilah's short attention span with its intricate letters swooped like bat's wings, pictures of a skull-like bat that reminded her of Zazo, evil sun and moon. There was a small ashy mark burned across its surface, letters that she couldn't make out. When Delilah sailed her finger across the words she immediately felt something trying to reach out from a world of brimstone and grab her hand.

Rez heard voices. Not *the* voices, but Clive and Lynk. He opened the dark room door to see Clive and Lynk arguing as usual. It was a loud blur about spilled chemicals, broken machines, ripped photos and ruined passions. Destruction. Clive was right side up, sweating profusely; the sun streamed in bars through the one window, filling the crevices of his pure English face with delicious yellow light. Lynk hung over him, a tangle of hair, black Grinders up against the wall, torn black T-shirt covering his drenched torso. And before Rez could say anything the entire room went still. There came a huge camera flash like a shockwave.

And then . . .

Clive went insane. He stood fast and ripped his shirt off; Rez saw that pale skin, those slatted ribs collecting sunlight. He slashed his nails across his chest and neck, his one arm with the bare bone tattoos, so hard that the blood welled in the angry tracks.

"Get it out of me!" He yelled. "GET IT OUT OF ME!"

Rez ran to Clive and shook his bony form violently. He saw that his arm was marked up with the words *YOU GO TRYING TO CONTACT THESE THINGS AND THEY WILL TAKE ADVANTAGE.* And in that instant Clive seemed to snap out of his trance. An EVP recorder and full spectrum camera dropped from his death grip.

"It . . . it . . ." Clive breathed heavily, the blood beginning to drip. "I thought it was in me . . ." Clive couldn't catch his breath. It sounded like he was singing a bad song.

Lynk turned. "Let me help you, Clive."

"No. Leave him alone! What happened here . . . Clive? Tell me."

But Clive didn't listen; his eyes immediately found Delilah, who was standing guard as if ready to brawl again.

Protecting me, Rez thought.

"Who's the girl?"

"My *sister*."

"Smashing."

And then Clive's eyes darted for the T70 around Rez's neck as if he could melt all of its mechanical insides and drink it like photographic knowledge. He all of a sudden felt it burn, felt it's weight shift like a haunted metronome, wanting to be touched by experienced hands. It made Rez feel weary and faint, but behind him Alex loomed, and the touch of his hand created a strong dark static between them.

"Is that a . . . no it can't be . . ."

"Holy shit!" Lynk said startled. "It's a T70!"

"Well, yeah, it was my father's camera."

"Bloody hell . . . that really is one! Didn't know they were still around," Clive said as his eyes sailed over Rez's head and in Delilah's direction again.

"What're you looking at?" Rez asked.

Lynk's face reddened. "Yeah, what?"

Clive's face sharpened. "Wasn't looking at no one. Calm your bums."

But Rez knew he liked her.

"I think we better go into the living room to talk."

They drank coffee, an expensive multi-layered blend that threw hints of Arabica tinged with okra across Delilah's palate. It was a symphony of flavors, an orchestra of woodwinds and harps in

Delilah's mouth. She never knew coffee could be so exotic being that she was used to the mud she drank at all the Violet Hill diners.

Rez handed everyone Star Wars mugs. He owned a whole bunch; half were vintage and half were manufactured when the prequels were released in theaters. The final battle between Darth Vader and Luke Skywalker was in Delilah's hands; the Emperor and his invincible lightning was in Rez's grip. He mimicked the words *UNLIMITED POWER!* until he got the entire group to say it also.

"POWER!"

Everyone else drank from the Millennium Falcon and the Death Star. Rez could nerd out all day when it came to Star Wars, how the saga had the biggest influence on CGI more than any other movie series in history. George Lucas created a billion dollar franchise out of one simple little idea of racing cars, but with a twist about a galaxy far, far away. The pieces just fit.

The group let go of the chaos in their minds for a little while. Delilah relaxed, certain that her dreams wouldn't find her in New York City. Well, as long as she didn't sleep. She couldn't bear thinking about that screaming red-raw mouth, the pale legs sticky with vaginal blood and placenta, and the screech of babies as if chewing themselves out of the womb. It was the best reason not to sleep. Staying up all night wasn't as bad as everyone made it seem anyway; it was actually enlightening, freeing.

Delilah was stuffed on the loveseat next to Alex. Her legs were stretched out, and the tip of her boots met Clive's dirty shoes like mice sniffing one another. Their eyes locked for a moment, but Lynk nudged Clive's shoulder to break his attention. She noticed that there were some bad issues between the boys and she didn't want to be another one. But when Delilah lost those thoughts, Clive's eyes met hers adoringly; Lynk's met hers with a searing curiosity.

They were past introductions already, the who's who of Delilah's band, who played what instrument, who liked to party and who liked what drink. They all played jokes on one another to lighten the mood and slammed through a twelve pack of PBRs like water, talking about music, books, and the ghosts on Arkham's film. Delilah talked the least, safe inside her own head, safe as her bedroom.

Hans had more pictures in his messenger bag: 5Pointz before it turned into the graffiti capital of the city, the dark little children that paid Arkham good money for photos with orbs in it. Delilah saw the little shining dots in all the black and whites, some with faintly skewed red eyes; she saw her future and past become clearer.

"He had good eye," Clive said.

"A fucking master for such a young age," Lynk added.

"I didn't know that Rez had a dad or a mum . . . or a *twin* sister," Clive joked. "He always made himself out to be born by wolves."

They both were tucked tight into a corner of the big smelly couch studying photos and playing with the T70, looking over all of its intricate controls. Lynk talked about throwing some batteries into the sucker and bringing it back to life, but Clive was more interested in what was already on the film stored inside the camera, putting the lens to his eye like some doctor searching for a disease inside a rotted organ. Delilah saw Lynk's legs brush against Clive's; his hair was atop Clive's shoulder. He eyed her for one moment and snarled. *Well, fuck you too.* Then Clive stuck a pillow between their hips.

"Let's develop it! I bet it's loaded with *Them!*"

Lynk opened the grip of the camera and slid AA batteries into the back with two sly clicks, taking out the old film tube and putting in a new one, drawing the film lead into the red start line. He turned it on and the mechanical kinks inside the machine squealed for a moment. He took a snapshot and the power of a small supernova filled the air. A white-hot wave coursed into Delilah's brain, made her mind fill with bad memories she knew nothing about, made her remember she was on a mission to find her past.

"The film cartridge icon still works on the LCD screen!" he said.

"So that's the camera that started it all," Clive said. "Only makes sense that we use it to call *Them* back."

"NO!" Hans said. "I've seen what it can do to people . . . that thing."

"Oh, bugger. Lynk, escort me back to the dark room. Let's get this film developed."

Lynk rushed to Clive, lifting him up and they both waddled drunkenly back into the dark room. Nobody said a word; all were curious to see what was inside that camera, even Hans, as much as he was afraid to admit it. But when Clive came back a few minutes later his face was wet and scarily red. Lynk was grinning, his swirled orange hair covering those honey colored eyes.

"It's rotted, the damn batch is rotted!"

"Better off that way!"

Then Hans told the story of why that camera was nothing but bad luck. No one questioned a thing.

"Sometimes I see a Shadow Man in my dreams," Delilah said. "Then again, sometimes my music brings it to me."

"Sometimes they're in mine too . . ." Rez said back.

Rez and Delilah made eye contact, a connection no one would be able to understand except them. She believed she heard Rez's thoughts for a moment, his blood whistling secrets like the sound of water dripping into a delicate sea shell. She felt their twin souls reach out and clasp like lovers, felt her razor scars itch and burn feebly. She saw Rez touching his scars too.

This is the time to use your brain, Delilah, use it!

"Hold on a minute," Clive said. "Now, I know I'm not crazy, but I think whatever destroyed the dark room did it at the same time you were playing at the club."

"Makes sense," Delilah said. "But why would my music channel through here?"

Nobody had an answer for that question.

"This Ouija board," Alex said. "It's got a burn mark on it."

"I noticed. But it's what we need if we want to talk to the dead . . . that is, unless you're Rez. And don't you know the legend of Ouija's?" Lynk asked.

"No," everyone said together like a string harmony.

"Ouijas are the bridge to communicating with the unknown. It's either they cross into our world, or we cross into theirs. It's a very simple concept. So in essence, if fire was a cause of death, fire will come to the board. Clive and I got it at Dago's party."

"And it's where we got the new equipment from too."

"You mean this busted thing?" Rez pointed to the small charred husk of a machine.

"Fuck!"

"When's his gallery opening?"

"Tonight!" Clive yelled. "But why should I go with all my work destroyed?"

"Because Dago said there'll be people there who we can talk to about . . . well, you know," Lynk said.

"It'll be good for all of us to vent. A little vacation from the drama."

Rez stood and put *Mer De Noms* by A Perfect Circle in the stereo: soft dismal rock to christen their breakfast bonanza. Delilah felt Maynard's melodies coil from the speakers and into her heart, jealous that she didn't possess the ability to growl or caress like him with her own voice, though Alex would disagree. He loved her voice and always said it out loud.

Clive complained, wanting to hear The Misfits or Black Flag, or *anything else*—but to no avail. He was outnumbered. Things could have passed for normal momentarily, but if for one second Delilah thought she found peace, it was over as quick as it came because Clive was truly staring at her now, licking his lips. She'd never admitted to liking a guy before, and it was rumored in Violet Hill that she was a bull-dyke, but Delilah knew what she was deep inside her cavernous soul, and that's all that mattered.

She wanted to let herself go in New York, wanted to fly, because enough was enough with just staring . . . but she was stopped by a sudden shadow that ran in front of her, a shadow swirled black and orange: Lynk. It was obvious he was jealous. And he even smiled about it! A sharp, *fuck you* kind of smile; a get-away-from-my-friend kind of smile. No loss on Delilah's part. But she did see Clive shift uneasily next to Lynk, saw that he was actually expecting her to come to him. Delilah changed the subject.

"So this is the place?"

She referred to a picture of Arkham standing in front of Helena's building, the 7 train above their heads, a junkyard at the end of the block and the building gloaming in the background.

"Yeah. But what's wrong, Delilah?"

"Don't you see it? There in the background."

Delilah made everyone look close. She saw a cloaked figure behind them, its scarecrow arms outstretched, fingers like black pinworms looking for meat to latch onto. No one said a word.

All she wanted to do was scream.

17

It's been over a day and she still hasn't called; neither has that little trendy snake of hers," Sheigh whined, sipping champagne from a plastic cup.

"It's as if we don't exist. Did something EAT them? A rat the size of a St. Bernard perhaps?" Billy joked.

"There're so many RATS in this dump!"

"She's too busy getting fucked up with her new shit-bag fans with the stupid names!"

"I just don't fucking get her. When she sinks her teeth into something, we have to sit around and wait like we're one of her obedient little animals!"

They were blasting sludge metal and didn't give a fuck about the time. *The Power of the Riff Compels me!* Billy was on the floor running his fingers through patches of rum stains on the blue carpet; then he was staring up at Sheigh, who wanted to do nothing more than step on his stupid bony face. All three bodies remained unchanged, unwashed; Billy in his filthy blue jeans and black bandana, Jimmy in his Guns n' Roses T-shirt and converses held together by electrical tape.

They smoked and drank all night, and when Sheigh came to her senses she realized that her head had been in a blur and that Delilah and Alex had abandoned them. She pulled at her unwashed hair and stared at it in the mirror. The humidity in New York made it curl in ways she never knew possible. A shower might've done her good, but she didn't give a fuck about hygiene; being dirty was her personal form of expression. It was all about her new surroundings.

The city was still so dark below. Through the grease vapors smeared across the window she saw narrow walkways bathed in soft crimson light; people shuffled along, their mindless conversations rising in the wind like bad whispers. The vapors made everything look faintly runny, sharp. There were so many strange and magical

157

names to the streets and bars, much like the people here. Each town held its own deranged secrets; every corner was dulled with a festering of faith. Lafayette, Canal, and Pell, those streets sounded like they belonged in London or Paris. Eldridge, Essex, and Stanton sounded like they belonged in The Lord of The Rings. Delancey, Orchard (an uncanny similarity to half the band's name), and Division certainly belonged in Narnia or Tatooine.

So many dark corners and clubs, and Sheigh wanted her band together to explore this vast territory now that she had the energy. But the pickup was in some underground parking garage, black and exquisite as The Bat Cave, and getting it out would cost a tip. Fuck it. She'd walk with the guys, finding the best place to score some good bud and drink all the craft beers the city had to offer.

Certain that three Pennsylvania hicks would be quite the noticeable bunch in the big city, her town came creeping up behind her eyes. She saw all of the trees in Violet Hill now, black birch and tall oaks with wild branches, saw them flooded with moonlight and hunched over like the buildings here, blocking the sun. They would listen with green ears and talk back with brown mouths, breathing dirty city air, dripping leaves like tears laced with anthracite dust. For the first time in a while she thought home was the best place in the world.

Big cities are scary and filled with so many foreigners you forget that you're in the U.S.A. The streets are a puzzle with many missing pieces: pot holes as big as car tires, open doors leading into a building where demon-whores live. What a mystical place. But Sheigh knew her band would fit right in, and that soon they'd rule the night and be happy, though her longing for Alex and Delilah made her angry. She hated waiting.

"What're the actual requirements though? I can't get through half the damn contract!" Jimmy yelled into the phone, pulling at his yellow hair.

He was talking about the deal with Carl Hirshman, the man who was ready to hear all of their music and sign them to Coil Records if they showed enough potential. Judging by the glorious uproar from Electric Orchid's performance—hands in the air, vacuous faces elated—Carl didn't really need any more proof. He was just playing the bureaucracy card. *We have to pays fees?* Sheigh heard, then, *UPFRONT?* Billy snatched the phone away from Jimmy and slammed it on the cheap receiver.

"What the fuck was that for?"

"We're gunna play hard to get. I've never heard of bands paying fees to sign a record deal. Have you?"

"This economy is shitty, maybe they're being precautious?"

"Shitty economy or not, our pockets have zero dollars in them. We've got nothing to offer them other than music itself. If they want us they'll have to come running in our direction."

Sheigh laughed. Billy was right. Why would they have to pay a fee? That was preposterous. She lit a Camel with her Zippo, watched the flame loll orange and beautiful as sweet tobacco swirled into her lungs, flushing out of her nose.

"I wanna draw," Billy said.

Sheigh didn't pay attention to him; her senses were stuck on the carnival of sights outside her window: the atrocity of crime, the peaked-pale faces partying on rooftops. Billy pulled out a set of silver and black markers from his messenger bag and began drawing like he played his drums. Outstretched arms, dead flowers wrapped around a skull and looping barbed wire tattoos, scrim of flesh still in need of color. Sheigh watched his skinny arm paint the walls, covering the flowered water stains. She knew of a place where graffiti lovers could hang out, drawing all day and then spray painting all night. Perhaps she'd take Billy there to kill some time.

"Why the hell do you want to draw right now?" Jimmy asked.

"Makes me feel better. You want me to start pumping again?"

"NO! You haven't stopped since we got out of the damn club. I mean, guys, are you ever going to get fucking serious? Or do I have to play baby-sitter all the time?"

"What's there to get serious about?" Jimmy yelled. "No parents, no school. NO RULZ!"

Sheigh laughed, figuring why the hell not join the camaraderie. That was when she saw the dark bullet jet across the wall, a bullet with sickly long legs and a fat black back. It crawled into a pile of leftovers by the bathroom.

"The fucking roaches are big as mice here. Sickkkk."

She squashed it and scraped the guts across the carpet leaving a greenish smear. This made her feel better about Alex and Delilah, crushing little nasty leggy things. With champagne flowing through her system, Sheigh almost forgot, on top of all the annoyances of the night, that she had her period: a disease that made her want to rip her uterus from her body and hang it up to beat like a piñata. Jimmy never cared about her time of the month though; he liked her red and filthy between the legs.

There were two safety pins lodged in the arms of her coat, and so with nothing else to do she decided to pierce her own ears. She dipped the points in the champagne, and then heated them up with her Zippo until they were neon red and shoved them through. She watched the blood crust into a scab around the metal, and washed it off with beer. She was happy now.

When Billy was done drawing he darkened his eyes with cheap make up and played with his nipple ring—a golden ankh that he said was from Egypt. He bought it at the Steeraway Street summer flea market. But they knew nothing was real if it came from Violet Hill.

"I wanna go out. I'm bored and hungry," Sheigh said, still staring at the bleeding darkness below.

"Are there any parties going on?"

"All over. Rooftops, clubs, dive bars."

"Let's go out and look for ourselves," Sheigh said.

"Judging by this crummy part of town there'll be plenty of them."

"Sun's almost up, the freaks are bound to come out now," Billy said.

"That's how I prefer it."

The sun was getting ready to rise, stretching new shadows over the city. The wedding cake buildings were set to lose their darkness; the electric-blue glow of the stars was fading. A new echo told the night life that their parties were about to come to an end, but that the after party was just beginning.

Sheigh tuned her bass as she waited for the boys. Billy and Jimmy were brushing their teeth and washing their mouths out with Jägermeister. Their jewelry jingled on their bodies; synthetic black rings covered most of their fingers. They looked ready for another show, but this time they wanted to be the patrons and not the band.

She played a Black Sabbath riff, but stopped when she felt a tickle across the back of her neck. She turned and saw nothing but the dirty walls. After, she applied silver and black nail polish in front of a long mirror; the kohl liner made her look like a raccoon and the dark blush clouded her small cheekbones. She was ready to cause mischief, just like the little depressed kids back home would, little punks who lived for anarchy and jerked-off to the thought of martyrdom. But then Sheigh noticed the dark marker line on her shoes.

"You drew on my Grinders you numbskull."

"It's black marker and black Grinders, quit yer whining."

Sheigh threw a musty pillow at Billy.

"Where are we going anyway?"

"Out to find Delilah and Alex."

"THEY COULD BE ANYWHERE!" Jimmy yelled.

"Well if we don't start now, we'll never find them."

"I wanna' go somewhere to drink and hang out."

"There's a graffiti palace in Queens that I read about. It's called 5Pointz. You'd like it Billy."

"Are we taking the pickup?"

"No . . . mass transit will do."

"With what money?"

Sheigh fumbled through her pockets, sliding out a shining blue credit card marked AMEX in silver.

"With my stupid father's credit card."

Heading down Rivington Street, arms draped around one another, clothes like Halloween costumes, the trio seemed quite the spectacle in the wee morning hours. They slipped past mom and pop shops selling lace and leather, fabrics and costume jewelry; doors squeaked open and people sat lazily on their lacerated porches, stress-lined small faces stared into space, wondering when they could just relax, or smile.

This place wasn't the typical small town they were used to; it was populated with the clack of high heels running into the boutique stores, with prowlers sucking their teeth for the night's kick. Cars packed the one way street; the worst kind of demons certainly lived between the buildings here, Sheigh could feel it; demons that Delilah talked about in her dreams.

Their boots echoed off the pavement and into the open windows burning candles and incense. The tenements rose high above them, a painter's palette of colors taking over the tight streets. Each turn brought them to a new curving block, the shops becoming more frequent, the smog thickening. A group of kids that might as well have been little fan girls of *Theatres Des Vampires* sat alone on a corner talking in hushed voices, gaunt pale forms with witchy fingers, clicking sharp nails against beer bottles. They caught sight of the three little trouble makers walking in their direction and began to whisper.

"I think that's Electric Orchid," a vampire-faced youngling said.

"They wouldn't be here," a girl hissed. "They're famous now."

Sheigh pushed passed them not wanting to be seen; she could smell their beer vapors and it made her think about cheap champagne, of sour white grapes poisoning her palate. Was this the first taste of fame? Billy and Jimmy didn't even notice, their noses were out for food, and it was Jimmy who said the smell of strange food was teasing his stomach into starvation.

Spices flushed out of hole in the wall eateries: roasted Afghani lamb, Cambodian Kampot pepper, cloying Thai chili paste, the sticky white scent of melting mozzarella, and a touch of curry; they could hardly pronounce any of the words. Then they heard alien voices mingling all the languages of the world, sounds that their Pennsylvania town never knew existed. It was amazing to see businesses alive and kicking all hours of the night.

"Everybody here is from another country. No one speaks English; white is a minority."

"That would be the statistic of the real world, Billy."

"So you're saying Violet Hill isn't the real world?"

"Pretty much."

"Those little fucking kids almost made me lose my appetite," Sheigh snorted, changing the subject. The issue of race never interested her, never influenced the way she lived her life.

"Why are you worried about them?"

"They said our name . . . didn't you hear them?"

"My mind is on food, and on booze," Billy said.

They were passing beneath a construction site tearing apart a gothic looking Synagogue, the graffiti so rampant that no words could be made out; power washing couldn't save the old brick and mortar. It seemed everywhere she turned something was marked by graffiti, so it was very easy to understand that she had to take Billy to 5Pointz, the Mecca of aerosol paint culture in a city that has shunned it nearly to suicide.

There were so many brick walls in New York that she figured *why not spruce it up for free?* But the law is a wrathful entity. They all laughed, smoking their cigarettes and not worrying about Delilah and Alex for the moment. Their bellies rumbled; their hearts were curious for the city. Down a few more blocks they found a pizzeria and invaded its insides. Marinara sauce bright as fresh roses bubbled over cheese and a flat hard crust, something Violet Hill could never get right, and it was so stupidly simple.

"This is truly the city that never sleeps," Billy said.

"There's something in the water here, isn't there?" Jimmy asked the gnome-faced Mexican server, but he didn't answer.

"My gods, this is the best shit I've ever tasted! Get more!" Billy said.

They each shoved a few slices down their throats, chugging grape soda and called it a good time. When the server asked for money, all three looked at one another and bolted out of the store. They flew south, down the tight streets, passing the tiny nightclub where the *Theatres Des Vampires* children were hanging out. And as the server ran out after them, they heard him yelling at the wrong group of kids.

Sheigh, Billy and Jimmy were already gone.

18

Dismal lost hour when there's no night or day, when time does not pass but reflects, and the sky is slicked with moon and sun like abnormality. Time to head out, time to have fun with no remorse, regret or question, time to clear the mind of its constant poison.

Alex waited for Rez by the front door and listened to the rain pelt against the apartment window, trying to hide his emotions, his quivering hands, his hardening dick. Rez was quite the beautiful boy with his peaked black hair, his soft cheekbones, and his sharp bird's smile. He looked very much like Delilah now that he thought about it.

"You ready?" Rez asked quietly.

Alex simply claimed those sweet lips, tasting everything of heaven and liquor and cigarettes. They grinded against the door frame, shuffling into one another's body, hands traveling the muscles of their stomachs, their groins, and through the holes in their jeans. Rez's hand opened Alex's pants and reached in, squeezing his dick so hard Alex thought it would burst. *I want you*, Rez said over and over in his ear as he licked it. *I want you.* Rez's skin felt so good, so pure. Rez was definitely new at this love thing, but learning fast. And Alex was alright with that, for he came to New York to find love himself.

"Is this what it's all about?" Rez asked.

"I guess so . . . I mean . . . if you want it to be."

"You're so cute Alex, don't ever change."

Out the door everyone went. Clive led the pack as usual, clutching the T70 with rigor mortis fingers. Alex had never seen anyone with so much determination when it came to film cameras. It was almost maddening. Clive's face grew haggard as the hours stretched on, and his smile was not so much a smile anymore, but a careful sidelong grin like that of an insane asylum patient.

But Alex focused his attention mostly on Rez, their tightly gripped hands. The streets somehow grew wider; the windows in each building were like dappled sunlight streaming through a dark forest. Then Alex realized that it wasn't that light. It was Clive. He was taking photos crazily with the T70: the corner garbage cans, neighborhoods passing, anything. He laughed crazily too, laughed as much as Lynk frowned. Did Lynk ever talk?

"I really love this camera," Clive said. "I'm gunna show it off to all those assholes who'll laugh at me."

"Who's gunna laugh at you?" Delilah asked.

"THE PEOPLE AT THE GALLERY!"

They were in the bad side of Chelsea now, going cross town on 28th Street, heading to 11th Avenue. It was a maze of narrow walkways, scummy playgrounds, and lighters blasting alive in every corner to get the next fix. One side of the street was clean as a whistle; the other side a freaky filth fest of construction boards, metal chunks and blocks of concrete. A giant sign that said *HUDSON YARDS* was heavily graffitied; the buildings here were lined with people begging for change, people affected by the economy and the social disturbances of the city. Alex assumed this place to be the local ghetto the way people swarmed as if the plague, the way its dregs stalked the night like lepers in basketball shoes and huge hoodies offering the nightly sweets. The rain didn't stop the dealers; the nascent thunder didn't scare them. But it was ever so close; pissed off God trying to wash away the evil in the air.

Coke, got that weed, acid, what ya need?

"I don't want any of their shit," Alex said. "I wouldn't trust it if someone tried it first in front of me."

"Never buy from these guys. They lace their coke with sweetener and skimp you on the weed."

"Do they sell acid?"

"You mean *Lysergic acid diethylamide?*" Lynk blurted.

What was up with this guy? Alex wondered.

"From the ergol family of poisonous fungi."

"That's right, Lynk. You know your microbiology."

"No. I know my *drugs*."

Alex found Lynk to be truly weird, and not in the good way. But he knew it wasn't right to judge someone he'd just met. *First impressions mean everything*, he remembered Delilah told him once.

"Fucking hack!" Clive yelled.

Alex heard the voice dive into the black nothingness of an alleyway, saw that Clive was cradling the camera now, kissing it.

"Calm your ass," Lynk said in a hectic whisper.

And then behold, the night's prize. The Cabal Gallery was squeezed between buildings too old to be renovated, ramshackle built of mortar and muck, its masonry screaming industry's antediluvian. The huge windows were lit by skittering light bulbs, by some kind of controlled fire inside that tossed spidery shadows against the dilapidated walls.

They stopped across the street from the gallery, safe from the rain under an ancient elevated freight railroad, planning, thinking. It smelled of truck exhaust and the melted metal effluvium of a town forever under construction. Rez nestled into a steel beam and Alex followed. They embraced; sharp collar bones rubbed against one another, whiskey tasting lips became wet again. Their bodies glowed green beneath the spreading neon shadows. Alex heard the rain hitting the concrete like the shattering of glass.

No insanity for one moment.

"I guess that's the place?" Delilah said.

"Not only is she a looker, but she's got BRAINS."

Clive giggled and took a photo of the building. Rez ducked his head into Alex's shirt. At first he hadn't realized how powerful the flash was, but when the silver spots receded form his vision he realized that it was like watching a fallen star descend into his eyes, a ghost-white tidal wave of danger. *A way to call them in.* It made him faintly dizzy. But then they were walking again and Rez was dragging him hard, stepping over a huge puddle of flotsam and screaming neon; rats jetted like huge leggy insects with no fear of sneakers or car tires.

In front of Cabal the kids gathered 'round like clots in an artery: gutterpunks dressed in black, JNCO jeans swelling like the tide, hipsters in thrift shop rags, straight-edge kids with SXE tattooed on their wrists, emo kids with makeup slathered over their eyes, and clean cut types with money so said their seersucker suits. They had cigarette burns on their arms, flasks clutched in their grip and talked in crazy art-speak.

Past one huge door was the dance floor; music spiraled downward from good sized speakers above: a stream of heavy metal anthems. There was no cheap wine or decadent champagne to be found. After all, this wasn't your typical art gallery. A long bare wood bar was packed with thirsty patrons; taps of craft beer stuck out like bad colored hair. Seasonals and annuals, pumpkin, stout, bitter hops and heavy malt; the selection was vast. Alex swiped a bottle of Magic Hat Howl from a lone table, but it was warm and tasted too malty for his liking.

"I love the way hops taste," Delilah said. "Like a mouthful of spicy flowers!"

She ordered herself a Sixpoint Bengali Tiger IPA and Alex too. Drinks were free, so long as you tipped generously. They walked through the warehouse and became awed by the sights. There was fine art, sculpting stations, fire starters, photographers, spoken word poets and writers. Each section was sealed off by black curtains; cliques stood around like sentinels, veiled by smoky indifference. They wore their clothes and their attitudes from the societies in which they came: Athens, Maryland, New Brunswick, Boston and Philly.

Every time a kid slipped through a curtain Alex saw a sliver of action, a tease to every fantastic spectacle of this fringe scene, a scene that seemed to get stronger each time a light bulb clicked out. Somehow, everything in Alex's life lived in darkness. But it wasn't just the darkness he was thinking about anymore, it was these kids. Marginalized youth who called no place home, who called nobody a true friend. *His kind.* The gentrified world had ruined any last bit of culture in their lives, leaving them to drift place to place like sideshow freaks looking to sell a piece of their withered dignity to survive, anything other than to give in to the dogmas of the majority. But within the underground nothing ever truly dies, it may fade away, may die, but its essence is like ink: it never truly washes away once it's marked you.

"THERE HE IS!" A boy's voice said. "LYNK'S PHANTOM LOVER!"

It was a drag queen of some sort, the first Alex had ever seen. Dressed in fishnet and red high heels, this boy was the infamous Dago, mutual friend of Lynk, Clive and Rez, a boy who loved to change skins every now and again.

"You punks made it out, and with some new meat!"

"Yo, Evil D!"

"Been drunk all day. Craft beer gets me going!"

Dago's smile stretched forever long, crimson lipstick maniacal as The Joker's. Delilah introduced herself and he kissed her hand leaving a wet red mark. Rez introduced Alex; Dago did not categorize him as boy or girl and a great sense of relief mixed with respect filled Alex's heart.

"I see you newbies like craft beer. Where're you from?"

"Pennsylvania. We don't get drinks like this there."

"Ah, fuck me silly—you're the band that won the contract! Electric . . . something . . ."

"Electric Orchid," Delilah said flatly.

"Now permanent New Yawka's," Alex joked.

"Please don't mock that accent. Sounds foolish."

Everyone laughed because they knew Dago's sense of humor. Oh well, Alex tried, and Rez kissed him to make him feel better anyway. Dago was so happy to see Rez had found a new boyfriend.

"Clive, is that a T70?" Dago craned his long neck and reached his hand out. "Fuck me silly!"

"Yeah it is. AND it's *mine*," Clive slapped Dago's hand.

"Ouch, cock sucker. What was that for?"

"I told you it's mine. And if you call me Lynk's *phantom lover* again I'm gunna fucking bop you."

"Looks like that's not the only thing that's yours. Nice marks on your neck. Who did that . . . *your dear Lynk?*"

Alex saw Lynk get embarrassed; Delilah took a step back to monitor their behavior.

"I should rip your heels off and beat you with them, Dago."

"Or you could suck it up and become one with human sexuality."

"I have a sexuality, and it's not for you to play with."

Clive looked straight at Delilah.

"Just let me see the camera for a second. I gave you my fucking hunting equipment!"

"Fuck off, you drag queen. Your equipment was all rotted."

"Is that so? Then maybe you shouldn't go over to the Boston tent then. They're from the Massachusetts Paranormal Crossroads. They're all photographers, and have real *paranormal evidence.*"

"Don't you like those guys, Clive? The Atlantic ones, too," Rez said.

"Shut your pie hole Rez. I wanna know what big mouth Dago thinks those people can do for me."

"Don't you people call yourselves *ghost hunters?*"

Lynk nudged Clive lightly.

"Yeah, we do!"

"Well I've supplied the real deal! The choice is yours." Dago made his hands into the shape of a hex, his scarlet nails like old drops of blood. "Peace," Dago said, vanishing into the growing crowd.

"So what now?" Delilah asked. "Entertain me."

"I'm getting another beer and then doing a tour," Alex said.

"Load me up on number two. Six Point."

Rez grabbed himself and Alex a Weyerbacher Imperial Pumpkin ale while Delilah drank down her Six Point in a flash. Good way to celebrate the autumn season. The head was filmy, and the bartender even rimmed the glass with cinnamon and brown sugar to bring out the pumpkin spice flavor. It put Rez's mind into a comfortable space of a child's version of Halloween, almost forgetting his bad luck, his wasted past.

"Alright. I'm ready," Rez said.

He and Alex explored each tent carefully. Some were filled with black light and smoke; others were plain as your palm in front of your face. The Athens kids were all gothed out, drones in silver and black with knife-like features still living in the world of *Silk* by Caitlin R. Kiernan. The kids from Philly were clean cut, showcasing painted madness on acrylic that scaled a part of the mind that not even Rez could fathom. Their portraits were rage and fire; their choice of color was madness and agony that dared your eyes to avert, but you'd be so sorry if you did.

Come in, said a stick figurine offering beer and a smoke. The metal sculptors' tent was full of solder dust and clay paste, structures resembling whatever deviances clogged these kids' minds, bending metal to their will to form something as simple as a horseshoe, or as intricate as a hex.

"Tess could do better," Alex whispered.

"Incomparable indeed."

Melting ice creatures were next, rats and bats, and it made Rez freeze for a moment. Not the ice sculpture, but what was going on a few feet away. Clive stood with Delilah as she admired the Zazo-like creature. Rez saw Clive's hand reach for her waist, but that she pushed it away; Rez saw Clive whisper in her ear, looking over his shoulder carefully—for what, Lynk, a ghost?—and that Delilah actually smiled. Lynk wouldn't be happy to see that, and Rez wouldn't be able to stop himself from smashing his face in if Lynk tried anything stupid.

Finally they came to the photography tent. Immediately Clive began to mumble to himself, sad about his ruined photos. The photographers lined their work back to back; a single table had copies printed for sale, and a clothesline had the originals pinned up and laminated not to touch. This really showed off their talent for angles and precision. A crow haired girl was talking in her nasally Boston accent about a piece called *Circles and Shiners*, slung up on a homemade birch board easel, her camera gripped in her thin fingers. She caught Clive's eye.

"A T70," she said. "Haven't seen one of those in ages. Unique. Antique. Great for capturing *Them*."

She pointed to her photos, black and white hallway like some abandoned factory or mental ward, like something out of a Michael Meyers screen shot, and on the wall was a chimera door knocker with a bull ring through its nose highlighted in a sultry purple hue. The face of the chimera itself was outlined in white as if a skull coming through its skin and all around its head were little silver dots.

"A great looking piece," Delilah said. "Reminds me of real ghost hunters shit. I may've seen a ghost or two . . ."

"You probably have. Ghosts are real, no matter what people say."

"Might I interrupt? I've developed my fair share of print orbs: they're the gateway into another dimension . . . a soul passing through it," Clive said

"Ding ding! You can call it that if you want," the girl's grin became morbid, "but most people *think* they catch an orb and it turns out to be dust, water vapor."

"Is that a hint of snark I smell?"

"Jesus, Clive, what's gotten into you?" Lynk said.

Perhaps a little life . . . dark life, Rez thought.

"Well if you see it that way, then perhaps. But my work is solid. This was taken at an old factory in northern Massachusetts."

Clive put his big pale hand up for the girl to shut up. "I suppose you had the fanciest equipment; the latest Geiger counters, the latest EVP recorders and the lot. I had all that once, and I've had my own encounter, which left my work destroyed. I was supposed to have it all here tonight. Have you ever had your work *destroyed* on you?"

Delilah watched Clive with an uneasy curiosity as if she was starting to like this new rage and new attitude. That much was clear.

"No *thing* ever destroyed my work. I guess I'm fortunate. But to me, it sounds like you have poltergeist activity."

"You might be right!"

"Well, from my experience all I can tell you is that you have to take command of it or it will *take* command of you," the girl's sandal wood eyes spoke of premonition.

"She makes it sound so cheesy," Alex said to Rez.

"My entire life is cheesy. Ghosts, me with no past . . . no family. It's a fucking cheese-dick story."

"Don't say that," Alex said, moving one finger across Rez's cheek. They turned back to her conversation.

" . . . and you know, if you piss it off enough, like with a Ouija board or something to contact it, you'll get an answer, maybe not the answer you want, but you *will* get one. Go back to where your work was destroyed and face it. Go there and tell it you're not afraid."

"Thanks . . . um—"

"Helena, is my name."

"Alright Helena, thanks for the tip."

"Speaking of tips," her eyes sailed over to a small donation box studded in silver. "Be generous." She winked and began speaking to the next person wanting to understand her work.

Rez froze for one moment. How much more coincidental were things going to get? Alex finished his beer and threw the cup to the floor; Rez let his roll over his tongue. A table littered with small square advertisements for technogoth parties in the Lower East Side gleamed; fire claimed Alex's face as a performance artist spit gasoline from her mouth. He seemed unamused by that entire conversation; it looked like he wanted to play his Juno the way he was moving his long piano fingers in the air, the phantom synthesizer.

"Wanna get lost in here?" He asked Rez.

"Sure."

"If we get too lost, meet back at Clive's place," Hans said. "No curfew, of course," and he skipped away.

"You heard him guys, no curfew!"

Delilah walked in the direction of a group of kids with instruments on their backs and PA systems at their feet: her musical kind. They looked like they were setting up for a show. Lynk and Clive were arguing about the camera again, arguing like a couple on the verge of breaking up. Then Rez saw Clive jetting away towards Delilah and Lynk running in the other direction toward Hans. *At least everyone is paired up now,* he thought. *And I have the best of the bunch.*

"Look!" Alex yelled.

B-HORROR SHOW said the banner. *This is why I love this kid. He's smart, experienced and into horror!* They entered the tent and it was exactly as stated: every famous B Horror film was reinvented by twenty first century artists. Rez saw the Tall Man from *Phantasm* cradling the world in his hands, saw *Dawn of the Dead* zombies swarming a carcass and ripping out garlands of intestine like savory sausage. People drank Tenafly Viper Wine and transformed into strange little demons with organs for eyes and sharp nails for teeth. Every acrylic stroke was masterful; each interpretation was tawdry, practiced to perfection.

"Radical," Alex said, his eyes ablaze. "Gotta love horror films made on a shoestring budget."

"Exactly. The ones today made on bad budgets don't even compare."

And then a small voice interrupted.

"I can tell you something?" It said.

Alex turned. "Tell me what?"

The woman hobbled over. "You might be needing this one day, child. Only five dollahs."

She had very wiry hair and her black eyes scintillated like snake scales in dawn's light; sweat dripped into her hollow eyes. She looked like she needed sleep very badly, and the determination to sell whatever was in the beer bottle in her hands made her seem witchy. *Made from the riches of southern India, the sweets of central Europe, the exotica of the Amazon.* When Rez turned around he hugged her.

"Alex, this is Magda."

"Oh, pleased to meet you, I guess."

"Rezzy, honey, I was gun' sell this to your cute blood-sucking friend here."

Blood sucking? Alex was almost insulted.

"He just moved here. Don't scare him off Magda," Rez winked.

"A drink, then, deary? Lots of beer."

"Magda, are you drunk?"

"Jus' a lil' my sweet boy," she reached up and touched Rez's cheek, smearing her finger sweat down to his chin.

Alex and Rez said good-bye and bolted for the front door. But just before they jetted outside something happened and it stopped Rez in his track. In his mind there was a huge flash of a camera, a girl's seedy laughter and a line of faces grinning like the family he never had. It was his life's mental blur stalking him; three little signals no one would've noticed, but as they coalesced into one huge portrait

Rez's brain twisted, completely aware that something was calling out to him like a clue in a great big game. He never turned back, fearing he might find the answer.

Outside the gallery, no action but a few muttering punks walking up 11th Avenue. The streets smelled of gutter trash; the sidewalks were slick with the last of the rain, glinting like a dying lamp. The clouds were silver cotton mountains.

Clive looked at all of this, taking in the scenery: texture, wrongful angles and light, sensory stimulation. The minute details spoke to him, awakening the isolated photographer inside his soul. It was in this moment that he'd never felt so alive; the camera did something to him: an oracle speaking in tongues only he understood.

Fucking hack, he thought. *Stupid Bostonite and her snark.*

"I could just smash her," he yelled.

"Smash who?" Delilah said.

He'd almost forgotten that he'd come outside for a smoke with Delilah, almost forgot that his hormones had peaked since the moment he saw her. She was the most unpredictable, talented, most amazing person he'd ever met. Her presence alone sent a shiver through his bones; her music was something he'd never thought he'd like, but it reached out to him with a welcoming hand.

Her lyrics were mystifying; they lived within the cavern of pain. He'd listened to Electric Orchid's CD a dozen times. Every syllable was made of gold; every melody came with a slew of maddening images: a phantom with eyes like black holes, a stadium overflowing with thick ectoplasm. Each song was a spinning chasm that led you into a new dark universe. He could listen to Delilah's silvery voice forever, until his ears bled, until his heart imploded.

Do you realize that when you close your eyes . . .

This world is yours to divide?

Shed the skin and let her in

Inject reality with your sins . . .

Delilah's words were so powerful.

He thought that if Black Sabbath and Nine Inch Nails ever had a child, it would be the drippy, dreamy music of Electric Orchid. And if Clive knew anything about lust, about righting all the wrongs he'd done with Lynk, with Rez, it was going to happen through her.

Delilah was going to save him.

"What is it with film cameras and you? There're so many digital—"

"Film captures what we think we see with our eyes. The problem with digital is that it captures too much at once. Nothing makes sense when you're trying to point out orbs or vortices."

"I see."

"Cameras are the eyes that see all things we cannot."

"Meaning . . . spirits right?"

"When film is developed from a proper camera we see something *more*; it makes us ask questions. Touch it if you don't believe me. It was your fathers."

Delilah put her hands on the T70. Clive watched her small skinny fingers work the lens. She moved controls that she knew nothing about, changing exposure modes, shutter speeds, and film modules. She looked cute doing it too, delicate princess of the macabre. The rain made her hair naturally curl, made the pink streak through the middle dance, something she tried to stop with the straightening iron and Manic Panic hair dye. And when he looked again he saw the rain pattering against her pale cleavage.

"So tired," she said.

"Want to sleep on my shoulder?" Clive couldn't believe he said what he just said. It just plopped out of his mouth like dead weight.

"Do I want to . . . *what*? Doesn't Lynk—"

"I guess Rez *has* told you everything already. Lynk is not my mother."

It didn't matter what Lynk thought anymore, what Lynk said anymore. Best friends? Bonded by ghost hunting? Don't friends support eachother's needs? Lynk was never supportive of Clive's quest for a girlfriend, Clive's *needs* as a man, flesh and blood *straight* man! This time Lynk was not going to whisper in his ear, not going to ruin his chances with Delilah.

She's not all that great, Lynk had said. *She's broken, tainted. Look at the scars stretched across her arms; the pale flesh on her knees is destroyed. The look of pure disdain lives in her eyes. She will hurt you, Clive, suck you dry and leave you to hang like butcher meat.*

Now that Clive thought about it, now that Clive had a moment alone to study her, Delilah looked so much like Rez it was almost sickening. It crossed his mind for a moment that if he touched her, he would be vicariously touching Rez. *GAY GAY GAY!!!!* It made his mind spin and fill with a strange hate, something he'd never felt in his whole life. Clive often wondered what it was like to stay angry days on end like Rez did. But no, he never had time to think about himself because his two besties were always so needy, so whiny. And if he did think for himself, it was for his camera work only. *Rez is never getting it back*, Clive thought. *He owes this to me!*

But Delilah was a different fucking beast.

She's brilliant and I'm just a wanker.

He wanted her so bad.

"You gunna smoke or what?" Delilah asked, lighting a clove. "Running low."

Delilah handed Clive the lit cigarette and he gracefully took it from her. He was staring at her now, hard, staring like a hungry predator. She wondered what was behind those beaming blue-grey eyes. Even in the dark they were bright as new born stars.

"So that Dago guy, bit of a freak?" Clive joked.

"I've seen worse," she said as she inhaled. "Come to small town boondock fuckville and you'll see a whole new breed of human being, twisted from life brought up in a bubble."

"It was sort of like that in England for me. I only saw English numbskulls while my mind was itching for something more."

"I come from nothing. At least you had people to depend on growing up."

"*From nothing?*"

"You deaf or something?" Delilah snapped.

"My world is dark and cold. I'd give anything to brighten it up a little," said Clive.

"The flash of a camera . . ."

Clive's head bobbled softly, the smoke traveled through the maze of his mousy hair, shrouding his face. Delilah knew they made a faint connection then, knew that Clive was getting antsy, more anxious.

"My way of life is very lonely. Art has obliged me into solitude."

"Art is life's voyeur."

"Art is madness."

"I agree. Like your friend Lynk. He doesn't like me. I can read it off his face"

"He's just a selfish motherfucker. A true camp, but doesn't even know it."

"Camp?"

"May bad. He's flamboyant and doesn't know it. He's angry and doesn't understand why."

"I see."

Delilah sat against a crazy looking brick wall with too much graffiti on it. She pulled out a small flask from her messenger bag filled with the lucky Jäger they stole from Lydia's liquor shop. She took a swig and the syrupy, licorice flavor calmed her down. She thought there was even an herbal aftertaste. Delilah passed the flask to Clive.

What the hell did this guy want? Delilah just couldn't figure it out. His actions came off needy, maybe even flashy-showy. Did he have some complexity about girls? Was it to prove that he wasn't a homo? The thought made Delilah a little sick. Rez was Clive's best friend, and Alex was her best friend. They hit it off very easily, very smooth. How could she be friends with this guy who tolerated homosexuality as if it was a chore?

"Are you happy, Delilah . . . meeting Rez and all? There's a lot of promise here for you."

Want my social security number too?

"You're prying a little too deep for my taste."

"Sorry."

Delilah could read the thoughts masked across Clive's face. He wanted to take a picture; he wanted to kiss her. But then his eyes glanced across the wicked tracery of razor scars between the lines of her black tattoos, saw the crusted blood.

"Rez has the same marks," Clive said.

"Sometimes they burn," Delilah returned lightly.

"Did you do that to yourself?"

Delilah clicked open her butterfly blade, let the dim light of the alleyway skim across its surface. She brought the blade to her forearm and created a small gash, dipped her finger into the wound and swirled the blood across her arm.

"Delilah, stop that."

"Honestly . . . it's none of your fucking business."

"Twins are known to feel one another's pain, you know that?"

"Like ESP?"

"I don't know . . ."

Delilah chuckled, throwing her cigarette into a small black puddle. For a moment she could have sworn there were a pair of eyes watching her from its oily depths, and so she made Clive take a picture of it. Then Delilah changed the subject.

"So . . . you're like the best ghost hunter around. Right?"

"Not anymore."

"Everyone fails sometimes. Alex constantly reminds me of that."

"Understandable. But I shouldn't call myself a ghost hunter if I don't get any evidence."

"You've had evidence. It's how you made your name."

"But none recently . . ."

"Ah, like Rez with his writing."

"Exactly. He hates to hear the word writer. He doesn't feel like one anymore."

Delilah nodded. "So, like, if you know all about ghosts, then you must know about Shadow People . . ."

"They look out for a person when a bigger force is on its way. When something is getting ready to cause harm."

"Exactly. I think I have one following me in my dreams."

"But I thought you didn't sleep."

"It's only a matter of time before the body takes control, Clive . . ."

"I see."

"And have you ever heard of astral projection?"

"It's how a person's soul can travel the dreamlands, a place where wishes turn into curses, where death comes alive again."

"Sepulchral."

Clive's interest peaked. And so did Delilah's. If she really thought about it, Clive wasn't that bad of a guy. All of a sudden she wanted him to kiss her, to hold her body tight with those big strong hands. She wanted her feet to entangle with his, wanted their lips to meet and never let go until the end of days, until the great black ship rips in two and sinks to the bottom.

"Delilah, can I kiss you?"

"Yes," and she couldn't stop herself from saying it.

In a blur of water and blood her hands caught his throat. She pulled him on top of her, and, oh gods, his strength was beautiful. Clive's fingers trailed the bleeding mascara on her face and he brought the taste to his seeping mouth like an addicting poison. His tongue tasted of her salty sweat, blood, liquor and licorice.

It was perfection.

They went down like anchors to the filthy concrete, kicking garbage bags aside and letting rats run free. Delilah's hand instinctively went for Clive's crotch, a technique she learned from

Alex. *Go right for the fruit of the loom.* Their limbs wrestled like severed worms. Pants down, legs open, fairy wings, hands clutching Clive's dirty hair, pulling the beanie off, tongue tracing his jutting chin, sticky smear across his five o'clock shadow. Clive moved his hands down her concave stomach, pawed her strong groin, and Delilah felt her pussy throb as Clive's fingers tore through the fishnet. Everything was moist and tepid in her panties.

She was *enjoying* this!

Nothing could stop this moment, it was animalistic. Delilah lay back as he crawled between the soft of her thighs, the petals of her vulva wet and blossoming. Then Clive was going in for it, lifting her one leg over his shoulder and getting ready to ease himself into deep sodden territory, a pink flower bursting with sweet nectar for any bee to steal. But then all feelings halted. Delilah became haunted by the thought of Lynk's honey colored eyes, his long white fingers placing the blame on her.

She knew Clive could love her, could be with her forever. But what she also knew was that she was broken, not ready to fall into the harrowing guilt of a relationship. Even though she had come here to change herself, to become a new Delilah, the old one just kept biting through her skin. If someone was going to change, it had to be Clive, and Delilah only knew one way to do this.

Mutate . . . Change.

There're rules that can be broken . . .

Into dreamland.

Delilah gulped the magical air of New York City and let her husky-raw voice loose. A sweet cadence fell from those impossibly delicious lips, a song to summon fallen angels to claw their way up to Earth for a listen.

I'm taking this pain and wrapping it in misery . . .

A broken halo to hold over my history . . .

And then Clive saw the world as he knew it rip in two.

NO! Clive thought. *ALMOST HAD HER!*

An unholy chasm split and they were diving head first into the soft dreamy vortex. Clive felt both their bodies detach from reality like a butterfly exploding out the cocoon. Delilah's lyrics paved the way; her voice became a weapon in this dream world, her melodies were hissing daggers that sliced the air; her lyrics coursed like bullets through the universal vein of this place.

Up ahead he saw a stage surrounded by a bright galloping flame. Delilah took to the stage swarming high above, littered with stickers, guarded by wrought iron spire gates as if an outdoor arena. She was a gothic queen in his eyes. The band, her band—Electric Orchid—cued her in: it was time to dance. And so she began the song with her lips brushing sensually against the Vector microphone and her voice violating the night like venomous magic; her spit was glitter exploding across the crowd.

You are the architect of my distress . . .

The next time I fly, I'll drop my seeds across your sky . . .

The next time I fall, it won't be you who sees me crawl . . .

The kids cheered and roared in unison.

And then Clive saw the problem.

Everyone was frowning. Their faces were vulpine; their eyes were black caverns, holes so deep he could smell wasted brains. And as the music continued, so did their gyrating, slumping movements. They shuffled into lines, splitting the dance floor with boys on one side and girls on the other. A young zombie-looking kid with a Deftones T-shirt and white-lightning hair began to scream into a megaphone, pitched voice skimming above the music, and then began to hop around with puckered lips and buck teeth.

And then all of the men put on fedora hats as the girls began to undress, their peaked-pale faces grinning, their hair vibrating in the windless club. Skinny limbs jutted like huge fingers; perky breasts dripped warm rancid milk. The boys charged the girls and fucked them until the room smelled of sweat and come, of popped cherries.

Was this a tease?

But as quick as it came it was all over. Like a splash of cold water they were ciphered out; they were both all of a sudden fully clothed, faces flushed, hair disheveled. Just before Delilah ran away Clive caught the seriousness in her eyes: strong, unquestionable blue fire.

The room he could see moving around him, shelves like the Leaning Tower of Pisa ready to bury him with books. The ceiling was a waving ocean tide at sunrise, and he saw the sun through the dark curtains, streaming across his face. He was all of sudden back in the dark room; all sense of place and time was blurred, his mind was still twittering with traces of the craft beer.

Lynk held the small EVP recorder tightly. It was just about the only device that he'd kept with him secretly. When he touched it an immediate sensation pricked his skin. If this scene was to be looked upon, if one were to peak in from the roof at this early hour, they'd see only anger, and the pain of loneliness stretched far beyond repair inside Lynk's tired, pissed off eyes. They'd see the ghostly reminiscence of something unknown, but close enough to be made aware of.

It was uncontrollable.

Everything felt alone, the stock piles of paper, the hole in his heart, the gutted buildings outside the window, the parks and the sidewalks. Lynk's head throbbed dangerously, as if a blood vessel was about to pop and poison his mind. Something was stirring inside, changing and transforming his very being.

All he could think about was Clive leaving with Delilah.

My princess of the macabre.

She'd done nothing wrong of course, but Lynk had grown overtly possessive since the Dark Room incident. *Two incidents between Clive and I. We're destined to be together.* The speakers outside were playing the movie soundtrack to *28 Days*. Delilah had mentioned she wrote a song about that movie, so Lynk kicked a shelf until it toppled over.

Fucker.

Clive ditched him for the sniveling rodent's twin sister! Lynk's vision did a twist, half light and half dark, forming a silvery black string leading his mind back into the Dark Room. There was no fear to think about it. It almost felt like a calling, felt like he must go back inside and contact whatever it was: Dark Side. Through the rip of his black shirt, Lynk saw his bulging shoulder, perspiring out of fear.

I'm alone, Lynk thought. *So alone.*

Not too long after he said those words he hit the glowing PLAY button on the EVP recorder. He realized back in the apartment that it had been recording the entire time Clive and him were in the dark room. He couldn't remember exactly what happened in there, but now he was sure to find out.

Lynk put on his Skullcandy earbuds and closed his eyes, trying to recall the moment his memories went blank, the moment before the big come down. He cleared his jaded mind and let the EVP recorder implant the images in his memories.

The sound of static, a faint sweeping noise, but then banging, boots running up stairs with nobody there. Wood smashed like angels crashing to the ground still clutching their heavenly instruments. And then he heard Clive yelling bloody murder to open the door. The Dark Room Door.

Lynk's head began to pulse vicious as childbirth. The noises culminated into something dangerous: hushed voices made a small ensemble of sounds, fingers moved across paper, deciding when to tear. There were dark things crawling around, snake slither steps soft enough to disregard as a breeze or settling floorboards, but loud enough to let you know that they're in the room, waiting for your weakest moment to strike.

Then more white noise filtered through the headphones, simple movements that can drive a person mad, making them question the dark until they plunge into a murky depth of delirium to drown. Lynk instinctively held his breath, waiting for the big come down.

And then it was his quiet voice *shrieking*, and Clive's British accent begging for mercy about the ripped photos. A giant swooping sound sent things crashing to the floor. Lynk heard a haggard voice claim the room, and it threw something meaty against the door. A body. *His body!* And then it was dragging him up the wall, across the ceiling and down again. All of a sudden Lynk *remembered*. There was the hand gripping his ankle as if Freddy's claw; it pulled him up . . . and up . . . and up. His clothes tore and his voice swelled. Inside the headphones Lynk's ears welled with these sounds thick and hot as blood. And then there was blood, a great fat worm crawling down his neck.

Was there a face? No. He could only recall a great slouched thing black as coal ash, its sandpaper hands forcing his mouth open to rape his throat of his voice and will to scream. Scarecrow fingers . . .

He stopped the tape when the room grew chilly, darting for the door. He'd never been so freaked out in his life. The gallery floor was empty now, bare as a birthday suit. He kicked Hans' sluggish body draped over a chair, and they shot like arrows out into the insidious night.

The secret was safe with him.

part Two

The Soul selects her own Society –
Then – shuts the Door –
To her Divine Majority –
Present no More –

—Emily Dickinson

19

Delilah and Rez were entwined in dream. Their minds clasped; their brains became one fluid expressway of loss, heartache, destruction. A grotesque wasteland of hurt, angst, of never getting what you so rightfully deserved. A bloodied woman screaming brutally as she loses the battle of childbirth, of making mistakes and not getting away with it, of being talked down to, and never fully appreciating the niceties life has to offer, if there were any.

But with so many things to be happy for, you still can't smile, forget and pretend. Apathy is no fool. These are the feelings that permeate the tough ectoplasmic membrane of sleep. A dark and flowered place, a gash in the universe, a whorled labyrinth into the heart of exasperation. Rez found himself walking this black road, desolate road to nowhere. Then he realized that he was no longer in a duel dream; Delilah was not with him anymore, the screaming woman with the meaty cleft of a mouth was gone. He could no longer reach out with his mind's eye and see her, could no longer touch the walls of darkness to feel her. Was this the path to Arkham? Or was this the path to self-destruction?

This was just more of the dreamlands.

A Flickering blueprint sketch far down the dark path, much like the early stages of a comic book drawing. It was Alex. He looked beautiful, glistening with some kind of green slime, rot, soaked all the way through his long black coat. He was holding a knife in his hand and cutting down mountains of orchids. It seemed the flowers were everywhere. Huge petals hit the ground and shattered. Crazy swirled petals, comfortable petals, petals you could garnish a sweet desert with. Alex attacked them like Edward Scissorhands, but did not redeem his hideous look with fancy tree animals and perfectly cut lawns. This was the work of a crazed lunatic.

This was a rage Rez knew all too well.

Rez eased himself closer and turned Alex around slowly. Green eyes possessed by catatonia met his own; a tear of blood ran down that sharp face. His bones were emaciated beneath the skin and his hair had grown wild like the vines that take over garages, a tri-colored web. But Alex was grinning, canine smile of rotted teeth, a mocking grin as if Rez deserved to see this grotesque image, deserved to see his lover turn to rot because of something he must have done.

"You broke my heart, Rez," Alex said.

"I don't remember doing that."

"*You will,*" Alex hissed.

Rez touched Alex's face, felt a great shock of loss, a bullet of pain and then spitting rage. It was then he saw the change: swish cheese holes oozing like AIDS sores, wet and proud and cold. A skeletal hand grabbed Rez's face and forced his lips upon Alex's. They were like razors; his tongue was a deadcold slug as he wedged it down Rez's throat, deep into his gut, then up into his brain.

Alex was trying to steal Rez's thoughts, his memories.

"I'd kill all the ghosts for you if you'd let me."

Rez said nothing.

"This is what you wanted, right?" Alex's gritty voice rumbled.

"What do you mean?"

His long trench coat was open now, and Rez saw childish bones, those slatted ribs that sucked all light away like a black hole, that pale bony navel, and ultimately Alex's raging arousal. It was beat red, and there was spit-green chemical come all over his hand, infant's vomit. Then Alex ripped the piercing between his balls and asshole right out of his skin.

It brought relief to his face, the physical pain over the emotional. Just like Delilah with cutting. Smiling evilly again, Alex showed Rez a serrated X-ACTO blade. It shook in his hand violently. *What's mine is yours,* he heard Alex say. *Here is the big come down, Rezzy!* Starting at one shoulder, Alex ambled the blade across, then down his smooth poreless sternum until there was a squiggling ribbon of blood.

This is what happens when you love someone.

YOU FUCK IT UP!

"Stop it!" Rez yelled.

"You didn't want it anyway, so I'm giving it to you, Rez. I want you to have it since I have no use for it anymore. *What's mine is yours!*"

"Give me what?"

THE ABSENCE OF LIGHT

Alex's face paled to a living skull. Rez couldn't recognize his landmark features anymore: the mineral green eyes, the vampire smile, and the long, thin musical fingers that could manipulate a piano to make haunting notes. Alex was shape shifting into a shell of his former self, a gossamer of life and soul.

But Rez couldn't stop watching the blood now, drizzling thick and glinting. It had a tinge of gold in it, and all of a sudden looked delicious. Rez wanted to taste it, wanted a vortex to open up inside Alex, a huge red-raw entranceway leading him to the squalid throughways of Alex's veins and arteries. A place where he could escape this stinking life forever.

"Keep watching . . ."

Alex drew the X-ACTO against the bloody Y in his thorax again and Rez heard the scrape of bone, could feel it skid into his senses. He tried to stop Alex, but his hands went right through him like breaking a cob web. Slicing, jigsaw puzzle grind of skin and fascia separating from the sternum like lips, the serrated edge burrowing, streaked black with tears, twisted red with blood. Alex lifted the X-ACTO again and Rez saw the blood meld into one stream of pain across its scheming edge as Alex slammed it into his breastbone.

A hot scarlet spatter misted Rez's face. Alex's hand searched the gelatinous fissure like a grab bag, the red and white puzzle of bone and flesh. It made a squelching noise that Rez had never heard before, and at the same time he swore he could hear Alex's keyboard shoot from his chest, from his cadaverous soul. *My Personal Hell.* Plasma and blood twisted down Alex's arm in tendrils as he pulled out the dark apex meat and held it up for Rez to see, a great gob of tissue veined dark and thick.

It was his heart.

"I don't need this anymore now that you killed it," Alex said with a towering voice. "DO YOU EVEN WANT IT ANYMORE?"

"STOP STOP STOP!" Rez held his ears and closed his eyes.

DON'T YOU KNOW THAT I LOVE YOU!

Rez attacked the image with his fists. But Alex had already burst into a supernova, into a million camera flashes, fading fast.

Rez heard an echo of despair.

Alex was gone.

20

A few days passed. The physical cuts and bruises were on the mend, anxious minds softening, eggshell frail, turtle without a shell. Good time to ponder, to be patient. Good things come to those who wait. Rez let the dream slide away from his conscience when Delilah told him that she'd been there to see it, and that it all would be okay. Rez would not break Alex's heart . . . for now.

"I saw it. I was there," she said.

"I'm afraid to hurt him."

"Trust me, brother. Alex is a drama queen and a bit of a clinger. He'll not let you go. Trust me."

"Maybe I'm afraid to love . . ."

After that Delilah and Rez would not let themselves sleep. They spent the nights gleefully awake and the days drifting out of uneasy catnaps. They drank craft beer from the bottle; half of them Delilah couldn't pronounce, but she learned all about the extravagant flavors of hops and malt, hints of orange, cinnamon and chocolate. Drinking could set any mind at ease. They smoked Jimmy's blueberry salvia in tightly rolled joints and found that the high was much different than any strand of weed available; it made their blood tingle beneath their skin, made their minds ride the uneasy juxtaposition of dream and hallucination.

They caught up on a lifetime that they could never get back and found out that they both loved the beat poets, Black Sabbath, and horror movies. They talked about Electric Orchid, about how the music spoke to ghosts, how Delilah wrote her lyrics and how Alex wrote such psychotic piano scales. Then they dabbled into the blackness that was their twin nightmare: a screaming woman giving birth, of being born into a world that had forced them out of their mother's warm wet saddle too early . . . bloodied, barbed, and ultimately alone. They became brother and sister, and for once in their lives they both felt complete.

188

It was the best of times and the worst of times to tour the city. Best to do it alone, to learn where each bar was, each club, each music shop and candy store. To walk aimlessly in this land was her right of passage; to scrape its insides clean for all its slimy secrets was her birthright. She toured the Union Square Green Market munching on bittersweet Granny Apples, drinking fresh juices (all natural) and crunching upon oatmeal vegan cookies. The swirl of flavor was heaven. It was New York. It was life. Only in New York can you taste the world's greatest pleasures and treasures. You could buy tacos made by Chinese people, eat pizza crafted by Afghani's, falafel made by Americans and sushi made by *anyone* other than Japanese people.

She remembered when she spent a few hours staring at the East River: a black bed of water like a charred snake dancing for her. She walked the entire way from Alphabet City, forgetting that the trains were even there. She held a votive candle in her hand thinking about being born here—finally coming full circle, but how her bones would never rest until she found the answer to her birth. She set the candle afloat the water, watching the yellow point until a small wave smelling of boat fuel and dead fish put it out. *That was for me*, she had thought, *my new baptism.*

The most interesting towns were in walking distance from Alphabet City. The concrete turned to cobble on some streets, the alleyways became sparser in adjacent neighborhoods, and the muck was powerwashed off the asphalt on other blocks. Union Square, Flatiron, the East and West Village, St. Mark's, the High Line Park, Hudson Yards, towns with awesome names and even more awesome cuisine. It was all for Delilah. Towns where the freaks came alive, where the artists and hipsters could roam free. But where did the ghosts hide? Where did they thrive? It was a miracle if any were left; too many non-believers now, too many ignorant puppets who couldn't imagine any other state of mind than the Technicolor reality in front of their faces.

Too scared to imagine anything else.

Upon returning from one of her nightly strolls to Stuyvesant Town, Delilah spotted Lynk sitting beside the fountain in Oval Park. He'd been acting nothing but strange toward her since the day they met. They never had a conversation unless Clive was involved, and they barely said hello or goodbye. But it wasn't Delilah who was against any contact, it was Lynk. He avoided her like the plague.

Delilah was just getting used to being alone with her thoughts again, without Clive's essence squeezing her insides clean, without her dreams yawning open with carrion mouths. All she wanted to do was forget the gallery and forget that she attempted to like Clive. But it wasn't working.

"Hey. You're all alone," she said.

"You're a *thinker*, Delilah," he whispered.

His knees were tucked up to his chest and his hair was in front of his face. A marble notebook that was practically falling apart was across his lap. Delilah saw deep dark pencil lines scratched into the page, a fedora hat atop a shapeless head, a tawdry scarecrow face with shaded black holes for eyes and long witchy fingers that seemed to reach out from the page with a crazy 3D effect. On another page, a feral boy with long black hair was being dragged up a wall in a room with a thousand pictures hanging on clotheslines.

A Dark Room.

"Nice art. Didn't know you could draw."

"It's none of your concern."

Lynk stirred, slammed his notebook closed and turned his face from her. He didn't want to look at Delilah, didn't want her near him. That much was evident. What was his problem? Delilah shrugged it off and sat beside him, found a coin in her pocket and threw it into the fountain water, listening to the elegant metallic splash, the water's bubbling wishes. It was a beautiful warm night and listening to the water was nice.

"Something wrong, Lynk? You've not spoken a word to me basically since the day we met."

Lynk snorted, then whistled and threw his own coins into the water.

"Is this something all the city people do? Make wishes and throw coins?"

Lynk continued on with his coin throwing. She could see his eyes misted beneath his curtain of hair, see that his peaked face was red with the park lights shining down on him.

"Hello, Lynk?" Delilah nudged his shoulder.

"Don't touch me," he spit. "I don't like people touching me."

"Why do you always whisper? It's so annoying."

"It's how I talk. Should I rip my voice box out?"

"Wouldn't be a horrible sight," Delilah joked hollowly. "Not funny? Oh well, I tried."

"Not funny at all."

"You got the wrong kind of stick up your ass."

Lynk's head bobbed; his hair blew in the wind mildly. And then he turned to face her. He lit a cigarette with shaking hands and pulled out a small flask that reeked of the sharp odor of Wild Turkey Whiskey.

"I'm gunna make this short and sweet, bitch. I don't like you. Never have, never will."

The shock nearly stopped Delilah's heart. *Not.*

"Fuck you, Lynk."

Those words tasted good.

"You fuck with him again, Delilah," Lynk moved closer, his eyes reflecting danger, his alcohol breath pungent. "I'll kill you myself."

Delilah felt the words rip out of her throat as Lynk spoke again.

"He cried on my shoulder for two nights because of you. Cried on MY SHOULDER!"

Oh, gods! She had no words!

"And what's my prize? Nothing but a snot stain and the smell of him on my shirt. Nothing but the sweat and tears of his pathetic love for you."

"I already said—"

Lynk lifted his hand for her to shut up. "See, this is where you're wrong. This is where I stop the conversation. This is where I tell *you* what's going to happen from now on. You think you're tough because you got into your first New York street fight? You think you know this city because you take some pathetic nightly strolls?"

Delilah clenched her fist, felt anger boil over her senses.

"You got nothing to offer this city. Remember that. You and your stinking band."

"Back off Lynk. Back the fuck off."

"NO YOU BACK THE FUCK OFF! Clive is my best friend. *He's my everything.* You won't win his heart. I won't allow you."

"I don't fucking want—"

"Of course you don't, but he wants you—BADLY. He'll do anything to have you. But I'll do ANYTHING to keep him from you. I'll slice your throat, I'll break your fucking jaw so badly they'll have to wire it shut; I'll gut you like a fish. Got that, you little fucking whore?"

Delilah rose, ready to fight, but so did Lynk. They both stared at one another long and hard. Delilah saw he had no tracery of age, no stress marks to match the tired little misfit that was his soul. It made no sense. Was this kid a fucking monster or something? Was this kid really that much in love with Clive?

"You're a delusional son of a bitch, Lynk."

"At least I'm not a self-hating slut. A cutter. A fucking whiny little loser. I see a goal and I go after it. You see a goal and you crawl into a little fucking ball. Boo-hoo. Woe-is-me."

That was it. Delilah let her anger roll into a monster truck rage. She took a swing, saw her arm come around like the hand of doom, and thought she smashed Lynk in his jaw, or teeth, her hand hurt so badly. But when the adrenaline rush stopped and the puddle of stars before her eyes vanished, she saw that Lynk had actually *caught* her hand in mid-strike, and was twisting her wrist to the breaking point. His teeth were bared.

"Like I said before. Don't fuck with me, or Clive. I'll end you, little girl. I'll fucking end you."

The gallery wasn't as much of a bust as Clive had predicted. It gave them all the confidence they needed to head to Long Island City and get back to square one with all the hauntings that surrounded 5Pointz. Clive packed the ghost hunting equipment with a bad look upon his face. Delilah watched him punch the cameras into his messenger bag, watched him click the small tapes into the recording devices with pissed off fingers; his chattering mouth spoke nonsense. He wouldn't turn, refused to see her, no matter how much she looked at him. She wondered what was going on inside his head. What could he possibly want with her anymore?

Her hair was a black jungle of dreadlocks before her face, and it did a great job of concealing reality. She didn't want to see Clive anymore, or his eyes, those twin grey storms of pain and anger. She felt pretty guilty about what happened, felt it even more now that she knew Lynk's stance on the entire situation. But she had to pay the price, had to bear the reality of Clive's hurt, his embarrassment. But thinking of the way his lips came upon hers—wet and lush and warm, his tongue so far down her throat he could have tasted her dinner from last week, the way his fingers slid beneath her panties—she knew Clive was not for her.

It was wrong to play with a man's heart, she knew, but she had to see if her feelings were that of lust, or of curiosity. They were neither. Men in general were not for Delilah: love-lust was not for Delilah. Plus, she knew how much it pissed Rez off that Clive liked her in the first place, so she wasn't about to feed into the moment.

Lynk was a whole other chapter in the drama. His art was his madness; Clive was his madness. The misanthrope; the clown, the demon. Who knew what was really going on inside that brain? A billion ghosts swimming the waves of his neuronal pools; a billion stories of jealousy and rage.

21

Temptation has wings and it flies above the hand of reason. Pain has a tongue, and it laps at the heart until it throbs with pleasure. See it there in front of your own face, feel it like the touch of the most adulterous lover, like the dark.

"I got it!" Hans yelled outside Stuyvesant Town.

"Got what?" Lynk hissed.

"The peyote."

"The what?"

"*Peyote.* It'll enhance our vision. A zip-loc full."

"The famous cactus?"

"Yes."

"Start with me, please," hand upturned.

Control your anger, Delilah thought, *he's putting up a front. But what am I to do? It's my word against his.* This was not the kid who only a few hours ago threatened her life. He acted different, enlightened, happy. She was surprised to even hear him speak after all the threats he spewed, but that damn hectic whisper was still loud and clear in her mind. *I'll fucking end you little girl.* Little girl? Fuck it, she couldn't waste her time thinking about this; there were bigger fish to fry, as in getting to Queens and uncovering her blank past.

Delilah crossed the street and stood away from Lynk, who was leaning upon a smashed streetlight and chewing his peyote caps. His thoughts could be read across his pinched face: fuck Delilah and let's get on with the ghost hunt. It was to be his lifetime's achievement. Beneath the dull light Delilah saw the glimmer of a long silver chain, followed by a pendulum shaped like a bat. Its wings flew like thin shadow; its face looked like Zazo's.

"An Icarus Machina necklace," Lynk said.

"A what?" Delilah questioned.

He would not look at her, only at the bat. "A Pendulum. It moves when a *presence* is near . . . you know, like *GHOSTS*."

"Wanna know something?" Hans interrupted. "It's taken me two decades to go back to that building. If you saw what I saw back then—"

"Think about it this way . . . it was *meant to be*. Clive and I'll get the ultimate ghost hunt, you'll get your redemption, Rez and Delilah will find out about their . . . whatever it is they're looking for."

Two stumbling bodies rushed out of the building: Rez with his messenger bag and William S. Burroughs paperback clutched like a gun, Alex running pencil fingers through it like he played his Juno. They were both pleasantly drunk and gibbering.

"Our *existence*, Lynk," Rez said.

"Right . . ."

"Delilah," Lynk said, holding up the Ouija board.

Is he talking to me? First words since the fountain. Anyone noticing?

"I want you to use this. It's the bridge to communication."

"I don't want this to turn into a game of 'Captain Howdy.'"

Lynk sighed. "If you give something a pen and paper to write, *it will write*."

"Lynk and I'll set up shoot while Rez and Delilah work the Ouija," Clive said out of nowhere. "I took the liberty to upload your CD onto Rez's iPod, Delilah. Hope you don't mind . . . if you even *care*," he whispered."

"I don't mind."

Gods, he's relentless. Someone please numb my mind!

"Got smokes?" Delilah asked Hans.

Hans let everyone have a go at his zombie-hand pipe which was stuffed with the last of the blueberry salvia, good enough to mask the trip through the sparkling thoroughfare of Times Square. He passed around the peyote as well. Delilah had never heard of this drug; she thought the caps looked like dead scrotal sacs, and smelled like them too. But she ate a few without even asking what the effects were. They tasted brown and vile; somehow she knew it was only a matter of time before she was going to hallucinate, before Arkham's world would open like a deep wet chasm and lead her to the answers of her cursed existence.

If you're going to do it at all, might as well do it hard.

"Hey Rez, remember when you said nothing good can come out of Pennsylvania?" Clive said.

"Guess I was wrong."

"SO WRONG!" Alex exclaimed, kissing him hot and wet and sweet.

Rez blushed.

The walk was a bitch but it made Delilah's excitement peak to know that she was going to take a train soon. *The real lifeblood of New York.* She liked the idea of doing something unpredictable, the explorations of trains and side streets she knew nothing about, because everything back in Violet Hill was so very predictable. She would weld a road map of New York into her mind.

Delilah stopped thinking when she heard chattering people, when the streets widened and the stars became blanketed by an electric-white sky. In Times Square gaudy tourists looked for famous hot dogs and sugared peanuts, walking stupidly in pairs, bulleting every language in the world. Above, a pap smear of moon was visible, below the windows were sallow like a forest of electric. Delilah wished they were lit by candles, like ones she used to burn in Violet Hill, but here in the big city everything was about vampire voltage.

For the first time in days she felt a wave of homesickness flowering in her chest. She missed the comforting darkness of Violet Hill nights, the silence breeding in the green diamond cascade of fireflies, her oak tree with the one twisted limb and the rope light swirled across the ceiling in her bedroom. She missed the blade, too.

No . . . she *mustn't* miss the blade.

Before the entrance to the train, Delilah read a street sign that read 42nd Street and 8th Avenue. This was a street that juxtaposed madness and money, where a triangle never added up to one hundred and eighty degrees. It would drive Lovecraft mad! Then Delilah hit her first problem of suburban awe when she heard a foreign word, making her feel extra stupid: metro card.

"You ain't afraid of a little loud subway station, are you Delilah dear?" Hans asked.

"Absolutely not!"

"Like a bomb shelter," Alex said.

They ran into the huge entranceway built by colored florescence, bad pizza vapors and fried food. Rez handed a slim yellow card to Delilah which felt like she could crumble and throw into the trash.

"Use it like a credit card."

"Credit card?"

"Slide it through the metal receiver."

But Delilah had never used a credit card, so Rez did it for her. *Great. You don't even know how to use the most important way to travel in your city of birth. Good job, Delilah!* Down filthy stairs into the basement of Manhattan, past mildewed walls, speed walking like real New Yorkers through a long white tunnel made of tile and cheap pressed glass. Each steel beam above their heads had tiny billboards nailed to them. *SO TIRED*, one said. *JUST GO HOME*, said another. *I am home*, Delilah thought. *WHY BOTHER?*

It was a whole new city down here.

Dregs of street musicians lazed with their terrible instruments and made sketchy music. They had Rastafarian dreads and drug-thinned faces; punks in leather wore chinking spiked lapels and brass knuckles. A religious black zealot was howling scriptures and passing out tiny pamphlets to uninterested people about 666, whoremongers, adulterers, sinners and Sodom's children. Gone were the sweet candied peanuts and the briny scent of hot dogs; everything was drowned out by the sound of the metal screech of a train's brake system.

"Off your soap box, mate," Clive said to the guy as he passed.

"REPENT FOR YOUR SINS!" The man's nostrils grew wide as black holes in his face.

Suddenly there were more stairs that led them into a muggy oblivion, and people actually rushed to go down there! Two number 7 trains were on either side; bright green circles marked the local train. *Huge metal worms*, Delilah thought. *Is this what Arkham and Helena did as kids? Ride trains to pass time?*

Now I'm doing it.

She saw the lights pulsing in the air, swirling and twisting like chartreuse-colored insects. The peyote was beginning to work. Delilah couldn't help but to think about how the trains hurtled themselves through the tunnels to their destinations, how they just kept going. She thought about Rudy, the Mole People and The Midnight Meat Train. Were the Mole People here? Would they come out and grab her? This city had a heartbeat all its own, a deviant soul as well. What was stopping someone from strapping a bomb to their chest and pressing the trigger? Absolutely nothing. The insanity was right here, halted only by a hair's thickness of the law.

It could come to life at any second.

"Rez, is this where the Mole People live?" Delilah asked

"Don't know . . . a bit of a myth in these parts. But there's a good book about them."

"Have you ever seen one?"

"Honestly no, but I know people who have."

"Maybe one day we can find some . . ."

"Sure thing, once this mess is over," Rez smiled.

The train doors closed and the hum of electricity and metal skidded across Delilah's mind. She wondered how many ghouls were hidden between the floorboards, how many fingers were severed off during the train's construction. She sniffed the air for the smell of burnt flesh electrocuted by the infamous third rail. These thoughts would make a great Fellini film.

"What a fucking crock of shit that guy was talking about," Delilah said, stern.

"Yeah, but get used to it here," Lynk said.

"We have religious zealots in Violet Hill, but not like that. He was just fucking rude."

"Like the damn Amish!" Alex yelled. "Jimmy would agree."

"People don't stop until they're heard," Rez said. "You should see them handing out pamphlets and preaching at other stations."

"I'd rather not. I think I'd vomit," Delilah laughed.

"So how long until the Pointz?" Alex asked.

"Only a couple of stops from here," Lynk said with a fake vampiric smile, the planchette twirling in his hand. His hair hung over his face hiding an inner ghost.

"You've never been in an underpass, right Delilah . . . Alex?" Rez asked.

"Nope."

"Then be prepared to feel your ears pop when we transfer to Queens as we go under the river."

"What?"

"You gotta hold your nose, close your mouth and blow to pop your ears," Alex said, sliding toward Rez, dangling from the silver pole stupidly.

"Yeah, something like that."

Delilah made her mind ride the people on the train. The faces bordered on the plain, the languages varied. Strange English accents could be heard. Rez said they were native to the outer boroughs: nasal Queens drawl, tough Bronx twist, Brooklynese and Staten Italy. Delilah took in the sounds with a grain of salt, remembering that she was in a big city and that this was not her small town where everyone was generally the same. Alex was probably thinking the same thing, angry that people categorized him with a gender.

But what were they supposed to do? These people didn't

understand issues of fringe kids, their depressed state of minds. They didn't care for some fag who lived a genderqueer lifestyle, nor about a boy who could hear what others could not, or a girl who sung with a sibilant voice that opened doorways to other worlds, to the dreamlands. Who wanted to take the time to decipher something that was too shocking to compute in their small mind? It was much safer to stay within the circumference of their own circle. *Stick with what you know*, as they say.

And it was in this moment that Delilah knew she'd become a true New Yorker. The children of Violet Hill could never survive here: the cemetery stock and the factory snails. They all lived by the darkness of the town, followed the religion of tragedy, of hate. That kind of nonchalance wouldn't last on these streets of New York-fucking-City. Here, one had to be very careful; assassins came in all shapes and sizes, all colors and creeds. They are your best friends and your tour guides, your street vendors and patrons of the local bar. Eight-year-olds selling dollar chocolates could rip you off without notice. And with this understanding, she finally felt like she fit in.

"Let's just not turn this trip into a cheesy horror story: family moves into haunted house and doesn't leave, even though they can see the bad right in front of their faces. Daddy goes crazy and—"

"Those stories have already been written. I'm looking to write a whole new one," Rez said.

"And we got all these goons with us anyway," Delilah smiled.

"Uh-oh, here it comes!"

Delilah felt her ears pop, her head get heavy. She could hear the train snaketwisting through the tunnel now, the shriek of metal scales swiping dirt and ancient muck: the song of the city's underground. The tunnel was so long, so fucking dark that you couldn't see out the window next to your face. Delilah was a little paranoid that she was going to fall asleep, or get stuck living with the Mole People.

But then gone was Manhattan as the train came above ground. She could see wedding cake buildings lit by shimmers of sodium lights and arcs of windy stars; the Empire and Chrysler glistened like two giant fangs in the night; a giant teal Citibank made of windows the only thing resembling Manhattan on this side of the river.

"Welcome to Long Island City," Lynk said.

"*City of Evil*," Clive sung.

The train filled with more people at the 45th Road and Court

House Square station: a purple haired queer with a broken cigarette between his blue smeared lips, a Chinese peddler with paper cuts for eyes, and a mariachi band wearing rainbow lapels singing about *desesperando amor*. They pushed and shoved, and Clive was all of a sudden leaning against Delilah. She could smell the must of his unwashed T-shirt, his dirty pants, the oils of his hair and the filthy beanie that flattened all those English curls. He simply looked at her, sad, let down, angry, as if he was just waiting for the day to feast all the way up into her red-ripe cavity.

"There it is!" Lynk said, pointing out the window as the train slowly passed the building. "5Pointz."

It was dark and old, slicked with moonshine and near ready to crumble. Deviant aerosol graffiti shimmered; a tangle of bubble letters scaled the collapsing fire escapes, sword fighting nymphs and a *NIGHTMARE ON TD4 STREET* mural dedicated to Freddy Kruger. Delilah's eyes saw a skull with a top hat elevated by a huge white hand and almost fell back as its eyes met hers, turning toward her as the train sped away from it. Below was a wall of famished fallen angels outstretching their lurching limbs from the concrete. *Zombies!* Alex and Rez said together. She knew Alex loved them, especially from Fulci movies.

Deeper in the dark western distance an ominous cantilever bridge appeared; it was a web of metal glittering against the inky night and stretched like a whore across the calm East River. *59ᵗʰ Street,* Hans mumbled. So many names to the towns, bridges, so many trains to memorize above ground and under, so many boroughs to get through! Delilah didn't even know where to begin. But as the train slowed a Silvercup Studios sign appeared; red neon leaked through the train's windows like blood, making Delilah's translucent hand glow pink. Suddenly the train doors were opening, *Queensborough Plaza* said the operator, and *start west* Lynk said as if William Lee from *Naked Lunch*.

"Enjoy the walk and its dark perks."

"Great . . ." Alex said, tightening his coat around his skinny body.

"All we do is follow the train tracks to the Pointz."

There wasn't much excitement heading *west*, at least none like in *Naked Lunch*. When Rez's feet met the crummy pavement he felt Long Island City spiral into his bloodstream and dangerously twist.

Everything crackled like white noise, weighted with memories he never knew he had.

What a different place tonight.

He wasn't paying much attention to the signs; 23rd Street was the last one he saw, praying that behind some dingy corner raging penises would appear and splatter green chemical come over the gibbous moon. But there was none of that. There was only Lynk, the most boring of tour guides, irrelevant facts and clichéd notions about Queens: scummy, poor people, the world's true melting pot, the most diverse piece of land in the United States.

This is Delilah and Alex's first tour of an outer borough and Lynk is ruining it. They've taken mass transit now among other things, and they became rock stars over night. They're home, finally, after forever. The sights were limited, the streets were old but being paved over; brownstones had boards in their windows; broken slats let streetlight leak in. Rez didn't want to know what was inside those lonely buildings. The blocks zipped by; artist's studios with huge windows invited passerbys into their worlds. A few thugs who wore their pants on their knees and thick gold chains on their necks reminded Rez of the guys back at the nightclub. Thankfully, they wanted no part of the scary white demons in makeup and black clothing.

Suddenly 5Pointz gloomed across the street.

It seemed this place was kept alive by some suppressed magic waiting to burst, by the whispers of every soul that had once passed through here, waiting to share their insidious story. They crossed the street as if stepping into a new world, darker and quieter on this side, the roar of the train drowned out by the hungry silence. Rez saw the Space Womb gallery, pink and black like Delilah's hair, New York art at its most decadent.

Their boots scraped across bejeweled sprawls of broken glass; the warehouses were husks being rebuilt. Rez saw the same artistic presence slashed across every metal garage shutter, a fringe scene not known by the commercial world. POET in swamp green; NEVER SATISFIED tagged brightly below a photo of a scary looking owl. Crane Street was a perilous block that led to a dead nowhere. Susurrant sounds swished like spray paint; the hissing of camera flashes loomed around them. Subliminal voices begged for a friend; strung out druggies searched for a new needle. Rez heard it all: arguments and old wars, voices.

Clive stood sentinel with the T70 in his grip, snapping pictures like he was under some kind of possession. 5Pointz, though more compact than any building in Manhattan, was a lot scarier. The phantoms of drive-by shootings still lived here; gentrification couldn't save the soil, but it was trying. The building had rows and rows of factory style windows lit by kerosene lamps and were mottled with little holes that coruscated light and murky smells to the street. Languid sounds could be heard from inside them: the flutter of pigeon wings, faint swipes of paint brushes on canvas, the electric snap of white noise from blown speakers. Sounds of desolation. Rez closed his eyes and listened for any minute voice of Arkham to call out, any ephemeral sound that would lead him in the right direction.

"My father lived here?" Delilah asked.

"He did, many years ago," Hans said.

Lynk opened the full spectrum camcorder and began recording. Delilah and Rez stood next to him and watched what was going on through the purple LED screen. Nothing but queer shapes and stringy light. *It's what we humans can't see*, Lynk whispered. *Them*. And then he walked away.

"This place gives me the creeps," Alex said.

"It does give off a *bad* vibe."

Hans placed Rez's iPod into the portable speakers and played *Pretty Hate Machine*. A delightful ensemble against the disquieting turbulence here.

"Should we be this fucked up going in?" Rez asked.

In front of 5Pointz directly now. Rez saw the parking lot was scrawled in rookie aerosol, a mural of biohazard spray paint cans, and in the far back a bright scheming Joker and Batman in the distance. *Arkham Asylum*, Rez thought. *What artist would want to live here? One looking for cheap rent, duh!*

Lynk pushed past the heavy front door and a *WELCOME TO 5POINTZ* sign in silver spray paint was brightly lit, *THE INSTITUTE OF HIGHER BURNIN'*. Rez felt the building's colored shadows loom over his shoulder as they moved inside. Broken shelves held dried flowers; Rez saw orchids and lilies; Alex began to pet one of them, and it seemed the petals livened up, moved. But a slew of insects vomited out of the vase and scuttled to their pulsing-wet nests large as baseballs. Silverfish and their thousands of legs darted up the walls.

"A dump," Alex said.

Zazo, for the first time moving from train to land, had begun to stir. Delilah let him go and he zipped back and forth on his thin lace leash uncontrollably, little bullet in a sky pregnant with oncoming doom.

"He's sensing something important right now," Delilah said. "He's leading up to where the fire happened!"

Delilah rushed up the crumbling stairs. They all followed her lead like good little children. When they reached the top floor, a small voltage light flooded against the door. Its ratty hinges squealed; the center was bent nastily inward, perhaps from when the fire department broke it open to try and save its burning occupants. And then Delilah was pushing past everyone with a violent fervor, following Zazo into the dark.

22

If there were any ghosts inside Arkham's loft, they'd hardly have a place to hide. It was a squalid and huge space where rivulets of light perforated like tiny diamonds through the factory windows dusted in soot. Guitars lay like liver spots with their necks smashed in half, the strings chinking together by an imaginary wind. Gnarled wraiths of psychedelic band posters were tacked to the ceiling, dog-eared and curled as if still trying to avoid the fire. A wretched pile of vintage records lay, their covers ripped to shreds. Pantera's *Cowboys from Hell*, Ministry's *The Mind is a Terrible Thing to Taste*.

The mind is pretty terrible, Delilah thought.

A scorched couch lay in the center, its velour skin hanging loosely on the cage of wood. To the right was a spacious kitchen: bland tiled floor and wood cabinets streaked with the souls of orange flame. Wires slung down from where there must have been a ceiling fan, curled as if ready to hang one's self. They were throwing hooked shapes onto the nearby walls.

A spiral of shadows, Delilah thought.

The kitchen sink was overloaded with mold; the drain was ringed in archaic rust. To the right on the bare countertop a knife lay, followed by crushed beer cans and Chinese take out cartons.

Loiters.

"Hold my hand, Delilah," Rez said.

The air tasted vile as decaying dust. Delilah stepped in carefully, certain that one wrong move and the boards beneath would yawn wide, hungry, bear jagged wooden teeth to grind her bones into ivory pulp. But would he be waiting on the other side, dear old dad? Would he even know who she was? Delilah imagined Arkham here, mourning the death of his family, sleepless eyes, too painful to blink or sleep because he knew *They* were coming for him.

And then he lit the match.

"It feels dead in here, but . . . alive, like your mind wandering in purgatory," Clive said, taking a photo with the T70. "I'll set up everything. This is the first time I'll be using music to wake up ghosts."

It was the most excited state of mind Delilah had seen Clive in since the gallery. He was in work mode, *art mode*, and it took precedence over all spaces and ranges of reality. He set up the iPod speakers adjacent to a tripod holding the full spectrum into the corner and laced strings in any hole in the wall he saw; Lynk ran a few cameras through and let them hang, twirl, for a good panoramic view of the loft, and set them to record mode. The Olympus recorder and the Geiger counter were safe in hand.

"The window, Lynk," Clive nodded. "For a sign."

Lynk hung the Icarus Machina pendulum on the dirty window via a simple hook; Delilah hung her dream catcher as well, kicking away the rolling papers moving across the floor like tumbleweeds. Windows, like any human would use, are great entrances and exits for ghosts.

Delilah left Clive and Lynk to their vices and decided to continue her tour with Rez. In the back of the living room were baggies full of multicolored paper towels and spray paint cans. *Huffers?* She had briefly tried huffing in the girl's bathroom in high school because she figured cutting herself during class would be too noticeable. But all the spray paint did was coat her throat with propellant like bad oil.

"What a dump," she heard Alex's voice echo.

"Still smells of chemicals," Hans added.

Zazo came back to Delilah's shoulder when she stepped into the foyer, and there she saw Alex walk slowly across the crumbling floorboards, making his way to the warehouse sized windows and scratching out *ELECTRIC ORCHID* into the soot. Now the moonlight truly filtered in, black as the air, branding everything it touched with a phantom layer of fire and brimstone. Alex spread a few orchid petals on the ground as if throwing them down into a grave.

"Turn off the music. I need to think," Rez requested.

Rez squeezed Delilah's hand then; their blood pressure unanimously increased, their twin heartbeats locked together by a single vital artery for this discovered past, present and future. *Together*, Delilah remembered. Finally all of the keys in Delilah's dreams were fitting into their respective locks. Perhaps Rez's writer's block would let up after this. But what would they need to find for this to happen?

"Hear anything?" Delilah asked him.

"Not really," Rez said as he sucked on his Djarum vanilla clove. "Surprisingly quiet . . . dead."

"Maybe fire *does* kill *Them* . . ."

Rez stared through the blackness for a moment. Delilah watched his eyes work helplessly, heard his wayward breathing, saw his head shake as if something was scrambling his channels. Maybe he was finally tripping, maybe the peyote was swirling his brain into a vile mix of repressed memories and needs.

Deadly petals with strange power.

Delilah broke his concentration, dragging him along the perimeter, ducking through holes peppered by chitins of plaster and cicada chrysalises. Even the insects had no places to hide here, no chance of survival. Rain had damaged the ceiling; flowered spots of water rot and sagging insulation hung like wet pillows.

"Whoa . . . what the fuck is that?" Rez said, pointing down.

It was beneath the window, aching black and gelatinous form, moving: shapeless or a shape shifter. That might have been where they found Arkham's body curled and charred to scrawny bones. That might have been where Helena breech-birthed her children. Delilah suddenly heard the shrieking sounds of her nightmare, saw the huge white hand reach into the redwet cavity and pull out a living, bleeding child. The ache in her soul was like lead.

Feel it, Delilah thought.

But what would it be like? She remembered what Nicholas Weiner felt. *Not suction or true sensation, but an insubstantiality, a fever dream . . . if you could rub hallucination on your skin.* But by the time Delilah bent down to touch it the dark ashy cloud was gone. She brought her finger back to her nose and sniffed it. The smell was pungent, reminded her of anthracite particles. But it wasn't. This smell was made up of every ash and chemical essence weighted with a man's torment for ruining his own life, his children, gone shriveled and tuft by his own flame.

Suicide.

Delilah's razor scars burned now, and Rez nodded to let her know that his did too, but that it was because they were separating. Nothing could stop the shift of paths in which they were being led. They were controlled by their separate nightmares, their separate anxieties. Delilah: moving toward the bars of light pooling in the hallway next to the front door. Rez: back to the group.

Delilah watched Rez fade away.

But then Zazo began to uproar, echolation shriek of something terrible ahead. *Stop, Delilah. Stop.* Delilah couldn't stop walking into the phosphorescent stream. It called to her as if the shimmering path of lighter fluid as she imagined Akham's fire bursting through here. All of a sudden there was fire, and lots of it. But she remembered the peyote, its dry bland flavor, its *power*. Tiny microbes came to life inside the whorls of her brain, ringing it dry of sweet blood. She saw sketchy images, squiggling things as if dreams breaking through reality. But then her reverie was snapped away by a tight grip on her arm.

"Delilah, let me come with you," Clive said with a baggy face, the look of borderline psychosis.

"You've not spoken a word to me in three days."

"I need this. *I need this ghost.*"

"No. This is my life."

"*I am part of your life now.* Only I know how to see *Them,* and they're seeing you."

"Get the fuck off my arm, Clive."

Clive let go. The last thing she saw was his head of scruffy mouse hair and a fiery glint in his grey-blue eyes. Gone. It was better to be alone. She needed to do this on her own. Clive was simply getting in the way.

The bedroom was small, four walls and a good sized window, square room tiny enough to keep her safe, to contain her dreams as if in a magical vial. A mirror was draped with dried orchids, orchids like her band name and Alex's decadent tattoo. The smell was long since decayed in here, shot through with a crazed man's essence.

Faded décor and more acid rock posters covered in dust swarmed the ceiling; cartons of take out were left by looters, soaked in a fermented puddle of Colt 45. Delilah could smell the sulfur of malt liquor. She'd gotten used to craft beer so quickly it sickened her to think she ever put something so cheap in her stomach. A shelf of books lined the back of the room, filled with maddening titles about photography, art magazines and the LSD-laced worlds of William S. Burroughs.

They're here.

Delilah felt an unimaginable amount of pressure building inside her skull. Faint, so tired all of a sudden, and she began to lie down.

The floorboards met her face cold and alone, the peyote fucking with her mind full-scale. She heard the iPod playing Electric Orchid's debut album. Delilah all of a sudden heard electric snap and sizzle. No, not electric: insect wings.

Zzz. Zzz.

It was all golden, wonderful music. Knowing that sleep wasn't far away, that dreamland was impending upon her, she remembered what Alex told her about Black Sabbath. This made her unafraid of what she might see, if some ghoul would take her to Arkham's lair. Delilah closed her eyes and hummed a melody with her galvanizing voice. Her flesh vibrated against her bones, parted like snake skin, and she was free at last. The ectoplasmic body began searching the bedroom.

"The basis of the board is that the energy of the user attracts the energy of the unconscious spirit. Boards are the great magnet," Lynk said.

Everyone surrounded the Ouija, cross legged, cigarettes their only source of light beside the moon. They were all very interested in what was going to happen, their eyes pale and focused, faces firm and respectful. They all knew that questioning the dark did not make them insane. Rather, it prepared them.

"She wouldn't let me follow her," Clive said.

Lynk rolled his eyes and gritted his teeth. "*Leave Delilah to her maledictions.*"

"Whatever."

"Anyway, *do not* ask it odd questions. YES or NO only, and one at a time. That's very important, especially when we're shooting. The inner workings of a camera are as intricate as life starting as a seed. You take a photo and who knows what you'll get; who knows what you're really capturing. Just like you don't know if you're making a boy or a girl when you're procreating, taking a photo is never guaranteed that you'll catch a proper ghost. It's a cat and mouse chase."

"SLRs are built based on the design of lens, mirror, shutter, film, sensor matrix, focusing screen, condensing lens, pentaprism and the viewfinder. They outweigh all other photographic devices by far," Lynk added.

"Those are really important factors in capturing the right things, the proper angles and colors, and this camera is the poster boy of it all," Clive held up the T70. "In simple terms: when you take a picture, light passes through the lens and is reflected by the mirror, then transmitted onto the focusing screen. The condensing lens and internal pentaprism reflects the image as it appears in the viewfinder. When you take the picture, the mirror structure moves, the focal plane shutter expands and the image is stamped onto the film. Very detailed, very precious. Does anyone understand this?"

They all nodded dumbfoundedly.

"Well, at least they got the picture. Ha, get it?"

Then Lynk put his fingers on the glass planchette, asking simple questions aloud. *Are you here? Will you talk?* Nothing at first. Only the annoyance of waiting, feet tapping, huffing and puffing. But then the sound of a chair's legs snapping, a cool wind filled with white noise. The round ball of ectoplasm was unlike anything Rez had ever seen. It was a miniature sun, a cold spot and an eyeball all in one. From some angle in the room Rez felt the eye roll in its oily socket, felt his father beaming down upon him. Everyone gasped. *Do it again, I beg you,* Lynk said. Clive snapped a photo of it with his Nikon, quicker than anyone could imagine, always ready when it came to the ghosts.

"Fascinating," Clive said.

"Being in here gives me the chills," Hans said. "Reminds me of too much."

"Do it again, Lynk."

Rez tip-toed to the tripod holding the full spectrum camcorder. The little purple screen was pointed at Lynk and very alive. He saw that something with dark long fingers was moving towards Lynk, something with a cankered tongue and blistered lips; its eyes were the same glow as the orb. But when he looked away from the screen it was gone. He opened Arkham's book for a clue about Ouijas but found nothing. *A book of poetic junk!* That's when he lost interest in the ghost hunt; the guys made the entire process seem too campy.

He walked into the kitchen with Alex behind him, checked the cabinets, moving his finger across the burn streaks. Nothing but stacks of non-glare photo paper and a row of vintage Star Wars mugs. *Arkham was a Star Wars fan!* Rez thought he felt a tendril of his father's black aura run through him coldly just then, and it made him lose his balance in a cloud of ashy dust, leaning against the near counter.

"Rez? What's the matter?" Alex asked from behind.

"I don't want to talk."

Talk a little, Rezzy. Don't you love him? His bad luck mocked him.

"Fuck off!"

Alex slipped his arms underneath Rez's torso, icy touch so familiar and yet so strange. When his tongue came past his lips, Rez tasted the poison of alcohol and clove infused spit. It was most wonderful and yet the most disastrous taste in the world. Rez pushed him away. But Alex wouldn't give up; his pale green eyes remained stern and dark behind the blots of makeup, makeup like a dissipating *bruise*. Rez wanted to create a real bruise all of a sudden.

"Don't do it Rez, don't hurt me."

Rez slung his arm back as far as he could, back as far as his mind would take him, and shot it forward like a bullet. His fist plowed into Alex's mouth in an arc of terrifying rage. Rez felt Alex's lips meet his knuckles softly, felt his sharp teeth cutting through all of that sweet pink flesh. Alex stumbled, raising his hands high, his fingernails slicing the air black and red in the defensive fallback.

"There," Rez said. "Now get the fuck away."

"No."

Alex came back, ghost steps across the floor, blood like grape juice on his thin lip, and held Rez tight. Rez all of a sudden wanted to taste that blood, the glittering pink drizzle. He wanted to know what it would be like, how sweet death would taste. When they kissed Rez only tasted corruption and betrayal. The elements of this place.

"What's wrong with you?" Alex said.

When Rez blinked it was all over. Fake images: a dream of looping psilocybin imagery in the center of his brain. He noticed Electric Orchid's music was playing softly in the background.

"*The music!*"

"Hey!" Alex said. "You fell asleep standing up. You're not well."

"Get out of my face, Alex!"

Rez found himself panting, sweat beading off his head as if he'd just took a shower. He wanted to be alone, wanted to listen to all the fantastical sounds so he could decipher them. There were so many *voices!* He thought he heard an iota of his father calling out to him from his dead world. But he turned and gripped Alex close to him instead, heavy coat just too big for his wire-thin bones, and collected as much of Alex's scent as he could. Then he asked him to go, final, that he had to look around alone and was better off that way, and Alex complied, moving into the living room with the other three.

THE ABSENCE OF LIGHT

Delilah, I need you.

Razor scars burning, face cold as if cradled by a ghost, lips sore as an open wound on the mend. A searing anger swelled inside his chest, heavy as the ash of memories inside this place. It turned his brain into an enemy, made it pound against the fluid-filled lining of his skull. The peyote was melting his mind into a puddle of bad memories. And that's when he felt a new feeling.

Feed me.

He threw his Moleskine to the counter and opened up the betraying pages. Nothing but nonsense doodles and scribbled words that could only be read by Rez's eyes. But this loft was now his dark temple, the perfect place to restart his creative mind. The ball point pen was like God as he began his writing tornado, page after page. But the Moleskine wasn't enough; he used his own skin as paper, blotting words until blood and ink twined down his arm, words that wouldn't make sense until morning, perhaps never.

But they had to be written.

Over his tattoos the pen slashed, across the small bones in his hand like speed bumps the nib defied skin, digging until he drew blood. Rez was a Book of Blood; The Illustrated Man. Best of all, the words were finishing themselves. But it was all in vain. *Tricks, these are tricks.* Deep in this scorched excuse for a kitchen something much bigger and hungrier was waiting, a permanent blackness that held a pulse, that could think clear thoughts; most of all it had knowledge.

An *evil* knowledge.

The Dark Side.

It was what had gotten into Arkham; it was what fucked with Clive and Lynk in the darkroom. If Rez stared into the walls long enough he knew that he would be able to see them before he heard them. They would writhe and form hands, a mouth for chewing to bring him closer to understanding what went on here two decades ago.

Suddenly he felt a million eyes watching him from a distance, sneaky orbs waiting for dinner like in *The Hills Have Eyes. Those huge boxed windows would let in a lot of moonlight if the soot was washed off,* Rez thought. And the light would show the monsters; they would have mouths screaming with twisted voices telling him the secrets of this place. Then Rez felt a huge surge of electric speeding through his veins like a flash of a million cameras.

It was time to let them in.

Rez ran for the window. Fists clenched, battered skate shoes skidding across the rotted floorboards, he had to meet the eyes and the pale and listless faces behind the glass! But then someone was stopping him with a bear hug: Hans. Rez saw his black filigree chain swinging ear to lip; it looked easy enough to rip out of his face.

"What the hell are you doing?"

"The eyes!" Rez said.

"What eyes?"

"Arkham's!"

"Um, guys," Lynk's pipsqueak voice.

"Not now Lynk!" Hans chided.

"I'm pretty sure that this place is making us see things."

"WHAT!"

"Like . . . you know, things playing with our minds, using our vulnerabilities against us."

"We didn't have to come here to understand that there're things out there that break boundaries and seep into places they ain't never touched yet," Hans said.

Breaking boundaries . . . places they had never been to yet. That meant at anytime anything could come through the membrane of time and space, like a fetus breaking from the placenta, and claim you. That meant that these things had been following them all along, that the dimensional plane could be opened by a simple flash of the camera.

Then the glass planchette moved without anyone touching it. It skidded over letters recklessly, then flew off the board and screeched across the floor until it hit into the hear wall. Then fire. Small bright flame washing over the Ouija, shark tooth dance, concealed only to the circumference of the board; black smoke shaped words of warning in the air.

And then Lynk's face locked onto Rez's, mouthing something bad, very bad about ripping Delilah's insides out for stealing Clive away from him. Rez turned to Clive and he had the T70 in his hands, announcing that he'd make a portfolio of her murder because she didn't want him like he wanted her. Lynk grabbed the knife from the counter; that horribly rusted knife. He stuck out his tongue and drew it across until his blood beaded like a glittering red horizon. Rez could hear the sound of sharp metal cutting into meat.

Taste her!

Kill her!

"Did you hear what he just said?" Rez yelled.

Nobody paid attention.

Lynk marched to Arkham's bedroom with his hands outstretched, his fingers curled, wanting Delilah's soft pale flesh. He would slit her throat and listen to the sound of her voice spill out in gold-red rivulets. He would drink her magical blood.

And then it was over.

"Calm the fuck down!" Alex said. "You fell asleep again! When's the last time you caught some shut eye?"

"I gotta get out of here; we gotta get out of here!"

"STOP!" Hans demanded. "I KNEW THIS WAS GOING TO HAPPEN!"

"It's him, he's gunna' kill my sister!"

"No one's killing anybody!"

They all stared at Lynk who was busy moving the planchette stupidly across the board, minding his own business. It was obvious whatever was in this room only had a taste for Rez. He was the only one who saw the fire.

But then, the scream.

She saw the tripod bag first in her dream world, haunted by the memory of Arkham's life as a photographer. An advertisement for a band at a Lower East Side club was tacked to the wall, bad ink job by the printer, just like she used to design for Electric Orchid shows at The Grin. Piles of photographs were scattered as if someone or something had recently been scavenging through here. She couldn't make them out; they'd been developed quite terribly. On the dresser a pack of cigs lay, still warm to the touch as Delilah's fingers spidered over it. *Warm like an rapport.* She knew about apports, how they can show up at anytime as a sign of ghostly activity.

Dad?

She stuffed them in her pocket, planning to smoke them until death brought her and Arkham to meet. *My Personal Hell*, he would say. The thought claimed her mind. Now everything that inspired those lyrics came rising out of the smashed walls, spraying over her like aerosol paint. This place made her insides birth new music, made her never want to leave. Four blighted walls to protect her all day and night.

What would be the harm in staying? She could pump out new melodies, tilling her brain until she passed out, until she died as fashionably as *daddy dearest.* Left in here too long and the music would be all that mattered anyway. Air and sun would not exist; only the gossamer hope of dad reaching out with ghostly fingers would feed her vitality. In here she could *kill.* Kill like father had done to mother.

Suddenly a jolt of pain, blue tendrils behind her eyes.

She felt it!

This place was inside her, influencing her mind into madness, into Dreamlands and Nightscapes. If she didn't leave now this place would keep her like it did Arkham and Helena. Then she heard the thud like phlegm against brick. Delilah turned to the closet, feeling it call her, sucking her soul into its core.

The door was the cheap sliding kind, and when Delilah pushed it to the side the entire thing came off the hinges and slammed into her head, pink and blue-black flash before her eyes. A warning? Her face was wet—tears or sweat, she didn't know—and as the dust settled, as the windows stopped their frail glassy shudder, Delilah saw a lone duffle bag: a bolt of light at the end of a long tunnel.

It was muddy and cold as if excavated from a century-old casket. She saw divots of bone. Human or rodent? It looked more like a contorted human finger, one that could place the blame, one that didn't want to go deep into the cold soil. Delilah reached for the broken light switch in the room and, miraculously—it worked.

A purple neon sheen washed over her, the same color as today's twilight . . . but what was feeding this room electricity and not the others? Delilah reached down to the bag. *Warm,* she thought, and unzipped the top portion and stuck her hand inside, ready to face her personal hell. The emotional torture would surely begin its downstream

And she screamed.

The crew jumped over the burnt couch and ran to Delilah. She was lying on the floor in a painful position; pictures were strewn across her torso and covered her face. Rez pushed everyone out of the way, feeling quite blank after what had just happened, but happy to know Delilah was alive . . . at least. But when he saw the pictures he knew why she was crying. They were revelation, a nidus of Delilah's nightmares.

Helena: her face obscured by a profuse amount of blood, her hair sticky with goblets of gore. A great gout of clear fluid slicked the floor, swirled with a dark substance; a white hand was wrapped around her neck as another jabbed between her legs, pulling tiny legs out of her bloodied fold of sex.

Murder!

Breech birth!

Rez drew his sister close to him; Alex covered her shivering body with his huge black coat. She laid her head on Rez's shoulder, holding her brother tight. He felt every searing tear drop, colored by the eyeliner, drying to a crayon smear on his skin.

" . . . some tubes of film here, too . . ."

"I'll develop them," Clive said, taking all of the tubes in his hand like bullets.

"This is bad, bad, bad," Lynk said.

"Oh, Arkham . . ." Hans whispered, dropping his head to his chest.

Clive put the tubes of film into his bag and scooped up the other photos scattered on the floor. They made their escape, forgetting about the Ouija board, forgetting about the dream catcher. Clive stroked Delilah's hair on the way out and no one noticed Lynk's dark jealously except for Rez. They all walked back to the 7 train in silence, not stopping to stare at the pair of red eyes peering from behind every metal column, the hand of doom ready to purge them into hell. Rez wondered what lunacies the photos were going to bring.

23

Darkness curtails the investigation; darkness coalescing, blotting the jagged road ahead. Good time for recollection, bad time for emotions. Some darkness is as insignificant as your shadow mocking your every step, whispering beneath your feet as a sheer nothingness.

Sometimes it's alive.

A green flame pricks the dark and lights a bowl-piece packed with sweet Lower East Side grass; a twisted hand grabs for more. The smoke swirled into Rez's mouth, imbued in his lungs. Alex took a hit and the ephemeral daggered flame suffused creamy light across his black hair, his shadowed features. But suddenly a shrill sound; something splat to the ground: garbage dropped from the windows above. Rez looked up—but not with his eyes—and heard a riotous whisper claw its way down the dirty brick wall, the sound of his engulfing dark dream.

Need a hit. How much? Come to me.

Feel me.

Take me.

No. He wouldn't feel the dark, wouldn't let it slick his soul as if corroded oil. Not like it had done to Arkham. Then a huge creature shot out from the garbage pile, a cat that had once ruled this side of town, the Queen of the Damned, but now just a sad lumpy feline. Rez read that cats can protect people from ghosts, that they were the keepers of the underworld.

He hadn't seen any action in this alleyway since the law had begun cleaning up Alphabet City. No one came into these parts to express themselves anymore, to escape society. The graffiti was gone, the smell of crack/cocaine long since faded; the silver strike of needle plunging into wasted vein was now a dead trend. Regulation and rule deemed graffiti a crime. Its dogmas were spread across the advertisements lining telephone booths and subways. Cops bust any punk kid holding an aerosol can faster than a dealer with *I'M SELLING TO TWELVE-YEAR-OLD KIDS* tattooed on their forehead. The only thing left was voices searching for an ear to live in.

Twilight. Perfect time for voices.

Rez looked up at the sky and saw a huge aubergine scarf stretching across the dying buildings, awakening the dark over here, keeping the light steady over there in this pitiful excuse for an alleyway. Daylight had just slid away like beads of sweat, and its excess shined upon Alex. Another day gone. Once, Rez could hide here from his bad luck, safe place to think, to curl with his trusted Moleskine, sorting out plot lines, characterization and wasted themes. Here his mind had collected thoughts and turned them into stories that he sold to *Weird Tales* and *Cemetery Dance*, stories about kids who dwell aimlessly in nightclubs; artists who swirl crazy colored oil on canvas, pictures that come alive. It was a part of his life that he no longer knew. Wasn't a writer supposed to write?

Rez had done nothing of the sort in months.

The wind rattled hideously; fast food wrappers formed a tiny tornado. Since 5Pointz Rez had been noticing every particle of life, every element that makes us tick; too aware of his own senses, his own physiology, frighteningly sensitive. The dark that he used to joke about when reading novels of horror and suspense could no longer be taken for granted. It was truly *alive*, and it could not be controlled. It was its own entity. It had to be questioned.

It's a scary and cold world, Magda used to tell him. *Don't get lost in that kind of puzzle.*

But for now he was spending time with Alex. He watched him rub his fingers against an engravement that Rez had nearly forgotten about. One night drunk as ever, lonely and looking for something to do, Rez had scratched his name into brick with a dull screw driver. Alex's bony fingers sang across the smooth edges, humming an Electric Orchid tune. He'd bit his nails down to nubs on the train ride back to Alphabet City and one of the cuticles was a shallow iridescent frown of blood.

"We lost them," Alex said. His breath was pungent with the stench of warm vodka, two eyes burning like remote stars in a lost universe. "Drink?"

Rez swilled the piss-warm vodka, liquid fire spreading down his esophagus, bursting in his stomach.

"I have a fucking headache like no one's business," Rez said.

"Hearing something?"

"Too much. It's like a billion conversations at once."

"I wish I had that kind of talent."

"No, you don't. This is a curse."

Alex turned uncomfortably. "So you're saying ignorance is bliss? You're the most informed person in the world!"

"No."

"Then what—"

"I just can't be bothered, that's all."

"It seems you never can." Awkward pause, and then, "Rez . . . what did you see in there?" Alex asked glumly.

" . . . I don't know . . ."

"You know."

"I'm having trouble remembering . . ."

"Think!"

"I'm trying! I'm no good at this shit, and I have a head—"

"Then I'll fill you in! You fell asleep standing up . . . woke up screaming . . . the music was going . . ."

Rez pressed his hand over Alex's mouth. "It's like . . . blackness . . . okay? A fast spreading blackness fast as fire . . . the absence of light . . . and . . . then I'm scared. I'm scared Lynk's going to kill Delilah."

"Oh, come on. Lynk's a sloppy vagina."

"I'm not kidding Alex. My brain won't let me to remember it all. But I'm filled with these . . . flashes of fear."

"You were definitely in a trance. Haven't seen anything like that since the days I watched Delilah's extravagant battles between dream and sleep."

"Do you think my dad was under some kind of spell? Some kind of mind game? Did music call it out?"

"Stop calling him that. His name is Arkham. That's it. He was never a real father."

"But without him I wouldn't be alive. I owe it to him to find out."

"You owe him nothing. Those pictures prove it. He abandoned you; he killed—"

"Yes I do! I owe him EVERYTHING."

"Gods, you're just like Delilah, forever tormented with this constant itch."

"You just don't know what it's like to have nobody!"

"No, but what I do know is that you don't have to be bonded by blood to be a family!"

Rez's heard jerked. He saw a light, Delilah's face, and then Clive's. "You don't get it! You don't have this need for answers weighing down your heart like I do."

"You still got one of those?"

"Fuck you, buddy."

"I get it alright, I get it real good. I've been Delilah's best friend since ninth grade, and what you're telling me is nothing she hasn't told me already."

"What's that supposed mean?"

"Nothing. Forget it. Point is, like I said, family is not all that 'blood is thicker than water' bullshit. Sometimes your friends are there for you more than your own stock. Think about it."

"I don't have any stock to think about . . ."

"Here we go again. Open those beautiful eyes! You have Clive, Lynk, Hans, me and Delilah. What about Magda? She's been like a strange mother to you!"

Rez stopped drinking the liquor, realizing that what Alex was saying was true. He'd had a family this whole time, but he was too busy wishing for Arkham that he couldn't see the beauty in front of his own face: the fact that people had loved him, kept him safe.

"Alex, you're right. I'm sorry."

Pale green shutter in Alex's eyes. "Softened you up, did I?"

"Perhaps. I'm just sick, so sick with all these bad feelings."

"Ah, my perpetual pessimist!"

"Shut up."

"Well then, let me tell you a pessimistic story."

"A story?"

"A legend in my home town, of course!"

"The one where you and Delilah tease that thing in the basement?"

"No," Alex said stern, staring at Rez with a force he didn't expect. "I never talk about that story . . . creeps me the fuck out."

"What's the point if it's not a ghost story? I wanna hear something that connects the dots."

"Nostalgia . . . now listen."

Alex and Rez sat, their backs sliding down the building's edifice, graffiti like deflated balloons hanging limp across the brick wall. *LaSt OnE LeFt IS A RoTTeN EGG!* and *LOISADA FEVER!* They lit cigarettes, watching the sky get darker and darker, watching the small square windows above gleam like spangled masks. *Story telling is good for the soul*, Alex thought. *It keeps traditions alive. Rez should know this, being a writer and all.* It was something the city and its perpetual hunger for change could never understand. It was something a city rat could learn from a small town boy.

"It's about *The Pocono Chopper*."

"Pocono Chopper?"

"It's the classic campfire horror story!"

"So your small town is near The Poconos?"

Alex rolled his eyes. "Kind of . . . we get all the slush of lost tourists looking for the ski slopes, finding only bars, the cold, and the anthracite factory."

"Sounds pretty industrial to be called Violet Hill," Rez said, his pale hand gripping Alex's leg.

"It is. One day we'll go there. So anyway, about the *Chopper*. The Poconos is the one place lost tourists always ask about, so it's no guess that—"

"Wait a second. I just realized something. Your band name is a flower, and so is your town. Question is: do flowers even grow there? I imagine Pennsylvania as some frozen strip of land, or mountain. Especially the way you describe it . . . like it snows ash or something."

"Of course flowers grow there! I grow orchids in my basement; violets, daisies and lilies show their faces in the summer. We *do* have all four seasons."

"I didn't know."

Alex found this moment to be one of the most sentimental Rez and he ever had. He couldn't stop himself from grabbing Rez's choppy black hair, gliding his tongue across Rez's lips. They were thin as razor wire and delicious as summer lollipops, and Rez returned the gesture, feeling Alex's ribs, running his hands to Alex's groin.

"Oh, you city people and your preconceptions of the rest of America. It's very funny."

"Cut it out now. Get back to the story."

"Yeah, so the Chopper is a tale told by all the adults to scare us little Violet Hill kiddies so we would never wander around outside at night, or talk fresh to our parents either. You see, it was rumored that The Pocono Chopper loved to cut out tongues, but not only that, he was known to dissever people limb from limb . . . while they were alive!"

"Bull shit!" Rez said.

Alex heard Rez's echo sail away into twilight above them.

"He was a wild man who lived in the woods supposedly, so deep into the forest that nobody could ever find him. He abducted tourists and left them on side roads stuffed in heavy duty garbage bags; he took townspeople and did the same, but always with a forewarning."

"Which was?" Rez said more interested.

"The sound of an axe, of course. You knew he was coming when you heard the sound of swiping metal."

"Hmmm. Creepy."

"And with the bitterly cold Pennsylvania weather at his disposal, police couldn't smell any decay or rot."

"That couldn't happen here. Too many people. And the weather's temperamental."

"That's the beauty of it all in Violet Hill. Our seclusion drives us to constantly question one another."

Constantly question one another. Alex suddenly realized how good he felt talking to Rez, and he knew Rez felt the same. He'd found the lover he'd always dreamed of, always wanted. It had been ages since he thought of his life this clear because he'd done such a good job at fucking his brains out before thinking about trust, about a relationship. Rez had sewn shut all of his lifetime's emotions, but together they could revisit the burning memories.

"I'm hungry," Rez said. "Let's get something to eat."

They skipped out of the alleyway, the night streets their gloomy guide leading their fevered hearts into the wild. The Halal cart stood alone on a scraggy corner, silver box trying to sparkle, grease vapors of roasting meat and spices calling out to Alex's sense of smell. Something exotic was being born. Rez ordered a falafel sandwich and a ragged brown hand passed Rez a little beige pillow called pita stuffed with a mix of mescaline salad, fried chic pea balls, sliced onion and a lot of tomato.

"This one's for the pretty girl," the man said, throwing a soda Alex's way.

Pretty girl, Alex thought. *I can get used to that.*

Rez bit down and then gave it to Alex. The falafel tasted like every spice of the Middle East rolled into one. A fistful of herbally fried chic peas, cold fresh tomatoes and slimy Tahini sauce rushed out the side of his mouth. It was heaven.

"I've never tasted anything like it," Alex said after taking another bite.

"I'm glad. That's one of the perks of living here. Now pass it back."

When Rez grabbed the Falafel out of Alex's hand his butterfingers missed the mark and it fell to the cement in a wet splat. But the taste of verdant vegetables and fried chic peas was still there, a hurricane of flavors mauling his palate.

"FUCK!"

"Don't worry about it."

"I always screw things up!" Rez yelled.

"I said *don't worry* about it."

"You just don't get it. I'm fucking unlucky."

"I know how to make you lucky," Alex said, unhooking his silver orchid necklace. "I want you to have this."

"I can't . . . accept that. It's your favorite piece of jewelry."

"It's for you, okay?" Alex smiled.

He put the necklace on Rez and it looked great upon his neck. Then Alex pulled Rez's arm hard and they skittered away from the sandwich. At a bodega Rez purchased a six pack of Magic Hat Hex Outrofest. More craft beer was fine by Alex; he couldn't get enough, and so he took a swig, watching all the eyes of monsters look back at him from the label.

Eyes of monsters. Eyes of monsters.

As the beer settled in Rez's stomach it seemed to take a crash course in his gut and uncoil into his nerves. A new feeling spilled like hot oil throughout his body. It wasn't fun or good times ahead; it was something to do with Alex: his new friend understanding all his fucked up emotions, becoming something more. Alex accepted him. Alex passed no judgments against Rez. He would not point his finger and call him stupid, would not tell Rez he was too unlucky to be cared for, too ugly to be loved. Alex wanted to talk, to open their hearts together, kiss the fine curve of Rez's throat and worship his pale skin.

But what business did Rez have liking Alex this much?

Ah, there you go Rezzy, the negative ninny!

It was always easy to write these kinds of cheese-dick love scenes in a story. You could make people do and say what you wanted because you are GOD when creating the plot. But in real life there is no Microsoft Word, no eraser to take away bad parts, the parts that hurt. The power of the pen is not all that powerful here. Suddenly his Moleskine burned from its dark core in his messenger bag.

Feed me, it said. *Words! Words!*

Why do I even carry this piece of shit anymore?

Then a rushing crosswind cut into him like a razor; it whipped Alex's huge coat open and blew his hair around crazily. If one were to look at them now from a high rise window or rooftop they'd see nothing but peace and understanding. But that didn't last. As Rez looked down an alleyway, he saw the flash of red reptilian eyes within the vampiric shape of Lynk's head, the glint of a trench coat wet with blood. He blinked and it was gone.

"I just saw . . ."

Alex turned. "Saw what?"

"Never mind."

"Come on, tell me. The sound of the night is so fresh."

Rez thought about what Delilah had said about trust issues from being adopted. *Given away by the first heart that was supposed to love you unconditionally.* She was right, and Rez supposed it would be a while before she showed her true feelings. What would Delilah really be like if she let herself go, let her true feelings flood the world? Would she have invited Clive to be her boyfriend? Clive didn't handle rejection well, didn't handle anything well these days.

It was a very toxic mix.

In fact, being rejected made Clive mad-insane, especially because of all the gay rumors, and the way Lynk tricked him out of getting into any relationship with a girl. Was he working on Clive right now, telling him how bad Delilah was? No matter. Delilah could handle herself. She was tougher than he, tough as the mother who fell in love with a murderer and carried his children until death parted them.

Rez was simply not going to get himself involved.

All of a sudden the buildings became more gothic, ageless. Gargoyles could be seen above, and that's when The Marble Cemetery appeared. Its spire gate was sealed by huge chains twisted together and padlocked. Alex wanted in, had never seen a cemetery that encased its dead in so much marble.

"I'll scale that sucker," Rez said. "Did it before, and can do it again."

"No," Alex said, hand tight on his arm, gentle squeeze, and smiled as if up to no good. "Watch and learn the skills of bored suburban kids."

Alex fished his hand deep into his coat, pulled out a safety pin and paper clip. He stretched them into long thin wires and stuffed them into the huge lock. With a few fancy turns the gears gave way with a single oily click and the heavy duty chains were at their feet. Alex slipped his skinny body in first, androgynous angel-devil still marveling over the sights of the city, the sights Rez knew like the back of his hand.

Night greeted them coldly in the graveyard. An essence fat with premonition lie in the air as the cemetery wind brushed across their faces like an eerie welcoming. A towering tenement was swarmed in an all out war of lime green vines with cascading droplets of morning dew.

Each marble stone was like a land mine holding so many secrets of the dead, waiting to explode. The few trees here spread far and wide, wicked limbs dusted with dead seasons, coming down as far as the ground to touch the frequent mourners or to perhaps choke the two wandering loiters. Rez could feel something wanting to come out of the dark.

Come in, the cryptic voice hidden beneath the soil said. Rez took his hand off the stone marked KIP BAY and listened again for any murmur, any blind echo. There were none. They only came when he touched their final resting place.

"I like St. Johns better," Alex said.

"How do you know that cemetery?" Rez asked quizzically.

"I took these from the dark room. This too."

Alex showed Rez the photos: Rez at St. John's the night Clive and him got so drunk they couldn't find their way out. There were also the photos of Rez at the Museum of Natural History. Rez saw the castle turrets gloaming in the background, the windows lit by strangely shaped lights. Not lights . . . orbs!

"If Clive saw these that'd make him really happy."

"He's busy trying to develop all those tubes from the loft. He wouldn't even notice these."

They were holding hands now because it was safe within the land of the deceased; the dead never had much to say when it came to sins and sexuality. They had bigger things to worry about, like the worms.

"I wish I had my cell," Alex said, "to call Delilah to see if she's alright. She needs me by her side."

"Clive says the same thing about me . . . that I need him around so I won't do something stupid. But it seems he's forgotten about me these days. Well, come to think of it, ever since he laid eyes on the T70 and Delilah . . ."

"Damn. If you feel bad, well, imagine how jealous Lynk feels."

"Oh, let's not even discuss that rat right now," Rez gritted his teeth. "Just thinking of him trying to make Clive . . . *like* him, fills me with . . . ugh, forget it. Thinking about how he hates Delilah . . ."

"Okay," Alex said, his plain accent coming out strong. "Forget him. But I'll tell you this . . . if Electric Orchid takes off, consider yourself taken care of. You won't have to be so angry anymore."

"If I ever write again and get a book deal then ditto."

"You will . . . Hey, Rez?"

"Yeah?"

"Thanks for understanding me."

"What do you mean?"

"You don't call me boy, or sir, or kid . . . just Alex. You remembered, and thank you." Alex leaned over and kissed Rez softly.

"No, thank you, for being so patient with me. I know I'm a pain in the ass and hard to deal with."

"It's a breeze."

Then Rez grabbed his stash of Sour D from his pocket and stuffed his bowl piece. They kicked off their shoes and sat atop Alex's big coat. They settled down to practice that talking thing again, that kissing thing too.

"Smells like the apartment," Alex said. "My coat."

"Yeah, it actually does. Like hangovers and stale smoke."

"Rez? I have a confession. I took something else."

"Took what?"

"Well . . . I remembered the day we all went back to your apartment, the day Clive and Lynk were arguing over the destroyed photos. I saw the camera there, still recording. I figured out that it recorded the whole incident."

Alex pulled out the full spectrum camcorder.

"Oh, fuck Alex. Clive will go crazy when he sees this is missing. It's one of his favorites. It captures all light that can't be seen by the human eye; it's how they see ghosts."

"Rez . . . don't you want to see what's on the tape?"

"Yeah, I do actually."

Rez turned on the tiny LED screen. It blinked madly, the blue pause screen bright as sunrise, curtains waiting to open up to a show.

"Press play . . ." Alex said nervously.

Rez did, and there was not much to see, not much to focus on: just black, the absence of light. Then it was the dark room. A storm of papers were falling everywhere; the shelves were being tipped over by a phantom strength. And there it was, scarecrow form, long black fingers tearing all of Clive's work. Its not-smile was sinister, insidious.

Then Rez heard Clive's throaty voice talking about The Misfits, how he missed the show last Halloween and would make a return this year. *Best night to party is on devil's day!* Alex gripped Rez's hand, closed his eyes when he heard Lynk's heavy whispering voice, frightened about something. It was a Blair Witch moment.

Heavy wet footsteps and a lot of wind . . .

Then there was a strange light, purplish and vivid as something gripped Lynk's hair and threw him in front of the camera. His eyes came into view, deep honey colored, filled with hate and hurt. Clive muttered something uncontrollably, pissed off about the ripped photos, the spilled chemicals. His screaming made Rez's head burst; thick wormy blood rolled out of his ears. And then the camera was knocked to the floor with a hard smack, recording nothing but the ceiling.

Alex squeezed Rez's hand tighter when the black mass swarmed like storm clouds. The screen blurred, but when it cleared Rez heard Lynk shrieking, saw his body being dragged up and across the ceiling. His hand was outstretched, begging for Clive to help him, but he never did.

"Shut it off," Alex said.

"That was fucking nuts."

"I think Lynk was right about the weakness thing. It's using it to get into our heads. Misery loves company."

"Misery loves *music* and company."

"Fuck man, I just wanna keep drinking. I should be four brewskis in by now."

"Kafka once said that one cannot cheat on his loneliness with intoxication, for it is all they have, and when the drugs and alcohol dissipate, it will be all that his peers have as well."

Rez hardly paid attention. "An ironic quote to say the least.

Which means there's only one way around this . . ."

"Around what?"

"Stop loving."

"What?"

"Everything around me always turns to shit anyway. I'm used to it, Alex."

"Nothing's changed!"

"Everything's changed. I'm starting to really like you, but if letting you go stops this thing from killing us, I'll make it happen."

"Out of the question."

"I mean it. I like you so much that I've been having dreams that I break your heart over and over. I'm going to ruin you."

"You're a goddamn drama queen, Rez! Dreams are just that . . . DREAMS!"

"Ugggh! I don't know how you do it."

"Do what?"

"Deal with me. You're incredibly patient. I've never met anyone like you."

"Rez, I'd do anything for you."

"Then keep away." Rez avoided all eye contact. "IT'LL TEAR US APART!"

"Nothing will ever do that!"

Rez threw his head back and laughed.

"What's so funny?"

"Your conviction is astounding."

"You're a grade A asshole."

"I'll smoke to that."

Rez sparked the green flame again and took more smoke into his mouth, pulling Alex close to him and releasing spicy tendrils into Alex's mouth. The shotty reminded him of how they first met, how their lips first touched, how the butterflies in his stomach never seemed to end. Alex dragged his finger across Rez's soft round chin, and then kissed him on the mouth, hard.

A wind picked up, swirling leaves and dust into their faces.

"Be nicer to me," Alex said.

"Lightweight! Time to head back."

"*Shhh*—I hear people!"

Rez tuned everything out around him except for the noises, the dead rustling from unwanted sleep beneath him. Alex was right. There was something to be heard, a huddling of voices, heavy footsteps, drunken footsteps, coming closer, closer, closer.

"Can you see anything? Hear anything?"

Rez only saw the twisted tree limbs above, the violent battle of vines on the buildings. But then shadows were creeping his way. Long ones, short ones, like the dead coming to life beneath their feet to take them to their world with gnarled bony fingers and appetites fit for a king. Rez grabbed Alex, a fright reflex he never knew he had, and he closed his eyes, wishing for all of this to stop. But before Rez could focus on a single coherent thought, his stomach turned and his head began to ache again as his mind automatically latched onto something: Delilah.

And he heard her scream, too.

24

Back in the apartment darkness was thick and invading. The *no remorse* kind of darkness. It was just how Rez remembered it from the loft. When his eyes adjusted he saw Zazo darting above, then felt him land upon his shoulder and lick the lobe of his ear. Rez comforted Zazo, but his attention was soon taken elsewhere.

Weird dragging sounds and heavy footsteps. Lynk? A monster? Someone was huffing and puffing; a form was breaking through the pitch black, something pale and monstrous; something with deep blue eyes and a face made of bones, something familiar. It was Clive, and he was pulling Delilah out of the dark room; her body lay limp in his grip, her legs were fanned out and her head rolled delicately between her shoulders.

Spidery hair touched the floor and her tattoos glinted red. Clive didn't even see Rez or Alex. He continued to drag Delilah, talking into the lens of the T70, lump of coal on a necklace. He lifted Delilah's limp little body like a ragdoll and rolled her onto the couch, shaking her mad-desperately until she woke up looking very confused.

"What the fuck are you doing?" Alex jumped toward Delilah.

Clive stuck out his hand. "It's alright. She'll be fine. She fainted."

"Delilah?"

Her eyes were the clearest blue staring up into the blackness. But at what? What was she seeing? What bloodied nightmare paraded across her vision? When Rez looked up all he saw were the posters. *TOOL* and *A PERFECT CIRCLE* in neon, *SANDMAN* and *KING CRIMSON* covered in the dust. Rez wondered what Robert Fripp would say, how his guttural English accent would sound. Would he play "Discipline," the maddening instrumental that put listeners into a psychedelic craze? Would it put them all into a state of vulnerability?

But then Rez caught Delilah looking at him—as if she'd forgotten who he was, though; like she'd discovered something so big, so huge that it was all she could think about, that it clouded every particle of her brain, her memories. She was a different person, and he didn't know why. Not until Clive spoke.

"Don't touch the light switch. I managed to develop the old film tubes."

No lights because he'd strung up the photos across the back wall by the Salvation Army curtains on small clothesline: living art, a garland of lights missing a few bulbs. Eight-by-ten prints of Delilah's nightmares, of Rez's nascent reality. The murder: premature birth by the wicked hand of their own father. Surely Arkham hadn't calculated this, surely a man would not want to demonize the mother of his unborn children and kill her. But Rez could see the agony in plain black and white, see the reflection of remorse displayed within his mother's bruised eyes, the way her mouth frowned, the way the geyser of blood slicked the floor black.

Arkham had closed the final chapter of his life by capturing the moment in which he'd murdered his girlfriend, then lit the loft on fire to kill the ghosts in his head. There were tons of flames in the pictures, huge and wraith-like. They burned Rez's eyes even though that fire had been long since extinguished.

"Nice afro," Alex said, sitting next to Delilah, rubbing her head.

"Where were you?" She snapped.

"Out in the alley with Rez."

"You stink. You left me!"

"Delilah—"

"Stuff it! Like we don't have anything else in life to do other than fuck around," Delilah's face was grim, and even through the net of dual-colored hair her eyes were huge: twin blue hurricanes ready to destroy land. She was nearly crying.

"Shit, D, relax." Alex offered a hug.

"No, Alex. I bet you haven't even looked at the pictures yet. Did you?"

Rez looked at the photos again. It pained him to be so fucking aware of them, pained Delilah too. Their birth was founded upon nothing, upon misshapen love, madness, insecurity. That's when he saw the blood streaked across her cheek, dried smear of red so wrong against that pale face. It came from her own arm, a crimson river running across Delilah's tattoos.

"You're cutting again!" Alex yelled.

"Fuck off! I'll slice myself to fucking ribbons if I feel like it!"

THE ABSENCE OF LIGHT

The photos had turned her into a monster. Rez didn't recognize this new Delilah beast, this soulless, brass-hearted bitch. But it was all for good reasoning, obviously. How can the realization that one came into the world by treachery and bad blood make them happy? This life, this bane existence of never truly feeling fitting in anywhere, all had meaning now.

Delilah and he had been born to be invisible, entities, phantoms. Rez remembered how natural it felt to run away from all the families that pretended to care about him, how he hung onto to solitude, how becoming it felt to be a drifter, a vagabond; a simple, peaceful soul on the road. He was meant to be a loner, for his own family had abandoned him straight from the sopping red birth canal. He felt so violated, so wronged, but righted all at the same time. It was a mass of feelings that weighed heavily upon his soul. And if *he* couldn't stand to look at this black and white reality before his face, he cringed wondering what was going on through Delilah's jaded head.

He felt eyes all of a sudden upon him, and voices ringing in his ears. It was Delilah. Her stare was locked dead aim on him, burning blue eyes like back at the show. He didn't need to know what she was going to do; she was already screaming inside his head, already broken without even saying a word. Delilah was going to run away like she rightfully deserved.

"The rest of it's rotted," Clive said, staring at a new person: Lynk.

Rez didn't even know he was here. Did they hurt Delilah? But when he saw Hans Rez lightened up. The old man was glued to the back wall, black leather jacket a chameleon effect, his yellow feathery hair a slash of color through the dark. Hans was visibly shaken, taken back by the reality that he'd tried hard to forget. He ran his hand through his hair; Rez heard the jingling of the bottle caps pinned to his shoulders, and the glittering squeal of Electric Orchid through Hans' Skullcandy earphones: grim synthesizers twisting over Delilah's velvet vocals, pinch harmonics smashing against thrashing drums. Nothing seemed to make Hans happier than music. But there was a weariness going round the room: everyone was watching one another with wide eyes, marking one another as if they were the enemy, and the other way around.

"Still, even in death, he had a fucking fantastic eye," Lynk said.

Lynk clipped a few photos free and rushed away to the dark room as Delilah snapped back into reality. She busied herself with a brush and ripped a piece of cloth from the couch, dabbing the excess blood off of her sore arm and rubbing it between her legs.

Blood like birth.

Rez thought about all that had happened in the past few days: the ghost hunt, his lust for Alex, and the ghost on the full spectrum camcorder. He couldn't get the image of Lynk being dragged up the wall out of his head, and how he screamed that something was getting *inside* him. It was like that sick scene from *Wes Craven's New Nightmare* when Freddy played "Skin the Cat" with Julie. He thought about Delilah too, and how Clive had turned from calm to crazy-obsessed over her. Delilah could've cared less, and that seemed to make Clive want her more, in a sick way.

"He never wanted us," Delilah laughed, the most obscenely mocking laugh Rez had ever heard. "What a fucking joke my life is!"

"The darkness feeds on weakness," Lynk blurted as he came back out of the dark room; the flickering Halloween lights from outside made his hair scintillate. "And we're going to call that out now. We're ready."

"We've no other choice. The other batches are rotted. The fresh batches."

All they had to work with were the ones already developed, still drying, and there was no time to string them together to make a portrait of death. Not like Delilah was allowing anyone to touch them anyway.

"One thing we definitely want to know," Alex interjected, "is what happened in that room. We saw Lynk on—"

"I can't remember," Lynk panted.

"Where's the camera, Alex? Show him. *Make* him remember," Rez said.

"YOU TOOK MY FULL SPECTRUM!" Clive yelled.

"I did!" Rez said.

"Bloody . . . nosey camps!"

Alex opened the tiny LED screen and pressed the play button. Nothing happened at first, but then the machine's insides did a clicking and clacking, suddenly dying. On the far side of the room the television turned on with an electric snap and suffused everything with white static, made everyone's face translucent down to the bone. It was like hypnotization.

"It's broken! Just my fucking luck," Rez yelled.

"YOU BASTARDS!" Clive yelled.

"Better buy us a new one," Lynk hissed.

"We didn't—"

Delilah stood and went to the window to light Arkham's cigarettes. Rez knew that she was seeking a strange inner peace; he saw it in the way her face pruned as if in terrible thought. Everything inside his body seemed to burn; his eyes, his heart, his feelings for Alex. He realized that he hated when he was this angry; it made him want to smash babies in the face. But it's who he was, and he needed to journey through this moment alone to accept this fate.

We can do this, Delilah. It will end no other way.

"I'd call them *Decadence in Bliss*, if they were my own," Clive said.

"You'd mock the murder of my own family? Fuck you, Clive."

"Mock it when you break my expensive equipment."

"Kiss my ass," and Rez threw the camera at the wall.

"Break it all you want. It's fried anyway, Rez. I want to redeem myself. Dago's laughing right now as we speak. For more reasons that I want to know."

"Who the fuck cares what Dago thinks?"

"I do."

"But you have this," Rez took out some old photos, dog-eared, going yellow with age, from finger prints. "Alex managed to save these . . ."

Clive's eyes filled with tears.

"I—"

"Save it," and Clive tore the photos to shreds. "If I don't have the proof from 5Pointz, I want nothing. NOTHING!"

"But—"

"I don't give a toss at what you're about to tell me. I know about film—*you* don't."

Rez gave up the conversation. He wasn't about to argue what Clive said. If the photos were no good, then they were no good for a reason.

"Rez, just listen to him," Delilah said from the window.

Clive's grin stretched wide, powerful. "See? Delilah knows I'm right."

Rez stepped away and went in the kitchen to wash his face. He felt as if the smog of the city was caked on his skin. Alex stayed with Delilah, rubbing her shoulders and whispering in her ear. Rez all of a sudden remembered a cut-up from Arkham's book.

Love began to curdle at nine, and it is a fact that wind had brought dreadful havoc.

He couldn't help but to realize that it was beginning to storm outside, and that the time on the stove read nine p.m. Then there came a small wind from behind him.

"You know I love her. Your sister," Clive said from behind him. "But she doesn't feel the same."

"What's Lynk got to say about it?" Rez scoffed.

"Don't be a fucking cunt," and Clive turned Rez around, face aching into his. "I don't give a toss what Lynk thinks anymore. Delilah is for me!"

"Give it up, man."

"But you don't get it," he grabbed Rez's arm, pressing into the razor scars. "I need her! I've never loved anyone like this."

"Ow, that hurts you British fuck face!"

Clive let go. "Sorry mate, but I need to set mi-self straight. I've never met a girl like Delilah. I can't play around anymore. I need to be an English gentleman and settle."

"You're suffocating her."

"I'm protecting her!"

"From what?"

"From hurting herself!"

Rez walked away, annoyed at Clive more than ever. He watched him from the kitchen, then Delilah, then the camera around his neck.

Something was seriously off about Clive.

Daylight faded. Everyone slept heavily, letting the reality of the photos settle into the jell-o of their minds. The room smelled of the last of their weed, their beer, their cheap wine. Delilah saw Alex and Rez asleep, curled into a cute little ball of flesh, chest to backbone, feet entangled in a sweaty knot. They were both so happy. She stayed awake as usual, studying the photos, the unease in her mother's eyes, the way those big white hands came down like lightning and ripped her from the womb.

He never wanted me, she thought. *This city never wanted me.*

"Can we talk, Delilah?" Clive, the emotional wreck.

"Talk about what? How your friend wants to kill me? How he hates me?"

"Fuck, he got to you already? Don't pay any attention to him. He's been doing this for years."

"I ain't scared of that rat-faced numb skull. Never will be."

THE ABSENCE OF LIGHT

"Please come with me to the dark room. For privacy."

He pronounced it *prih-vacy* and Delilah thought that was funny. She accepted his offer and back into the dark room they went. She hadn't realized how dirty it was until now. There was scattered paper and spilled chemicals everywhere. Clive opened the T70's cartridge and placed the new film tubes onto a shelf for developing, all of which seemed to be *moving*. Were her eyes betraying her? Clive shut the door, turned on the safe light and locked eyes with Delilah, staring hungrily. Delilah knew exactly what he wanted. It was something she wasn't going to give up without a fight.

"It's all magic in here. Like a great black Disneyland."

Delilah looked at everything around her, amazed at how much shit Clive stuffed in here without it all coming off as cluttered. Everything had a proper place: extra cameras, film rolls, chemicals lined in alphabetical order on thrift shop shelves. The room held a clear odor of poison, but then she saw that the lone window was nailed shut, painted over in black, going grey.

No ventilation. Great.

Delilah still felt like she was flying. She realized that a small trickle of peyote was now opening its eyes in her system. She could feel the drug crawling through her blood vessels. She touched her lips and rubbed off some of the black lipstick, then reapplied it. Typical for peyote users, sensory organs are on high alert, everything you touch, taste and smell is exponentially registered in the brain.

Clive opened a draw and showed her his stash of 'shrooms, saying that she should take some. Delilah wasn't in the mood for anymore hallucinogenics, but Clive ate two stems down in a quick crunch with no problem. All of a sudden she felt eyes watching her, looked up and saw art magazine cut outs of half-headed people, big hands engulfing faces in black and white; a Misfits poster was peeling off the wall. But it wasn't that at all. Hidden between all the regalia was a perverted Hustler centerfold; a girl with big blue eyes watched Delilah as she eased her own fingers into the spongy pink folds between her thighs.

"Delilah, I want you," Clive said in his sweet accent. "I never wanted anyone in my life like this . . ."

"I can't help you. We're not meant to be."

"But why? We're perfect for each other."

"In your eyes."

"You kissed me . . ."

"It was a *mistake!*"

"Please . . . one more shot. *Please.*"

Begging turned Delilah off more than anything.

"I can't . . . because I'm leaving."

"LEAVING!"

"Will you shut the fuck up? I don't want to wake Rez and Alex."

"Why? WHY? Delilah you can't. YOU CAN'T."

"I can do whatever the fuck I damn well please."

Clive's face got tight as a knot. "Delilah, please!" Clive snatched her arm, pressing against the scars. "Don't go."

Delilah hadn't been in the presence of someone with so much strength and desperation since her "father" smacked her across the face when she called him a cocksucker for throwing out her National Geographic collection.

For crazy girls! She remembered he'd said.

She pulled her arm free and it sent Clive stumbling toward his shelves. The lowest one crashed to the ground, sending a splash of chemicals everywhere. His breathing increased, his mouth became agape. He was pissed off, screaming now. She could smell the rot of the moldy mushrooms on his breath. But she wasn't paying attention anymore.

She was walking away.

It was then Delilah saw his eyes glow like storm clouds, saw his face sharpening into a scarecrow grin; the scratch marks on his neck were beginning to bleed bright red blood. She heard a slow moving sound above her head, like a broom brushing across bare wood, rats running inside pipes. Something was awakening, getting stronger in the dark room. She looked up at the ceiling and saw blinking stars like the whites of eyes as she exited the room. When she looked back at Clive she saw it.

Cloaked figure.

Scarecrow hands.

Bloodshot eyes.

Clive's eyes.

25

Rez opened his eyes. He could smell Alex's hair, could smell the fresh midnight air. *How long have I slept?* His mind was eerily at ease. Clutched in his grip was not the usual paperback book, but Alex's silver orchid necklace. It amazed Rez that a piece of Alex could level him so. He hadn't dreamed, hadn't thought about the pen and paper, the torture of possessing no creative process. If not for writing, what could he call his own? What was his creative outlet? What could a person depend on when life brought you down, when death took away the ones you loved, when sadness came out of the deep dark closet to claim you?

Nothing without writing. But maybe Alex.

Alex stretched and yawned. His tongue was bright pink; his teeth were yellowed from the clove smoke. Rez kissed him, so sweet in the morning, so warm. Alex's small skinny feet rubbed against Rez's legs, and for a moment Rez did the same thing back. This boy, this beautiful boy was his, this sack of bones covered in skin and hair and tattoos was all for Rez. Nothing could stop the need to hold Alex tight, to feel his skin brush up against his own, to smell that sweet spicy breath, to feel those lips like orchid petals.

He loved him. Could love him forever.

Did he love?

Delilah.

Rez wondered where she was. He couldn't make out the licorice smell of Jäger, or the constant incense that seemed to be part of her womanly scent. No, couldn't smell a thing, couldn't see a thing his morning vision was still so blurry. Alex's hand found his shoulder, brought him back down to sleep, covering them both with his big jacket. But Rez couldn't sleep anymore. He was focused on trying to figure out how he'd knocked out so fast last night. What happened to his insomnia, his love for watching the moon fade to glistening sunlight? Then he remembered: the photos. Anything was better than looking at those damn bloody photos.

"You alright, Rez? You're stiff as a board," Alex said.

"*Shh . . .* I hear something."

"Voices?"

Alex sat up; he heard the sounds too. Someone was crying. Big, loud gulps, so much so they were almost choking. Rez saw Lynk's EVP recorder on the couch, a couch that had just cradled a body. His headphones were there too, and when Rez put one to his ear he heard the snap, crackle and pop of footsteps crossing dried foliage. Rez figured that's how ghost hunters came to hear ethereal conversations, listening to tapes over and over. Rez wondered if he was hearing something on that tape, but when he focused it wasn't that at all. It was something in the dark room.

Hans was passed out with a PBR in hand listening to music on his headphones. Nothing was going to wake him at the moment, not even the sounds of crying. Was it Delilah? Rez remembered how upset she was, how nasty her mood became. Was she cutting herself again? He hated to think she was, to imagine the flesh so bare, so terribly scarred.

Then the sound of familiar voices. *She's no fucking good for you, Clive! I'm glad that she's gone! You can worry about girls when we've done our jobs as ghost hunters!* Alex and Rez ran as if they read one another's mind, both instinctively towards the dark room. Rez loved that about Alex: always out to help someone. They found the dark room door wide open, and that's when Rez caught a faint trace of Delilah's smell, fading. Then he saw the culprit crybaby. Clive: his face uneasy, stretched and crimson, wet with fresh tears. Lynk was above him pointing his finger like a wicked witch.

"Clive, what's the matter?"

"She's gone . . . fucking gone!" He was holding himself, his knees pushed up against his chest.

"I'll handle him, Rez."

"The fuck you won't!"

"SHE WHAT!" Alex yelled at Clive.

"She . . . she kissed me . . ."

"Clive is MY FRIEND!" Lynk yelled in that horrible sounding voice.

"Where did she go, Clive?" Alex asked.

"Shut that pretty face of yours, Alex. You've no business here."

"His business is *my* business, and Clive and Delilah are MY

BUSINESS!" Rez retorted, livid.

But then Clive held up his hand for everyone to stop.

"Left . . . said she was going home . . . couldn't stand the photos."

"Un-fucking-believable. We gotta go after her," Alex gritted his teeth. "She's going to drink herself into a coma; she's going to slice herself to death!"

"Clive, listen to me," Lynk demanded. "She's no good for you! She'll destroy you!"

"No . . . no! She'll love me!"

"She's ruining everything! Ever since she came here things have been getting worse!"

Clive stood. "I'M NOT GOING TO LET YOU TALK ME OUT OF THIS ONE!"

Clive stormed out of the dark room, smashing everything in his path. They all followed.

"What did she say to you last?" Rez asked.

"That she had nothing to live for here and that—"

"SO YOU JUST LET HER GO?"

"She *confided* in me!"

"You imbecile, she doesn't give a flying fuck about you!" Lynk said.

"But . . . she told me all about Violet Hill. I can find her there."

"You don't know shit, you English goon! Only I know where to find my fucking best friend! None of you do."

Alex was fuming. But oddly it was nice to see he had a nasty side, nice to see he knew how to show it. It hurt Rez a little that Alex didn't think he had the brain power to find Delilah back home, but it was a hard truth. The truth hurt a lot these days, if not for him, Delilah the most. Rez knew that he shouldn't have let his hormones get in the way. He couldn't help but to blame his relationship with Alex for why he didn't go to his sister's aid sooner. Lust had blocked him from becoming truly *close* to his own sister, close as twins in the wet womb. She was the only flesh and blood he had! Something had to give, and if it wasn't the fact that he needed to find Delilah, it surely would be him and Alex.

Their demise.

Everyone is doomed to take the big dirt nap.

What does all of this matter?

But this was beside the point. Delilah was gone, probably cold and alone on some seedy bus waiting to take her back to her

Pennsylvania hell. Her *personal* hell. How could Clive just let her go like that? He wasted precious time pouting like a baby rather than going after her. Now she was probably scared, lost in the train tunnels looking for Mole People to come snatch her, or in the streets picking fights with whomever looked at her the wrong way. She was too dangerous even to herself.

Why leave the comforts of this new life? Why so quick to assume that the pictures from the loft were the answers to her existence? It made no sense, but if Rez had learned one important characteristic about his sister, it was that she was feral, spontaneous, and quick to make a decision. She didn't think about any consequences; *living in the now* was her motto, the blame for a girl who cut herself.

Rez thought about his own suicide ghosts, the malleable meat covering bone, flesh that he'd come to forgive since he met Alex, flesh that for once in his life he didn't want to break free of. But what about her? She was too angry to come to such terms. It was easier for Rez to accept the things in life that he could not change. He'd been doing it forever.

He remembered the way her eyes met his back in the apartment. They were clear as daylight; they were on a mission', a mission to run the fuck out of this new nightmare called New York, the nightmare of truth and no redemption. Redemption? What, revenge on a twenty year debt? Remorse for a family that had never been?

"I'm leaving," Alex said.

"I'm not letting you go find my sister alone."

"I can take care of myself."

"Not on my watch."

They all ran out. Lynk remained behind, a mere scarecrow in the dark, forever patient, but growing angrier.

Delilah ran.

Through the streets the night-wind took her. She zipped past train stations and jumped over the wobbling feet of bums laid out all over the pavement. There were no trees here, no spongy ground to lie in and watch the mice roll over her hands playfully, the ants skip up her arm until they bit her armpits, her shoulders. She thought about 5Pointz, all the ghosts of her life, all the linear answers she had sought after now in the palm of her hand like some fragile egg she just couldn't bare to crush.

THE ABSENCE OF LIGHT

Delilah lifted three bottles of Jäger from the closest liquor store she could find, downing the first in a sweeping gulp that set her guts on fire and made her hair feel like wavy tendrils before her eyes. It was a great way to start the journey home, great way to numb the long road ahead. The store clerk mistook her for one of the regular crack heads and demanded she leave, and Delilah couldn't blame him as she caught her reflection in a nearby mirror: ratty, disfigured and dirty, a hopeless glimmer in her eyes, the crooked jaw line of a constant frown, her soft face runny with black tears. It was a girl she once knew, a girl she thought she left back in Violet Hill.

She saw Alphabet City in the distance, fading fast as Violet Hill did all those weeks ago. Treacherous to watch by foot, Clive's building seemed to loom in the back drop of night sky and never quite disappear. But with Zazo on her shoulder, she could do anything. She wanted to all of a sudden blow it up, wanted to see all of those pictures burn like they should have two decades ago. The thought of all her demons exposed and vulnerable for any eyes to see, to violate the privacy of one man's journey into murder, haunted her. Thinking about people's reactions to the truth of her existence made her furious. And so it was time for another gulp of Jäger; Delilah found no issue with finishing off the second bottle . . . that it might actually kill her.

"The truth is a piece of shit," she mumbled.

She was born to bad blood, and so what was the point in staying? *Rez*, she thought. *Stay for Rez.* No. He had Alex now. Should she have fetched him before she left? Sad to say it didn't even cross her mind; she was too sold on the thought of returning to Violet Hill and digging herself a hole to sleep in forever. There was nothing left to discover in New York, nothing left to imagine, nothing left to *hope* for. Home is where the heart is, but her heart was drifting, and her home was hell. Delilah thought about her bedroom, all the posters on the walls. Trent Reznor's eyes glared like fire in her memory; M. Shadows screamed like a tyrant rising from the earth's molten core; Otep's girl goes grrr! At least they could keep her safe. Her bedroom was her womb, the place where she could hide from the world, drink her pain away, *cut* it away.

The butterfly knife burned in her pocket; blade that slashed her own flesh, blade that took care of the thugs who tried to harm her new family. *New family.* Where were they? Did they put the search warrant out for her? Forget it. Delilah looked at her arm instead. This atlas of agony was something they couldn't understand. The scars mocked her; each one had a different meaning.

They were the reminders of each time she'd tried to take her own life, and oh how treacherous her own skin was. Each time she cut slightly deeper, testing the vessel that is the human body, the dermis, the subcutaneous flesh to see how far the blade could reach before she severed a major vein, an artery, how much jelly she could expose without ripping her arm clear out the socket.

Delilah put her hands into her pocket and rubbed the dull edge of the blade, realizing that it had become grittier. She never cared about rust, but it was something Alex always warned her about. The side effects of tetanus didn't scare her; her muscles could contract, her lungs could turn to stone, but as long as she could watch the blood spurt like a rich red fountain, she was alright with it all. Her blood was music and it was how she warmed her cold soul. Delilah remembered Alex telling her that the human body is a puzzle of flesh, and that making the pieces fit was fun and amusing. But she wanted to tear those pieces apart; she wanted to make sure they could never come back.

The Bolt Bus was huge. Just one fucking dollar and she was happily on her way out of the city and welcoming back the coldstone comfort of Pennsylvania. If Alex, Rez, or her band had any sense in the goddamn world, they would leave her be, let her sulk in the pleasures of drink and solitude, of forbidden dream and of questions answered, which had now died hard. She hoped that they were all occupied with their adolescent charms, their pitiful prank wars and liquor stealing games, their make-shift karaoke nights. It was then the bus door closed, the engine hummed and the sickly sweet sensation of Jäger put her mind at ease. The thought of being in a permanent twilight claimed her mind; she rested her brain, fully aware that she was never going to be the same Delilah again.

26

Sheigh, Jimmy, and Billy straggled down strange streets, deciding to be known or not. It was always a battle between stealing all the attention or creating it. Along these parts were buildings that needed renovations badly, darkened by fires past, boarded windows falling apart. People partied illegally, all at the expense of the construction company that was set to demolish and reinvent the space.

They had never smelled air so sulfurous, nor saw places more skewed. They rode random trains all night, trains that were now tagged with Billy's name and poorly sketched orchids across the seats and windows. They learned the paths to myriad towns; they thought metro cards were great, and thanks to the American Express they bought unlimiteds.

They jaunted: Financial District to Inwood, and even Brooklyn; they circled Williamsburg for a matter of ten minutes because at dawn nothing was open; the bars seemed dead, just like its wispy patrons. They were on a mission anyway: to find Delilah and Alex and get to 5Pointz so Billy could draw until his fingers gave out. It was the best way to kill time for free, according to Sheigh.

Billy thought he saw a pair of hot red eyes pressing into him, eyes that Delilah used to say she dreamed about, but he let that go. He used to make fun of Delilah for using her dreams as an excuse to show up late to shows, or to be a plain old bitch. Maybe she wasn't that crazy after all, and he remembered clearly the look on her face the night they won the show: revelation, understanding. Had she talked to a ghost? Had she seen one?

"Ha! did you see that fucker's face chasing us out of the pizza joint?" Billy said.

"I've never done anything so fun in my life. I feel like I can take over the world!" Jimmy yelled.

They were in Chelsea now, chivvying in and out of streets

aimlessly, the night's grand mystery. They ate food out of trucks that tasted alien but left their palates salivating for more; third world spices lingered in the back of their throats like a cocaine drip. Everything in New York was scrumptious; everything was so new they never wanted the feeling to end. On the narrower blocks people gathered like rats around a festooned block of cheese in dive bars and clubs; even the diners were packed. The metal crunch of guitars could be heard, and it made them want to play a show. There was talk about a train track that had been turned into a walking park where you could buy treats and hang out in a city summer beer garden, or walk a dozen blocks and just be free.

"That park's called The High Line," Jimmy said, reading a tourist pamphlet under a street light. "We could go there, or just go to Queens already."

"I feel like drawing," Billy said with a fish face.

"But look, a gallery!" Sheigh yelled.

Cabal: languid neon.

"We might as well check it out. Things don't last long here."

"Well if one thing is for sure, New York is an ever changing beast. It's amazing the speed that things birth and die."

"We should enjoy everything while it lasts, especially these food trucks. So delicious."

It was a scary thought to understand that one moment you could be comfortable, then as quick as a pinched flame your comfort could be pulled out from under you. Change comes in many forms, adapting like a chameleon to its new surroundings. It never literally hurt, but getting used to it did.

"Think we'll ever get in touch with Delilah or Alex again?"

Sheigh stopped. "We have to. We have a record deal awaiting us."

"The five boroughs have eight million people to search through. I'm gunna get sick doing it."

"If you didn't get sick from the drinking water, you're good."

"Actually the water is known here for being some of the cleanest."

"Bullshit. This city is the capital of muck trying too hard to be posh. It doesn't work."

"What do you know?"

"Shut the fuck up. *I know that.*"

Billy laughed. "That's what you think!"

"LOOK!" Sheigh yelled. "Quickie anyone?"

Daylight was beginning to stream, the night's ghost tucking into bed, and with their bellies full they had a new craving: a good bottle of liquid fun. Sheigh noticed it first, twenty-four-hour liquor store, shimmering mirrors and neon as if calling their names. Nothing made their hearts race faster, their adolescent souls scream louder than the rush of stealing.

"You know how it goes, boys!"

The store was too bright inside, smelled of wood and spilled wine. The counter person was half asleep watching a Korean soap opera. Billy clapped his hands and awoke her with a jolt, demanding that she show him where the Zinfandel was. That was the signal for Sheigh to pocket the bottle of Jäger and jet. When they ran out Billy took his permanent marker and drew sloppily across a wall and the woman began to yell. Anything to distract her thoughts from the stolen bottle.

"Our morning has just begun," Sheigh said. "Breakfast anyone?"

Rez didn't know one person with a driver's license, so his search for a quick way out of the city had died before it even started. People here used the pleasures and treasures of mass transit to thrust them from place to place. Living in the city meant you didn't need a fucking car, didn't even need a bike to get you from downtown to Brooklyn, from the Bronx to Queens. Chump change bought you a metro card; an MTA map was all one needed to survive.

"I won't have any of it," Alex said. "We need a *ride*."

"Where are you taking us?" Rez asked.

"It's a surprise."

They were running down Rivington Street. Hole in the wall restaurants and nameless hotels was about all he could see. But this place, as everywhere it seemed, was being cleaned up. The rats and roaches ran from the business owners and boutique workers powerwashing generations of slippery grime, vomit stains and broken glass from the concrete.

"I know the hotel is here somewhere." Alex gritted his teeth.

"What hotel? They're all shit," Clive said, taking photos as usual.

"I have the keys, but don't fucking know where it is!"

Alex said that the band had parked the pickup in the hotel's lonely parking lot. After a few more minutes of chivying through narrow blocks, pulling on his hair and smoking himself silly, Alex finally landed upon it. HOTEL ON RIVINGTON smack in the middle of Ludlow and Essex. Posh inside, but piece of shit outside. Clean up, clean up, everybody everywhere! It loomed against the sky, dodging shreds of pale cloud, trying to touch the never ending stars. The entrance to the garage was on the corner, lazily guarded by a man too busy picking his nose. Rez saw how dark it was inside, how quickly Alex and Clive were swallowed by all that black. Before he followed he looked back up at the hotel, at the stars. *First time I've seen stars in a long time*, Rez thought. *And they look like eyes!*

"Behold . . . the pickup!" Alex said.

Beat up piece of shit, puke yellow in color, sticker-scarred, scratched, dented and evil. *HOLE IN THE SKY!* Sabbath's fallen angel, *THE FRAGILE SLAVE FOETUS*, and some kind of milky rainbow jism shooting Pink Floyd's *Dark Side of the Moon*. *ART SAVES!* bubbled like vomit. The trunk was black going blacker, amps and chords jumbled. The front was a mess of beer cans and cigarette ash. Shit was just everywhere, out of place. Rez nearly fell into a laughing fit.

"Couldn't have come out of anywhere else but white trash Pennsylvania," Rez said.

"Whatever," Alex said. "Love it or leave it."

"What will the band think when they find it missing?"

"My gods, they'll paint the fucking town red!"

They all jumped in, Rez in the middle with his hand in Alex's lap and Clive's arm hanging lazily out the passenger side window, his mouth busy with a cigarette. Alex eased the puttering truck out of the lot and began tormenting the streets with skidding tires and clove smoke. Everyone's adrenaline was racing. The pickup rocked and rolled as hard as the music that blasted from the speakers as they sped away from New York and onto the highways leading them to Pennsylvania. They were all hilly and full of pot holes as if broken scabs.

Familiar bridges passed them, the highways were soaked in wavering lights; florescent knives stabbed Rez's skin. Moonlight dappled the road, Alex's face, his gritted teeth. It made Rez realize how empty his life would be without Alex, that he'd come a long way with him in the short amount of time he'd known him. Why would he want to go back to the life that had done him no good? Why was he so damn afraid of truly committing?

Delilah. It was all about Delilah right now.

"Those photos were spectacular," Clive said. "She doesn't even know it. Doesn't understand it. Maybe I—"

Rez lowered Otep's "Home Grown" to hear Clive.

"What's there to understand? It's in plain black and white," Alex said.

"Well, Alex, you *would* think that. There's more to photography than just staring at a picture and saying how pretty it is. It's an equation. The way the photographer places his subjects, the angle . . . oh never mind. Who am I to even fucking talk at this point."

"Right . . ."

"No, Clive. Tell me," Rez said.

"Each of Arkham's pictures were telling a story, offering another piece to the puzzle of his demise."

"What?"

"You know that book, that little book you hold with all of his terrible poetry inside of it?"

"Yeah."

"They all match up to the photos. *Journeys end in lovers meeting, love began to curdle at nine.* If you looked hard enough, you would've seen a clock that said nine p.m. You were born at nine p.m., at the end of a journey between two supposed lovers."

"I don't get it," Alex said.

"You're a bloody musician and don't get art?"

"It's a different creative process . . . much different."

Rez thought about creative processes. When was his mind going to soften? When was the writer's block going to stop nesting nasty electric in his brain?

"So he did predict his death . . . with those damn cut-ups," Rez said.

"Looks like it, mate. But this isn't about that anymore. This is about getting my girl back."

"Your girl?" Alex giggled. "You've got another thing coming."

"A weird girl I'm in love with."

"LOVE!" Alex slammed on the breaks, sending beer cans and equipment screaming to the front. "Delilah doesn't do *love*, Clive. Don't you understand that about her?"

"What's that supposed to mean? She could be my princess, my babe."

"No, she can't be any of that until she's good and ready."

"I think you're wrong, Alex. So wrong. She showed me her dream world . . . she kissed me!"

"Sounds like you got a bad case of the love-bug."

"We almost . . ."

"Shut the fuck up! WHEN WILL YOU LEARN?"

"I know she wants me . . . she just won't allow herself."

"I think I'd know my best friend better than you. She isn't going to budge. Not for me, not for you, not for anybody . . ."

"Except him," pointing to Rez.

Rez sunk down in his seat and sipped a piss-warm Colt 45. It was literally like drinking piss. He didn't like the argument between his best friend and his lover, especially if the argument was about his twin sister! It was lunacy.

"I'm keeping to myself if you haven't noticed."

"You know I'm talking the truth," Clive said

"When we find her," Alex said, "your worries will be over. She'll prove to you that she doesn't want you. *Not now, or ever.*"

Clive pouted into his hands; his hair fell over his face like a freakish brillo pad. Rez patted Clive's shoulder as Alex sped back onto the road. It took a good minute for Clive to lighten up, and then his focus was not on the conversation anymore. His eyes were drifting across the ceiling of the pickup, at all the cigarette burns, water stains and bad pictures drawn in marker.

Alex blasted Electric Orchid now, a song called "Flesh of Eve." Delilah's voice sounded distorted but still hypnotizing; Alex's keyboards remained haunting. The guitarist mocked the hallucinatory scale of King Crimson's time signatures, his guitar down-tuned to all the levels of Hell like Sabbath.

Does he have one less rib like they taught the kids?

Was it to save you from your sins?

The Flesh of Eve claims the snake . . .

And somehow I'm the mistake

Looking out the foggy windows there wasn't much to see, from what Rez could make out on the night road before them. Everything seemed to billow and metamorphose. New York was gone and the pickup hummed his mind into a relaxed state. A good two hours passed, slow lanky hours spent thinking, spent with all the mind boggling music, the crappy FM rock stations.

Before Rez knew it all he could see were mountains and dying shrub patches. Rez wondered what little scary places were hidden between the mountains, towns not touched by twenty-first century architecture, devoid of land lines and electricity, towns with Indian names but not one Indian in sight. Rather, as Delilah and Alex had already told him, the towns here would be filled with Amish and anthracite; the oak trees would tower over their bodies, drooping limbs would attack a passerby like Dorothy and the living Apple Trees in Oz. The sky even grew blacker here, if that was even possible, like the shapeless things inside the loft. They all had a new respect for the dark . . . now that they knew it was coming after them.

Rez focused his attention outside the window, his dark hair dangling in front of his eyes like a ripped curtain, focused on something. It was huge and black, charnel house of some sort, windows smashed in and no visible door beneath the moonlight, stars like pin holes in a black jacket. Pinwheeling watermills dripped stagnant water, a ghost commanding the abandoned factory to work, and Rez knew Clive would want to get in. It was the least he could do, cheer him up a little. He ordered Alex to stop, lowered the music and listened in for any voices.

"Clive, look."

Clive's face immediately became in tune to the sight.

A possible hunt!

"Hear something?"

"A whole maddened conversation."

Fork in the road, dirt like flour beneath their boots, dark clouds thick as New York City smog. A thousand looming trees and a hundred million dead bushes outlined the perimeter; with each step they crushed dried twigs and dead leaves, the worst ingredients for a cheesy horror flick. The entrance was destroyed by fire, fire like back at 5Pointz; fire that plagued Delilah's dreams, Rez's nightmares. Odor like spoiled meat, how death would smell. Two rooms too dark to see. In the foyer nothing but a huge rotted rug and an assembly line of small dark stones, ashy.

"Anthracite," said Alex.

"It reeks in here," Clive said, taking a photo.

Cobwebs were strung corner to dark corner; mother spider lay in the middle of the silken hex, her sharp black legs spread vile as a clock, her web intricate as a dream catcher. Its hairy abdomen pulsed wickedly, violently; it was a wonder when she was going to strike for her beady eyes were so black they glinted red. Then Rez saw that she was only protecting her dinner, wrapped in tight little cocoons like silver bullets frozen in time.

A crisp wind blew past them filled with voices. Rez turned his head to the spiders in their webs, seeing the flash of eyes, pomegranate bright, and then a body descending like a dragon from its spiraled castle. The face was that of a scarecrow, hidden in the darkness of its overcoat. The black mass was aimed right for Clive's torso but Rez pushed him to the side; the T70 slipped from Clive's hands.

"You numbskull!"

"Sorry, I saw . . ."

Good job, a voice said. *Round two?*

"It's time to go. They know we're here."

Rez led them back out the door, the sound of dripping water and crunching shrubbery so innocent, but overlaid with premonition. He let his mind focus back on the music. If he tried hard enough, Rez could see the lights back at the show, stroboscopic arcs and every color of the evil rainbow exploding like Delilah's tragic lyrics. Her words whirled through the grooves of his brain as if corrosive thought. He missed her. Missed her so bad. Was the Colt 45 that potent? Did it fuck him up that easily? When he opened his eyes he felt as if the walls were closing in around him, as if his father's stare was pressing against his mind from incalculable angles.

But it was over.

"You fell asleep," Alex said.

The guitar howled; a bass line crashed through the speakers as the pickup came to a sudden halt. Alex's grin was dazzling and sharp; his movements were jittery. But it was only because he was opening the door. Finally, they had made it to Violet Hill.

Black and silver land, the moon's light filtering through towering trees like a dirty window pane. The air of Violet Hill crisp and clean, but puzzling as the fork in the gravelly road. The darkness was so grand that the moon's protuberant light and its dozen of asymmetrical faces couldn't wash it away.

Delilah awoke to a familiar smell, a familiar taste. It was Jäger dabbed with blood. She'd been picking at the scabs across her arm, letting the crusted pieces melt over her tongue as she slept. Even in sleep she was prone to hurting herself, prone to letting her nightmares get the best of her. Were they nightmares if they were all true now?

She stepped off the bus and ran, forgetting how barren her town was. She'd had gotten so used to life in New York—the flooding lights, the depthless crowds of people—that she almost forgot what it was like being raised in such a lonely atmosphere. There was simply nothing here—no clouds of smoke, no cars like speeding bullets, no vampire voltage. Violet Hill was such a small space within the map of the earth; it didn't encompass any true land mass, didn't give back to the world and feed selfishly off its monetary bosom. Not like New York, anyhow.

Delilah was now on Steeraway Street. She bolted past every storefront, every house and every trailer raised high upon cinder blocks. She skimmed over the gravelly roads, rushing through the one bane cemetery that buried every lonely soul here. She thought to stop for a minute, to admire the pale jutting stones, the endless flowers that grew wild and free. But ahead she saw her favorite field of sunflowers all dried and dead in this October frost, tall brown stems, heavy circular heads wishing for the sun to liven them up.

The boulevard was dead, lit by weak street lamps and a few lonely bars. The only sound was the electric sizzle of neon lights. Her body hummed like a throng of insect wings, like Zazo's wings. Zazo was high above her on his leash, a happy predator taking to the inky sky. Delilah held his leash so tight her nails left little red crescent moons when she released them.

Her side of town, the poorest section, Worship Street. Beer cans and old bags of chips lay open and vulnerable. Beer and snacks were popular among the townies here, the goonies, the crowds who thought bisexuality was a trend, who thought hanging out and smoking Marlboros while talking cheap beatnik poetry was exotic. At the end of Worship Street was another fork in the road, one leading to a mud marsh, the other to her goddamn Victorian excuse for living quarters. There she saw the oak tree with the twisted branch. Right where she left it. It was nice to come home, to see things unchanged, safe—safe from New York, safe from hell.

Delilah climbed up the branch, then onto the lattice that led to the balcony before her bedroom. She thought for a moment the lattice would give out. It had been rotting since she could remember and her father refused to paint it, refused to even put lacquer on the damn thing to help repel moisture. Every time it rained or snowed, the thing would get a little weaker; the riotous vines would snap another row, claiming a new spot as they grew against the house. Processed wood can only last for so long before it rots and cracks, then ultimately falls apart.

By the time she made it to the top she was out of breath, severely hung over and dehydrated as fuck. Her mouth was coated with anthracite dust; her boots were filthy with mud and grass stains, her fishnet leggings were ripped from ankle to knee. She let herself rest against the balcony, imagining how life would be if she'd never won that New York contract, if she was never a musician, a sister, a daughter to a psychotic family. It would be peace in the dark.

Her eyes felt so heavy, so betraying. They wanted sleep, but Delilah wasn't going to give in. It was too cold to sleep anyway; she'd freeze out here by the time the sun came up. So Delilah took a moment to herself, gazing at the vista before her house, behind her, all around her. There were the distant hectic lights of Steeraway Street, the dark rockets that blasted from one side of the field to the next, tiny nameless animals running from the huge owls circling the sky.

Everything here was just how she remembered it. She knew how the shops in town would smell, how the food would taste. There would be the piney scent of newly fashioned wood tables; coriander potpourri would swell inside the Amish shops where nothing but weird homemade treasures were to be found. There would be pierogi and fresh carrot juice, hot mashed potatoes laced with garlic and parsley. If she thought about it hard enough, Violet Hill had a bit of culture of its own, but a culture she damn sure knew paled next to New York.

But this was home now, again, after forever. Her true home. It was safe here. So fucking safe she could vomit. No more surprises, no more long lost past, no more mystery. Nothing! It saddened her to think how much she'd come to love Rez, her only flesh and blood, and how much she'd come to love Hans as the uncle she never had. But it was an ash of memory.

Ashes.

Arkham's cigarettes were still in her pocket. She flared one to life and let the carcinogens do their duty and kill her lungs, let the smoke swirl out her nose. It helped with the hangover, helped with the disgusting taste in the back of her throat. Of all the smokes in the world, Delilah loathed these, but *had* to smoke them. They possessed a certain stinging quality; a potent poison had to have been laced within the filter. And when she really broke it down, Arkham's cigarettes were stale as all hell, but being that they were *his*, she'd make them taste good and last forever.

Delilah wondered if this bad brand would ruin her voice, take away the one thing that connected to her a hundred lost souls in this town. Her voice was the town's temple, that diamond-like growl, that scrim of flesh in her throat melodious as much as it was tainted. She was the savior, a goddess among insects, among the ones who had no place to hide amongst the sheep. But she didn't revere them back. They were all bland in her eyes, didn't understand the true rage she tried to force down their throats with her music. They never helped her cope with her pain, the cutting, the unanswered past.

Don't you do it; you're not even you yet.

If you do this you'll never have the chance to try again . . .

Her arm was a blaze of crisscrossed red and black. The moon made her tattoos glow faintly grey, shot through with wet gore. She'd allowed her scabs to dry, but tonight she'd open them again, open them within her room. Delilah turned around and went to open her window, finding it locked, barred by that same piece of wood she used to close her parents off from her room for privacy.

Locked out by your own findings! Idiot!

Locked out for good reason. Delilah had to blink twice before she realized that her room was not the one she remembered. There were no halos of green rope light tacked to the ceiling, no candles with their pin point flames to keep her warm. The lace on her bed was gone, her desk was cleaned and waxed, the graffiti scrubbed away and the stickers were in the process of being pulled off. Her stereo was missing, and her books, *The Scream, Books of Blood, Strange Angels, The Witching Hour, Cities of the Red Night,* all stuffed claustrophobically into boxes. Everything else was piled high against the wall, the wall that used to be covered in magazine cut outs, posters, ticket stubs and magic marker graffiti. The memories were all gone. No more music, no more Trent Reznor, Sabbath, Otep, Glassjaw—all gone!

You are impossible, Delilah: the Princess of Denial.

She'd come back for this? An empty memory? Delilah realized that she'd worked herself into a cold sweat, and that her hand ringed condensation upon the window. Her parents had packed all her shit, never wanting to see her return. They got their wish. Or was it Delilah's wish? It hurt, hurt so fucking bad . . . but if she thrust the butterfly blade in it wouldn't hurt so much.

The first scab she found was still moist, long and moist and *rich.* She clicked the blade open and let it *sail across the stream* as they say, because *down the river* meant sudden death, *down the river* meant puncturing spongy vein and muscular artery, meant bleeding painfully and miserably. She didn't want to go in that fashion. She just didn't want it to hurt anymore.

Where was there left to go now? She couldn't return to New York, couldn't face Rez again, his sapphire eyes, his harsh opinions. She couldn't face Alex and his wits, or his fair opinion. There was only one thing left to do: drink. Liquor thins the blood; maybe her arm would drip scarlet rivulets for all eternity.

The last Jäger bottle was safe between her legs. Delilah threw Arkham's cigarette down and began to guzzle the brown liquor. The Jäger felt fucking great singing her insides. One thing she realized about Jägermeister was that not only did it have a great licorice aftertaste, it left a lingering blaze, a blaze that surely could start a fire inside.

Fire.

She smelled the faint burning of leaves, like summer camp, like those smelly garbage cans that burn all night in the streets of New York to keep the bums warm. But it wasn't that at all. Delilah had thrown the cigarette down without putting it out, and she'd missed the garbage can; instead the cigarette fell into a desiccated pile of leaves.

Arkham's ghosts!

The blaze took to the sky, fascinating to watch while she was getting a nice buzz on again. But soon her fun turned glum as she heard the screams, the weary footsteps. It was her parents! They came stumbling outside. Mother in her pink night gown; father in his wife beater and stupid tighty-whities. For a second Delilah missed them, for a second Delilah was going to call for their attention, but instead she hid herself in a dark corner drying the blood with her black shirt.

"Put it out!" Mother yelled, a child's fit.

As they battled the blaze Delilah picked herself up and shot down the lattice. She bolted for the night, not looking back, afraid that four eyes would notice the flash of pink and black dreads, the moonpale glow of skin, the scabbed arm and knees. Before she cleared her property Delilah caught a reflection zipping past her peripheral vision, and it made her legs stop short. Something had indeed found her when all she wanted was to be invisible.

A flare. Red eyes.

THE ABSENCE OF LIGHT

Brake lights.
Jimmy's truck.

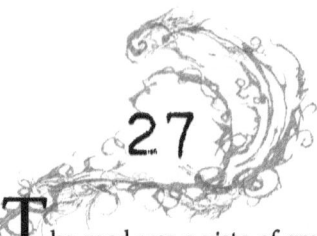

27

The road was a vista of gravel; the trees were charcoal towers. Everything was soft beneath his feet, a place where the dead could rise and taste fresh air again. Rez thought about taking a dirt nap so he wouldn't have to worry about the burden of love, or Delilah the runaway.

He could see Violet Hill clear as daylight. Past the ratty town limits sign there were smudges of lights and a low growling sound from the one huge building with dozens of xanthous colored windows. The Gheligg factory: Violet Hill's anthracite producer and its biggest employer. *Delilah's father works there*, Rez knew. *So this is what a small town feels like?*

Like the dark here now, in this empty space, writhing and waiting to become a monster since there was no light to challenge it. Just like the blaze in Arkham's loft, it would eat them all. How Alex preferred this sepulcher of a town over New York City was beyond him, but he was damn sure going to find out.

"She might've gone to her house. Maybe my house," Alex said. "I don't even know where to begin."

"What would she do at your house?" Clive asked.

"Dance with my orchids of course. She loves them."

"Orchids? You got a green thumb?"

"Alex has a very handy green thumb. Growing orchids in Pennsylvania takes precision. This environment would kill them instantly otherwise."

The pickup skimmed the roads, spitting out smoke, the gas tank getting low. The smell of pine and tree sap was strong. Rez remembered the smell of all those fresh cut trees in the city during the Christmas season, slowly dying to satisfy a hollow holiday. But here in Violet Hill they were all over the place, alive and safe and strong in the ground, not strung up for sale, bleeding sticky sap all over the place. Then they pulled up to Alex's house: drearily plain house that seemed to be standing on stilts.

"So tall," Rez said.

"My grandparent's."

They all got out of the car and followed Alex's lead. The second Rez put his feet on the ground he felt immediately out of place. *This town doesn't want me here*, he thought. Alex fumbled through his keys and realized that he'd left the set for his house back at Clive's apartment. There was no way they were going to get inside, not unless they broke a window or rang the bell. Given the hour, Alex was not about to wake his grandparents.

Looking around, Rez felt like he could hear every single animal trekking themselves to some deep hole, their teeth crunching bark, every breath of the trees and swish of blood forced through throbbing arteries. Running away or trying to stand against the newcomers? If he stood here long enough Rez was sure that the blackness from the loft would find him, the fire too. *All darkness is related*, he thought. And this darkness would spray over him like aerosol paint, would grow as huge as a planet until there was no life or sun left, or air to even hope to survive on. Rez thought maybe his finely tuned sense for the dark was related to magic, but then gave it up, laughing on the inside.

"There's a window by the basement. Delilah would've gone through there."

The green crunch of pine needles brought them to one tiny window. Rez thought about that movie *Haute Tension*, how that poor French farm family was brutally murdered by a whacky truck driver, but which actually turned out to be through the vision of a psychotic lesbian in love with her best friend. Could Lynk do something as sinister as that? But Alex's tricky hands caught his attention; he was working a small bar into the window and it clicked open easily. Alex was first to go in. Clive waited outside to smoke himself silly, the trashy photographer on a mean mission.

A cold grey glow of moon spilled upon the basement floor, sailed up the cinderblock walls. A giant wrinkled sheet darkened a diaphanous tribe of orchids, and they all seemed to be moving, writhing, reaching out with desperation to touch Alex; they rose and fell, twisted left and right. Rez had never seen flowers so beautiful, so rare and unique. These flowers were Alex, they were his children. He remembered what Alex had told him about orchids. *Dangerous and delicate, but only I can make them dance.* Would they dance for him right now?

There was not much else to see in the basement, nothing out of the ordinary. It had a musty smell and the floor was a bit soggy, but it didn't give Rez the sense of urge to run away, not like Alex. He was in a severe rush, rugged footsteps and nervous breathing. But then Rez saw how light truly changed down here, how the powerful moon threw everything it touched into shadow. And then he saw it: the basement closet.

It wasn't her ghost, Alex had said.

Rez could not tell if the door was open or closed, but he took a step further to find out. *Youngling,* a voice said. *You smell sweet.* His breath and voice became tangled in a knot; he wanted to call out to Alex but he was suddenly gone. Rez's mind spun; the salvia he smoked on the car ride was making him hallucinate. He stared the door down, saw it twitch. Strands of brown hair hung from the door knob; an oily eye rolled in its socket from deep within the twisting void. Then the door was teasing itself open, and a small band of smoke twined around his wrists as Rez put his hand on the doorknob to stop it. That's when he heard a small chattering voice, a little girl talking about music, about a grand piano as the door exploded and pushed Rez to the ground.

"REZ!" Alex yelled.

He was disoriented and confused for one moment.

"I felt her . . ."

"Who?"

"The woman in the closet."

Alex held Rez's head in his lap. "I told you not to think about that damn door. You give it attention and it will give it right back."

"But it was amazing."

"Not more amazing than this!"

Alex pointed to an empty wicker cabinet.

"I don't get it."

"Delilah came here. I was right."

"What do you mean?"

"My jar. It's gone."

"Jar?"

"My jar with the special orchid petals in it. It comforts her, brings her back to a place where she can feel safe."

"So what do we do now?"

"Get to the one other place that makes her happy. Follow me."

THE ABSENCE OF LIGHT

They teetered on the town's edge. Suburban neon differed so much from that of the city, but this quaint little boulevard still reminded Rez of 8th Avenue. The sky above Steeraway Street blazed; the smolder of city air was breathed out of their lungs momentously. They hit up local bars and eateries. Everyone knew Alex, Electric Orchid, and so they enjoyed comped food and drinks. They drank Birch Beer and deemed it bitter; they ate Amish potato salad, hog maw stuffed with sausage and huge pieces of shoofly pie that was a bit too sweet for their New York taste buds.

"That's Alex," kids in black whispered.

With their bellies full they traversed the main boulevard. The streets were mostly cobble; grass wilted, vines peeked trough the cracks; dried leaves crunched dead orange songs beneath their feet. A lot of dollar stores and Laundromats, small farmer's markets and bars. This spoke of the people's income, of their withered hope and dreams. A fat woman with a blank face, beady blue eyes and a turkey neck was staring at the stars as she leaned on her old lady cart. She didn't even notice Alex's impassive wave.

"Lots of people know me here. Small town problems."

Clive took a few photos of the Amish forts decorated with elaborate gothic hex's, their huge peaked barns where they vended fresh jam, brown eggs, homemade fire places and pierogi. Down at the end of the road was the Gheligg factory, the slums. Lacuna Lake was where all the tragic stories of tiny living lights came from, the only thing supernatural that Violet Hill would admit. *Like swamp gas or orbs.* Clive took to climbing a weeping willow and let his weight sag the branch down until it hit the water, taking more pictures. The Sideshow Music shop lay adjacent and Rez saw rows of records and rock music figurines, horror comics, collectable magic cards and ancient editions of *Sandman*. The store reminded him of Sounds and St. Mark's Comics. The basement to the shop had a shabby studio. Electric Orchid recorded their first set of singles there.

Worship Street was a dead end. Dilapidated housing and trailers set up on cinder blocks was all that there was to see. Old antennas jutted from rotted roofs; there was no life there. A silver Volkswagen with its windows smashed in housed a sleeping punk, maybe a shriveled old man, but Rez couldn't make it out to be certain. Clive took some shots with the camera. Never a dull moment in a ghost hunter's mind. Still shots of this quaint little town, something to add to his portfolio.

"The Skeleton Grin?" Rez asked.

"It's the home away from home."

Rez almost forgot that he was on the hunt for Delilah. Everything was so fresh and new, he didn't want to remember his endless journey into pain. The Grin was guarded by a very tall man babbling to a few young patrons. A Black Label Society leather vest covered his torso, edgy looking sunglasses his face and black grinders on his feet. Even his natural blond beard was died black; his eyes were so pale they pierced through the glasses. His name was Yosef Klurn, and Alex had said he was the coolest guy around, had opened The Grin for the kids who would have otherwise been running the streets and robbing thrift shops or supermarkets to pass time.

"Yosef!" Alex yelled.

"Hey, piano man! How's New York? How was the show?" Yosef's eyes were wide and curious.

"We won! And I made some new friends along the way."

"Good. Glad to meet you fellas. I'm Yosef, owner of the Grin."

"Has Delilah been by?"

"You mean she ain't glued to your hip?"

"Did she or did she not?"

"Yeah, she came in not too long ago. She wanted to party."

Alex stormed in, followed by Rez. Clive only had one thing on his mind: find Delilah. Apologize, make amends, whatever it may be. *Don't let her get away this time; don't let her say good-bye. Good-bye means god-be-with-you and there is no fucking god.*

The club reminded Clive of all the little dirty holes he used to hang out in south London, the Lower East Side, places where punk was founded, where heavy metal had smashed all of the bones of Blues music into ash, where people who never felt accepted by society could careen and be apart of a distinct family not bonded by blood, but for the love of music, movies, books.

The Grin was that kind of place.

He half expected it to be a shithole, but Yosef had put time and money into it. The PA system was almost too good; the dark glam was perfect; the neon strobes and black lights top notch. Here you could smoke indoors, a nice break from the rules of New York, and their smoke threw spirals into the air like twisted strands of DNA.

Clive saw crazy looking kids with wiry hair and face piercings that took in light as if an electrical current. Depressed kids, metal heads, druggies, kids who drew on their converses, who decorated their bedrooms with scary posters and wrote stories that dealt with evil and the death of society; kids who wore glittering spikes on their necks and pounded makeup over their eyes until they looked like pissed off football players. They all had sharp faces hiding skewed bones.

This was a sea of every rooftop junkie he'd ever partied with, a sea of absent minded individuals who gave up studying for the SATs or the GREs. Their wrists were scarred, already sick of life and its hardships; their faces concealed a familiar inner anger. They reminded him of Delilah: kids with no one to guide them, with no ear that would listen to them. Kids who followed forgotten trends and had no place to fit in.

A couple of bone-faced girls stared at him with impassive, drunken eyes, but when he stared back they went back to their terrible dance of heavy metal. These bastard kids of eighteen or nineteen wouldn't even give him the time of day—so what made him think Delilah would?

Fuck everything.

Where was Delilah? Partying.

Partying.

"Let's just find her," Rez said. "This party bites."

"I know it's not as exquisite as New York, but here it's a little homier."

"As long as we can smoke inside . . . whatever."

Clive thought their conversation was bogus. They should've only been thinking about Delilah. He felt his blood pressure rise, felt his heart clench in his chest, threatening cardiac arrest. Clive had never been this stressed out in his life, not even when all the little campy wankers in his social circle thought him and Lynk were mates. That was enough to piss off *any* macho straight guy. He felt his thoughts reach out and crunch someone's head, a random head. *FIND HER!!!! FIND HER!!!! NOW!!!!*

Clive took a walk around the club. The walls were marked up in homage to music, madness and forever youth. *CRIS GIVES GOOD HEAD/MASTERS OF REALITY* was written in clean ink. Magazine cut outs of dead rockstars were arranged in a funeral fashion; flower petals were pinned to their sweaty hearts. A huge memorial to Dimebag Darrel was in the center; a shaky string of joints was glued by his obnoxiously smiling face. *REVOLUTION IN HIS MIND! 1-866-666-6666.* There was a crowd of girls putting black lipstick marks on the windows just as a band was leaving the stage—*Cradle My Rage* so said their painted banner. They looked straight out of a Pantera video, circa 1994, with their tired denim jeans and ripped muscle shirts, oily hair down to their shoulders.

Alex sat at the far end of the bar, drinking a Rolling Rock, and handed Rez a Natty Ice. Clive saw Rez take a sip and spit the beer out on the floor. Spoiled by the craft beer, he assumed; even though they were drinking free tonight thanks to Yosef, their taste buds yearned for the magic of craft beer. There was nothing like Dog Fish Head, Magic Hat or Weyerbacher. Here in the boonies you were stuck with the piss, and the cheapest version at that. But the little fuckers here didn't know the difference, didn't care. Why should they? There was no reason to leave, no money to push them out or change this town. This was a stagnant place, Clive realized, and he couldn't wait to get the fuck out.

"Why don't you get yourself a drink?" Rez said.

"I don't want this piss."

"Get a Jäger bomb."

Jägermeister. Delilah's favorite.

"It'll rest your mind."

Suddenly the bar flooded with too many pale faces and too many hands flashing their dollar bills for lovely intoxication. Clive waited patiently for some of the crowd to dissipate. He could smell their armpits and their dirty feet, their beer breath and their hairspray of the moment. Soon a few ducked away, sipping wine from plastic cups, giggling and squealing to the music. Clive lit a cigarette and moved a few steps forward, then almost fell over his own feet.

He saw Delilah.

At the bar she was playing with strangely colored orchid petals, the petals that Alex spoke about. Zazo was laying on the countertop, cradled safely by her hand. She was swarmed by her rhapsodic fans; her spidery tattoos shimmered beneath the lights; her face gleamed with the lust of a true drunkard. And that's when Clive saw that one of her forearms was scratched beyond recognition, bandaged and bleeding. Thick lines of red seeped through, pulsing in time with the shattering music. She'd been cutting!

Clive tried to get through, tried to move these kids away but they were like leeches to Delilah's wounds. They were a barricade of flesh and bone. They all screamed for her to perform, pointing at Alex like he was the skeleton key to the ancient lock in her musical brain. But she paid no attention; she didn't want any of this. She was much like Rez in that sense, killing herself and everything around her because of her longing for a true family. It was simply amazing how they both were alike.

Delilah turned for a moment; Clive raised his hand high, saw the sad droop in her eyes, and then she turned right back to the bar. Had she noticed him? Would she notice him? How could she with all these kids around? Why would she? Not unless he did something so drastic, so stupid that it would force these kids to scamper away like roaches from the poisonous stream of bug killer.

Clive knew exactly what it had to be.

The first body he saw was a girl with absinthe hair down to her lace-mounted ass, her mouth busy with a cup of beer. Clive smacked the cup out of her hand and thrust his fist into her face. He saw the blood shoot in the air, felt her teeth meet his knuckles, before he realized that he'd used all of his force and knocked her square to the floor. A couple of kids caught what he'd done and they all came charging with their fists clenched and their pocket knives drawn, ready to kill the stranger in their bar.

He hoped Delilah would stop them.

But the brawl began. It was the moshpit that he could never imagine. Teeth and nails came for him, pulled his hair; fists smashed into his skull. *This is what a skull-fuck feels like?* It all happened so fast, so sudden. But he was fighting back, fighting hard. He bit into the shoulder of a skinny boy who would have otherwise knocked him in the face with a bottle of Rolling Rock. He kneed a fishnet-covered girl in the stomach who was just about to use her sharp nail filer to stab his eye.

Soon they outnumbered him, coming too fast, too synchronized. Then Clive heard the music cut out, heard the voices get louder, heard the girl's screams echo as far as outside. Then there was Rez's desperate, demanding voice, but it all sounded terribly wrong, hollow. There was no sight of him! Clive put his hand to the side of his head and realized he was bleeding badly; all of a sudden remembered being kicked in the side of the head by some goonie, some little devil in dirty converses. Clive was dazed and confused now, but through it all he could only think of Delilah, and the fact that she didn't come to save him.

She stayed at the bar, ignoring the voices and the brawl. But as long as she ignored everything it made Clive feel a little better. That meant she was naturally a secretive person, unable to let herself feel completely comfortable within her own fucked up skin, let alone feel comfortable with a would-be boyfriend. Gods, she made him feel crazy! Then Delilah snaked away from the kids and their wet pink mouths, their big hungry black eyes, and descended upon the front door.

"DELILAH!"

"Don't say her name you creepo!" a girl yelled.

Finally Alex and Rez came to Clive's aide and broke up the brawl. They all listened to Alex without question.

"WHAT THE FUCK IS GOING ON!" Rez yelled.

"I saw her . . . I saw her . . . and she left!"

Rez's face scrunched. "You saw her?"

Gripping Rez's wrists harder, "I swear it . . . and she didn't react . . . she didn't help me."

"Help what?"

"The fight."

"Where did she go now?"

"The front door."

Sweat dripped thick as blood from Clive's temples, smearing down his face. Rez bolted. When he wiped it away and came to his senses he saw that it was really his own blood. Clive didn't feel right; a premonition was in his chest, his heart. Nothing was making sense. For a moment he forgot he was in love with Delilah and the T70; for a moment he was the old Clive again. He almost felt at home, almost could picture himself sitting in the cold English rain at night, not giving a fuck about anything in the world, snapping photos of crumbling buildings, dreaming of making it big in America.

But then the music came on: "Scream" by The Misfits.

Back to insanity.

That's all Clive wanted to do: scream. It would make him feel much better. And when The Misfits was over, the DJ spinned through Deftones, Radiohead, and Tool. The entire crowd went nuts when "Lateralus" came on.

Spiral out, keep going!

With Rez going after Delilah, all he could do was wait. He found

THE ABSENCE OF LIGHT

Alex talking to a couple of musician friends and sat on the floor by his feet, cradling his own head. A few kids spit on him, but he didn't care. The girl who he'd punched sat with a red-stained rag on her face, her eyes speaking of a million curses to be placed upon Clive's soul. But Clive only thought about Delilah, his dead heart worn like shreds on his sleeve. And nobody noticed the blaze brewing in his eyes.

28

Lynk flipped through a book about fucking with spirits. It was an ancient thing covered in flaking leather. *Human skin*, he thought, *of the person who fucked with the wrong ghost*. The ink looked like it had been scrawled with a quill pen. *How to become one with an entity. How to make sure they're really there . . .*

This kind of hocus pocus would not work, Lynk knew. Only the ghost in 5Pointz would lead him to the ultimate truth: that there is more than one reality and that life after death truly exists. No one was going to take that away from Lynk. Not Rez, not Delilah . . . not even Clive. He didn't essentially *need* proof that the afterlife existed—he'd known this his entire life—but to convince others he needed evidence in plain black and white.

Soon his eyes became heavy; a rip tide swirled in his brain like the worst hangover of his life. It made the faintest beam of light painful. There was so much visual stimulation in Hans' apartment, and Lynk angled his mind toward it momentarily. The man seemed to be holding onto every last morbid thread of his youth: industrial posters of brittle skulls and neon guitars glowed beneath black light, markers and instruments piled in all the corners, crushed PBRs were left to rot, stinking of sulfur on the table. Hans was inside his bedroom causing havoc. Lynk heard the black shatter of old records, drawers being emptied, the dry paper crunch of posters being stepped on.

He scanned more pages, lighting a Camel. They were getting better and more descriptive. But then a shrill sound of thunder, the sky suddenly pregnant with nascent lightning. Gone was the candy-streaked sky of twilight to fat black clouds. And that's when music came from Hans' room: Ziggy Stardust. *Making love with his ego, Ziggy sucked up into his mind.* The pitchy voice of Bowie and the grinding girly guitar riff was sheer magical luminescence. It could compliment any night.

THE ABSENCE OF LIGHT

Lynk shut off the lights and pulled a candle close to him, its orange apex lighting the way, listening to the rain patting slowly at the window like a devilish song. His pointed face remained busy and fascinated by the scriptures, eyes sentinel as jewels scanning the book, fingernails painted silver today instead of the usual onyx. Each time he flipped a page the votive flickered and his eyes were pinched with pain.

A ribbon of hair lay over his tired eyes, and when he moved it away he suddenly remembered the moment he had decided to run away from home; far, far away and never return. Thinking about how much he truly hated his parents and their hippie world view filled him with a familiar anger. Hans reminded him of his father somewhat: skinny know-it-all of a man not wanting to grow up. His father was more like the brother he never wanted; his mother was sort of just there, existed to talk about stories about the *All You Need Is Love* era.

Their world view wasn't dark enough for Lynk, wasn't insightful. They were proud of flower power while he was screaming to end the world with all his might. Lynk didn't want that life. When he escaped he decided that he was going to keep a journal of his adventures through Brooklyn, but he hated writing so instead he bought a cheap film camera and began cataloguing life as he knew it, finding a new appreciation for the city, for himself, especially when the orbs showed up. He knew then it was fate to be a photographer, to find life after death. And in a city of over eight million with a sordid, filthy history, life after death is rampant. When he signed himself up for photography classes, Clive was the only one who understood Lynk's work: the vortices, orbs, elementals.

Clive.

He couldn't help but to think about the Dark Room, couldn't stop wondering why Clive left to go find that little bitch Delilah. Were they watching him now, those ghosts? Would they want to taste his insides again in the moment before he collapsed and . . .

Nothing.

Blank. Memories erased from his brain. All of it was overshadowed by a small fire of jealousy growing in his gut. It blocked his thoughts. A hot sour taste rose in Lynk's throat: beer bile. He needed to lie down, to think about how this could have all gotten so fucked up. Clive's lust for Delilah seemed truly limitless now. Had she been there for Clive like he had? Snap his fingers and *POOF*—there Lynk was, awaiting Clive's demands. Gone was the hope that one day Clive would wake up and just say *fuck it, I love you Lynk.* Gone!

Lynk grabbed a handful of his hair and pulled it in time with Bowie's squealing voice, his pain. Deep in the bar's flashy core that night, Lynk remembered the colors running together messily, the liquor swirling in the air. All of a sudden the juke box had played The Misfits and it made Clive get crazy. Soon he was pulling Lynk down the narrow stairway and into the bathroom barely big enough for two people, and Clive was pulling out his flushed white cock, beaded with a pearl droplet of come, and Lynk's mouth was opening . . .

Enough.

Bewitched.

Clive was in love with Delilah and he had to accept that. *Ditched me for pure Pennsylvania pussy. What a fucking tool.* Delilah: princess of the macabre, rock n' roll rebel dressed in the skin and bones of a girl. Clive was like every other guy out there, obsessed with women, their hour glass figure, and their naturally soft skin. He was too scared to take a real chance with someone of the same sex, too prideful to admit he had even let Lynk touch him. *Blowjobs*, Clive had said, *don't make me gay.*

Fine.

One day Lynk would probably have to watch them get married, and Delilah would surely spit out a hundred babies with shadowed eyes and frayed hair. Clive and his Queen of the Rodeo would live in Wonderland and he would become mad as the hatter, bitter as the taste in his mouth, his thoughts. Lynk wanted to vomit. And of course, of all the fucking coincidences in the world, Delilah had to be related to that sniveling rodent Rez. But that didn't mean he had to like Delilah . . . didn't mean he had to be *nice*.

All was bearable before Delilah. But now watching Clive claw for her, listening to the crappy poetry he spit for her, made Lynk sick. Clive liked the chase. And so that was that. Lynk stopped thinking about his life as Ziggy Stardust came to its glittery ending. He was amazed how a person can run through jealousy and turmoil in all three and a half minutes of a song. It felt more like an eternity to revisit those feelings.

Lynk's fingers moved back over the book, skimming over words and sponged up the goods inside the pages. He and Hans had that one thing in common: the trust and respect for knowledge. They had talked about it on the walk over to his apartment. You don't realize how far apart towns are in Manhattan until you walk them because there's always a train to cut your trip at least by half.

He sailed his vision over to Hans' books, the titles sticking out like sore thumbs: genre horror, splatterpunk, tales of UFO's, Magick, and the truth about the 2012 prophecies. And then there were the VHS videos, rows of cassette tapes broken, film draped over piles of other paraphernalia like an endless black tongue tasting the sweets of the old world.

"I got it!" Hans walked up to Lynk's lazy-limbed form on the couch. "You okay, kid?"

"Yeah . . . fine."

Not fine. Not cool. All Lynk wanted was to be normal. But what was normality? Who were the normal people? Those creatures that think everyone should follow the same trend, wear the same clothes and become hypnotized by the same machine? Lynk laughed to himself knowing that nothing in their empty lives lasts forever. What will they do when their money runs out, when the malls close? What will they do when the world stops churning out the technology that keeps them on high doses of *Ignorance is bliss*?

All that shines turns to rust, shrivels into nothingness, then goes dead and cold. Your hands will move through it like dead air, and in that sense, life itself is very much a ghost.

"You got your flask?"

"Yeah. It means a lot to me."

Lynk saw a simple brown leather trimmed flask. He couldn't tell what was so special about it.

"This was the flask that Arkham and I used to drink out of when I snuck liquor out of these cabinets as a kid."

"Now I see the sentimental value," Lynk said with a bowed head.

"You sure you're alright? You seem upset."

"I'll deal with it. Are we going back now?"

"Sure, whatever you want." Hans' eyes darted to the book in Lynk's hands.

"Once upon a time I was searching for something like this, when I was younger and into magick."

"You gunna use it to talk to the dead?"

"Don't make it sound so campy."

"Oh, but it is in a certain, decadent way."

Lynk began to yawn, "Let's get out of here. I'm tired."

"Tired!" Hans' eyes pierced into Lynk's. "There's no rest for the

WICKED! Drinks are in order."

Hans made it his business to move quickly, putting on his boots, packing his cigarettes in his jacket pocket. Lynk couldn't argue free drinks.

"Hurry it up Bela Lugosi!"

Lynk cracked a smile. "Most people call me Nosferatu; you're the first to call me Lugosi."

"I was never a Nosferatu kind of guy, I always preferred Lugosi's Dracula."

"Me too."

They stormed out of the apartment and hailed a cab from the people-smogged streets of Ninth Avenue. Hans told the driver St. Marks and jumped in, staring at the shape shifting buildings like the leaves of autumn as the taxi sped downtown.

"Where're we going?"

"You'll see."

Hans fiddled in his pocket and pulled out his zombie-hand hash pipe, flaring his drug store lighter to life; all the dark resin in the center glowed orange. Lynk took a hit and the smoke made his head stagger back—biting his throat—but it flowed into his lungs smooth as satin, erasing the headache instantly. He held in the smoke as long as he could stand it, releasing it slowly. The cab driver didn't even bob his head in protest; he was smoking a Hookah.

When the taxi screeched to a halt St. Marks splashed darkly before them. People were running away from the rapid rain. It made car lights squiggle, made the neon signs of small businesses glow vapid as if a warning. Lynk loved it, reminded him of the Brooklyn dive bars where he used to relax his mind. Hans paid the cab driver and began to get antsy as his eyes fixed upon the sign painted across the black wood.

5 SHOTS OF ANYTHING FOR 10 BUCKS.

Demons in Lynk's mind opened their fiery eyes; claws clutched his heart, stealing his breath. OF ALL PLACES!

"Why did we have to come *here?*" stopping in the rain, pissed off, wet as a rat.

The bane of Lynk's existence.

"It's where we first met! Lots of memories, lots of things to discuss. FREE DRINKS! Get in, get in!"

"Memories are the key to insanity," Lynk said, slipping behind the velvet rope. "We could've gone anywhere. Mars Bar, Knitting

Factory, Lucy's . . . CBGB's."

"Couple of years late there, kiddo. Forgot that CBGB's been gone? And Mars Bar will be gone in no time. This place is a ghost of sorts already."

"Don't change the subject." Lynk sniffed the air as if this place had been waiting for his grand return. "This is the place that Clive . . . that I . . ."

"I don't want to argue," and Hans put the special flask to his lips and sipped, his eyes widening. "Wow that's sour! Now come on!"

They straggled in damp and cold, former rock dive shimmering with banquette leather, riotous with a vagrant mix of patrons: Yuppies with their money flying from their sticky fingers, aged crowds of the beat generation and Blitzkrieg Bop trends. They were all here for the same liquor deal to burn in their bellies, but all on opposite shores of opinion and status.

"Been working on and off here for about two decades. I used to hang here with Arkham and I still like to think of it as our place, no matter how much it's changed."

"Why do you want to torture yourself even more?"

"What am I supposed to do, sit back and cry? I've done all that. Things will pan out."

Then Lynk let his mind slip into the past momentarily, remembering music, riots and slimy hook-ups. "What was this place like before?"

"It was great! The best joint to drink and see a show; a true dive bar that didn't let anyone tell them what to do. Now you can see what happened."

"Like everything else, we must accept this change. We should've known these things don't last forever. Out with the old and in with the new."

"The same can be said for your hatred of this place."

Hans' words wavered, hit a huge nerve in his chest. Lynk's heart froze; his face became hot.

"How the fuck did you know?" and when he let his breath go everything went fire red.

Hans just nodded, slipped behind the bar and set up ten shot glasses. Old Number 7 for himself and Jäger for Lynk. They were at the foot of the bar, able to take in the panoramic view of the place: rows of black benches, tables in the back, a huge LED screen playing nonsense television. Lynk made sure to turn his head away from the stairs leading to the stink-fest bathroom. He'd hold his piss in forever before returning there. But something in him ticked, and it made his mind play tricks on his heart, turned his brain into a machine controlled by nefarious phantoms.

"I used to party all night here," and Hans passed over Lynk's round of shots.

Lynk tried to talk but the words came out like spit. The need to visit the infamous bathroom was beginning to work its way into his bladder, into his weird, jaunty movements. Hans caught on, giving him the look of a let down party-goer as he arranged his shots side by side: bitter amber fire in small glasses. Lynk swilled them without taking a moment to think, wiped the excess across his lycra shirt, then through the belt loops in his pants. He just realized that he wasn't wearing his studded belt; that must have been the reason why his body felt lighter, or was it that the Jäger shots tore his insides up? Then the juke box at the other end of the bar began to play The Misfits. That was it.

"I gotta go to the bathroom."

"It looks like it, kid . . . all jittery and shit."

"Alone! Don't follow me."

Down the intestine tight stairs, graffiti and archaic posters peeling from the black brick walls, and it was only a second before Lynk locked the ratty door behind him. His brain boiled in his skull like gumbo; his eyes became lost within the splay of scrawled messages along the walls, the frilly advertisements for random sex.

Then he realized nothing was how he remembered it.

The bathroom was clean, remodeled for the yuppies. The grit, the evil, the music . . . gone! But why could he still see it all plain as daylight? The small mirror above the sink was still stained opaque with trails of soap scum; the stench was still ungodly, but a little sweet as Lynk registered his recollection: Clive's bones nestling into his, big hands ruffling through his hair, Dresden-blue eyes innocent and loving.

Lynk punched the sink and his rings cracked the porcelain. He caught his reflection in the mirror, mutated into a tired, vacuous face; veil of hair concealing eyes bleeding for night. It was a look that he knew meant harm. And then Lynk wasn't Lynk anymore in the reflection. The stroboscopic light sculpted his face into a new being, something black and vehement: a skin of envy. A shadow lurked over his shoulder with faint red eyes and a sharp face; snaking-cold hands invaded his skin. He couldn't move a muscle; he was waiting for something to claim him: the hands of a lover.

He gripped the lip of the sink as the black scarecrow phallus lolled toward him through the hectic lighting scheme. It glided across his lips in a smelly smear of blood and come. Then it morphed into a dagger and plummeted into his mouth, stabbing his brain and teasing him with the memory of Clive. Lynk felt his thoughts being violated, felt his heart punch through his chest, felt it run up his throat and choke him.

He saw Clive again; he saw Delilah happy as a pig in shit.

He wanted to kill her.

And then a hammering sound.

"It's been a half-hour!" The voice said behind the door.

There came the sound of wood smashing and security all over Lynk's body, pulling him away from this poison and to the safety of fresh air. He could see Hans shaking his head. By the time he got to the top of the stairs, Hans was dragging Lynk out of the bar and into the misted night.

"Time to go, lightweight!"

Hans could never understand the plight of love. It seemed the man was asexual. He never talked about men or women. So Lynk let his mind bathe in memory, let his heart rest knowing that he'd be seeing Clive soon . . . *and* his black princess, Delilah.

Delilah was quick as an arrow, sly as a thief, but Rez caught a glimpse of her before she left the club. He couldn't mistake the pink and black dreads, the bat on her shoulder, and the spicy smell of Jägermeister that lingered off her body. He told Alex to stay behind and keep an eye on Clive. *I gotta handle her myself.* Delilah's obsession and oppression with family and forgotten roots was exponentially larger than his own, a territory that Clive often claimed to be an arid zone of nothingness within Rez's soul. But if his was such a dreary place, then Delilah's must be as infinite and deep as the universe.

"Delilah," Rez said, the cool breathe of this Pennsylvania night licking his cheeks.

She didn't pay attention, too busy looking at the sky, dazed and confused, drunk, rubbing an orchid petal across her smooth flushed cheek, then across her scarred arm. The moonlight ravaged her features, shone upon her sadness, her madness. Rez knew that if he could do one thing, it was to keep his sister calm, for he was part of her angst, her bleeding turmoil, as much as she tricked herself into believing he wasn't. But then Zazo caught onto his voice and flew into Rez's open hand.

"My baby," Delilah said, and then, "you found me. Congratu-fucking-lations."

"Why are you doing this, Delilah?"

"Doing what? Coming back to where it's *safe* from all that chaos?"

"Safe in the boonies? The place you loathe?"

"Yes."

"You're home's New York. You know this."

"Know WHAT? I know NOTHING! He didn't want us! HE RIPPED US FROM THE FUCKING WOMB!"

Delilah's malice hissed out of her mouth like smoke. Rez grabbed her hand to comfort her, his sister, this girl who was his only flesh and blood, and yet he didn't even know who she was anymore. She would not look him in the eye with curious intent and demand him to answer questions and crack jokes, not like she had back in the city the night of Electric Orchid's show. She would not protect her family and friends with her skilled butterfly blade, but most of all, would not allow Rez inside of her heart, or Clive, for she might've ripped it out before coming back here. Delilah was a shell of her former self.

So who was this creature string back at him? A girl of rage, a girl made of bloody fire. She was Arkham's daughter, as he was his son, but Delilah was also someone much different. She was much bigger than this angst, bigger than the ease of giving into self-destruction. She was her own creation, her own malediction, and yet she hadn't the power to face the black and white nightmare that had sent her from this tiny industrial hell into the city that never sleeps.

"Let go!"

Rez almost forgot he was holding her hand, so fragile and cold as if he was holding hands with a chrysalis. But when he blinked he saw that it was only hers, and that he was holding it so tight his nails were digging into her skin creating small half-frowns about to fill with blood. Blood like on her arm, blood that would soon spill if Rez didn't bring Delilah back into reality.

Not that there was much reality to be had. Clive was bat-shit crazy. He wasn't laughing these days, wasn't creating art either. Usually if Clive hit a bad patch, he'd take Rez out and go on a serious hunt in the closest gutted tenement he could find and search its contents until the voices made Rez's head ring, until the darkness actually *posed* for the camera. After there would be drinks and music, the smell of chemical baths and spicy lower east side grass. Tonight Clive took back an infinite number of beers in the club, started a fight and didn't even apologize for it. Something very unlike Clive. Who was Clive these days? Who was Delilah? All that remained was madness everywhere Rez turned.

"I won't go back. I swear I won't. He didn't want me. He didn't want YOU EITHER!"

"Keep your voice down."

"Nobody tells me what to do, Rez. Nobody."

"You wanna talk to Alex? He's inside . . . Clive too."

Delilah spit crazily on the door. "That fucking pansy."

" . . . and he says he's in love with you."

"Good for him. He'll never have me."

"That's what Alex says."

"Alex knows me better than I know myself . . ."

Rez took a careful step closer, didn't want to push her buttons more than he already had. He could not bear the thought of losing his sister, or her hating him, or her killing herself. And then a tiny implosion sounded behind his eyes, dawning the realization that he just might've grown up yet again. In his head he was running away, proud to finally be free with nothing but a notebook in his hand, a godforsaken pen and a six pack of Magic Hat. He was all of a sudden back in Alphabet City shivering that winter night Magda found him and put a moth-eaten coat over his bony shoulders; he was partying the night of 666 and Clive was there, the old Clive, and he was taking pictures again. He was laughing again. Then Rez was in the apartment he didn't pay for, haunted by all the foster families that never loved him.

But this was what it truly was: it was time for Rez to do the caretaking, time for him to lead the pack rather than to lag behind it. Rez would take Delilah into his custody—the duty any sibling should proudly take up—from this moment forth; he would protect her and pledge his allegiance to her more than he already had. He would do the same for Clive, and he would forgive Lynk for all his bitching. This time it was different, this time it was deeper than blood. It was about heart, and Rez had finally discovered through Alex and through his nightmares of losing him, that he *did* have one after all.

The pictures from the Pointz scrambled within his head. He saw his desperate mother slimed in all those regretful gouts of birth-blood, all the bite marks across her arms and legs, the furrows of rage that Arkham had ripped into her. But Rez would not cater to that mentality, would not allow himself or Delilah to be claimed by that meaningless rage. Rez knew then that he was safe, but to convince Delilah was a whole new task.

Standing closer, Rez could smell the pure stench of liquor on her breath now, the dull tobacco smell of old cigarettes. *Arkham's cigarettes.* Her cold sapphire eyes met his again, and somewhere a voice was waking from a century old slumber, a voice stuffed with sarcophagus dust and the remains of an escaped mummy. *Mommy.* Rez took a deep breath and coughed as he imagined inhaling all that dust. But by that time Delilah was already kissing his hand and waving good-bye.

Oh no you fucking don't, he thought.

THE ABSENCE OF LIGHT

They were on the boulevard; Delilah was jetting, but there was nowhere she could run. He heard all of her footsteps through the scary silence, could follow the stench of Jäger no matter how far ahead she got; Jäger lingered in the air, was thicker than it. He gazed upon all the neatly placed shops, the plate glass windows and the badly painted doors. Everything was really old and needed renovations badly. Touch the rotted wood with one finger and the splinters could go so deep you'd need surgery to remove them. He read the signs: *MILLIE'S PIEROGI, AARON'S MOVIE MANIA, JONY'S CRISPY BBQ CHICKEN AND JAMS.*

"I've never seen you this drunk, Delilah. Please stop!"

"I don't even have a place anymore! They took it all down, they cleaned it up!" Delilah stamped her feet.

"Cleaned what up?"

"MY BEDROOM! THEY CLEANED OUT EVERYTHING! IT'S ALL GONE!"

"All the more reason for you to come back to New York!"

"Whatever." Delilah raised her arms high.

"Look at your arms! Cut them up real good this time."

But before Delilah could answer a big voice yelled; biker boots ran their way. A great shadow loomed like the tide in the street, and then Rez saw that it was man that could pass for Zakk Wylde on steroids: Yosef.

"WHAT HAPPENED INSIDE MY BAR!"

Delilah turned. "Have no fucking idea."

"No idea? Those were your stinking New York friends."

"I have no friends!"

Delilah's eyes spun like tornadoes. She was lying, of course. She lit one of Arkham's cigarettes, but before she took her first drag Rez snatched it from her. She was quick on the defense; her fist bashed Rez upside the head, and her teeth bared as if ready to chew him up. Her nails clawed for the damn thing and she shrieked until Yosef stopped her. When Delilah calmed Rez smoked it for himself, curious to taste what Delilah had become so addicted to: stale cancer stick, smoke like diesel fuel, taste of slow suicide in his throat.

"Both of you are acting like children!"

Delilah turned away and hummed an Electric Orchid tune, one Rez hadn't heard before. Her melody was shot through by a fast tempo where Delilah's voice seemed to reach pitch levels that defied the scales. Her body even seemed to glow, orange neon outlining her head, arms, legs; holy shaman waiting to be taken into divinity.

"Not paying attention to me, Delilah? I should've ratted your ass out, girl, when your parents first came to see me. But instead I told them you were abducted by aliens and sprayed them with the hose . . . and *this* is how you treat me and my bar?"

"Yosef, I'm sorry, but . . . shit. I'm not in a good mood."

"I can see. You've been cutting again."

"SO WHAT. My life is dead. LOOK!"

Delilah shoved photos into Yosef's face. Black and white fire claiming the walls of the loft, a vicious pyre doing what it does best: eat. One thing Rez knew about fire was that its life depended on the consumption of everything around it, never stopping until it curls everything around it into ash, finally dying out. Fire is a vampire of sorts, so beautiful yet so dangerous as it draws you in with the knowledge that it could hurt you, but that you'd *like it.*

"Arson," Yosef said.

"How the hell did you know?" Rez asked.

"Did you two think you're the only gifted kind? This place is full of them."

"Can we go somewhere to talk?"

"Anything you want, dear boy. Anything for Delilah's brother."

Yosef's motorcycle was big enough to fit three people, Harley Davidson limited edition that shot down Steeraway Street like a giant roaring bullet in the night. He ignored cars and signs, ignored street lights, nothing in the way but the cold stars like a night game of checkers. It was past midnight and the town was dead; the trees were alive but trying to hide their heartbeats.

The Harley growled on a path to the outskirts, a road flanked by the start of a mountain and overgrown bushes brittle as dried roses. Nobody ever came this far out, so far out so the caves met you with huge black mouths lined with jagged rocky teeth and an evil intention to invite you in, but never let you out; so far out so the insects doubled in size and animosity. The road seemed to go on and on; the trees became sparser and the cornfields huddled together from the cold. Rez spoke of The Pocono Chopper and Delilah cackled a horrendous mocking laugh, but Yosef was happy to know he'd gotten to understand the tales of town, why they were made up and why they lasted for many generations. Story telling was a past time that would not die in Violet Hill.

Then a small dark green barn appeared; a dozen hexes, dream catchers and pentagrams made of twisted metal dangled like puttering light bulbs. Delilah hadn't been here in years, not since she first became friends with Yosef. This place was Yosef's home, a safe haven for pow-wow and black magic, HexCraft. Yosef always had a penchant for this kind of craft, had cured Delilah's fevers many a time, her sore throats and hangovers. She once saw Yosef tease a butterfly from its cocoon, remembered how it ripped from that membranous womb. It was marked beautifully with dark colors that blossomed against all that Pennsylvania sky like a fresh stencil drawing. Delilah had never seen anything so beautiful in her life.

Yosef's love for magic was why he left Pennsylvania Dutch society, after finding that he liked the free life during his Rumspringa (the right of passage) more than the life of the Amish. He wanted fast food, cigarettes and electricity, wanted to read bad books and listen to ungodly music. So the Amish let him go without an issue and deemed him an English Sinner, knowing well that God would punish him. God was the ultimate decision maker, and this he must understand: that once you left the circle you left your fortunes and families inside it.

But all the fortunes Yosef ever wanted already lived inside his head, and they had no price. He never forgot the stories, the myths passed down through language, the magic made with the click of a finger. He'd been using magic years before that, sharpening the skills he learned through of all the Dutch Country myths that he wasn't supposed to know. But people talk and tug the grapevine for juice.

It was forbidden territory to cross when you're Amish because they always tried to kill miracles and replace them with the Lord. But when Yosef left the circle he began to indulge all that he had lost in his youth. He rocked out to Pink Floyd and Janis Joplin, smoked joints and played with fireworks. He lived the life he was born to live. He jarred dandelions in ethanol like Grandpa' did in *Dandelion Wine* to keep himself drunk and happy, but also did this with violets.

"Wait here," Yosef said.

The area was pitch-black; nothing could be heard other than the heavy metal drum of the motorcycle. Yosef jingled around a heavy set of skeleton keys until the lock clicked open with an archaic sound. Delilah couldn't see anything inside the house; everything was fogged, the ratty screen door was filthy.

"Delilah, I need to ask you a question."

"Yeah?"

"About Clive . . . ?"

"After the gallery . . . something's really changed," Rez said with a rising terror in his voice. "He's not . . . right. I'm worried for him."

Delilah stayed quiet, turning her head away, her face catching the dappled moonlight through the trees. Rez just didn't understand the plight of a girl whose religion was spite and reprieve. Perhaps he was a little too naïve to get it.

"I don't know how to explain it, Rez."

"Just try. Just try."

"It's NEVER going to happen. That's all I can say. He'll never have me. I'm only saying this once. I don't love . . . at least not for my own benefit. I protect."

"Does this mean you won't be his girlfriend?"

"Girlfriend?" Delilah laughed mockingly. "I wouldn't touch him to scratch him."

She felt sad for Rez momentously. He was smack dead in the middle of the drama between his best friend and his sister. And there seemed to be no end, seemed to be no other way but to spiral down. But then a bunch of thin points appeared inside of the house, taking on a mischievous glow. Candelabras. Delilah jumped off the motorcycle taking Rez with her, moving to the door, slowly. Their eyes unfolded at the wonderful and peculiar sights inside of Yosef's home.

Hands atop around a glass counter, candlelight vigil, fingers like pale sausage links covered in silver rings and painted black nails. The small barn was cramped, had a faint smell of Djarum Vanilla cloves, spices kept too long in a jar and even a form of decay.

"Hear any nonsense in here?" Delilah asked Rez.

"Not trying to listen."

But Rez saw a manner of many things: aberrant collectibles, potions and plants that no one in Violet Hill wanted to talk about. Glass cabinets bordered the wooden walls, ones that hadn't been opened in a long time which were guarded by a net of pad locks and thin bicycle chains; loads of cryptic papers sat atop them like bad bibles. Glass bottles were lined everywhere. Weird named botany lay within and was labeled with the ghost of scratchy ink. Ancient notebooks, bird bones encased in glass boxes, and jars filled with gummy substances came with arrogant smells that punched you in the face if you sniffed close enough. Then Rez saw Delilah do something he would never do for fear he'd break everything around him. She dipped her finger into an open jar that read *VIOLET ETHANOL* and put it to her tongue, not caring if it was poison, or something that could cause a deadly allergic reaction. This is what made Delilah unique and so inclined to darkness

Goblets were chokingly full of dust; glass rooster ornaments guarded the top of all the cabinets and roses on a huge thorny vine. Books stuffed cover to cover were on every shelf, titles of mystery and hell, hexenmeisters, Aleister Crowley, H.P. Lovecraft, compass rose magic as well as the Sixth and Seventh Books of Moses. Those were Yosef's most revered texts.

Rez lit a candle and perused the inside of a glass cabinet, but found that it was empty. It amazed him to be here, in this small town, in this magical place Alex told him about. Did the Pocono Chopper live here? Would he hear the sound of swiping metal soon? What was Alex doing now? Kissing a twink back at the club?

"Little dusty in here," Rez said. "Ancient."

"I can't care to clean. Too busy living."

Rez suddenly realized that Yosef had the slight touch of a foreigner in his voice.

"Where's your accent from?"

"America."

"No . . . really."

"My English is bruised with Pennsylvania Dutch. It was the language of my birth, but I don't remember it much other than reading."

Then Rez went around again like a kid in a candy shop while Delilah busied herself with candle. She was burning the ends of her hair together. Atop a wood shelf he found an old copy of a book; inscribed on the front cover were the words *Whoever carries this book with him is safe from all his enemies, visible or invisible; and whoever has this book with him cannot die without the holy corpse of Jesus Christ, nor drown in any water, nor burn up in any fire, nor can any unjust sentence be passed upon him. So help me, God.*

Burned up in any fire, Rez thought.

"It's changed a bit since the last time you came, Delilah," Yosef said.

"Very much. But it's still . . . comfortable in here. It'll be good to sleep in being that I don't have a home anymore."

"Sleep in?" Rez interrupted. "You're coming back to New York with me."

"No, I'm sick of dreaming. Sick of the nightmares."

"We all fall down, but it's who picks you up that can change your life," Rez said, hurt.

"I'm done chasing a dead dream . . . done chasing what never existed."

Yosef lifted his one sharp pinky nail and dug into his teeth, throwing away part of sandwich he ate earlier. "Done chasing what you were always meant to know . . . don't you mean that, Delilah?"

"The darkness is my best friend, but she's betrayed me and I don't ever want to ever see her again."

"You are a child of darkness, Delilah, and the light is straight ahead if you look for it. The truth."

"The truth is a piece of shit and the light burns my eyes."

"The truth is what sets you free. The truth is what makes you a better person."

"THE TRUTH TURNS YOU INTO A GHOST," Delilah snapped.

She took a seat by the front glass counter. Jars stuffed with bright yellow balls like jaundiced eyes hung on the ends of long green stems, floating in fermented juice: Dandelion Wine. Another set of jars were labeled CAT'S CRADLE and ROOSTER'S BLOOD, but Rez couldn't dream about Byzantium and Bradbury's Green Town right now. If Rez really thought about it, this place could be a convenience store of magic and mayhem. Dollar store and ShadowScape tarots filled a display cabinet. There was a wretched Queen and delirious King; there were disfigured numbers and many other glum characters displayed. But inside the counter was where the true prizes were. Arcade dinosaurs, cheap ping pong paddles, whistles, neon bracelets and bubble gum galore, but everything was covered in dust.

"We came all this way to bring you back and we won't leave until we do so. We can beat them, Delilah. Beat them good. We know the truth now. They can't hurt us anymore!"

"He speaks eloquently, Delilah."

She had no words. Rez could see that she wanted to run away again, but to where? There was only one choice: back to New York. It was the only way to douse the fire of her nightmares; she would have to walk the burning path to find Arkham and demand that he let her go, and let her brother go too.

"I can see it in your face that you're ready to face it, and I know how you can do it, Delilah," Yosef said.

"Music," they all said together.

A wind picked up; a few candles blew out. Dull smoke danced in the mildewed room. Arkham calling out to them? That's when Rez touched a Ouija board-looking device, a metal structure that seemed to be some kind of typewriter meant for capturing voices, phenomena, and it rang to life scribbling like an earthquake reader on an old piece of paper.

"That's an old heart rate detector; *lie detector*, to be exact."

"Used for what?"

"To make sure people aren't lying!"

"I thought it was a Oujia board."

"Careful. Oujias are the great magnets. They'll come in like ticks and leeches and suck you all dry."

Rez disregarded what Yosef said. He was watching Delilah grip a jar so hard that the glass cracked, bleeding gooey liquid onto the counter that smelled of summer and allergies and stuffed noses.

"His mind was set on fire," Delilah all of a sudden said. "Set on suicide for what he'd done."

"Fire never helps anything, never creates. It only eats, consumes, and never knows when it's satiated until it has curled everything around it into ash. Then it finally dies. Anyone who plays with fire is destined for death."

It all clicked in Delilah's head; Rez could see it in her face. Her tears were Arkham's flame going down her cheek. It was time to go and burn the ghosts away.

"Take us back Yosef. Arkham never wanted me, and now it's my turn to show him that I don't want him anymore."

When they pulled up to The Grin a group of metal heads were brawling. Two girls ripped into one another's faces; their boyfriends slammed heavy fists into torsos and fat necks. Yosef ran to the melee and pulled kids apart; Rez heard the tear and snap of band shirts and cheap costume jewelry. Delilah slipped through the front door and ordered herself two more drinks, then gathered Alex and Clive. Rez rushed to the bathroom, his bladder heavy with beer, his mind burning with the thought of fire.

It reminded Rez of every city stink-fest he thought he would be escaping in a cute little small town: nonsense pink urinal cleaners that smelled worse than piss, walls caked up in mold, sticky with spilled liquor. A girl and two guys were talking loud and slipped into the only sticker-scarred, graffiti tattooed stall. *BUT MYSELF KEEPS SLIPPING AWAY!* and *SHIT ADDS UP AT THE BOTTOM!* was written in intrusive white nail polish.

"We need some excitement in this town," the girl said from the stall.

"Let's kill someone tonight," the boy said back.

"Fuck me first," she begged.

Rez heard the slide of lycra and the construction paper rip of lace over sweaty hips and calves as "And All That Could Have Been" by Nine Inch Nails slithered reverb and clean guitar chords through the thin walls. Rez saw the scribbled poetry of pain shaking on the mirror. The permanent cloy of spray paint in his nose clogged his thoughts.

One boy stayed back, waiting by the urinal, a twinky boy in black jeans and a bright green Glassjaw T-shirt, smiling evilly and licking his fingers. His small chin was jutting back and forth maniacally; Rez knew he was coked up. But the boy's dark eyes marked him from the cracked mirror, the low voltage light skewing his features. Rez realized that he was horny, horny enough to do something stupid, to taste another boy's spit, another boy's salty sweat. *Cheat on Alex.* How many boys had Alex tasted? Rez didn't have enough fingers and toes to count.

Don't you remember that I love you? The dream had said.

Was it all happening now? Was the beating apex muscle in his chest not strong enough to stop the temptation? The sudden realization crashed upon his soul. Love is for the kind of people who can rationalize and compromise with a partner for the sake of trust, companionship, and Rez had neither of those talents: the baubles of lust were everything he imagined them to be, but in his dark and cold world it was the smallest of furnaces.

Then the demon's hands were at his throat, and the mouth was lush and warm as it kissed the back of Rez's neck, nibbling at the hairs there.

Alex?

No.

"You smell great," the twinky boy said.

Rez couldn't move, could only stand still as the lithe beauty in black touched him deeper and deeper. The boy smelled faintly sweaty but sweet, sweet as clove cigarettes and coconut rum.

"I could hold you all night, I could be yours. Kiss me."

The boy turned Rez around and his mouth steamed like an iron as their lips met, tongue invading and squiggling around his teeth and gums. Rez tasted cigarettes and the sour crystal drizzle of cocaine; it was a wrong flavor. But that didn't mean that Rez could resist it. He couldn't convince himself to stop; his dick was too hard, his hormones were spinning out of control. The boy grabbed a handful of Rez's shirt and the silver orchid necklace went straight to the tiled floor; Rez ignored it. These sweaty lips, these sharp hip bones, this messy hair in his grip, all for him.

And then the hoarse yell.

"REZ!"

It was Alex. Rez saw him bend down and pick up the necklace.

"You got your tongue in the wrong fucking mouth."

The boy pulled away from Rez quickly. "Alex Zweig! Where the hell've you been?"

"TOMMY!"

Rez saw Alex's razor lips curl against his quivering teeth, pale green eyes filling with hurt. And he saw the boy's sheer surprise. *Ha-ha, cat got your tongue?* Tommy tried to talk to Alex, tried to touch his face, but Alex wound his fist back and plowed it into Tommy's face. Rez saw his orchid tattoo swell with rage, saw all the veins in Alex's arm bulge. Tommy flew backward into the bathroom stall and the girl and boy inside didn't even care, too focused on their fucking, the girl's long pale legs in the air reminded him of Helena's.

"Piece of shit! You'd do anything to keep me away from you!"

Break my heart . . .

"Alex . . ."

"Don't you know how to appreciate the people who do *good* things for you Rez? I mean, I could care less that you kissed Tommy of all people, but to not take care of something I gave to you . . . that hurts the most."

Then Alex was gone. Rez chased him outside and caught the end of an argument between Clive and Delilah. Clive was in another state of mind, entranced in a new psychotic way, bony shoulders bunched up and cragged. He looked about ready to explode.

Back in the pickup Alex drove like a lunatic, not stopping at any lights, not caring if anything came in the way of the car. He could have passed for mad-insane the way he was lost in his own brain. Rez wondered how many terrible thoughts raced behind the highways of Alex's mind. *You broke my heart into a million pieces.* And maybe he did. So Rez stuck his head out the window to taste the last traces of Pennsylvania air. His hair became a black kite flying in the wind, wind like daggers that smelled of anthracite, the dust of blood, and ghosts.

30

ackson Avenue again, curving into Davis Street. The sinister graffiti writhed against 5Pointz, scintillating across a black vortex sky.

Halloween night.

Hell bound.

"Leave us here," Rez said.

The faces behind the windows were lost and mercifully unhappy. Rez and Alex barely exchanged glances; Delilah ignored Clive's touch, and how he begged her not to go without him, without the proper equipment for the ultimate hunt. But she would not hear him, the sibilant signal for her necessity of solitude.

Next stop: the answers to the rest of her life.

Delilah walked toward the door, clutched Zazo as she stared down the skull and top hat picture. Rez watched his surroundings carefully, more aware and afraid of the dark and fire than ever. Thoughts were drowned out by the guttural roar of the 7 train; the snap of electricity brought all the paintings to life tonight: fighting gnomes attacking with huge barbed wire weapons, Zeus plowing his sharp lightning bolt into the earth and demon armies raising their claws.

"This is my chance to get the ultimate thrill; the answers to life after death, and you want to be alone?" Clive scowled.

"This is our life . . . our story," Rez said.

"She hates me. She bloody hates me, and used me like the tool I am."

"Just fucking go man. It was hard enough getting her to come back."

"Yeah, yeah."

And then they were gone. The last thing Rez saw was the shimmer of Alex's pissed off face and the crazed look sprawled upon Clive's face. Such is life lived in anger. Then Rez noticed that his tattoos were soaked with fear-sweat, gleaming. Delilah took his hand and he saw that she was holding back tears, so much so that if she blinked too hard her kohl concealed eyes would drip black rain.

Dearest Delilah, too tough for her own good.

A metal garage shutter slammed and it brought Rez's mind back to reality. A wire-haired boy riding a silver BMX stared at him with reddish eyes, laughing insidiously as he spit red aerosol. The sudden urge to open up his old scars came to him, to drain away the annoyance of the night, the fright, and Alex. Just like Delilah would have.

Kill the ghosts already inside him.

He was dizzy. Rez felt horrible about what had happened in Violet Hill, but some kind of relinquishing feeling let him know that breaking Alex's heart was the right thing to do; it was why he couldn't stop himself from that gorgeous mouth, that lolling pink tongue beating against his own. Rez had searched his entire life for true love, and family, and he broke it off the moment he found it. If he could survive that, he could survive anything inside the loft, survive Arkham's demon-plagued world.

The room was like a great black maw, ravenous for the two tethered souls entering its digestive tract. Finally alone, just them and the pulsing black, blood to blood. Through the windows the seldom gleam of street light mingled with cool blue moon shadow. Black light slicked the rotted ceiling and red neon hit the complaining floorboards; one long fluorescent bulb split the kitchen in two as if *daddy dearest* was lighting their way back into his final resting place. *He wants us to see*, Rez thought. And all that light blasted upon the Ouija, patient and silent coal-black words smeared across the board. Rez saw the glass planchette resting atop the word NO, and that the iPod was blinking.

"Let's clear this place."

They pushed the dead couch against the door so that no one could get in, but more importantly so no *thing* could escape. Delilah pulled a huge blanket out of her messenger bag and with it came the smell of magic, patchouli, ginger, and dirty old bat. When he sat upon it, Rez felt like he was touching the back of an ancient sphinx, soft as silt atop the Nile.

Zazo sat upon the countertop, observing the room around him.

Scarier than a bird and more evil than an owl, his thin brown wings outstretched like some membranous cocoon, waiting to warn them of anything suspicious. Rez heard the haunting metal ball click of a shaking aerosol can, but then remembered he was in the heart of contemporary graffiti culture.

Delilah lit two swirly green candles that she lifted from Yosef's house with Rez's jet-flame lighter and set them in cloven hoof holders; the flame points were tiny orange daggers. *Flames that Arkham had succumbed too.* She put one candle on the lone windowsill below the pendulum and dream catcher that hung like dead fingers. Tiny symbolic knobs were nailed into the wooden frame; a stretched silver shadow spilled across the floor where *ELECTRIC ORCHID* was wiped into the soot.

Then Delilah scampered to the bedroom, leaving Rez with the sound of nothing, of terminal darkness. It was an unsettling silence twisted with the essence of ash and sadness, of a million souls and drops of blood, and fire. Rez opened and closed Delilah's spiral notebook, wanting to add a touch of his prose inside, but he was blank. Then he flipped through pages of Arkham's cut-up book, skimming his fingers over random passages, too many to look at, too much to decipher. *Just come out already*, he said to himself.

And then he heard them.

The voices toyed with his thoughts, replayed them in his mind: Lynk being dragged up the wall; him and Tommy breaking Alex's little pale heart. And then he saw them crawling like reptiles to avoid the light. Rez fished in his pockets nervously, found two more peyote buttons and ate one in a terrible crunch, saving the other for Delilah. In his head he couldn't help but to hear Darth Vader speak.

You underestimate the power of the Dark Side.

Yeah . . . right.

Delilah came back to the blanket quietly; her lace top was torn nastily, her pale cleavage showing. No wonder Clive loved her. She was beautiful, even more beautiful with the cigarette in her hand—laughing again—bird's smile like Rez's own.

"What's so funny?"

"I found the novels that Arkham used for the cut-ups."

"No way."

Delilah pulled out three tattered paper backs, all covered in dust. *The Shining, At the Mountains of Madness,* and *The Haunting of Hill House.* Rez looked through all the pages, smelling that ancient book smell that pinches your nose.

"Figures. All ghost stories."

"He was sending all the signals. He knew what he was doing. The Shining ends with a great big bang of fire; At The Mountains of Madness is obsession; The Haunting of Hill House is the most classic ghost story."

"I understand that now."

"And Helena . . . her name is in the books too. Helena Addams."

"Like the famed family."

"Well, if you want to get truly technical, they were based on Ray Bradbury's Elliotts."

"Those weird people living in that spectacularly gothic Illinois mansion; never coming out during the day . . ."

Delilah threw her head back and laughed at the top of her lungs, Pennywise the Clown sound

"Gimme a stogee please."

Rez sparked the cigarette to life, Arkham's smoky life swirled into his mouth and throat.

"You know, we're a part of this place now. I feel like it doesn't want me to leave," Delilah said.

"There's no escape from it, there's never been."

"These ashes," Delilah picked up a pile and let it fly from her hands like pollen, "are apart of us, his blood was spilled here, it's our blood. Our sadness, our shame; our yearnings have built this place. But I'm going to knock it down. I can't live this way anymore. I won't let my dreams control me, won't let them drag me down. He never wanted me."

"Delilah!"

"Shut the fuck up when I'm talking! For all I know he never wanted children, which is why he killed her."

The candles flickered madly as Delilah yelled, a dying heart's last gulp of blood, calling out the ghosts.

"Deli—"

"Rez," Delilah took his hand, noticing that his was identical down to the nail polish, "promise that we stick together, and no matter what happens we won't let each other die."

"You didn't have to tell me that," and he gave Delilah the last peyote button.

"Deadly petals with strange power . . ."

"So now . . . how do we begin?"

"Press play on the iPod."

Clive barely got his keys into the lock before he saw the flash of Lynk's hair and caught the smell of cheap beer.

"YOU'RE BACK! WHAT TOOK SO LONG?" Lynk's face was sour. "It's always about her, isn't it Clive?"

" . . . gunna put my foot in your mouth if you don't shut the fuck up," Alex said.

"I'd love to see you try."

"I WON'T WATCH ANYONE FIGHT!" Hans said. "Lynk, you need to rest."

"Fuck off, all of you."

Alex ran to the couch and dug his hands into his pockets. Hans followed him and they fell into deep conversation. Clive felt a little sorry for Alex. After all, Delilah had done him wrong the same way too. He knew then that twins were truly connected beyond a cellular level; it was metaphysical, so much so that they both could ruin the lives of everyone that loved them and be okay with it.

Clive let reality sink in: he was done chasing Delilah. It was time to be his own man. An explosion of bad thoughts teased him like a cankered tongue: the Dark Room, Delilah and losing the ultimate ghost hunt. It was time. Everything burned in his chest. Photos, the cameras, the chasing of ghosts, Delilah's dreamland. He scanned the posters on his walls, heard Electric Orchid's music in his head. And now he would lose it all if he left Delilah and Rez to their haunts within 5Pointz. There was simply no way he was going to let that happen.

"I'm not sitting around any longer, Clive. This is our fucking chance to finally get it . . . to show the world we're the real deal."

The real deal, Clive thought.

"Ghosts. Heh, I kinda' feel like making a homemade ghost tonight," Clive said.

"I know exactly what you mean," Lynk grinned. "She isn't the leader of this pack."

"I know. I know," Clive said.

They were huddled against the window now, faces squished against the glass and their breath making little clouds that obscured the city below. The door was the key to freedom. It felt like life was finally summing up. The equation of love and lust and friendships did not have to be answered. It just had to be let go of. Clive wanted the camera, end of story. He wanted Delilah, end of story.

"It's like that girl from the gallery said. We need to call it back if we're to be successful. We need to be there. This isn't Delilah and Rez's mission anymore; it's ours!" Lynk said.

"Delilah doesn't want me, but I want that ghost. Get the equipment."

Clive's mind ran through his own shadow, a long and hilly road flushed with wasted light, a spiraling song only Delilah could sing. Heaven? Hell? Dark Room? He didn't know. It was all happening within the millisecond flash of a camera. Everything was clear now, clear as pictures slung up like pieces of a fiery map. Delilah would not live in vain. Rez would no longer be Clive's little pup.

The burn. It felt great!

Take me.

"Time to get rid of these two bozos," Lynk said.

"Alex has the keys. Can you drive?"

"I can attempt," and Lynk grabbed the frying pan from the counter as they went over the plan.

Alex was the first target: wrapped up in his trench coat, bag of bones so frail a simple wind could crush him. Lynk connected the pan to Alex's temple in a quick upper cut, then to the back of Hans' head. Both were down for the count. Lynk flew out the door like a bat out of hell, his candy colored hair luscious as blood dried on pale skin. Clive felt his hands burning then, his mind moving in a wrong direction.

Cat chasing the mouse, chasing the cheese.

The couch was an endless ocean into dusty paradise. Hans had drifted off to sleep with his big earphones on; Clive and Lynk were talking in the kitchen beneath murky light, their faces thrown into shadow, their eyes wet with displeasure and bad plans. Alex welcomed the couch with delicious sleep to soothe the ache in his chest.

I came to New York to conquer love and all it did was conquer me. The irony was almost too much to handle; the deceit was enough to rip out the hair that he'd taken the time and patience to grow out. But it was the truth that set Alex over the edge, and it was Rez's own words that haunted him.

THE ABSENCE OF LIGHT

If letting you go stops this thing from killing us, I'll make it happen.

Had he done it? Did Rez contemplate the end of their relationship? If true it was a sick thought, but reality is the sickest entity of all. *I'll ruin you. I'll ruin you. I'll ruin you. I'll ruin you.* The words wouldn't shut the fuck up! Love was his enemy now; Rez had ripped it right from his grip and squashed it cold, had shown him how much it could hurt.

Naïveté was not one of Alex's characteristics, but it was most definitely a characteristic that guided him when it came to love. If Rez so was so quick to let the mysteries of the universe and the horrors of his life guide his thoughts, then Alex was perfectly okay with letting himself go as well.

He hadn't used it in years, but he'd kept his X-ACTO knife with him at all times. The same blade to tag along with Delilah when she used her butterfly knife, his tool to defy his own flesh and blood. Here we go again. Ain't no better time to destroy one's self than on the eve when the heart was the last organ in the body to guide you.

Alex exposed his pale arm and ran the blade carefully along the edge of his wrists. So sharp he didn't feel it, but saw his own skin part, saw the delineation of flesh, the flourish of reds and whites, the sticky smear of blood that's left behind. Would it be the sweetest escape to end all woes, all of life's carnival deceits? To go out in this fashion was quite dreck, but it was his only choice.

But then two shadows grew behind him, two scarecrows with their hands held high and a circular weapon descending upon Alex's head. *Was never meant to take my own life*, he thought. *They're going to do it.* Then the giant saucer crashed into his skull, and Alex went straight to sleep.

Rez hit play and "My Personal Hell" swooped out of the speakers as grand and black as bat's wings. It echoed within the empty space, ran rampant through the rotted holes in the roof and spiraled around them as if made of magic and bone dust. Alex's Juno coursed through Rez like nails down a chalkboard, pernicious keyboards belting a starburst rhythm; Delilah's lyrics were of the elements.

. . . learning to gloam above tragedy . . .

. . . did you even want me?

Music is the key to souls, as souls are the key to the heart and the heart is the key to the mind.

"Haunting," Rez said.

"The Oujia," Delilah pointed.

Rez moved his finger over the burn patterns. It was a message he couldn't decipher, a message that wasn't meant to be known as the planchette scrambled over a dozen letters.

"Shit," Rez said.

"I don't think we're supposed to use it like this. I have a feeling we're not looking for answers. *We are the answers.*"

Delilah was right. Every lump of ash Arkham left behind was right here in Long Island City. When the time was right, Arkham, or whatever happened that night two decades ago, would come through this scintillating dimension.

"Fuck this place," Delilah said.

"Fuck it with a ten foot pole!" Rez said back.

It was then that the dream catcher hit against the window and the piles of ash began to move; their cigarettes turned to orange flames twisting in the still-dark air.

"It's coming," Rez said.

He pulled Delilah close, protecting her. All of a sudden she was pulling his head down; her arms were wrapped around him. She did not want to be protected; she wanted to be the protector. Then a slam above their heads, the sound of glass grinding into dust, sledgehammer rage peppering ash on their shoulders. They were leaning back as if instinct to avoid danger, and that's when Rez tasted charred flesh, burnt wood, and sadness. Then he heard it again, and it wasn't from above, it was at the door! Something was coming in!

"I understand now! FIRE! It's what they need to come."

Delilah threw her cigarette into the blanket and a small flame rose quickly, flames like Arkham had started, flames coming back for his children! She threw all of Arkham's books in the pile and the fire ate them up quickly. Rez, on a brave whim, threw the book with the cut-ups into the small blaze too. It made a small explosion of liquid yellow and orange as if every ghost, every shred of darkness that lived within those pages was coming to life.

Smash again to the door, twigs crushed by truck tires; crystal candy crunched by teeth. Even in this barren town, noises like that could attract attention, and as Delilah stood to investigate the noises the door whipped open. Two bane forms rolled in, two familiar forms darkened by something unimaginable. One was tall and scrawny; the other was a net of black hair streaked with the color of pumpkins, face like the tip of a knife. Their intentions screamed danger as they swarmed, their fists flailing, their hands holding sharp objects.

Delilah instinctively whipped open her butterfly knife but the wave of fire washing over the room was too bright to fight. A rain of razors slashed their faces, across their eyes bleeding tears, across their throats in glimmering scarlet frowns. That's when Rez felt it: peyote trick, 5Pointz trick, the drug working fast, digging their psyches twin graves. His muscles were atrophying, his bones snapping; his soul was lifting from his very skin as was Delilah's. Left only was a deafening silence like the end of days, and melodies enveloping them safe as an embryo as the fiery roundabouts came, crossing the fevered membrane of reality and dream.

Lived it all before, but watch me live to tell . . . that this is My Personal Hell!

The infinitesimal ghosts began their descent.

31

Something wrong.

Rez's soul didn't slide free of his flesh, didn't rise through the still-dark air and into breaking dawn. Instead, he remained in the cornerstone of this x-ray dark world of insanity, a place where Lovecraft's geometry would not sway. This is where it ended, where it was never meant to even exist.

There was the smell of burning, the cold fish reek of dream ghosts, ectoplasms. His senses were pricked with the feeling of being watched, like that feathery breeze teasing the back of your neck and when you turn around nothing is there but the fading footprint of your night stalker.

He saw Delilah asleep, the lone candle throwing flat dark shadows over her curled form, reminding Rez of the pile of ash that was Arkham's last essence. And then Rez remembered how the astral body leaves the physical one behind. But was this dreamland? If he was here, then Delilah's body was *out there* roaming, lost, alone. He'd promised to stick with her no matter what, and what kind of brother breaks that kind of promise?

A BAD ONE!

He had to find her.

Up his knees went, bones like a machine, and his spine arched toward the window without thinking. The dream catcher was gone, and when he touched the place it should have been a dark energy rushed through him. He all of a sudden felt Delilah, her soft skin, saw those sapphire eyes blazing. He heard Electric Orchid's sepulchral echoing music as a spittle of fire stole his attention. Luscious, fresh flame.

But then he saw something else. The dark energy manifested and reality dripped before Rez's eyes like rain. There was a puddle of blood glowing black beneath a cold sun; there was a woman's pale legs slimed in gore and two tiny bean-forms at the tip of her shredded vagina squished and smeared like insects.

Life is over when they die. When you die, a voice said.

Then it all vanished like turning pages in a book. But would it be the book he'd eventually write? *I won't fall for this,* he thought. *I'm going to count to ten and the pain will disappear.*

One ... two ... three ...

It didn't stop.

He burned inside and out; not like the razor scars, but like being held over a large flame. Rez remembered what Lynk had told him: this place was going to test his weaknesses. And when Rez snapped to his senses he finally realized that he wasn't dreaming, that this was all real. FIRE! A wall of brightness grandiose and gaudy. It threw flowers of black smoke around thick as diesel fumes; it took over most of the living room, thrashing against the walls, pushing into the windows.

Encircled by the great inferno was Delilah, and it was looking to steal her soul with crawling, burning fingers like it did Arkham. And then it wasn't just Delilah, but something else. Scarecrow statue, angry, yellow eyes like a wolf. It was Lynk and he was holding a thin pointed weapon as if to stab her. Rez was not about to let that happen.

He bolted for his sister, would jump through the mouth of flame to save her, but was all of a sudden faltered. A blaze of stars corrupted his vision, though he hadn't fallen or hit his head on the floor. He was suddenly winded, and his arms went numb as his entire body was thrown to the far side of the kitchen with a muscular throttle. His temple smacked the edge of the counter and put a good dent in it; his face met the floorboards with an unwilling impact. Rez tasted blood in his mouth. His own salty blood. And that's when a face he knew all too well descended upon his starry vision. It was the mask of a friend, his once best friend, his only brother.

"Bloody bastard," the voice said. "You put lies into her head!"

Delilah's world spun before her eyes, ripped in two, and pulled her headlong into Arkham's nightmare. She saw the dark roads and hills of dreamscapes, a clouded sky of meat and a gelatinous black hole like a bitter birth canal. A faint smell of fire pinched her nose, but she figured everything in Arkham's nightmare was a bit burnt.

There was no sense of time or place. All places and passions and people that made up her life mingled like a batch of insects burrowing into a corpse; a plethora of memories ciphered from her brain and into the treacherous air. The walls and boxed windows stretched and writhed into different shapes; crumbled copies of *Diffusion Magazine* and vintage newspapers turned pages by themselves with a dry clicking sound. The destroyed instruments were spinning together a jangling tune of coat hangers raging across broken strings. A jagged time signature ripping downward spirals into the universe.

Music.

Her body moved weightlessly; liquid bones churned beneath her skin, tadpole limbs. She saw Rez sleeping on the blanket and when she tried to touch him, to bring him into this nightmare, her hand went through his body like electricity collected across a metal surface. Delilah's fingers felt the meaty pulse of his heart, the velvet blob that was his liver, saw all of his queer shaped organs and the huge sausage link that was his intestine. And then she was all of a sudden cupping Rez's mind, precious black gem, cradling it careful as you would a bejeweled Fabergé egg.

Soon, a voice said, just like Rez talked about. *Voices.*

Then she saw the first blink of red eyes in a corner, followed by a skeletal hand. It had been burned by Arkham's fire and it was imploring her to come. The hallway was a cornucopia of neon, candlelight and blackness; it was shrouded in smoke like a rock club. When she arrived at the door a huge black velvet curtain covered it; curtain like in the back room of The Skeleton Grin, curtains from the apartment she had been born in.

She imagined this as the door that leads to Wonderland, Narnia, or The Funhole. Delilah stepped inside wearily; an ominous rainbow of music coiled around her like the living trees from *Evil Dead*. Inside was full of empty liquor bottles, crushed posters and the faint echoes of music. At the bar the taps were burnt tongues vomiting beer; the cups were made of eyes and cameras. A swirl of light and smoke licked the walls in shades of dead crimson flame. Like instinct Delilah was ready to perform, ready to kill her voice and taste the creamy blood in the back of her throat for music. Was there ever any other way to call them back other than her words? Was there any other way to fuse life and art than death?

She saw a shadowed figure, then two.

The woman had long pale legs and jet black hair that fanned

across her soft face and gleaming blue eyes. The man was bony and young looking in his leather jacket and painted black jeans. It was her parents, and they were alive as if they had stepped right out of their own black and white world of destruction. Their arms were outstretched; their faces were oblivious to this reality. That's when Delilah saw that the skeletal hand belonged to her father as he begged her to come to him.

They stood to let Delilah pass, clapping their hands with tears in their eyes. Were they fans? Did they like the music? Was it Electric Orchid that had brought her to them, or them to her? They said no words, shared no secrets, and offered no apologies for the life they had left her with. She was faintly curious to know how they sounded, if they carried the distinct accent of New York, or if she had gotten her talents from mom or dad. But Delilah knew if she crossed that invisible boundary she'd never be able to return to her living body, that she'd be stuck in this dreamworld forever with living the life of abandonment.

DREAM.

As much as she hated them, Delilah was unable to decide. Stay with the parents she never knew, or run the fuck out of dreamland and return to life with Rez, her one and only family member. *Rez*, she thought. *He's out there alone.* It was now the easiest decision in the world to make, especially when she knew Arkham never wanted her in the first place. So she turned away from them, back to the clear fiery light. Behind her the ghosts of her parents succumbed to the flame, burning the last bridge that would ever connect them to her. In an instant they faded into the darkness which they belonged.

Then she was back in the living room and ready to claim her sleeping body. There was a typical Skeleton Grin boy of black on black clothes with tie-dye nails, a metal crossbones necklace and too much gel in his dreadful peacock hair. His lips were a twisted red slash; his eyes were filmy white, and he held up a crumpled piece of paper.

"Won't you sign it since you're famous now?" He asked.

"I'm not famous."

"Oh, but you will be. You'll be a thing of the past in no time. People are always more famous when they're dead."

Delilah snatched the paper away and dipped the ballpoint pen into the open wound on her arm, signing it in blood. A thing of the past? Well blood is forever. It may fade to a dusty orange, it may flake away from cement, but it can never die. It will seep into whatever crevice it can find and survive like a bottom feeder.

That's when she noticed the huge thing looming behind her. That's when she heard the slamming of metal, the breaking of wood. She had no time to react before the boot came shooting down like a flaming comet, catching her in the back of her legs, paralyzing her momentously.

"Bitch," it said.

She all of a sudden felt sunshine bathing her face, teasing her skin with a tan that she never wanted. No, not sunshine. Fire! Pinwheeling flame, bright loops of orange slicking the walls; black smog choked her. It was everywhere. When she found the living room again, Delilah was encircled by fire and it threw too many shadows about the walls. But through it all she saw Clive and Lynk holding cameras and knives.

I have to fight.

"What're you gunna do now, Delilah? The Princess of Denial," Clive said.

Delilah realized her butterfly blade was in the palm of her hand; she was ready to brawl. She flipped it across her wrist and did a simple thumb opening. Before she even had the knife gripped tight in her hand Clive was already wielding his knife toward her. He was controlled by a strange mutated darkness that trailed behind his every step. A different shade of dark, not the absence of light, but more like all colors rolled into one.

His blade rose and she didn't see it cascade down with a silver evil grin until it was too late. She felt the metal crack clear through the side her ribcage; a spatter of blood surged free from her body, bright crimson ribbons like curtains opening to a show, and the force brought her body down hard, back into real time.

There was no more pain.

It was Clive. His hair was a wraithlike jungle before his eyes concealing a face lost in anger and obsession. The kitchen knife he held was gripped so hard a million dribbles of blood stained that white, white skin. He streaked his own blood across his white shirt.

"It's time for me to live again, Rez."

Rez needed a moment to think clearly. "Live for what? You've been living!"

Then Clive kicked Rez square in his stomach as if he was punting a football. Rez felt bile and blood rise in his throat, burning.

"Clive . . ." His voice was singed by the bile, by the choking smoke.

"Oh shut the fuck up. Don't *Clive* me. Just understand what you've done to my life! Understand what she's done!"

Rez relented to stand, but did so anyway. He needed an out. As he got closer to Clive the voices grew louder; his brain became a puddle of nothingness between his ears. He saw the blinking-dark presence floating around Clive in his peripheral view, scarecrow like, controlling Clive as if a puppet made of meat and bone. Rez caught the flash of his father's face, but realized that it was only the shadows of flame. Perhaps this was Arkham's residual haunting, never able to leave the place that last saw him alive.

"She doesn't want me because you told her I was gay!"

"I didn't say—"

"So I'm going to let her die. Soon that fire will eat her up."

"NO!"

Then Rez heard the most hopeless laughter he'd ever heard in his life, straight from the mouth of his former best friend.

"She doesn't want me . . . so why let her tease me any longer?"

"I won't let you," Rez said. "I'll kill you if I have to."

It was the hardest thing Rez had ever said. *Kill my best friend.*

"You're a weak little cunt who couldn't kill a fly!"

Clive darted his passionless eyes across the way, marking Delilah. Rez could see the reflection of the blaze in them, and the reflection of his knife as well.

"Death is where you two will finally find peace. I'll bestow that upon you both."

"Put it down."

"WRONG, old chap," lifting the blade high, drops of blood falling off the side. "I don't listen to you anymore. I don't take care of you anymore."

Clive took a step forward and Rez stepped in his way. Anger did not fit Clive's face. He was never the type. But it didn't matter who or what Clive was anymore; Rez's instincts came alive and he knew he had to protect Delilah, at all costs.

"You know, I thought you'd always come around," Clive snarled. "But you're just too fucking selfish, *Rezzy!*"

"What the hell are you talking about?"

"You think I should just live alone, with you and Lynk my whole life and not find love? ARE YOU MAD?" Clive's eyes were webbed impossibly red, pupils like an oil slick across concrete.

"NO! It's Lynk that's done all of this! LYNK!"

"Shut the fuck up! Wrong, wrong, wrong! Don't lecture me. Don't fucking lecture ME!" Clive bashed his bloodied hand against the countertop. "I'll gut you first, and then her," Clive put his hand into a fist and knocked it on his head, clicking his tongue.

"Fuck you."

"No, fuck you! And since you insulted me, I'll fuck her brains out and force her to love me. After I've had my piece . . . she'll have my permission to die."

And then Clive slid his body across the countertop toward Delilah. But Rez found a strength inside his tiny bones that only a love for a sister could conjure. He grabbed Clive's arm and pulled as hard as he could to stop him. The force of Clive's body smashed them into the crumbling cabinets. But Clive was quick to get back on his feet and sprung one leg forward, landing it straight into Rez's nose. The floorboards splashed with fresh, warm blood. For a moment the world went blank. All he saw was Delilah, hoping that wherever she was—in the bedroom or encircled by flame waiting for Arkham to come out of hiding—she could protect herself, because Rez didn't think he was going to win this battle.

Clive picked Rez up by his shirt and threw him head first into the smokestack of blankets and books. He landed right before the flame could lick his arm and suck him into hell. From this view he could see Delilah still tucked into a fetal position, her body swarmed by Lynk's angle-less shadow. There was nothing he could do to stop him from pressing the needle compass into her neck, her chest. *I'm sorry.*

The fire was at the window now, pushing against the old glass with such a force that it exploded with a roaring sound. Rez was knocked back by a phantasmic push and his head bashed into the rickety floor. That's when he saw that the Ouija board was moving uncontrollably: the skull with wings slithering from side to side and laughing out loud maniacally.

But he was on his feet again, his adrenaline kicking in. Fight or flight . . . FIGHT! But it was what his peripheral vision saw that made him stop. It was a black creature with pink membranous wings: Zazo. Too late. That's when he saw Clive's knee lifting, felt his ribs crack as Clive's leg pistoned into his chest. Rez was all of a sudden on the floor again, looking up at that burning sky. Clive's boot was pounding upon his skull again and again. He heard music, he heard voices. His teeth clattered like piano keys; blood slimed the side of neck, dripping out of his ears. Before Rez's consciousness gave out he saw the wormy thing crawl in through the window, felt it flutter over his body, felt the arms of a woman cover him, felt hair like billowing curtain sucking him into her world of destroyed dreams.

Everything is going to burn. Fire will take care of it, he thought.

Then the world he knew froze in time as Clive's boot rained down oblivion and a blue-bolt of aneurism pain spread in his brain.

He spiraled out.

When Clive was finished with Rez, he spat upon his best friend's face. Huge wad of phlegm blackened by the smoke, and he watched it drip down his cheek, slide over his lips, mixing with blood. He knew that to spit in someone's face was the ultimate insult, and Clive was very much into insults these days.

Then he walked over to sleeping Delilah. *Caught in her little dream world*, he thought. *Only one way to bring the soul back to the body.* His hand was controlled by a demon and he allowed it to bring the knife down, allowed it to plow into Delilah's torso. Her blood was amazingly hot, amazingly beautiful. It slicked her small sharp face, brought about a glitter to her unraveled dreads and a sheen to her lips. Clive kissed those lips, licked the blood away and thought he might do it again, and again, forever until this fire ate them both up. There was nothing to stop them now.

"I imagined it coming out gold or something," Lynk said.

"It's red and delicious."

"Just don't kiss her again. If you do that, she's won, even in death."

Then Lynk scrambled to set up the tripods and faster-speed film cameras. Clive smiled for them all with teeth streaked in Delilah's blood. This was to be a video of ghosts and broken hearts, and art's madness.

"What do we do now?"

"We wait for *them* to come out now. If this is their father's final resting place, you know as well as I do that the damned thing will come back . . . will show its face."

Brightness glissading; a billion suns blazing. Somewhere in some past life, she saw this same kind of dappled light. Light like birth, light like waking up in the morning to murder.

Delilah's eyes bolted open. The world was a filmy rip tide of red and glistening shadows. A dark shape quickly descended upon her, grinning, shaded by long black hair swirled with pumpkin highlights. It was Lynk and he was taking many photos. She saw Clive there too and all the tripods set up with fancy cameras, the EVP recorders begging the air to crackle with phantom conversations, and the full spectrum camera recording all of the spectral lights within this strange reality.

She spurt blood as she coughed, let it slide down her chin. It was almost impossible to breath because of the smoke and the wound in her side, and it wasn't a second before Lynk's long white fingers were on her throat, fingers burning like holy water on a demon.

"She survived!"

"Off her!" another voice: Clive.

"I knew we should've slit her throat."

It was now or never. Kill or be killed. Delilah managed to knock him away with a quick elbow jab to the neck and jetted for the door, but like a dumb girl in a B Horror flick she tripped over the couch and her head met the front door with a meaty clap. Pale eyes descended upon her like owls; gnarled fingers pulled hair out of her roots. She instinctively kicked a leg up, and her Doc connected right to Lynk's face. She heard the crunch of cartilage, the snap of breaking teeth.

"BITCH!"

It screamed in a voice she didn't know, voice of the dark side. A shadow gloamed in the darkness, but when her vision cleared she saw it was Clive, and that his eyes spoke of sadness, redemption, anger. He smelled faintly of something decayed, a kind of grayish death like a mummy. Was he rotting from the inside out?

"DON'T YOU LOVE ME????"

His right fist came out of nowhere and smashed into her temple. A great flash flooded her vision, dripping like stars. Her knees buckled, her legs spread hopelessly. Clive's elbow jammed in her throat and his other hand was moving up her thigh and ripping the fishnet stockings. One finger prodded the spongy pink center between her legs, finger like a knife going through her.

"Sweet as can be," he whispered. "Your little dream world can't help you now, you cunt."

He was too strong to fight off as he spread her legs and pulled her into his crotch which burned like the circle of fire. His tight grey jeans were unraveling; his cock was hard in a flash; the engorged head was pink as a seashell with a lone pearl droplet of come teetering on the edge.

He was going to rape her.

"OFF!" Lynk snapped. "She's playing with your mind again!"

"I just want one more taste before we let her go," and Clive gripped her ankle hard, stretching her leg up to her chest.

"No!"

Clive obeyed Lynk and kicked her in the side. Lynk saved her dignity, and for that she hated him less. But it was still two against one with no place to run. Delilah rolled over to catch her breath and it was then she felt the burn of the butterfly blade call to her. She slipped it out of her boot and made it dance the dance of metal. She raised it high in one scheming silver arc and sailed it across Clive's face. A freshet of blood stung her eyes, wet her lips. He roared and clutched his bastard, bleeding face. Lynk screamed in terror and aided his friend's huge wound, dripping, wet. Delilah ran as fast as she could, mustering up the last of her energy. She circled the loft now, desperate for Rez. But every step she took they were behind her, looming, grunting, and seething, taking pictures with the T70. She tasted Clive's blood and smoke.

" . . . fucking slashed me!" Clive yelled

"You can't hide in here!"

She ducked beneath a broken wall and saw that she was back to square one. It was the pile of ash where Arkham had died, and there she found Rez curled up in a fetal position sucking his thumb, barely awake, barely alive, but when she touched his bruised face his eyes bolted open.

"We have to fight," he said. "They . . . can't be saved."

"We'll die in here, there's too much fire. We don't have a lot of time."

"There's only one thing I can think of," Rez said. "Just follow my lead."

They ran back to the living room. Lynk was missing now, but Clive had his big knife in hand now and the T70 around his neck glowing like a target. His face was awash in beads of crimson that took in all the light of the fire. Rez ran for Clive in front, and Delilah went behind. All three tackled one another, managing to loosen Clive's bloodied grip of the knife. That's when Rez snapped the T70 off its leash.

"Is this what you want?" Rez said.

"NO! You bloody fool— I'll kill you!"

"I'm sorry, Clive . . ."

Rez wound his arm back and threw the camera out the window. For one moment Clive's soul seemed to be innocent again. But he was already after it, possession, obsession. Everything stopped for one moment, all things coalesced; every moment in the making was beginning to take shape. Delilah knew this was the end of it all. She saw his body lift in the air like magic, and then drop quickly to his demise. Three stories down. Head first. It was over.

"We gotta get out of—"

THWAP!

It came out of nowhere, two-by-four swung like a baseball bat, and it bashed Rez upside the head with a loud wet clap. He was down for the count. Delilah wanted to scream, but before she could Lynk came launching out of the darkness. He lifted Clive's big kitchen blade in the air, slashing maniacally, hitting into Delilah's wrists as she blocked him. She brought her leg up and kneed him in the groin, thinking for a second that Lynk didn't have any balls being that he didn't scowl in terror from the force of her knee. Then she slashed Lynk across the cheek with her butterfly blade. And that's when she felt it: the heat of Arkham's fire boiling inside her blood, razor scars pulsing as rapid as a suicide.

"It's *down the river*, not *across the stream* you dumb fuck!" Delilah yelled.

Lynk just stood there and smiled; she could see his teeth stained red through the glistening meat of his cheek.

Delilah felt his eyes bleeding into her.

"The eyes are the window to the soul, and I can see right through yours. Goodbye, Delilah."

"Fuck you."

"Don't you know what goodbye means? God be with You."

"There is no God, you asshole."

Then everything was usurped by a shower of heat and darkness as the fire towered over their bodies. Sunspots burst like all of the pantomime eyes of her nightmares. Delilah lifted her boot high in the air and plowed Lynk in his chest. He fell straight into the seeding flame, and when he tried to escape she saw the fire grow big burning hands like a carrion plant opening its petals of doom and pull Lynk into its ravenous world of brimstone.

Delilah picked Rez up and pulled him to the door to safety. For a moment she could taste polluted New York and was happy to. But all of a sudden there was a strange hot weight pulling her down, and a crawling, burnt thing atop her. Its face was scarred by Arkham's flame; napalm-sludge melted in time with its waning heartbeat. Enough was enough. If she let Lynk win, Rez would die, and so would she. That would mean living happily ever after with daddy, the daddy that never wanted them in the first place!

With the last of her strength Delilah's fingers instinctively grabbed Lynk's throat. Any singer would know all the intricate muscles and bones of the larynx—hyoid bone, thyroid cartilage, and trachea rings—even if they didn't know what it felt like to be a murderer. But Delilah could not stop the reality when her nails began to break through Lynk's skin. Her eyes saw only death and destruction, saw Lynk and Clive's treachery that pushed her to use all the strength in her hands until Lynk's neck cracked like dead twigs in her grip. His head bobbed to the side and his tongue hanged limp as a dick out the side of his mouth as she pushed him back into the blaze. She saw his face give into sweet death, that ultimate nothingness, yellow eyes all anger, all flame.

32

easing sound of laptop keys, quill ink dripping to paper. Rez awoke; his mind felt relaxed, slack, the meat of his soul free of the night's weight. Any last trace of ghosts was now lost within daylight. Yes, daylight, it lit the vista of dusky buildings, the webby bridge in the west, a yellow-gold sheen that cleansed all the evil of the world. It came with a cool breeze that washed over his body.

There was nothing but sky above him, sweet and cold autumn sky. And that's when the throb in his head came back to life; that's when he also came to realize that the sounds were not laptop keys, but the crackling of burning wood. It was 5Pointz bursting and boiling with unstoppable fire.

An eyesore of blood was scattered across the cement, glittering atop piles of glass, dark and rich as pomegranate juice; angry blood. His mind filled with a million jagged images as he rubbed the back of his head where Lynk had hit him with the wood. His hand came back with cold greasy blood. Old blood, so the damage was minimal, but his face fucking ached. And then like magic a familiar long black trench coat wafted the odors of clove cigarettes, coffee and alcohol sweat. It was Alex, and he was lifting him up off the floor to his feet and his lips—oh his lips so sweet and tasting of heaven.

"Pieces of shit!" He yelled. "You okay, Rez?"

Then he was telling Rez that he forgave him for what he'd done, that it was okay because Alex understood the temptation of hormones, and that he wanted to go far, far away from here. But everything was slow and drunk; Rez couldn't make sense of the commotion there were so many things going on at once. Delilah's band was lazing around too, their arms crossed, feet tapping the floor impatiently: three pairs of tangled limbs, three sweaty blots of famished looking bodies.

"What a way to spend time in the city!" A girl yelled. Alex called her Sheigh.

The other two, Billy and Jimmy, turned their faces toward Rez, grinding inquisitive teeth as they scanned for any symbol, any feature or wrinkle around the eyes that would verify he was related to Delilah. They all reeked of the city, the bones of fallen buildings.

"He hit you guys in the head with a frying pan?" Billy asked.

"Not HARD enough, obviously."

Rez stood fully and that's when he saw the true carnage. 5Pointz looked about ready to crumble; the smoke was so thick half the town was engulfed. The 7 train had stopped service.

"DELILAH!" Rez screamed.

"She's right here," Alex said.

And there she was, towel stained with blood on her forehead, smile so happy to see her brother. They hugged, tight, happy to find that all of this was over.

"Are you burned?" She asked.

"Surprisingly no. But fuck me I have a headache."

"Any voices?"

Rez took a minute to listen. "No . . . they're all gone."

"Well then don't look in the mirror for a few days. Lucky you still have your teeth."

"Will someone tell us what the fuck happened?" The band said.

All five heads moved toward the building again. Rez heard something tick in his mind, a strange whispering voice. He remembered Lynk being thrown into the flame by Delilah, thought of his charred husk devoid of blood, meat, and imagined crushing it with his boot like a rotted vegetable bulb for what he'd done. But the voices told him something else, to look in a certain direction, to where Clive was.

And then Rez turned his head.

"Don't look!" Alex pulled Rez back. "It's not pretty."

"He needs to see, needs to know so we can move on," Delilah said.

Delilah pushed Alex away and escorted Rez. He almost couldn't bear it as he remembered the way Clive smashed him over and over with his boot, how he tried to kill him. Still, Rez almost vomited when he saw his best friend dead, his smashed face turned up and blotched with a flowered bruise from the fall, his skull cracked open like an egg and curds of tender brain leaking into his hair. His legs were bent in an awful position and his long arms were broken at impossible angles.

Next to Clive was the T70, broken in half, but it was as if even in death Clive was still yearning for the damn thing. A roll of film lay next to Clive like a scintillating carpet, exposed to light. No one would ever know what was on that film. But it didn't matter anymore, the story was complete. A true tragedy of jealousy, rage, love: all of the things that can kill a person if they let it control them. Obsession leads to aggression, and aggression turns to vulnerability, and vulnerability forms darkness, the absolute moment of no return.

"I'm sorry Rez," Delilah said.

Rez completely ignored Delilah, ignored his pain. "Where's Zazo?"

"With us!"

Jimmy, Sheigh and Billy had brought a jar of insects and Zazo was feeding on a long and leggy caterpillar of some sort.

"It was her the whole time. She was our shadow person, protecting us against Lynk and Clive. I understand now."

Rez understood too. He knew that Shadow People lurked around only to warn people when a bad presence was on its way. He remembered that Hans had told him that Helena had a Shadow Man too, but sadly it couldn't protect her from Arkham. The dark had taken over his soul too quickly, much like how it claimed Anakin Skywalker in Star Wars. Rez's head suddenly felt a little better.

Everyone walked out arm in arm into the desolate parking lot. Halloween was over and it seemed that Long Island City had lost its dark magic. Davis Street was a dustbowl except for the sounds of nascent fire, crackling wood and whaling sirens getting closer and closer until the entire block was a bright sea of red and blue. The gang jumped into the pickup and watched the town fade away, watched it burn.

There was no funeral, just boxes packed and lingering worry about where the next move would be, where Rez would live. Clive had distant family that flew his body back home; Lynk's parents conducted their business like shadows and buried their son's crispy corpse in some wacky graveyard far away from New York City. No formal police investigation took place, none that Rez knew of anyway.

"Can't believe he's gone," Rez said.

In the Dark Room, *that* Dark Room, and the boxes were piling high, labeled and ready to be shipped away. It had a bad look to it now that it was bare, devoid of Clive's everything. Rez kept some old pictures, the posters, memories distilled in time. The after burn of spilled chemicals resonated like bad liquor in Delilah's mouth. She couldn't help to think about the moment she had with Clive out by the Cabal Gallery, and what he'd said to her. *My world is dark and cold. I'd give anything to brighten it up a little. Art has obliged me into solitude.* Clive would never have to worry about darkness for he would forever be obliged into fire, forever burn with Lynk. He will never be alone. The time him and Delilah spent together was special, but not one that filled her with grief. Clive made his own decisions, trekked his own path to death. It was ironic to think Clive did everything in his power to get Lynk out of his love life, but in the end they had died together . . . forever.

"They wanted something to latch onto, and they found Lynk and Clive," Delilah said. "So don't feel so bad, Rez." Delilah held her brother's hand.

"He was my best friend . . ."

"I'm here for you, Rez. You're my brother. I love you."

"Where the fuck will I go?"

Home . . .

Delilah thought of the city outside the small window, forever changing, and wondered how she was going to make the rest of her life here. The butterfly bandage on her hand and head itched like hell, but anything was better than stitches. Something about a needle pulling black nylon through skin freaked her out. She was too pale for that anyway; it would have made her look incongruent. So down her fingers moved, soft against the area just under her ribcage, the place where Clive had plowed his angry blade. She knew there should've been a deep gauge, a gaudy wound exposing tender meat between her ribs . . . knew that she should've been cooped up in some uncomfortable hospital bed, her body shifting uneasily beneath the stiff sheets, her veins hooked and barbed by intravenous with some generic anesthetic rushing into her blood.

But it wasn't that at all. She hadn't bled out, hadn't drowned in blood and died right there in the middle of that fire. Clive had simply penetrated the dreamlands once again, the place she'd shown him first hand. So what remained of his anger was only a tender spot; a discoloration as if a blob of ink forever trapped under her pale skin. Delilah didn't know how, but she *knew* it was going to be there forever: a reminder. A dark souvenir. She understood this, just like somehow her life had been spared by *Them*. And though she didn't fully understand *how* it happened, she didn't really care. Being alive was what mattered most, and for the first time in a long time . . . it was something beautiful.

She rummaged through her pockets and found Arkham's cigarettes and decided to crush them. She didn't need him anymore. That's when she felt the pinch in her fingers, like lightning running up her arm her hand was so sore. The memory of her fingers pressing into Lynk's skin, cracking his neck like charred timber, left her feeling strange inside, but hardened.

Looking at Rez, then gazing by the door and knowing her band was there, Hans and the airy city out the window, Delilah realized love is what really matters at the end of the day. Without love there's no life, and without life there's no love. A palindromic concept. Part of the hardships of growing up is facing what you never thought you could. And for Delilah, she'd just lived it. In the city you could be anything you wanted to be, and Delilah wanted to be happy.

"Rez?"

He looked up, abashed, huge bruise across his face. "Yeah?"

"Let's go, okay? Let's go and live."

She pulled Rez out of the room. The past was a smoky smear of emotions about to fade; the future was what it was all about. For once she did not have to fight with her heart as she smiled. It felt all of a sudden natural.

"I love you, Delilah. My family."

Then the smell of coffee filled the air and Alex was handing out cups. Billy, Jimmy and Sheigh sat around lazily on the floor, flipping fast through copies of *The Onion*. They'd never seen a newspaper that mocked everything from Aliens to the current President's policies, and how it was kept in circulation certainly surprised them. It was better than a tabloid magazine for sure, but *The Onion* never quite made sense. It was an upside down world inside those pages.

"I love your new piercings Sheigh," Delilah said. "The infected look brings out your features."

"Whatever. I remember when I pierced your ears. Did a fine and dandy job or else you wouldn't have gauged them!"

Sheigh talked about their adventures in the city. They had barely had enough money to eat, but had gotten so good at shop lifting that they always had a full belly of Colt 45 and snickers bars. They went to

The Museum of Natural History and saw dinosaurs, ancient gems and sea creatures—for free! They were planning to return soon.

Hans' aging face reflected a happiness that could be seen in the small lines around his eyes, the creases in his cheeks. He had found an inner peace, had his two kids with him that he had searched for his entire adult life. They'd be with him forever now. Everything was surprisingly copacetic.

With everyone sipping their coffee like campfire hot chocolates, they all were becoming closer than ever without even knowing it. Zazo licked some out of Delilah's cup, shook his head and zoomed back into the air as if the caffeine had electrified him. In a year's time all of this would be looked back upon and only dredge up a molecule of fear. It would most likely be laughed upon.

"Everything's packed," Rez said.

"Lynk's stuff too?" Hans asked.

"Yeah. Looks like I'm back to the park. But it feels, I don't know, it feels good."

"No, you're staying at my place. Everybody can stay there as long as they need to, and I mean it," Hans said.

"I don't want to impede."

Rez took a long deep swig of his coffee, his eyes moving between Alex and Delilah, and she saw the confirmation in his face: he loved them; he would do anything for them.

"Let's just go; I can't stay here anymore. Too many memories."

"Everyone out!" Hans clapped.

"No, wait!" yelled Delilah. "After a nap. We can deal with this in a few hours."

"Sleep, Delilah . . . *you?*" Alex asked.

"Yeah, for once I can do it safely," and she looked at her new family and smiled.

Delilah chugged her entire cup, disregarding the burn, and her eyes clicked out to the sound of Hans putting Electric Orchid in the stereo. All of a sudden she felt renewed, finding a woman inside of herself she never knew was there, a woman who could overcome angst and self-loathing. She slept the best sleep she could remember, free of woes, free of nightmares.

Epilogue

Tompkins Square Park. Twilight filtering across the expanse of people and cobblestone, purple plasma sneaking between black iron gates and up into the drooping trees. A wholly evil place of new age yuppies juxtaposed next to bohemians. Gentrification will soon rule this place, as it has done to too many towns north of here.

Rez: Moleskine in hand, cigarette in mouth, dreaming of an ice cold beer and a falafel to share with Alex. He'd just finished drawing weird shapes onto his skate shoes, mocking the teal musical scale tattoo on his arm, the raven quill. He was knuckle deep in a new piece of fiction, finally with a clear head. It was a short story but could be extended into a novel if he worked on it hard enough. It was one based on cameras, dark emotions, a blackness that held a strong pulse and hungry enough to claim weak souls. It would be his best story because he had lived it.

The gang straggled on the benches inhaling the misty autumn air, relaxed. Alex's head was in Rez's lap, and Rez's fingers traversed through his hair. Jimmy announced that Coil Records had come into contact with him again, and that they had met the demands of the band, and would be signing them on with a pretty sweet deal. Five figures! Maybe Rez wouldn't have to beg Evolution for his job back.

"What's mine is yours," Alex said.

Delilah screamed when she heard the number and sparrows jetted out of the trees behind them, reminding Rez of how fast Zazo moves. Billy and Sheigh began to dance—one girl with big knotty hair a shade of deep indigo, pale bones hidden beneath black lace, and one hick-looking kid with the weird skinny body and crossbones bandana on his head. Jimmy grabbed his crotch as two skateboarding chicks passed with their stereo blasting Glassjaw.

"Ditto," Delilah said, smoking her cigarette slowly.

They'd discovered through it all that they had become a family. Delilah kept repeating that you don't need to be bonded by blood to love one another; it was a lesson she learned from being in New York. Blood doesn't constitute a family, only love does. They didn't need the recognition or approval of anyone else but each other.

Rez felt the weight of his bad luck sizzle away, though there was a surprising pale spot in his heart where Lynk used to be, and a deep hole for Clive. He would miss him the rest of his life. In his mind he could still feel the moment when the glass broke and that cold wormy hand moving across his face in the friendliest gesture, a goodbye, farewell; it was great to have known you. Rez would keep that moment in his heart, to himself.

The gang bickered, argued, all the things that you nit pick because you know one another so well, petty arguments because you love each other. So this had to have been magic, for it seemed their hearts all craved the same things. For once Rez felt he could have good things in his life, and that the bad would not come like a tidal wave and wash it away.

He looked at his arm and wished for the razor scars to vanish, wished for magic to do it. Delilah nodded in agreement. Maybe if he stared long enough he could make them disappear. He gave up after five seconds. It didn't matter anymore because in this city of millions upon millions of people, he was just an ant, and ants never get noticed, so he didn't have to worry about any stupid stare or caustic, snarky words.

Through all the pain that their adventure brought, they came out on top. It was the power of hope, really, that had saved them. *Chance*, like Hans said, mixed with the magic Magda always talked about. But it couldn't save Lynk. *Poor Lynk*. And Clive? *Let's not think about it anymore*, he heard Delilah say. *The ghosts died with them.* They wouldn't come back for Rez or Delilah . . . at least for now.

But Evil has no boundaries. As long as there is Good, Evil will exist like a shadow lurking behind your every step. It's a part of the balance of life: the good and the bad, like *the force* in Star Wars. It isn't meant to be challenged, isn't meant to be predicted. It's just there. The only thing one can do is respect it because once you think that you've got one up on Evil, it comes back three times mutated and bites you in the ass, or swallows you whole.

"You know, you were absolutely right about Lynk," Alex whispered.

"Meaning?"

"That he wanted to kill Delilah."

"Will the cops ever find out how they really died?"

"Not if anyone talks. And judging by our group, no one ever will."

"You're right. Now kiss me."

Alex slid over to Rez; their thoughts mingled, their eyes locked, their hearts joined as one. One day they'd get away, live a forever summer like in Bradbury's Green Town. But for now it was just twilight and Alex's mouth tasting of freedom, of the last dark flavors of ghosts, bad luck, the new flavors of autumn, and a happier year.

"Alright lovebirds! It's time to get drunk," Hans said. "I know a place that's got a special tonight, and I'm sure the band can drink free as long as they play a set."

"Yes! I want to play. I feel like it's been a while," Delilah said.

"We're always ready."

Everyone walked arm in arm with their respected lover or friend. Rez watched Delilah smile—bird's smile, Arkham's smile, his smile—the tattoos over her arms glowing in the cool night. He watched Alex's face, so content, still so sharp and pale and beautiful as if sculpted from ivory. He loved him. And then something splat on Rez's shoulder, runny and white like snot. Rez stopped for a moment and looked up, seeing a flutter of brown wings take way to the endless sky.

"I hear that's *good* luck, Rez," Delilah said, "when birds shit on your shoulder."

The land around them seemed new and old at the same time, like the beginning of a good story, and the buildings looked alive tonight, just like 5Pointz. Rez watched his shadow stretch long and thin in the park lights. And for a second he thought about the hungry blackness. But there were eyes watching him. Rez looked up and saw it was only the stars, so many tonight, corrugated crystals of white fire lucent against the darkening sky, like nothing he'd ever seen before in this city of lights.

Delilah's Lyrics

MY PERSONAL HELL

Emptiness speaks eloquence
In this nest of hate where I thrive
Cannon tongues and crooked lungs
Grind me down to wet dusty strife
Brought up in the excess of fake
With nothing but my identity at stake
But I'll free myself
Let the phantoms fly...
Watch your corpse burn and die!
I'm buried alive, crawl
A living ~~ecstacy~~ for this tragedy
Now ~~go~~ watch me live to tell
This is my personal HELL!
MY RAGE is under construction
But it demands full consumption

ELECTRIC ORCHID

28 DAYS

Stinging English rain
Lit by a dead sun...
Put the devil on wholesale
Now you've nowhere to run
28 Days was all it took to ruin me
To drown in the blood and kisses
28 Days 'til I ruin thee
Your G-d is impartial
Brick and mortar idol
Biased bastards on the run
Keep sucking the tridil
As the gates of heaven tumble

NO WAY OUT !

Suicide lies, WE still seek
Knife in the eyes
Never been so meek
We shall rise and creep

SEED ASYLUM

A River runs through me
My blood uncontrolled by gravity
A generation of hate
Learning to gloam above tragedy
Old you even want me?
I'm an asylum of seeds
Spreading my infectious needs
In this garden of eden
built upon Sodomy...
No longer your happy little slave
No wage can make me behave!
You are the architect
Of my distress
But I'm the one who chooses to digress
The next time I fly
I'll drop my seeds across your sky
The next time I fall
It won't be you who sees me crawl

ORCHID

ELECTRIC

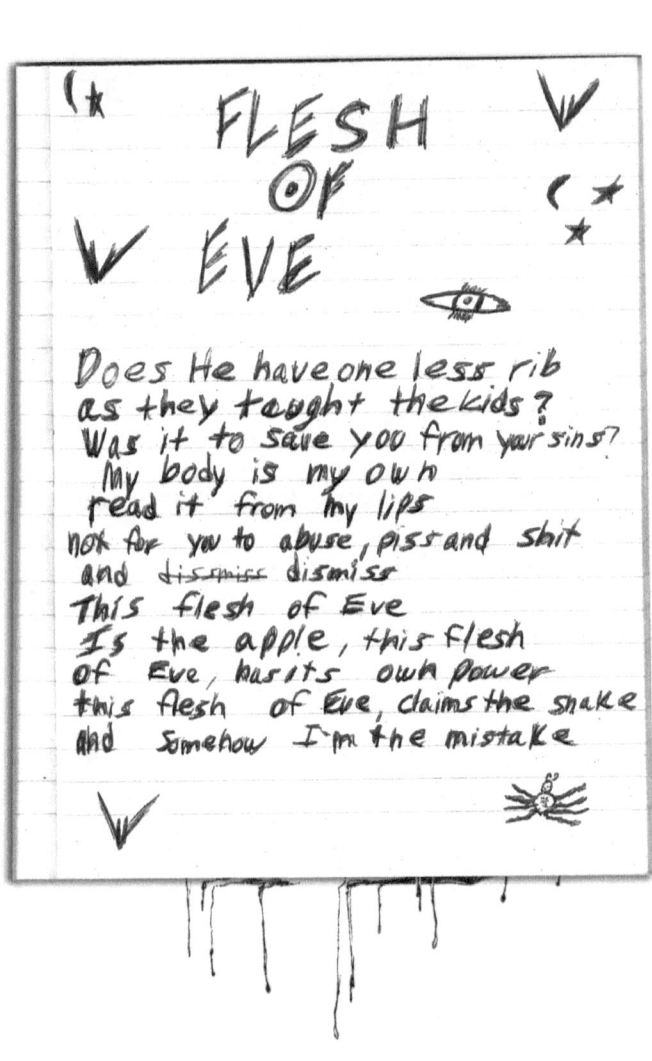

FLESH OF EVE

Does He have one less rib
as they taught the kids?
Was it to save you from your sins?
My body is my own
read it from my lips
not for you to abuse, piss and shit
and ~~dismiss~~ dismiss
This flesh of Eve
Is the apple, this flesh
of Eve, has its own power
this flesh of Eve, claims the snake
and somehow I'm the mistake

CATATONIC

Do you realize that when you close your eyes
this world is yours to divide?
Shed the skin and let her in
Inject reality with your sins
Hide what you are?
For a laughing martyr
But all is becoming, numbing
The world around me is shuddering
I've seen the light in this night
My senses overload
I've seen pleasure and felt sound
And now my conscience explodes
They say darkness is the absence of light
But without light everything is alright
The ~~stars~~ twin stars will shine bright
They still believe in me tonight

PHOTOS & FANTASIES

She's invisible ...
Reflected in a tilted mirror
Built by lies, demise
She will never win her prize
This will never resign
Only in pain will she realign
She wants a place, ~~out~~ but to
tear down your signs
Tears of blood, dreams of glum
Dark fantasies of daughter and son
Wishing like ~~a~~ blind faith's tomb
Watching the world strike down her muse
But words are the key to ~~surviving~~
Stronger than a blabbering bible
She's divisible ...
In two she can reign
But one and she's done and dead
This isn't the last time she's felt any
dread...

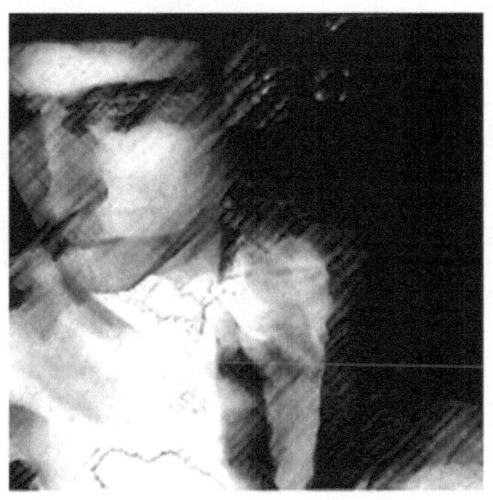

J. Daniel Stone is a 25-year-old juggernaut of a writer born and raised in New York City. He does not eat meat, believes in equal rights and absorbs as much art and science as he can. You can find more of his work via *Abomination Magazine*, *Blood Bound Books*, *Pink Narcissus Press*, and more.

In 2010, the legendary horror review site *Hellnotes* deemed him "Psychologically insightful."

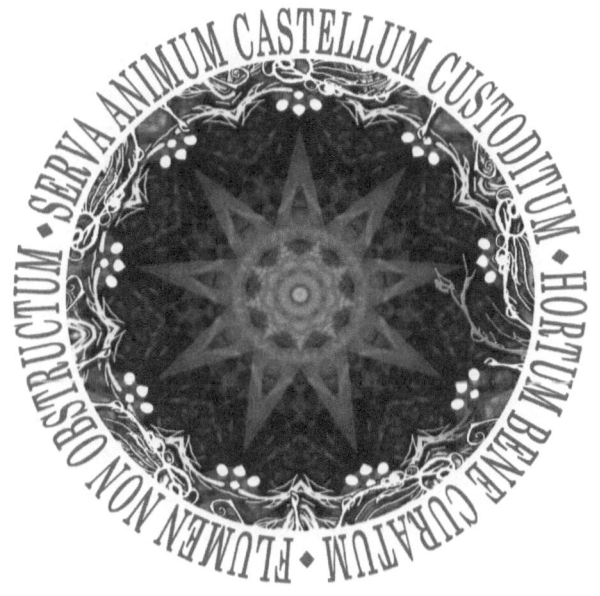

Did you enjoy the book?

We welcome all feedback and queries.
Villipede.com